The
Collectibles

For Patty

In memory of Joseph Kaufman, my father and first doctor, and Robert Hutchins, my friend and second doctor—each a wonderful husband, father, and old-fashioned doctor who cared.

Acknowledgments

First is Patty, for her love, graciousness, keen eye and ear, and for always believing in what I can do. My deep gratitude to my son Jeffrey for his love, critical analysis and input as we discussed ideas for *The Collectibles*; and to my daughter Kristine for her love, candor, support and patience for my literary enthusiasm.

My appreciation to Jane Hight McMurry for her belief in this story. Many thanks to Anna Contino for her early work on behalf of *The Collectibles*.

Many close friends – you know who you are – encouraged me in writing *The Collectibles,* and I thank each of you. I especially thank my dear friends:

- Ann Kalkines – you have been there from day one in connection with this novel. Thank you for your support, input, all of the phone calls, discussions and encouragement – and your unwavering belief in this story, and my ability to write it.
- George Kalkines – for our life-long friendship, your endless generosity and all of your encouragement and input.
- Steve Braff and Marty Braff – for all of your manuscript comments, support and encouragement.
- Diana Holdridge – for your continuing support from early on, as well as your input regarding the manuscript and its revisions and, as always, your encouragement.
- Andy Miller – for your enthusiasm and support in connection with early renditions of this story.
- Paul T. Miller – for your many years of friendship and for teaching me much about the intricacies of the automobile business.

- Dr. Robert Brownlow – for your insights and keen perception, appreciated through the haze of a great cigar on the porch.

I wish to thank Meredith Preston, Harley Sacks, Terry Sacks, Rev. Edward Connett and my dear sister Laurel for taking time to read the manuscript and giving their valuable insights, editorial comments and support.

My gratitude to Joan Lester, from whom I learned valuable writing lessons and Nikki Kalkines for her support and sharing her professional mental health expertise as applied to one of my characters.

My deep appreciation to Linda Rohrbough for taking the time to talk to me, encourage me, teach me and read and edit my book. What a wonderful person and teacher.

I am grateful to Nancy Berland and all the members of her team for their edits of my manuscript, design of the cover (Thanks Jeanne!), understanding, help and guidance. Nancy's edits taught me the need for and value in revisions. Her efforts clearly made this a better book. I also thank Nancy for referring me to Antoinette Kuritz and Strategies. Antoinette has been a major help on a host of levels in connection with the manuscript, marketing, and distribution.

I also thank Patricia Rasch for her format and book design, and photographer Patricia Ann Roseman. What a team. Your support meant the world to me.

If in the friendship I speak of, one could give to the other, it would be the one who received the benefit who would oblige his friend...

—*Montaigne, Of Friendship*

CHAPTER 1

Joe

The words Joe heard that night would define the rest of his life. The wind had finally relinquished its hold on Bald Peak and light was growing scarce, the sun swallowed by the vast acres of Adirondack green forest. The full moon was visible through the tall pines as Howard Buckingham and Joe, his fifteen-year-old nephew, found the protection of a small cove.

Joe and Uncle Howard repeated what they had done for years after a full day of hunting, trapping, and then fishing for their dinner in the fresh mountain streams. They built a makeshift lean-to of fallen trees and branches, braced it against the side of a jagged rock formation and started a small but adequate fire to cook the fish, brew the coffee and, finally, warm them before sleep. Joe treasured times like this when he could have his uncle all to himself, the mountains quiet except for the wind and the occasional wolf's howl.

"You know what you say sometimes about there being truth up here," Joe said. "What's that mean, truth in these mountains?"

Howard was a full-sized man who, when his head was not bent down lookin' for snakes, stood six-foot-five inches tall. He wore hunting pants held up by a two-inch-wide, forty-six-inch leather belt slightly curved at the top and bottom and fastened by an honest brass buckle. Not the fancy rodeo type but a simple brass square with three prongs to pass the leather through and hitch to the holes. His shirt was soft wool with flaps over each breast pocket. Over that he wore a weathered deerskin jacket that hung below his waist and just the tops of bright red socks that Joe's Aunt Lettie had knitted showing over his high leather boots.

"Well, son, these hills don't lie. They're beautiful, but they ain't forgiving. If you make a mistake up here, you can die. Animals make mistakes and die all the time. Men, too. Only the strong survive, the ones that protect themselves. It ain't just the animals; you can see it in the fish in the streams and in the trees. It can be cold and raw and windy and whipped. It can also be calm and clear like tonight. There is a certain... I don't know, what you might call *rhythm* to it all up here. I have seen it all my life. The animals know it. The woods know it. No one's fooling anybody up here. It is what it is. Treat the mountains and the animals with respect, listen to them, and be prepared, and you'll be all right, and never alone. If you don't, you won't. That's what I mean about there being a truth up here."

Howard pulled the collar of his jacket around his weathered neck while at the same time using the toe of his right boot to nudge a log in the fire. No matter how many times Joe tried, he was never able to make a fire grow better with the slight nudge of a log. He watched Howard carefully remove his red and tan cap and brush his hand over his balding head and then criss-cross his chin.

Howard caught Joe's look. "How you doin', son?" When Howard asked you how you were doing, it was a big question, not to be taken lightly but answered straight out.

Joe thought for a while and tried his foot on a log, which promptly caused four other logs to fall away from the fire. After he'd gotten them all back in place, he replied, "I'm all right, Uncle Howard, I guess."

Howard seemed to ponder that answer as he rose and selected four nearby sticks, looking them over as if only those four would do. The ritual was familiar to Joe as he watched his uncle unsheathe his hunting knife and, using the handle, pound the sticks into the ground, each a yard from the fire. Next, Howard sat down on a log he had pulled up to the fire and slowly unlaced his boots, placing them upside down on the sticks. Then he removed his wool socks and hung them up to dry as well.

It was Howard who'd given Joe his first pair of high leather boots. "Them boots are your foundation in these hills," he told Joe. "Take care of 'em, they'll serve you well."

Joe stared at the fire, not moving.

Howard looked at Joe again and asked, "What's botherin' you, son?"

"Well, to tell you the truth, Uncle Howard, I've been doing a lot of thinking and, no matter how much I think about it, I really can't change."

"Can't change what?" Howard asked in a gentle tone.

Joe's eyes continued to lock into the fire. He heard what Uncle Howard had asked, but no words came out in response. Just silence. Howard simply waited and, finally, Joe looked up from the fire and directly into Howard's eyes. "Can't change the fact that I'm average, and I'm always going to be average."

More silence.

Howard finally stood up, walked over to Joe and, kneeling down, put his hand on Joe's shoulder. Looking into his eyes, he said, "Joe, it ain't been easy for you with your mom and dad gone at too young an age. Your Aunt Lettie and I love you like our own son. I wonder sometimes whether we've been good 'nough for you. We prayed many times askin' for help from the Almighty. Lettie and I couldn't be more proud of you if we tried. We think you're a fine young man. Lot of people 'round here think so, too. You talk about not wantin' to be average. I ain't the reader you are, and I don't know all the words you know. But it don't seem to me that you were average when you won the All State swimmin' meet last month. You ain't average in school, 'cause you're at the top of your class, winnin' all kinds of learnin' and athletic awards. You already got them colleges writin' to you about scholarships, both for your grades and your swimmin' and wrestlin'." Howard looked up at the moon, stood, turned and added, "I don't call it average when you went down into that crevice and brought that young fella from New York City back up after he fell in and broke his arm. Funny name. Started with a 'P.' You saved that boy's life."

That was more words at one time than Joe could remember Howard ever saying.

"His name was Preston. And you had something to do with saving him, the way I remember it," Joe replied with a grin, stoking the fire.

"You did the savin', I just did the haulin'. Anyhow, don't be changing the subject. So what's average about all that?"

"What I mean, Uncle Howard, is, well, I'm five-foot-nine, and I'll
probably never be taller. I can only lift so much, and I sure can't do
the carrying like you. And I listen to the way you talk to the men you
guide, and I see the look in their eyes and hear the tone in their voices
when they talk to you. They don't just respect you, Uncle Howard,
they idolize you. They're never going to be like you. I'm never going
to be like you. And I don't think I'm going to be like them either. I
hate being average."

Joe watched Howard get up and walk around the fire, stretching
his arms and neck. He went over to the lean-to and laid out his sleeping bag in front of his backpack basket. He arranged a few more of
the pine boughs on each side of the lean-to and prepared himself for
sleep. But instead of crawling into the lean-to, Howard came over to
Joe, put his hands around Joe's shoulders holding him square, and
again looked straight into Joe's eyes.

"Son, you're right. You can't help bein' average. But that don't
mean you can't be uncommon."

"Uncommon?" Joe asked.

"Yep, uncommon."

"How do you be uncommon?" Joe asked, amazed that Howard
had said this much to him and praying that he was not pushing his
uncle too far.

"Well, I'm just an old mountain guide, but seems to me there are
three ways. Do what the other fella can't. Be what the other fella ain't.
And then help the other fella."

"That's it?"

"That's enough," Howard replied, and crawled in the lean-to.

Joe thought about his uncle, how he had worked these mountains
he loved since he was a young boy, how he'd lived for sixty-eight
years outside the small town of Mineville, on the eastern side of the
mountains in the foothills, in a large, two-story, wood-frame house
that he built with his own hands. Winding behind the house was a
fresh brook, home to endless numbers of trout. Behind the brook

were seven small green-and-white wooden cabins he had also built. These cabins were rented from time to time to the business executives and others who came from the cities to bag a deer or catch a big trout with the help of Howard as a guide.

They returned year after year, lured by the majesty of the mountain and its bounty and by Howard's competence, charm, warmth, and grace. They felt safe with Howard. There was Aunt Lettie's humor and mountain cooking, too.

Increasingly, Howard had allowed Joe to come on these trips. The executives, or "city fellas" as Uncle Howard called them, were, for Joe, a window to another world. Joe loved to watch them as they struggled through the narrow passes. First Joe noticed the difference in the way they talked. Not only the words they used but the sound of the words. What Uncle Howard called their "New York City way of speaking." Then there was a difference in the way they walked, the way they moved. It was hard to explain, but there was something in the way they acted that gave Joe the impression that they had seen it all, that nothing could surprise them. Finally, their clothes were the kind Joe had only seen in catalogs, sort of fancy and finished at the same time, all new and expensive. Joe felt they lived in a different world.

Occasionally, they would even say a few words to Joe. They could not keep up with Howard, though he had them by fifteen or twenty years. At night, they gathered around the campfire, watching Howard cook. While usually tired, they were expansive, at times euphoric, as they recounted their experiences during the day. They missed their shots, lost their fish, or found their traps empty, and acted as if they had conquered the world. Eventually, in one way or another, they would turn the talk to their lives and how successful they were in their business deals. Joe could tell from the way Uncle Howard kept taking off his cap and putting it on again he didn't care too much for the bragging part, but Joe wanted to hear it all. Where they went, their cars, their Lear jets, and especially their boats and where they would take them on the ocean. It was another world. Someday Joe would have a boat and drive it in the ocean himself.

Howard insisted on no alcohol during the day and indeed discouraged it altogether. But often, the flasks would appear after supper "to add a nip to their coffee," and that added fuel to their words. After Howard had listened intently to all of their stories, and told a few of his own, he would suggest it was time to turn in and "allow all the other animals in the mountains to get some sleep." Joe watched Howard carefully, taking it all in.

The moon was high and bright now. Joe sat by the fire watching it until the last ember died, replaying the conversation with his uncle over and over. The air turned chilly. His uncle's words burned hot in his mind. *Do what the other fella can't. Be what the other fella ain't. And then help the other fella.*

Joe crawled into his sleeping bag. He finally fell asleep, but not before making himself a promise. *I may have to go through this world being average – but I swear, I'll be uncommon along the way.*

CHAPTER 2

Preston

Hundreds of miles away and in a world apart, Preston, too, would hear words this night that would change his life forever. The only son of Peter and June Wilson, he had the misfortune of being born rich, and ignored by his father. From this father he inherited a tall, strong body with full shoulders, a well-proportioned and pleasing face, a full head of thick black hair, straight healthy teeth, and piercing blue eyes.

Preston's mother was an even-tempered, slight-breasted woman of thirty-seven who wore her thin brown hair in a page boy cut and a small amount of make-up applied to her eyes and sparse eyebrows. She had thin lips, slightly turned down unless she happened to smile. When she did smile, her pale translucent face took on a bright, less hungry look and, at times, she actually had a certain glow, especially when she saw Preston.

From his mother, thanks to her father, Preston would inherit a trust fund making him the sole beneficiary of 6.7 million dollars. His mother also inherited a sizable sum from her father, Rupert Gaylord, who had the good fortune to buy a large amount of stock in a little-known company named Haloid. Haloid became Xerox, and Rupert became rich.

Preston's father had been a promising young businessman when he persuaded June Gaylord to marry him sixteen years earlier. They were living in an expansive cooperative on the twelfth floor of 1040 Fifth Avenue, on New York City's Upper East Side that June's father had purchased for June when Preston was born.

June insisted that her son attend the right private schools; among the many subjects of Peter and June's arguments was the question of which would be appropriate. They had settled on Eaglebrook in Deerfield, Massachusetts for grades six through nine. He was now enrolled at the Hotchkiss School.

What seemed most important to Preston and many of his classmates were their backgrounds. What did their parents do? Where did they do it? How much money did they really have? Where did it come from? Would it continue to come? Did they actually make money from what they did, whatever that was, or was their money made from returns on their money? And, above all, would it last?

It wasn't hard to figure all of this out. It was a small group, after all, and there were only so many Michael Douglases, Samuel Kauffmanns and Hiltons.

The majority of the boys came from New York City, as did Preston. Preston could tell that they were from the city by how fast they talked, their body language, their attitude and the way they acted toward their teachers. They were rebellious, and underneath, they were all, in one way or another, angry.

While Preston knew that they, and he for that matter, were privileged, he wondered what the privilege was in being shipped off to private school, consigned to live with all these smart-ass kids, when what he really longed for was to have a relationship with normal friends and to spend at least some time with his mother and father. When Preston complained that he never got time with his mother, and even less with his father, June reminded him that his father did make an effort. "Preston, your father has tried," she said, but it was evident that she was trying hard herself to think of an example. Then, her face a bit lighter, she reminded him, "There is the business about those trips way upstate in the mountains. You know he tries to do that at least every other year."

His mother did not need to worry – Preston would never forget that trip last summer. While Preston appreciated – actually longed for – time with his father, he hated the fact that what little time he had was spent traipsing around in the mountains watching his father play hunter. Besides that, going into the mountains was not a vacation – certainly not the kind his friends enjoyed with their parents:

skiing trips to Aspen, the Swiss Alps, cruising the British Virgins or the Greek Islands. And the mountains were dangerous.

What was with his father and these hunting trips anyway? What in hell his father saw in going that far to bust their asses climbing around in the woods with some local hicks and freezing to death in some half-ass lean-to was beyond him. Why did his father seem to covet the respect of some poor mountain guide? And what was Preston supposed to do about the kid, kiss his ass because he got him out of a tight spot after Preston slipped, fell from the trail and broke his damn arm? They shouldn't have put him in that position in the first place.

"Ask him why it's a good thing that I never see him. Ask him why you never see him either. Why do you and he stick me on a shelf, first up in Massachusetts and now in Connecticut, visit me on parents' day and Thanksgiving, and have me join you at Christmas? Why is that enough?"

"You don't understand, Preston," his mother replied. "It's not that simple. These things are for your own good. I don't want you to make the mistakes... "

"What?" Preston demanded. "Go on."

"I don't want to go on," June said in a choked throaty voice. Preston saw her eyes begin to fill, and he feared she was going to cry. "I don't want to discuss your father in this way; I don't want to let him down. I will talk with him, however. I'll do it tonight."

Preston thanked his mother. He wished he could talk to his father himself, but either Peter wasn't around or, when he was, he was too busy doing "other things." What Preston did not understand was what these other things were.

"What do you do, Dad?" he would ask, only to be told by Peter in a vague but sweeping way, "I'm a businessman, son. I make deals, make things happen, manage money, that sort of thing."

Peter waited until a night when June would be in the right mood, after a steak dinner and wine at Mulligans, to educate her on the idea and get her support. Tell her about his vision for Global to import latex gloves into the United States. Unfortunately, the night he picked was the same one when June was waiting to talk to him and it was also the night that Preston happened to be home and had decided to position himself in such a way that he could hear their conversation after they returned from dinner.

Preston seemed to anticipate that his parents would continue their conversation in the study over Johnny Walker Red and ice. He crouched under the wooden cabinets in the narrow butler's pantry off the kitchen where he used to hide as a young boy. He could hear the exuberance in his father's voice.

"June, honey, I've spent a lot of time focusing on my next move, what I'm going to do, and I've really got one this time. I'd like to tell you about it."

June sipped her drink, leaned forward in her chair and looked at her handsome husband with a smile that failed to mask distrust. "Oh, wonderful, Peter," she said. "Please do."

Missing, as always, the complexity of June's response, Peter was delighted with the green light. "I've devised a strategic plan," he said, with pride and special emphasis on the word "strategic." Peter went on to explain that he had become aware that the United States and China had recently held a joint session on Trade Investment and Economic Law in Beijing. "I've researched the Sino-American scene from a potential market perspective, and, baby, I've determined that the Chinese are hot in the latex market." He flashed his best smile, hoping to convince June and himself of his confidence. "They're producing latex gloves right now, but they need the good old US of A to really fly."

"Don't they have a large population of their own to supply, let alone the rest of the world?" June paused, and then asked sharply, "How much do you need this time?"

"Only two million. The rest will be self-producing. And I can pay it back in less than twelve months," Peter said, trying to sound convincing.

"I don't want to talk about lending you money right now, Peter, and

I don't want to be. . . " *what did her psychiatrist call it? An enabler. . .* and she added, "In any event, what I want to talk to you about is Preston."

"What about him, and why are you changing the subject? Why do you connect Preston with helping me over the top with this business deal?" Peter thumped across the room with no specific destination in mind. He stopped at the antique end table, picked up the empty ash tray and threw it down again. "My relationship with Preston is just fine."

June stood up, drink in hand, and addressed her husband directly. "I think it's time we speak frankly, Peter. There is good reason to connect Preston to your deals because, while you're off chasing rainbows, you have a wife and a son who are unclear what you really do and who you really are. Do you know how many deals I've given you money for that were going to make you millions, in fact, amounted to nothing but debt? I'm not stupid, Peter, and neither is Preston, by the way. He asked me to talk to you, and I've been meaning to talk to you myself for a long time. I have decided that I'm not going to loan you any more money. And I want you to find Preston and have a heart-to-heart father-and-son talk."

Peter knew he had to be especially artful in how he managed her now. At the same time, it annoyed him that he had to go through all this just to tap in to what he regarded as her inexhaustible resources. He decided to take a different tack. "Okay, June. Take it easy. It's not a big deal. Relax. I'll talk to Preston. I'll tell him whatever you want. What do you want me to tell him?"

At this point, June, having poured herself another scotch, was sitting stone erect on the forward part of the sofa. She looked up at Peter with ice in her eyes. "All right, Peter, I'll tell you explicitly what I would say to him and what I would not say to him. I'll start with what I would not say. I would not tell him that, despite your good looks and charm and gift of gab, you are an abject failure. Notwithstanding your promises, you've failed to deliver on every significant business matter you've undertaken. You've nearly exhausted the money my father left me, with no money left for Preston. Thank

God the trust wouldn't let you touch the money for his education. You have my love, what's left of it, but you don't have my respect. As far as what you say to him, you as a father should be able to figure that out. You might try listening to him for a change. Ask him how he feels. Answer his questions. Truthfully, Preston loves you. He just isn't sure who you are or what you do, and he can't understand why you constantly push him away."

"Anything else?" Peter asked in a tone laden with sarcasm.

"Yes, Peter. You can explain to him that you will be moving out of this house. I have been thinking about this for some time. I know what you've been doing, and I am well informed as to with whom you have been doing it."

June stumbled over to her antique wooden desk against the wall, rolled up the top, and picked out an envelope. With a slight tremor, she handed it to Peter. "I still love you, Peter. God knows why. But I'm quite simply tired of it all..." In a deliberate but barely audible voice she continued, "There will be a divorce, and I will have sole custody of Preston. You've asked for money. Here is your last check from me." She handed Peter the envelope. "Call it severance or whatever you wish. Tom Sutton at Cromwell will get you the papers. It's over."

"Where do you propose I live?" Peter's face flushed and twisted. He collapsed on the sofa, immediately pulled himself up, and began to wander again.

"Try one of your ... friends."

Preston, listening, sat cramped on the floor, stunned. He had no idea that his father was carrying on with other women or whatever his mother was referring to. But what really shocked him was hearing his mother say that his father was an abject failure. At this point, hearing more than he had either bargained for or wanted, he slunk upstairs to his room, softly closed the door and, feeling guilty about eavesdropping on his parents, turned up the volume on his TV. He stood in front of his bed staring but not seeing his Porsche racing posters on the wall, his head pounding.

"What about Preston?" Peter cried.

"What about Preston?" June demanded. "Preston needs… has always needed… a father. Why don't you try doing that deal for a change? You can visit him any time you want. I hope it is not too late." Tears streamed down her face. "Go talk to him, for Christ's sake."

Peter stared at June in disbelief and then opened the envelope and looked at the check. Noting the amount, he decided not to argue the point. He slowly put the check in his pants pocket and sauntered out of the study and up the stairs to Preston's room.

Preston knew he was coming from the sound of Peter's wingtip Churchills on the hard wood steps but he remained sprawled out on the bed, pretending to read one of his race car magazines and trying to appear calm.

Peter went to the dresser serving as the TV stand, switched the set off, moved around the bed and sat down on the near end, edging Preston's feet to one side. As usual, he did not look directly into Preston's eyes and missed the tears.

"Pres, there is something I need to tell you. Your mother and I have decided to separate. I will be moving out. I want you to know that none of this has anything to do with you. I love you. You're a big guy, and you'll be fine. You have a large trust fund, as you know. Actually, you are worth more than I am. I'll see you often. Your mom has made it clear that I may, and I'm still your father. Sorry, son, sometimes these things just don't work out."

With that, Peter rubbed his son's head and put his right arm loosely around Preston's shoulders. Preston stiffened, words imprisoned somewhere deep within. Moments later, Peter rose and strode out the door.

Preston crawled under the covers of his bed, the recorder in his mind playing his own conversation with his mother, and that of his mother and father, over and over.

You don't understand, Preston. It's not that simple. I don't want you to make the mistakes… I don't want to discuss your father in this way… There is good reason to connect Preston to your deal… You have my love, but you don't have my respect. I love you, Peter, God knows why. But I'm… tired of it all… there will be a divorce…

You're an abject failure... You're an abject failure... You're an abject failure.

His thoughts were interrupted by a soft knock at the door. "May I come in, Preston?" his mother asked. "The door is unlocked," Preston said as he sprung up in bed and pulled the covers around himself as his mother walked in.

"Your father tells me that he has spoken with you," she said, perched on the edge of the bed. "Don't let this upset you too much, Preston. Your father loves you, as you know I do. You and I have each other, and we will survive this and be fine."

Preston awkwardly put his arms around his mother. "I'm not sure what to say, Mother. I really want to try to get some sleep. I need to think about all this."

"I understand, Preston. It's been a long day. I'll talk to you in the morning, dear." June quietly got up, sidled to the door, and gently closed it behind her.

You're off chasing rainbows... you have a wife and a son who are unclear what you really do and who you really are. Do you know how many deals I have given you money for that were going to make you millions?... I'm not stupid, Peter, and neither is Preston... You're an abject failure.

Preston, his mind spinning, turned off the light and stared into the darkness. He finally fell asleep, but not before making himself a promise. *I'm going to be a bloody financial success no matter what. I will never be an abject failure.*

Chapter 3

Thirty years later

The chancellor's words were drowned out by the increasingly loud sound of rap music that came from a black Pontiac speeding by. No one would have paid any attention, except for the confusion that came from the shot. Or was it a backfire from the car's engine? The crack startled Joe as he took Ashley's hand to guide her up the stairs to the Hall. She was holding back as if her dress were caught or she were being tugged by yet another of her admirers.

Earlier that afternoon Joe had felt the warmth from the soon-to-be-setting sun through the bathroom window as he struggled with his bow tie, rushing to keep up with Ashley in preparation for her big event. He knew that he had to be ready by six o'clock and could tell by Ashley's glance that his late start was, as usual, not appreciated. Over the years, he had come to understand and even appreciate her several editorial looks directed at him. She had, after all, only partially trained him.

He'd glanced over at her as she brushed her hair and applied the faintest amount of make-up. She had a face a guy could spend his whole life looking at: high cheek bones, sparkling blue eyes that highlighted full eyebrows, and silky golden brown hair.

Ashley applied unnecessary last-minute touches, while Joe slipped into his rack size-forty tuxedo jacket and stood before the full-length mirror on the bathroom door. He brushed his still-full head of salt and pepper hair, noting the increasing grey setting in at the temples.

He'd taken a moment to check his eyes, satisfied they were suffi-
ciently clear, indicating that his long day in grueling depositions had
not been enough to prevent his bounce back from the shower. He
wanted to look his best for Ash tonight.

Ashley wore a long black Armani dress. The diamond brooch and
pearls she chose were understated but perfectly suited for the charity crowd they would soon greet. Joe caught a whiff of Ashley's Joy
perfume. After fourteen years, he still felt excitement and stirring
when he saw her. But when she really turned it on, like tonight, he
was mesmerized.

Joe stood staring, trance-like, at their picture on the night stand,
he in his full Navy dress and she in a pale blue silk gown set off by
a simple diamond necklace and matching earrings. Ashley told Joe
that of all of her jewelry she loved those most because he had given
them to her when he really could not afford it.

"Joe, can't you move a little faster? What are you doing staring
at that picture?" As if realizing she'd spoken sharply, she added
almost in a whisper, "I have a surprise for you, but it can wait until
we get home."

Jarred by the tone in Ashley's question, Joe responded, "Nothing,
just thinking." Then he turned to her. "Ash, this is your night.
What's bothering you? What's wrong?"

"Sorry, I don't mean to be short. I'm a little edgy tonight for some
reason."

"Why?" He gently put his hand on her shoulder.

"Oh hell, Joe. A lot of things. It's complicated. I know it's my
night, and that's part of it. I realize we need to honor the donors,
keep their spirits up, all that. But these companies could afford to
give so much more, do so much more, really engage. Instead they're
happy to take the deduction, the press, and move on. The awards
highlight them and fundraisers like me, not the needs of those we're
trying to help."

Joe knew this was a time to just listen. As he looked at his wife, he
recalled the night they met. It was at a cocktail party in her home
town of Charleston, South Carolina, held in honor of the officers of

the *Trader*, then one of the Navy's new groups of nuclear submarines.

Neither four years at Annapolis, nor the years as a naval intelligence officer assigned to the Navy's fleet of spy submarines, had prepared him for the impact Ashley would have on him that night, or since. Ashley understood all of the nuances; she was an effective lady. Men, of course, were instantly aware of her beauty but they soon were equally impressed with her intelligent approach to any topic. Women simply loved her. She had a soft touch but things got done. They saw that she could be trusted and that she cared not only about what she was trying to accomplish but about them personally as well. They could feel her warmth and knew it was sincere. While Joe appreciated all of that in her, what he loved – and what everyone else loved – was Ashley's lack of pretense.

The cocktail party was scheduled for seven on the lawn at the entrance to Taylor Hall with the concert to follow. Ashley was to receive an award for her cancer crusade work from the National Lung Association, together with the university's distinguished "Medal for Life." It would have been impolite, to say the least, to be late for the opening ceremony.

The chancellor of the university had arranged for Ashley and Joe to be picked up by limousine. While Joe appreciated the gesture, Ashley fretted that it was a waste of university resources. Whatever it was, the car was waiting.

Joe snatched a last-minute glance in the mirror and noticed Buck, his German shepherd, in the background. Joe could see Buck's fully upright and alert ears and, of course, those penetrating dark brown-black eyes watching every move. Buck had joined Joe and Ashley as a puppy ten years before, in response to Ashley's anticipated loneliness and to add to her sense of security when Joe was first assigned to an extended Atlantic tour. Underlying Buck's arrival was the inability, despite the lack of discernible medical reason, of Joe and Ashley to have the child they longed for. The idea for a German shepherd had come from Red Barnes, Joe's roommate at Annapolis, his best man, and his executive officer on the *Trader*. As usual, Red was right. Buck was always there, following Joe and Ashley from room to room, ready to travel. His intelligent eyes were compassionate, alert, comforting. His strength was obvious, his love and devotion unconditional.

Joe softly commanded Buck to stay and told him they would see him later. At the same time, he playfully commanded Ashley to get going. "Come on, Ash," Joe teased, laughing and locking his soft hazel-brown eyes with hers. His voice seemed to blend his authority and his humor, all in a way that made one trust him, want to follow him. They shared a soft kiss and walked downstairs into the limo.

It was a fifteen-minute ride to the university, winding through the older section of Braydon, past the country club and under the arches formed by the eighty-year-old live oak trees. As Joe leaned back against the large, black leather seat, he took Ashley's hand and gave it a tender kiss. He could not help but reflect on how good life had been to him since a somewhat shaky start. He thought about his mother and father and hoped that somewhere up there, they were aware of how far he had come from Mineville. What would they think if they were riding in this limousine tonight? Would they have expected their son to be a prominent attorney, respected by his peers, judges, friends? Would they ever have thought he would marry a woman such as Ashley? He realized that he would never be accepted in southern society in quite the same way Ashley was, but he did feel taken in.

"Competence is respected here, that's what counts," Dr. Robert Worthington, their local doctor friend, had said upon Joe's arrival in Braydon years earlier. While Joe, coming from the Adirondacks, had his doubts about that, he'd come to feel that Dr. Worthington was right. The same had been true when he went to law school after the Navy, and especially as he handled more and more sophisticated legal cases over the years. Joe got the cases the big firms couldn't handle and was known far beyond the Southeast for being an exceptionally cool attorney under fire, one who could figure a way out that worked for everybody.

Joe watched Ashley make notes in preparation for her remarks and, at the same time, admired the azaleas just coming into full bloom that April evening. He decided not to interrupt her, to resist telling her again how tremendously proud he was, how deeply he loved her. He would tell her all of that and more later tonight. He wondered about the surprise Ashley promised, reminding himself not to allow his dream of their having a child overpower his expectations. Yet he could not suppress the hope.

The limo pulled up to the crowd gathering in front of Taylor Hall. A group of cadets from the Citadel lined the entrance, their white gloves and uniforms sparkling with swords at their sides. The evening was a perfect 68 degrees. Joe could see the glow in Ashley's eyes as she took the gloved hand of one of the cadets and stepped from the limousine.

Several young girls were greeting guests at the entrance; each wore a long flowing gown and a warm, full smile. Ashley was instantly surrounded by friends and well-wishers, for many of whom she had arranged large donations. Seventy-five guests were in place, engrossed in excited conversation.

Except for the faint sound of loud rap music, no one noticed the convertible swerving down University Drive, carrying five teenage boys. Nor could anyone smell their liquored breath or hear their adolescent arguing, laughing and shouting.

The chancellor welcomed the guests outdoors and enthusiastically invited everyone to enter Taylor Hall to begin the ceremony. He approached Ashley and Joe, bowed slightly to Ashley, and took her white-gloved hand, raised it slowly to his lips and kissed it. "You look stunning, Mrs. Hart. We are honored to have you here this evening." He motioned Ashley to lead the way.

As Joe took her hand, he looked into her face, first seeing her odd expression, then feeling the warm trickle of blood on his right arm. When he moved his hand and arm up to cradle Ashley's head, he felt more blood, mushy and warm. Ashley collapsed on the stairs. The primal scream began somewhere deep within Joe's gut, but when it finally erupted, he never heard it.

CHAPTER 4

What followed was pain beyond Joe's worst nightmares. He watched the following nights and days as if they were played for him on a sharp, fast-forward screen. The futile rush to the hospital by ambulance, the conversations with the doctors and later the police. "Sorry, Joe, I know this is rough. Do you know how many random drive-by shootings killed innocent people last year?"

Yes, the boys were caught. Yes, the boy who fired the handgun was arrested, and pled guilty. No, it did not make any difference. Yes, the shooting would be used to rally the anti-handgun laws and to support Braydon's anti-crime drive. No, Joe would not lead any anti-crime reform causes and was tired of explaining.

Then there were the conversations with Clayton Anderson at Anderson Mortuary about the details of the funeral. "I know this is difficult but there are a few matters we need to discuss and for you to decide, Mr. Hart." Joe found himself hating the details and hating the choices, especially the choice of the casket. He finally settled on a fine wood but wondered if that was for Ash or himself.

The staff at Anderson's greeted well-wishers and friends in the same gracious manner it had for the last one hundred years, and for Joe the funeral was a blur. He did recall and was surprised to discover how much he appreciated the many flowers. He had always sent flowers but until then never knew how much they could mean. It was toward the people that he experienced a lack of feeling, not for any want of their responsiveness. If anything, Joe pulled away from their reaching out, knowing that they only wanted to help, feeling guilty in his withdrawal.

Joe understood the funeral was important and faced it with the same discipline – instilled at the Academy and polished by the Navy – that he had employed all his life. Joe and Ashley's home was full of people bringing food, trying to help. During calling hours at the funeral home, all offered well-intended remarks and expressions of sympathy. Silence would have been more appreciated.

While hundreds of people came through the long lines, Joe did not remember any of it. His old Navy buddy Red Barnes was there, of course, at Joe's side, quietly anticipating Joe's needs and doing all he could to help. Red took calls from friends, clients, and well-wishers, most of whom he did not know, and did his best to take notes about who had called. Apart from struggling with some of the accents, Red was able to understand most of the callers. A few, however, seemed different from the rest, their conversations hard for Red to decipher. Somebody who identified himself as Johnny seemed to talk in a par-ticularly strange way. "Tell Joe Johnny called. Okay. Tell Buck okay." Red thought he must have been a nutcase.

Then there was a caller named Tommy Greco, who sounded like he was right out of *The Sopranos*. A woman named Missy, who was too upset to talk, just said, "Please tell Joe I love him and wish I could be there but... well, he'll understand." And a man named Harry, who said to tell Joe he was sorry, but he wasn't feeling well.

Finally, Ashley's burial. And then nothing. Joe felt as if a dentist had given him a full body shot of Novocain, administered directly into his heart. Ashley's parents returned to Charleston, people stopped coming to the house, and only Red was left.

"I'll be fine, Red. I'm okay. Go ahead. Need some time alone. Thanks for being here. As always, you've got my back. Got Buck, and he's better-looking than you anyway." In reading Red's face, Joe knew that this was not enough. They had been together too long. "Okay, look, I can't sleep and when I do for an hour or two, I see her... sort of like a dream... and I really want to see her. I know I can't. It sounds crazy. I wake up in a total sweat. Then I take another shower."

"You always took too many showers," Red replied with a smile. "Who is going to give you the save-water speech?"

"Thanks for your searing insight, Buddy," Joe said with a forced grin. "It probably all comes down to time. I'll be fine. I got an idea, Red. Why don't you get your sorry ass out of here and leave me alone?"

"Aye aye, Cap. I'm out of here, but keep in touch and tell me how you're doin'. That's an order."

Joe walked Red to his metallic gray Panamera Turbo. Joe looked the Porsche over and the two men smiled, shook hands and slapped shoulders. Joe spun at the doorstep and returned the salute he knew Red had given so Red would know he was fine.

But Joe was not fine. For many nights he did not sleep, only briefly dozing off. Believing Buck needed as much consoling as he did and thanking God they at least had each other, he tried to get his dog to jump up and sleep in bed. But Buck remained on the floor, on Ashley's side.

Joe constantly thought about his Uncle Howard and Aunt Lettie, the heavy responsibility they must have felt taking the place of his parents, killed in a freak lumber mill accident when he was ten. He loved his uncle and aunt dearly and he knew they had done their best. But he wondered what his mother and father were like, and what it would have been like to be raised by them, to have felt them. Even though he didn't know them, he'd always missed them. It was through Ashley – her love, her understanding, her acceptance – that he had finally come to peace over the loss of his mom and dad. And now he'd lost the compass that led him out of that place. How was he supposed to go on now? Why should he?

Joe felt that he was having a conversation outside of himself, but he didn't know where it was coming from, or where it would lead. He hadn't been afraid of much in his life because he had faith and always managed to determine where he was going and how he would get there. Now he had no idea where he was going and less of an understanding as to how, or if, he could get there. His training was kicking in on one level – push forward, get it done – and on another level he felt he was in a deep, black hole. He decided for the moment, at least, the best he could do was to keep moving.

Over the next six months, Joe threw himself into his law practice, finding the huge caseload helpful and the people gracious, save a few well-meaning jerks, who simply could not let the topic of his loss alone. He looked forward to the long hours, avoiding empty nights at home and meals sitting across from an empty chair. He learned he could be utterly alone in a group of three or a crowd of two hundred.

He thought about seeking the counsel of his minister. He respected Dave, found him easy to talk to and certainly understanding. He knew how valuable a minister could be under these circumstances, having observed how helpful the doctors and clergy were to the men with whom he served in the Navy when they got in trouble or were under unbearable stress. Joe realized the value of all this, not to mention the connection he knew Dave would make to his relationship with the Lord and the comfort and the support that would provide.

It was essentially the same story that was drilled into his head when his mother and father died, although he was too young to fully understand it. He heard it again when his Uncle Howard passed away, soon to be followed by his Aunt Lettie. But this time it was not enough. This time he and Buck were all alone and no words were going to change that. And there was no reason for it. No logic. Why? Why would a woman like Ashley, in the prime of her life, be killed by the bullet from a gun of a young kid she never knew? How could it happen? The whole thing made no sense and Joe could not, despite day after day of thought, make any sense out of it.

At first he found himself waking up and reaching out for Ashley or calling for her as if she were there. He found himself talking to her and asking Buck about her. In short, he felt he was losing his mind. Then he went through alternating periods of withdrawal, hostility and anger, listening to himself lash out at clients, friends or others in a way he'd never done before.

He was aware that he was doing it but what bothered him was that he couldn't stop doing it. He'd been pissed off before, yet for his whole life he had managed to be in control of his emotions. That was one of his greatest strengths and that's what everybody talked about who'd worked with him in the Navy and served with him on the *Trader*. It was one of the components of his leadership, an area for which he was most admired. Where was that quality now? Would it come back? He didn't know. Worse, he didn't care.

Wanting to communicate less and less, he shut down his email and cell phone.

So he asked himself, *was this the time to go see a shrink?* While Joe had on occasion dealt with psychiatrists on behalf of clients and friends over the years, he had never consulted one in connection with his own problems. Although increasingly aware of his depression, Joe sure as hell did not want to be medicated. He'd seen enough of that over the years, in and out of the service. He knew time was his only ally. He remembered his feelings of abandonment and despair when his mom and dad were killed, and found solace in having survived that loss. He would survive this one, too.

Your Aunt Lettie and I love you like our own son... I wonder sometimes whether we've been good enough for you... We prayed many times, asking for help from the Almighty... Lettie and I could not be more proud of you if we tried.

He had learned through Ashley to let go and to love flat out, without reservation or qualification, but now reservation and qualification were back. He drove cars too fast, slammed doors too hard, and apologized too slowly. He resented it when his friends implied – and some expressed directly – that six months was time enough to get on with your life. How the hell did they know? How could they possibly understand the life he and Ash had? How many had ever experienced that? Time might diminish the scar, but no time would ever be enough where Ash was concerned.

While he wanted to cling to everything to do with Ashley, he also knew he had to do something, make some change. He kept being drawn to the pain he'd felt when Lettie told him that God had taken his mom and dad, and they were in heaven now. Looking back, he knew he would have joined them if not for his aunt and uncle. He remembered Lettie's last words to him, that she loved him, and *"whatever you do, don't forget Jesus."* What Joe wondered was whether Jesus had forgotten him? Joe had faced danger and risk of death many times. After all, he would die at some point anyway. *Why not now?*

When he pushed these away, his thoughts turned to Howard and the mountains. Joe could feel the spray from the waterfall on his face. He could hear the rush of the brook and taste the trout. He could see Howard's smile, hear his voice, as if he were still alive.

There's a certain truth in these mountains . . . They're beautiful, but they ain't forgiving. Only the strong survive . . . Treat the mountains with respect . . . you'll be all right, and never alone . . . If you make a mistake up here, you can die . . . It can be cold and raw and windy and whipped. It can also be calm and clear.

Uncle Howard was long gone. So was Aunt Lettie. So were Joe's mom and dad. And now Ashley. They were all gone. All except the mountains. They were still there. It was time to go home.

CHAPTER 5

The limo driver dropped Preston Wilson and Casey Fitzgerald, his chief financial officer, on the south side of 1575 Broadway. They passed by the green marble walls and floor into the spacious elevator and up to the thirty-eighth floor. The elevator door opened directly into the venerable law firm of Whitcock, Stevenson, Brookfield, Berry and Brown.

Preston stormed into the reception area, General Patton in a pinstriped suit. Casey waddled behind. The receptionist, apparently used to clients under stress, quietly called Andrew Brookfield, a senior partner heading the firm's fixed assets commercial group. At the same time she directed Preston and Casey to the waiting area: an antique sofa accented by a table with an assortment of neatly stacked financial magazines, softly lighted by brass and leather lamps. As he waited on the sofa, Preston bobbed his knees up and down while he noisily flipped through the pages of *Fortune 500*. Casey studied two bound financial reports.

Brookfield was the attorney supervising Wilson Holdings, Inc., the parent company of Preston's vast new and used car network. Under various names and in various locations, including Atlanta Motors, San Francisco Autoplaza, East Bay Porsche & Audi, Manhattan Mercedes, Charlottetown Motors, and Houston Automax, Wilson Holdings was one of the largest multi-state mega-dealers in the country.

Preston threw the magazine back on the table and thought about making calls on his cell phone, but the hushed atmosphere discouraged him. The only reason Preston was sitting here was the urgency of Mr. Brookfield's tone in calling the meeting.

Preston hated the way Casey looked, but there was no man he trusted more with his money. Casey's horn-rimmed glasses with thick lenses fell down his reddish, bulbous nose. Thin blond hair stuck out from underneath his khaki hat. He wore a rumpled, gray three-buttoned suit. The buttons on the vest struggled to contain his shirt, red-and-blue striped tie, and massive belly. Over his suit he wore a khaki raincoat, even though the skies were clear that morning.

It was Casey's sharp eye that had picked up the too-good-to-be-true numbers on the operating statements of San Francisco Autoplaza; his shrewd questioning and persistence that uncovered the general manager's attempt to hide the capital losses.

The silence was interrupted by an older woman who asked them to follow her to Mr. Brookfield's corner office.

"Good morning, Preston, Casey. Glad you could make it. Would you like coffee, tea?" He came around his large cherry desk and offered his hand. Andrew Brookfield was six feet, one inch tall, on the slight side, and wore thin, gold-framed glasses in front of intelligent if darting blue eyes. Except for his thin, gray hair he carried his sixty-four years well, leaving one with the impression that his experiences at Harvard and later with the United States Commerce Department, followed by the Securities and Exchange Commission, were all taken in stride.

"No, thank you, Andrew," Preston said. "Can we sit at your table in the corner?"

"Of course, please," Andrew said as he gestured, picked up a yellow pad, carefully selected one of his three fountain pens from the inside of his suit jacket pocket, and strolled to the corner where they sat on comfortable straight chairs with high backs, gathered around a small, round marble table. Casey took a yellow pad from his briefcase and prepared to record every word that Andrew said at his billable rate of $680 per hour. "Well, Andrew, have you taken Wilson's temperature?" Preston asked.

"Yes, several times," Andrew replied.

"Let's have it," Preston said, looking at Casey, who was studying the parquet wood that surrounded the border on top of the table.

Casey, of course, had informed Preston of San Francisco's cooking of the books and said he regarded the situation as serious, a word Casey did not overuse.

"As you know, Wilson Holdings has guaranteed the debt of its six subsidiaries, and each has guaranteed the debt of the others. Accordingly, they are all cross-collateralized..."

"Except for East Bay Porsche Audi," Casey interrupted.

"Well, East Bay is the only store standing alone and in the black at the moment," Andrew acknowledged. "As you know," he continued, "the only franchises East Bay has are Porsche, Audi, and Range Rover. While these franchises are not down as much as Ford and certainly not demonstrating the huge losses being generally realized in Chrysler or GM stores, their volume is only average, and insufficient to carry any of your other stores, let alone all of them."

Andrew rose from the table and poured himself a glass of water from the Waterford cut glass pitcher. Turning to Preston and Casey, he continued the lecture.

"You have $16.4 million past due in cap loans in three of your stores, some going back six months. The banks are pressing... hard. In an off-the-record statement, the bank's counsel in San Francisco told me she thinks your operating statements are bogus and your dealership's are SOT. She is threatening to go to the manufacturers on the statements, and we can expect her to seek a Temporary Restraining Order to protect the bank. In other situations, some suits have already been commenced and it's foreseeable that more will follow."

"What's the good news?" Preston asked with a tight smile that never reached his eyes.

"We have had the privilege of serving you for many years. You like your coffee strong and the talk served straight." Andrew pulled his vest down as he made this remark. Casey looked over at Preston and rolled his eyes which, if Andrew saw, he ignored.

"This is a serious matter. What I have not covered yet are the audits. Each demonstrates non-payment under the terms of the floor plan. Our auditors are still trying to determine how much."

Andrew returned to the table, set down his glass, perused his briefcase, and pulled out a particular file. He then locked eyes with Preston, and said, "I want to review with you the condition of being Sold Out of Trust ... "

"We know what it means when we haven't paid the bank what we owe on the vehicles, Andrew," Casey interrupted.

"I'm sure you do, Casey, but our litigation department received a memo from our malpractice insurance underwriter directing that we must inform you as to the meaning and implications of SOT. Please bear with me." Andrew looked first at Casey and then at Preston. Preston nodded and Casey stared blankly at Andrew.

"I know you don't want to go through this and I'll make it as brief as I can," Andrew said. He then proceeded to explain to Preston and Casey, in mind-numbing detail, the nature and character of SOT, legally and practically, with all of its implications, including potential criminal exposure.

"Again, Andrew, we know what SOT is. The real problem is what can we do about it? Aside from all the technicalities, when do we get to the real world?" Casey asked. "Given the 2008 crash, the aftermath and all the other problems in our business, how many dealers do you think can really keep up with timely payments to the bank? That money is needed for operating expenses and cash flow. Our dealers are getting killed, sales are way down and the customers are hurting and upset. What are we supposed to do?"

Preston shifted in his chair, obviously uncomfortable, as Casey, seeing that Andrew was not offering anything, continued.

"Hell, everyone's scared. Never been this bad. If the dealer needs cash, he'll keep all the money from the sale – and use it in the business or whatever – figuring he'll pay the bank off later."

"I know you're upset, Casey," Andrew replied. "I've already told you I had no choice but to be able to say that I explained all this to you. We think that the amount could be in excess of eight million. The inventory has relatively small value when compared to the debt from the cap loans and the floor plans, and the value is dropping further because of the deteriorating market conditions. Plus the manufacturers want to get rid of many of their non-performing dealers. The wheels are off the car business and we see no light at the end of the tunnel. I'm sorry."

Feeling the sweat running down his sides and the middle of his back, Preston jumped up, hurried to the credenza, and poured a large glass of ice water. "We can always sell one or more of the stores, can't we?" Preston asked. "Ford, at least, is still buying stores back."

"Ford's not easy. No blue sky. Valuation in the basement. As far as selling to dealers, the timing's bad. The buyers will work you over, discount the assets, and work with the franchisor on permission for the transfers – and that's if they don't cancel the franchises, like Chrysler and GM are doing now. When they finally conclude their due diligence, you'll be six to twelve months out.

"I've already mentioned the expected Temporary Restraining Order in California. They'll seek an order compelling all of the proceeds be directed to the bank. We'll try to prevent the TRO, or at least have it modified so that ordinary business expenses would be first taken out by the dealership before money goes to the bank. Loans to officers, however, would likely not be permitted, nor would drawing out funds to help any of the other stores. There would be no profit generation."

At this point, Preston was pacing the room. "What about the value of the underlying real estate in those stores?" he demanded, throwing his pen on the table.

"I know you're aware that real estate's down across the board, some places worse than others. And I'm sure you know what's going on with the banks. The jury's not in on whether the bailouts will help or not. We argue about that every day around here. The only two stores where you own the real estate are East Bay in Chicago and Charlottetown. The North Carolina real estate is already encumbered by first and second mortgages, not to mention the Uniform Commercial Code's securing the collateral. There is very little, if any, equity remaining, particularly since the refinancing we completed last November for East Bay. The rest of the stores are leases, and the franchisors have been pressing your stores with such a demand for site improvements, I doubt that you have any real equity in the leases."

Preston rose from the table and strolled over to the floor-to-ceiling window overlooking the west side of Manhattan. He stared out, his nose close to the windows. He could see his breath on the glass. He watched the cars running like ants up and down the West Side Highway and the boats on the Hudson River. The sky was filled with planes servicing Newark, Tetterboro, and other airports. He looked over at Casey, who still had his hat on. Casey returned Preston's look, shaking his head. Preston could see moisture behind Casey's thick lenses.

"But, Andrew, what's our solution?" Preston demanded.

"Our group has reviewed this, not only among ourselves, at length, but also with our commercial people, our real estate people, our financial people and our bankruptcy ... advisors. Although they are not actually our people but a firm specializing in the actual handling of bankruptcy matters. While there have been some differences of viewpoint among the groups, the ultimate consensus is to file for protection under Chapters 11 and 13 of the Bankruptcy Code, with an individual filing under Chapter 7 of the code to follow for you and Marcia."

Hearing the name of his wife jarred Preston and added a new dimension to his growing fear. He wished he could stop the words rushing out of Andrew's mouth.

"As you are aware, Marcia has personally guaranteed the debt for all of the stores," Andrew said in a low voice. Preston slowly nodded.

"Except East Bay," Casey mumbled.

"Yes, except East Bay. But again, in the overall picture, that does not make a material difference. The problem is that in the filing of a Chapter 11 proceeding, which deals with the businesses only, there probably will not be enough unencumbered assets to survive the filing and be of use to you. Even if there are sales, the trustee in bankruptcy will be doing the selling. It will take years to go through it, and the banks do not have to wait at all before going after you and Marcia on the notes – and pursuant to the Personal

Guarantees – without waiting for the results of the suits foreclosing on the collateral. The only thing that will stop the tide is bankruptcy. By law, all the creditors will have to stop hounding you. They'll still be there but will have to work through a creditor's committee. And the Trustee."

"If we file for individual protection under Chapter 7, these damn banks will take everything we have. We'll lose our Trump Tower condo, our home, and we'll lose all of our stores and all of our real estate. What's left? Personal belongings?"

"You have no choice, Preston. Besides," Andrew said, playing his last card, "your best chance for keeping this civil is bankruptcy."

"What the hell does that mean?" Preston asked, knowing at the same time exactly what it meant.

Andrew entered into another lengthy lawyer-like dissertation, more in the nature of an Artful Dodger disclaimer, including why Chapters 7 and 11 might not work depending on how the SOT was viewed.

"Are you telling us we could actually go to jail over this?" Casey asked.

"Well, we assume that the money that would have otherwise gone to the bank to reduce the interest and principal on the loan for the flooring line went back into the business in one form or another. That the monies were used for operations and other legitimate corporate purposes. Any non-corporate use exacerbates the problem. Private parties, the Lear jet, personal yachts.... "

By this time, Preston, having heard enough, had already stood and was heading for the door. He turned to Casey, moving his hands to instruct him to pack his papers in his briefcase.

"So what you're telling us is we're screwed and there is nothing you can do about it. Where have you been?" Preston said, putting his hand on the large brass door handle and looking over his shoulder. "You've had no trouble billing the shit out of me. Probably paid for half this office. Come on, Casey, let's get out of here."

Riding down in the elevator, Preston slammed his fist against the elevator door, and turned to Casey. "You know what really pisses me off? We keep these guys high up in their fancy offices with all the glass, but in the end, they tell us to go down instead of bailing us out. I want you to find a smart attorney with guts who can figure out 'how to' instead of 'why not.' And I want you to find him now!"

The elevator door opened, and they marched out past the green marble walls, their shoes clicking on the marble floor.

CHAPTER 6

"Okay. I get it. What you want me to do is find a lawyer who specializes in automobile financing and understands SOT?" Fred Drucker asked Casey.

"I want you to do much more than that. Look, you're an experienced head hunter, right? I want you to talk with lawyers around this country who have experience in asset-based financing, automobile dealerships, commercial real estate transactions, banking, litigation. I want you to develop four or five solid recommendations for a bright and savvy lawyer who is an experienced litigator, understands business, and understands how to get the damn job done. A fighter. A fucking legal warrior. With balls. Get it?"

"Mr. Fitzgerald, you've got to learn to get over being so shy," Fred said. "Try to speak your mind."

"Where's the coffee?" Casey asked, getting up and looking around.

"Actually," the recruiter said, after pouring coffee from the silver pot on his credenza, "I know a man who was in the Navy who really was a warrior, and, in fact, is now a practicing lawyer somewhere in the South. I don't know what kind of law he practices, but I can tell you he's a leader, in fact a former commander, and he knows how to deliver. Surprisingly, he's a really nice guy. I'll check it out and find out what kind of law he practices, and maybe he can lead us to the right man."

"Okay. Just get it done. And after you find the right guy, have one of your investigators check him out. Mr. Wilson wants to know everything about the people he hires. Everything. Get it?"

"Yes, Mr. Fitzgerald, I understand. I'll get back to you shortly," Drucker replied.

Preston rode up to his co-op on the thirty-eighth floor without seeing any of the people in the Trump Tower elevator. *He takes my company's temperature and then tells me we're gonna die and there's nothing he can do about it.*

Marcia was listening to McCullough's *John Adams* while ironing one of Preston's Faconnable shirts when she heard the door open and slam shut. "I'm in here, darling," she called.

Preston sauntered to the bar, poured himself a Chivas Regal on the rocks and collapsed into his Italian brown leather chair, propping his feet up on the matching ottoman.

"Why don't you have Elsie do the ironing? That's what we pay her for," Preston shouted in Marcia's direction.

Marcia took off her head-phones. "I iron your favorite shirts, Preston, because you don't like the way they come out when Elsie does them, or when I send them out. Now, what's bothering you, Pres?" She unplugged the iron, trudged in to the large den, and slumped down on the ottoman. Marcia was in her late-thirties with dark brown hair and effectively applied make-up that made her look even younger. Her body reflected hours of working out in the private Trump Tower health club.

Preston watched Marcia as she sat down, giving particular attention to the way Marcia's body filled her brown wool skirt and sweater outfit.

"What are you doing today?" he asked, catching a whiff of her perfume.

"Lunch with the girls at Daniel. How was your morning?"

"Oh, same old. Meetings. Met with Andrew Brookfield."

"Really? How is old Andrew? Elegant as ever? Did he have his French cuffs on?"

"You don't like Andrew, do you?"

"I don't know. He reminds me of a couple of guys I worked with when I taught at Columbia. He's supposed to be a big-shot lawyer from an old line firm, Harvard and all of that, but I find him a bit of a snob. He needs to lighten up. Why were you seeing him?"

"We've got some business problems with the companies. He called Casey and thought we should go over the financials."

Looking at the drink in Preston's hand, she said, "It's a little early, even for you, isn't it? How serious are the problems?"

"Nothing for you to worry about," Preston replied. From the look on her face, he knew that she would worry anyway, particularly about his having talked her into signing personal guarantees, against her will, on all the corporate debt. He remembered all the nights when he'd assured her, "It's just a formality."

Preston abandoned his drink and headed out.

"Are you telling me everything, Preston? I really feel as though you're holding something back. We're in this together, aren't we?"

If she finds out how bad this is, and that I have not protected her . . . we'll be in real trouble . . . she'll freak out . . . she'll leave . . . I need to talk with her, but not now. What a mess.

"I've got a luncheon meeting at the Four Seasons Grill Room and then more meetings all afternoon at the Manhattan store," Preston called over his shoulder. "If Casey calls, be sure to have him get me on my cell."

CHAPTER 7

Even though Preston was in a meeting, he opened his cell phone.

"Yeah, Case, what have you got?"

"Talked with Fred Drucker, the legal head hunter at Antel. He thinks he has a positive search, but I'm not so sure. You want to hear it?"

"We need help. Go."

"Turns out he knew a guy in the Navy named Joe Hart, who was a submarine commander and is now an attorney in some hick town in the South. Drucker was going to get a short list of attorneys this guy would recommend to do the job. As a matter of course, he checks the guy out first. Five out of the six recommend this guy. They've all sent him work, heavy stuff, you know, the kind of cases they either can't handle or don't want to take on the risk. If he wins, they're heroes. If he loses, it's his fault. They don't know how the hell he does it. But he does it."

"What specifically does he do?" Preston asked.

"He looks at the same case they looked at, the background and financials, collateral, equity, that information. Then he figures out where he wants to go. They say he cuts through it and persuades everybody involved – even though they're all fighting with each other – to follow his plan. It really doesn't matter what the case is, as long as he's interested in taking it. It's not about money with this guy. If he needs to, he litigates, and he wins. But he'd rather do it without litigation. In fact, one of the lawyers I talked to told me a story about Hart defending one of seven above-ground swimming pool companies in a plaintiff's case in Federal Court in Syracuse. It seems that some idiot got drunk and dived from a second-story balcony into a four-foot pool, fracturing his skull and breaking his neck. He's now a paraplegic and will be in a wheelchair the rest of his life. Hart makes a motion for summary judgment before the judge and before any depositions are even taken. The thing that pissed the other defense lawyers off is that he won the motion."

"Why were they upset? Weren't they all on the same side?"

"Yeah, they had a lot of respect for what Hart did from a legal point of view, but what pissed them off was that he kept each of them from making over $200,000 in fees defending the case. It took a lot of guts."

"Did you ask how he got the judge to throw the case out?"

"Yeah, the way he did it was he compiled the sworn affidavits from all the witnesses that showed that the plaintiff was drunk out of his skull and caused his own injury by diving head first into a four-foot pool. He showed that the failure of the pool companies to warn that the pool was only four feet deep was not what caused the injury. Something about proximate cause or some other lawyer crap.

"Then Hart presents a financial study on the cost to the plaintiff, to all the defendants and to the court itself if the court waits until all the depositions of all the parties are taken by all the lawyers, which he projected to take over a year and a half, which apparently hadn't been done before. His cost projection was in the millions. He challenged any of the lawyers to dispute the projection of the costs, and they couldn't do it. So it went 'uncontroverted.'

"The bottom line is he convinced the judge to throw the case out right then. Not only that, the plaintiff appealed, and this guy Hart wrote his own brief and argued the appeal in the United States Court of Appeals right here in the city and won. And get this, he's done some heavy lifting for various mega-dealers around the country, straightened out some pretty big messes."

"Interesting," Preston said. "I wonder why we haven't heard of the guy."

"He's not your garden-variety lawyer. He only takes about one in ten cases. He doesn't advertise. He gets called in by the big firms, decides if he wants to take the case, and if he does, he gets in and out and sends the client back to the big firm. The big firms don't want to advertise that he bailed them out and he's happy to keep a low profile. He doesn't even have a website."

"So have you talked with this guy?"

"Well, that's the problem. We don't know where the hell he is."

"I thought you said he's in ... well, some town in the South. Why can't you narrow that down?"

"We did that. The town is outside of Charleston, a place called Braydon. We know where Hart lives, but we don't know where Hart is."

"What?" Preston demanded. "I don't get why it's so difficult to find a lawyer practicing in Braydon, South Carolina."

"Well, here's the part that gets really bad. It seems Hart's wife was killed in some random drive-by shooting. Can you believe that shit? He took it really hard, which I can understand, and he took off."

"Took off where?"

"Someone said something about the mountains, which makes no sense to me. We can put a PI on it and send him down to where the guy lives and see what he can find out, if you want me to do that."

"Casey, your man Drucker has a full investigative report on this man, right? Where is he from? Where was he born? Where did he grow up?"

"Believe it or not, this guy's from New York."

"If he's from the city and such a big shot, why haven't we heard of him?" Preston said. "Something's wrong here."

"This guy is from upstate, and I don't mean Westchester. The boonies. But there is something wrong."

"What?"

"We've got the best lawyers right here. Why should we go chase this guy? Besides, he's got problems, and we don't have a clue where he is. We're wasting time looking for this guy. Even if we find him what have we got? I think it's crazy."

There was a long pause on the line.

"Preston?" Casey asked.

"Yeah, I'm here," Preston said. "Let's think this through. From what you've told me this guy's a fighter, a former Navy commander. He does this kind of work, apparently well. He's not like other attorneys, sure as hell not like ours. You say he tries not to litigate . . . but when he has to, he kicks ass. That sounds just like the kind of guy we need."

"I don't know." Casey said. "Anyway, we don't know where he is."

"You said he's gone some place in the mountains. Some place in the mountains," Preston repeated. *Where? Where were those mountains my father dragged me to?* "Where does the investigative report show he's from, Casey? Where did he grow up?" Preston asked again.

"Just a minute," Casey said. Preston could hear him shuffling through papers. "Here it is, Mineville, wherever the hell that is."

"Hang on a second, Casey," Preston said, as he pushed his mind back further and further. "I'll call you back."

Preston excused himself from the meeting and went back to his corner office on the forty-fourth floor of the General Motors Building. He walked up to the glass and stared through the floor-to-ceiling windows. It was a clear morning and he could see the East River and part of the Hudson River, the George Washington, Triboro, and Queensboro bridges, the sun shimmering off the water, the buildings and the planes approaching and leaving LaGuardia in the distance. He loved that view, and he loved being up there. He didn't want to lose it. His thoughts turned to his mother and then to his father. He kept pushing back, further and further in his mind. He was not sure what he was searching for, but he knew there was something he was missing. Then he remembered his mother's words that horrible night when she told his father to leave. Some reference to his father spending time with him. Then it hit him. *"There is the business about those trips way upstate in the mountains."* Preston recalled one trip with his father, a guide and the guide's son. Or maybe it was his nephew. Whatever, Preston hated being dragged up there, the whole wilderness thing. He vaguely remembered the old man and the kid. *They were pathetic, but they did know the mountains.*

Preston called Casey back.

"I may know where he is," he said. "Get a helicopter. You and I are going to Mineville."

"Wait a minute, Pres. Mineville is where he grew up, but, again, we don't know where he is now. I have no information as to what mountains he's in. There are a lot of mountains: in the Carolinas, Virginia, the Appalachians, the Poconos, the Adirondacks, the Catskills. And that's just in the East. Maybe he went out West, who the hell knows? How are we going to find him? And if we do, how do we know he'll help us?"

"We don't have a choice; we've got to find him. If we do find him, I think he'll help us."

"How the hell do you know that? You act like you know this guy."

"I might. Years ago there was a kid my age in the mountains. I think his name was Joe. He lived with the old man, the guide. There was something about his father not being around. He had a different last name. It could have been Hart. We went hunting with them. He wasn't anybody but . . . well, if he's the guy I'm thinking of, maybe I've got a hook. You know what I mean?"

"Well, not really . . . but . . . whatever you say, Preston."

CHAPTER 8

"Okay, Casey," Preston said, looking at the map. "Follow Route 9 North. It's about fifty miles or so. We'll start there." He pointed to Mineville.

Two hours later they were looking at worn-out houses, dilapidated roofs, stores closed and boarded up or left with broken windows. No McDonald's, no KFC; a church, a grocery store, an old gas station, a tiny post office alongside a laundromat.

After a day it seemed as though Casey and Preston talked with nearly all of Mineville's 1,482 people, but no one knew Joseph Hart or any of his family. When Preston or Casey talked about hunting guides and getting into the mountains, everybody they spoke with had a different idea.

"I'd go up to Lake Placid and come back into the hills," one said. "Maybe he lived around there."

"You might try Saranac Lakes Wild Forest Whitney Wilderness," an aging woman offered. Another suggested Hamilton County, the High Peaks Wilderness. And so it went on.

One old man suggested they check with the hunting camps and guides to see if anybody "had ever heard of this fella Hart." He said to look for "that fella named after the mountain. What was his name? Yeah, 'Lockart,' that fella. Try to find a guide like him, someone who grew up huntin' and fishin' in these woods."

Neither Preston nor Casey had any idea how big the Adirondack Mountains really were. One guide they did talk to, while never having heard of the Harts, told them that the Adirondacks included over five million acres of big game wilderness to explore, hunt, fish and to enjoy the waters. While the enormity of the area was impressive, it was also daunting.

Preston told Casey to drive farther up Route 9 North. "I wish the hell I could remember the name of my father's guide who hauled my ass all over these mountains."

"If you ask me, I think you're chasing rainbows."

"I didn't ask you. And don't ever say that to me again. Do you understand? Never!" Preston could see the bend in the wheel as Casey tightened his grip. In all the time that Preston had known Casey, Preston had never talked to him in that manner.

Soon they arrived in the small village of Witherbee, four miles west of Mineville. No one knew of any Harts there. They decided to keep going west. The only encouragement, if you could call it that, was that the roads were winding more and the foothills getting closer.

They pressed on to the next little village. Again, no one knew any Harts. It was getting late, but they decided to try one more town. Casey drove on until they found a few houses and a small battered wooden sign: "Lord's Valley, Population Two Dozen." The largest building was a big green wooden house set off the road into the rocks and the hill, with seven small green-and-white wooden cabins behind it. The sun was setting now, with rays still shining through the trees and reflecting off a brook that seemed to run under or near the big house. There was something hazily familiar about it to Preston.

When Casey shut the motor off, Preston was immediately aware of the quiet. All he could hear was the babbling of the brook. An old broken-down Ford pick-up sat in the back of the dirt driveway, jacked up sideways to the house. Rotting wood steps led to the screened-in front porch.

Preston and Casey approached the house from the front, and as Preston knocked on the front door, he tried not to fall through the steps. No response. He banged again, harder. The door fell off its hinges and to the ground. A heavyset man with huge arms and upper chest, obviously in his twenties, appeared holding a

Remington 1100 Shotgun in his arm. "Can I help you boys?" he asked.

"I'm Preston Wilson, and this is my associate, Casey Fitzgerald. I apologize for the door, and I'd be happy to pay to have it fixed. I'm looking for an attorney named Joseph Hart. You know him? It's important that we find him. We were hoping you could help us."

"Most folks who come visitin' don't knock. They just come on in. It's the knock that got me worried. But you fellas don't appear to be a problem. Don't worry about the door. One of these days, I'm meanin' to fix it. Save your money. We don't need that neither. Now who is it you lookin' for?"

"An attorney named Joseph Hart. He'd be about forty-six years old," Preston guessed.

"Don't know no Attorney Hart," the man said. Preston looked at Casey, who was shaking his head.

"People hunt and fish around here, right?" Casey asked.

"Yep."

"You hunt and fish around here, right?" Casey went on.

"Nope."

"You know of any men who have come up here – men in their forties or so – to fish and hunt?"

"Yep, they come up here all the time, but I don't know 'em 'cause I work in the mill."

"Okay, thanks for your time," Casey said, as he turned around and walked carefully down the steps. Preston started to follow Casey. As he walked away, he heard the man say, "There was one fella who came up here to hunt and fish and stayed quite awhile. Nice guy. I remember him because he asked me how I liked this house and whether I could afford the rent. I told him I liked the house fine and the rent was real reasonable. He seemed happy to hear that, but I don't know why. Come to think of it, he slept in one of them little cabins in the back for three, four days while he gathered stores and ammunition to go up into the hills. By the look of it, he was gonna stay up there awhile. I don't know why they do that."

Preston turned and asked, "What did he look like?"

"Average, I guess," the man said.

"I don't suppose you know his name?" Preston asked.

"Nope, sorry. Guy with him just called him Cap."

"Why did they call him Cap, do you know?"

"No, I just have a wag." Seeing the expression on Preston's face he went on, "You know, a wild ass guess," and laughed. "Not to be smart or nothin', but I figured he might have been in the Navy by the way he talked, you know?"

"Why do you think he was in the Navy?" Casey asked, suddenly showing interest.

"'Cause when he asked me about the house and the rent and all he called me sir. Nobody ain't ever called me sir. I asked him, 'Why you callin' me that?' He said he was sorry, an old Navy habit. Then I heard the guy he was with call him Cap or something like that. Then they left. That's all I know."

"It's getting late," Preston said. "Is there any chance that any of those green cabins is empty? Could we stay there for the night? Do you rent them?"

"There's one empty at the end. I don't rent 'em, but some fella from Witherbee does. I got a key though. You want to rent it, it's ten bucks in advance. And you gotta be quiet, and there ain't no drinking. And stay away from the other cabins, these people want peace and quiet. Especially the lady in the third cabin. She's had a hard time, and she don't want no company."

Preston gave the man ten dollars, and he and Casey went to the cabin on the end. There were two beds, a table in between with one lamp, and a small bathroom. It looked good to both of them.

"We'll stay here tonight, Casey, and in the morning, we'll try to find a guide to take us up into these hills and see if we can find Commander Hart, also known as 'Cap.'"

CHAPTER 9

Preston had already showered and dressed when Casey woke at seven. A morning mist covered the trees and steam rose from the brook as the two men bundled up in the ski jackets they had brought along. They climbed into the SUV and headed west on Route 9. After about six miles of winding road, they saw a brown shingled house with three cars pulled up on the lawn and a wooden sign that proclaimed, "We cook the best for all the rest."

"You fellas lost or hungry?" the waitress asked, directing them to a table in the front of the large room, with a view of pines and the road. As they walked to their table, Preston and Casey could not help but notice a striking young woman bent over a table in the corner facing the road. She stared out the window through dark sunglasses that barely covered the bruises on the right side of her face.

"Good morning," Casey said to her as they passed by, receiving a slight nod and no smile in return. The waitress brought piping hot coffee. As they waited for their bacon, eggs, sausage and toast, Casey leaned over to Preston and whispered, "She may be the one the mill guy was talking about." Preston nodded. Their breakfast soon came and the men ate eagerly.

"You fellas get enough to eat?" the waitress asked. "Like more coffee?"

"No, thank you, we're all set," Preston said. "Tell me, is there a hunting and fishing club in the vicinity?"

"I don't know about the vicinity, but you could hit the Blooming Grove Hunting and Fishing Club with a stone from here," she laughed.

49

"Do they have guides there?"

"You'll have to talk to who's up there this morning, see who's around and who ain't. It's already a little late in the morning. Most of the fellas would've gone out by now. Maybe Larry's around, with his bad foot and all. Don't know. Go ask. Only way to find out."

Casey and Preston saw the white sign with black letters in front of the three-story wooden frame house with steep stairs leading up to the front porch. "There it is," Casey read, "'Blooming Grove Hunting & Fishing Club.'"

Hearing no response to their knock, they walked in through the unlocked front door. The shutters were closed, and the inside was dark and chilly as Casey called out.

"Can I help you?" A tall, thin man in his forties appeared.

Preston introduced himself and Casey.

"Larry," the man said. "What can I do for you?"

"We are trying to find an attorney named Joe Hart. We have reason to believe he's hunting or fishing around here, and it's important that we find him as soon as possible."

"You in a rush to hunt?"

"No, we just need to talk with him," Preston said. "Do you know him? Is he here?"

"This is a private huntin' and fishin' club," Larry said. "Sorry I can't help you."

Jesus, we come this far, sleep in a dump, find the damn club, and now this guy thinks this is the New York Athletic Club in the mountains and wants to protect its members. Preston took a deep breath.

"I understand, sir, that this is a private club. I don't want to intrude. We've come a long way to find Mr. Hart. We believe he is an attorney who can be of immense help to us, and we need him desperately. We would greatly appreciate your assistance. It would help a good deal if you could simply tell us whether you know him, and if so, whether he's here or where he is. Perhaps you could help us as a guide and take us to him? I met him years ago when he was a young boy in this general area. He was hunting with an older man, I believe his uncle. I will be happy to pay you – and pay you well – if you can help us find him."

"You was hunting with him? Can you remember the guide's name?" Larry asked.

"It could have been Howard ... or maybe Harold ... I'm not sure."

"Did this Howard have a last name?"

"I'm sorry but I have been racking my brain trying to think of his name. It was a long time ago." Preston said.

"Would ya know it if ya heard it?" Larry asked.

"I don't know," Preston answered, growing more frustrated by the minute. "Also, the attorney we are trying to find is sometimes called 'Cap,' perhaps because he was in the Navy."

"How about Howard Buckingham?" Larry asked.

Preston thought for a while and then said, excitement lighting his voice, "Yes, I believe that was it, now that I hear the name. It was a long time ago, but I think I do remember the name Buckingham because he told my father and me we could call him 'Buck.'"

"What was your dad's name?" Larry asked.

"Peter Wilson," Preston said, thinking how odd it was that he had never thought of referring to his father as "Dad."

"When were you and your dad huntin' up here? What year?" Larry asked.

"Well, I was fifteen. That was thirty years ago."

"And you think Buck was the guide for you and your dad?" Larry asked.

"I think so."

"Wait here a minute, help yourself to the coffee on the side stand. I wanna check the book upstairs," Larry said, and limped up the stairway at the side of the room by the fireplace.

Preston fell into the large, leather, winged-back chair while Casey poured himself a cup of strong coffee and flipped the pages of a hunting magazine. Preston assumed that Casey was wondering what in hell they were doing up here and whether they were on a wild goose chase. He regretted that he'd blown up at Casey in the car about the chasing rainbows remark. He knew what haunted him had nothing to do with Casey, who had always been a good friend. His thoughts were interrupted by Larry clunking down the stairs.

"Well, we have a policy against intrudin' in this club. It's private, ya understand? But seein' as you and your father actually met Buck and been huntin' these hills with him before, I reckon Joe would think it's okay to talk to you like this."

"Then you do know Mr. Hart?"

"Sure do. He's one of us."

"Can you find him?"

"What do you mean, find him?"

"Well, do you know where he is at this time, and can you tell us, so we can go to him and talk with him?"

"I know he came up here a few days ago. I know he was planning to go up into the hills for a while. I don't know where he was going to go. He didn't tell me and I didn't ask. So no, I don't know where he is in particular, but he's no doubt out there somewhere."

"How can we find him?"

"You probably can't. You could wait around here till he comes out and then he probably will get in touch with me or need provisions from Sarah. You could see if he would talk to you then. He probably would."

"Look, this is really important to us. We've got to find him. Do you think we could hire a plane and pilot or a helicopter and find him that way?"

"I doubt it," Larry said. "We're talking a lot of land here. The State Park alone has six million acres. Actually we don't think of it as acres. It's miles and miles of wilderness and wild country. The woods are thick, heavy. You ain't gonna see much from the air, and that's on a good day. How you gonna tell who you see from the air anyway, even if you saw a man or a group of people? It just ain't practical."

Casey suggested to Preston that they take a break, get some coffee, and talk it over. Larry invited them into the kitchen of the big lodge and showed them where the coffee pot was.

"Help yourselves, gentlemen," he said, excusing himself. "I'll be upstairs if you need me." He left Preston and Casey at the table, drinking coffee.

"Well, Casey, any bright ideas?"

"Yeah. Let's get out of here, go back to the city," Casey said. "This is like finding a needle in a haystack. It's beyond our control. We've got to let it go."

"I don't want to let it go, Casey. I can't. Think. What can we do? We've been in tight situations before. We've always found a way out. Why should this be different? It's got to come down to money. It always does. Think about it."

"Preston, this is not one of those deals where you make a donation to charity and get named man of the year. We're in the boonies. The mountains are big and we don't know where the hell this guy is. Larry doesn't either, assuming he really wants to help us. And I don't know if he does. Let's face it. We're screwed here. Maybe we can find another guy."

"There's not another guy, Casey. He's the one. That's why the hell we're here. But that's a great idea. Make a donation. We'll make a donation to this hunting club. Let's try that." Preston got up and went to the foot of the stairs and called Larry.

A few minutes later, Larry came down. "What are you fellas going to do?" he asked.

"Larry, I want to make a suggestion to you," Preston said. "I hope you will take it in the spirit I intend it. I would like to make a generous donation to the Blooming Grove Hunting and Fishing Club. I appreciate your trying to help us. I know there's no way to know exactly where Mr. Hart is. But I don't want to stop trying, and anything you can think of that we haven't would be greatly appreciated."

"Well, that's very generous of you, Mr. Wilson. Lord knows, this club can use money. If you want to make a donation, that's fine with us, and we'll be thankful. But that's not gonna find Joe. I can see that you fellas need to hook up with Joe. I don't know whether Joe needs to hook up with you, but that's not my business. Joe will figure that out if you can find him. He's been through a lot, and I know he's not looking for company."

"We heard about the unfortunate ... tragic ... thing that happened to Mr. Hart's wife. I'm very sorry. That shouldn't happen to anyone. I can certainly understand how horrible that must be."

"Well, I've been thinking about where Joe could be myself. If Joe were going into the park for a while, he would check in with the Rangers. He knows a lot of those fellas, and he would check with them and get a permit. I made a couple of calls when I was upstairs. He hasn't checked with the Rangers on this trip. That makes me suspect that he's heading for some private land. I know of a couple of areas – privately owned – that Joe likes. I'm not saying he's there, but I do know that he wanted to be alone. I figure he would stay away from the hikers, the climbers and all of that. He's probably staying away from the peaks and the trails. He knows how to handle himself out there, so he ain't limited to the trails. Fact is, he'd rather go off on his own. If I knew when he left, that would give me an idea how far he would get, again, if he went where I think he might have gone.

"I'll tell you what. You donate to the club, and I'll donate two days of my time. We'll take a walk to where I think he could possibly be. There ain't no guarantees he'll be there. You got to understand that. But I'll take you up there, and we'll see. Maybe you'll get lucky and find him. Maybe you won't. Whatever happens, it's a pretty trip, and at least you will have tried. That's the best I can offer you."

"That's good enough for us," Preston said. "We accept, and, again, we appreciate what you're doing for us."

"Well, I'm happy to help. To be honest, I'm doing it for Joe and his family. His uncle was a legend in this club. You said you met him, hunted with him."

"Thanks," Preston said, with appreciation and excitement energizing his voice. "When do you think we can leave?"

"Seeing as you boys are in such a rush, I would say we can leave at first light. Where's your gear?"

"What gear?" Preston asked.

"Well, you fellas might get a little cold up there, a little wet. You might like something to sleep in. But it's all the same to me. If you don't have nothin', I'll scrounge around here. Probably can find something you can get along with. You fellas go down the road to

Sarah's store and get what you want to eat and a bear canister to put the food in. I'll meet you out front by my red pick-up truck in the morning."

"Tell me about the bear canister," Casey asked, feeling awkward about the question and hoping it did not mean they really did have to worry about bears.

"It's a regulation now that, if you're going to stay overnight, you've got to keep your food in a canister. Sarah has 'em. No need to invite the bears in for dinner."

Casey shot Preston a look, but Preston was already up and shaking Larry's hand. "Thank you again," he said. "We'll see you in the morning."

Casey and Preston left, climbed into their SUV, and headed for Sarah's.

CHAPTER 10

When Preston and Casey arrived at the lodge just before day-break, Larry was waiting in his truck. They loaded the backpacks Larry gave them with their clothes and the food and water they had purchased, then bounced for what seemed like hours over the winding dirt road, the three of them crammed into the front seat of Larry's four-wheel-drive. The road followed Blooming Grove Stream for a while until it passed over an ancient wooden bridge and became narrower and rougher as they climbed higher in the hills. Finally it simply ended, with a rusted steel bar across what looked like a foot trail.

"Well, the easy part's over," Larry said. "From here, we go on foot. Joe likes the next pond on the south side. Maybe he's up there."

Larry led the way up the trail, which became increasingly harder to recognize. Preston, and especially Casey, had a hard time keeping up with their guide, even with his bad foot. Other than a lot of grunts, Casey never said a word.

"We've gotta keep movin'," Larry said. "If we find Joe, I'll be leaving you fellas. It'll take me a day to get back."

Casey and Preston were taking increasingly longer stops for a drink of water and to rest. Larry looked at them impatiently but waited, and then set off again up the trail.

It seemed as though Casey was finding it harder to breathe. Like he felt some tightness in his chest. He said aloud that he had to keep his promise to himself to lose weight.

Even though the sun was no longer visible, there was still plenty of light, and Larry seemed as though he didn't really know where he was going but there was no choice other than to trust him. Larry was saying very little and just kept moving. As they climbed higher and higher, deeper into the forest, Preston was second-guessing himself. *What if Casey is right about Joe? Right about this trip? I should be back in the city taking care of my business. What if Joe is troubled? He's obviously a drop-out. He has gone through some difficult circumstances, to say the least. What if he's not all together? What if he tells me to leave him alone? Or go to hell? Maybe I am chasing rainbows.*

Larry seemed to be picking up the pace. At one point, he climbed up on a large rock embedded in the side of the hill, looked down and to the left with his binoculars, and slid down again. "It won't be long. We'll be there soon."

"Be where?" Casey mumbled. These were among the only words he had spoken since they left.

"At Four Points Pond. That's where I'm hoping we'll find Joe. It's a great spot, kind of special. Very quiet and loaded with game."

Although there really was no longer any trail, Larry pressed on, making his own. They were climbing along large sides of rock that seemed built into the ground and looked like they had marble in them.

Out of cracks in the rock grew pine and spruce trees, some larger than Preston had ever seen. The air seemed different and so did the light. It was also getting harder for him to breathe. There were hawks coasting high in the air, and Preston's sense of smell was working overtime. Other than the sounds of water from streams and the rustling of the wind, there was quiet. More quiet than he had ever experienced.

At last, Larry stopped and turned to Preston and Casey with a big smile on his face. "You boys must be doing something right or else you got the Good Lord on your side."

"Why, what?" Preston and Casey asked at the same time.

"I believe we've found the man you're looking for," Larry answered as he kept moving.

"Where? How do you know that?" Preston asked.

Without breaking his stride, Larry looked over his shoulder at Preston. "'Cause Joe has started his fire."

"How can you tell it's Joe's fire?" Casey grunted.

"'Cause Joe makes a fire just big enough," Larry said. "And no smoke."

After another thirty minutes, Larry guided the two men down a steep path through rocks and trees leading to a large pond. The pond was fed by a waterfall cascading down the boulders. At the near side of the pond and the edge of the forest was a man sitting in front of a tiny fire with his back to a lean-to set against the rock side of the mountain. Larry whistled as they approached and Joe whistled back. Larry went up to Joe and whispered a few words that neither Preston nor Casey could hear. Joe nodded and motioned Casey and Preston over.

"Joe, this here is Mr. Preston Wilson, and the fella with him's name is Mr. Casey Fitzgerald. Fellas, this here is Joe Hart." The men shook hands.

Preston tried to reconcile the man he now looked at with his memory and the mental image he had formed. This was not the fifteen-year-old, scrappy, out-of-it kid he thought he remembered, nor did he expect that. On the other hand, he did not look the way Preston had anticipated. He was shorter, but with squarer shoulders and a stronger build. Yet, something about Joe prodded Preston's memory. He now remembered Joe's eyes, having stared into them in the crevice when Joe had been lowered down and struggled to tie a rope around him.

What Preston saw now was a fully mature man with the same piercing eyes but a cold face. He seemed to Preston to have a certain confidence and presence, simultaneously comforting and intimidating. Joe and Preston stood and looked at each other for what felt to Preston to be too long a time.

"Well, I've done my part, Mr. Wilson," Larry said as he set his pack on the ground. "There's two sleeping bags in here, two blankets and a tarp. That oughta do ya. I'll be climbing back down this hill now. So long, Mr. Wilson, Mr. Fitzgerald. See ya later, Joe."

Joe nodded and waved goodbye as Larry returned to the trail.

"Thank you, Larry," Preston called after him. "I'll settle up with you later."

Larry held his right arm up, and just kept walking.

"You guys came a long way," Joe said. "Why?"

"I don't know if you remember me, Joe."

"I remember. How's your arm?" Joe asked with a smile.

"It's doing fine," Preston said, not returning the look. "I wish I were doing as well. What are you doing up here all alone?"

"What makes you think I'm alone?" Joe asked.

"Well, I don't see anybody else."

"I don't think a man is really ever alone," Joe said. "Besides, there's a lot of animals up here. And you don't see Buck. But he's been smelling you and Larry and watching you for the last three miles. Buck is the reason I knew Larry was with you, and that's the only reason you found me," Joe said.

At first Preston was confused. Then he had the horrible thought that Joe must be confused. *He's been up here too long. I'm screwed.*

Joe looked at Preston, still smiling, and put two fingers to his lips and made a shrill whistle. Within seconds, a 125-pound, solid-black German shepherd came running from the woods, straight to Joe. Buck licked Joe's face, and then sat at his side, staring at Preston. Preston froze. While he had never had a dog as a child, he was not particularly afraid of dogs either. But this dog was big and dark and had a manner about him that terrified Preston. Buck, on the other hand, sat quietly at Joe's side with his large ears sticking straight up.

"Meet Buck," Joe said. Preston nodded. Casey moved slightly toward the dog and said hello to him. Joe nodded almost imperceptibly to Buck, and Buck went over to Casey and licked his hand.

Casey appeared comfortable for the first time that day, as though he was falling in love with the big, strong dog that he was now petting. Buck continued to watch Preston but did not approach him.

"How old is Buck?" Casey asked. "How long you had him?"

"Buck is eleven," Joe replied. "We ... he's been with us ... he's been around ... since my Navy days."

"You train him?" Casey asked, clearly impressed with the way the dog behaved.

"Buck never needed too much training. He's always had a pretty good idea what to do and how to do it. I did ask a buddy of mine over at the War Dog Training School at Fort Benning, Georgia, to spend some time with him and that turned out to be time well spent. He tried to get me to enroll Buck in the war dog program but we . . . I . . . wanted to have him with us. Anyway, I'm glad you like my dog, but let me ask you guys a question. Why?"

"Why?" Preston echoed, still leery of the dog.

"Yeah. Why?" Joe said, putting clear emphasis on the word. "Why are you here?"

"Because I need your help, Joe. I'm in a difficult position, and I need a smart, tough lawyer to get me out of it. You've had quite a career since you and I were last together. Very impressive. It looks to me like you're the one man who can help me, and a man that I know. I want to retain your services, hire you to pull my chestnuts out of the fire, so to speak."

"Do you need help, too, Casey?" Joe asked.

"Casey here is an old friend of mine and my chief financial officer," Preston said.

Casey nodded, mumbling something to himself.

Preston went on, "I hauled his ass up here because he knows all the financials and all the particulars about my companies. I figured that you would need access to all of that. That's why he's here."

"You figured wrong, Preston," Joe said, pushing a log slightly to its side with his boot, making the fire immediately burn stronger and brighter.

"About what?" Preston said.

"About my needing access to all of that. I don't need access to any of it, because I don't need to listen to any more about your problems. I'm sorry you've got problems, and I'm sorry that you've come all this way for nothing. You're welcome to put your tarp up and spend the night here, and in the morning, you can work your way back down the mountain. It's easier going down than coming up."

"You don't understand, Joe," Preston said. "I'm the owner of Wilson Holdings, which is a company that owns car dealerships all over the country. We have stores in New York, Atlanta, California, Chicago, North Carolina, and Texas. Big stores."

"Good for you," Joe said.

"Please let me finish, Joe."

"Why?"

"Because you need to hear the whole story."

"Why?"

"So you can ... "

"Preston, I don't need to hear the whole story. I don't need to do anything. You may need to do something or say something or address your problem in some way. But I don't. Surely, as a mega-car dealer with stores all over the country, you already have legal counsel. Probably a large firm. I'm sure they have given you advice. Whatever the problem, it is not my problem, and I do not want it to become my problem. I hope you guys brought something to eat, because Buck and I are about to have our dinner and go to bed."

Joe arranged some thin sticks across the small fire in the form of a wooden grill and then placed two filleted trout over the tops of the sticks. Buck watched. Preston and Casey eyed the cooking fish with envy apparent on their faces as they dug into their small packs and brought out canned Cokes and several sandwiches, which Sarah had wrapped. The three men ate in silence.

After their dinner, Preston tried again.

"Look, Joe, you obviously want to be alone up here ... or up here with your dog alone. I had no right to intrude. I apologize. I really didn't have a choice. I'm in a very difficult situation, and in fact, my businesses are going down. Yes, I have a large law firm, and yes, they have advised me. But, to be honest, their advice sucks. I owe a lot of money to a lot of banks, and all my big-shot lawyers can do is tell me to go bankrupt. I can't go bankrupt. I'd lose everything. I can't sell my properties because of the liens against them, and I can't refinance either. If I don't go bankrupt, my lawyers think there's a good chance I will be indicted for selling cars out of trust or bank fraud or both. Even if I do go bankrupt, I might not be able to discharge all my debts if the banks claim fraud. I haven't defrauded the banks or anybody else, but if I don't keep this civil – treat it as a civil matter – some over-zealous prosecutor could come after me on a criminal basis. Whichever way I turn, I'm screwed."

"You know, it's not the trap that kills the bear when he gets caught," Joe said. "It's the thrashing around trying to get out of it."

"What?" Casey mumbled.

Joe ignored the question, feeding the remains of the trout on the stick to Buck and watching him lick it.

"You're right, Joe," Preston said. "I'm between a rock and a hard place. I don't know how to get out of the trap. But from what I have learned about you, you not only know how to get me out, you've got the guts to do it. That's why you're the only one who can help me. Money is not a problem. I'll pay you whatever you want. Please. Please help me."

"I thought money was a problem for you," Joe said.

"I've got the money to pay you."

"How did you get here from New York City?"

"We flew from Teterboro by helicopter to Ticonderoga Municipal Airport," Preston said, "and then Casey talked me into renting a car from there. Why do you ask?"

"I thought we'd do better with our own car instead of a company car and driver up here," Casey interjected.

"Just wondered," Joe replied, obviously amazed at how rich business men continued to cling to their expensive toys even when their companies were going down. "Most of all, I wonder why in the world I should believe you, let alone help you."

"What do you mean?" Preston asked.

Joe sat down and motioned Preston and Casey to sit as well. They did, and Joe looked at Preston. "You've probably renegotiated your bank loans with your various banks personally and with your large firm lawyers at your side or even through them in the past. Correct?"

"Yes," Preston replied.

"How many times?"

"At least three."

"Three, each bank?"

"Actually, yes."

"And you're in breach with each bank now, right?"

"Correct."

"So the way I figure it, you've made commitments to your banks, failed to live up to those commitments, renegotiated the loans to ease the commitments, and then breached those commitments, twice, for each bank. So, essentially, you've lied to each of your lending institutions financing your businesses three times. You've probably lied to yourself as well." Joe got up from the log he was sitting on and walked over to the edge of the pond.

"Are you married?" Joe continued, picking up a stone and tossing it into the pond.

Preston nodded.

"Is your wife on the personal guarantees?"

Preston nodded again.

"Have you told your wife the full story of how much trouble you're in and that you're going down, as you put it?"

Preston slowly shook his head.

"So you've lied to her as well," Joe said. "Again, why should I believe anything you say to me? I think it's time we get some sleep and allow all the critters listening to this conversation to get some sleep as well. Don't leave any food around tonight or the bears will give us all a hard time. Good night, gentlemen."

Joe got up and carefully placed some pine boughs on the side of his makeshift lean-to and set out his sleeping bag. He came back and added three more logs to the fire, and then he returned to the lean-to, followed by Buck. Casey and Preston sat by the fire, neither saying or doing anything for a few moments.

"What do you think, Casey?"

"I think he's right, we've got to be careful about the food," Casey answered, clearly afraid.

"Forget the bears. What should I do? You know, I've worked all my life to get to this point. I've built a small empire, and you've been a big part of that. And now I'm going to – we're going to – watch it all go down the drain."

Casey looked up at Preston, who was now pacing by the fire.

"This is a disaster. We should never have come up here," Preston said. "I'm sorry I yelled at you in the car yesterday afternoon, Casey."

"You're under a lot of heavy shit."

"No, well, yes, but... beyond that. Something set me off. Something you said about chasing rainbows. I remember listening to my mother accuse my father of that the night he left us. My father was always on the verge of making the biggest deal, but it never panned out. Eventually, my mother made him leave. She couldn't stand it. I swore I would never be like him. That I would be a success. I thought I was. I don't know how I got into this mess. Now I'm going to lose it all." *I can't be a failure. I won't be a failure.*

"I know, Preston. I know."

"And then there's Marcia. That's the absolute worst part." Preston realized that he had begun to cry. "She's going to leave me, man; she's going to leave me for sure. I can live with losing my business, but I damn well can't live with losing her. And sure as hell, I'm going to do just that. Joe's smart as hell. He's right, too. I did lie to the banks, and I did lie to myself, and worst of all, I lied to Marcia.

"I've never talked to you about Marcia. She's really smart. That's what drew me to her in the first place, aside from that fact that she's drop-dead beau-... well you know what she looks like. She was the only woman who really got it, and fast. She was nice about it, but she could look right through a person and see what I didn't see. And she could do the same with other things, including business. Before I got tied up building an empire, or at least one I thought I was building, Marcia and I had wonderful times together. She really understood me and what I wanted to build. It was exciting. She made me feel special, that I could do the things I wanted to do. She was a huge help; she added a lot. And she was fun to be with. Still is, except that I haven't been around much because I've had to take care of business. I wanted her to have the best – high-end cars, a great condo, the best clothes. Marcia never asked me for anything. All she really ever wanted from me was what we had in the beginning. I can't stand the thought of losing her, and I don't know what to do."

There was nothing more to say. The two men stretched the tarp between two trees as best they could, then put the blankets on the ground under it with their sleeping bags on top. They crawled in, and tried unsuccessfully to sleep.

Joe also tried to sleep, but having overheard all of their conversation, he was having a serious argument with himself. He resented Preston coming up here and trying to dump his problems on him. Despite everything, however, he could not help but feel compassion for the man. But these mistakes were not made on his watch, or by his men. They were simply not his problems. *Maybe that son of a bitch in the Navy was right. Maybe I am flawed for getting too involved with other people's problems.*

Despite the observation being on the record, Joe knew that his FITREPS, the Navy term for fitness reports, had all showed high ratings for performance, that his position in the Navy had been secure. At the same time, he'd had to face the reality that because of the fraternization comment he would likely not have been promoted further and could have been headed for a desk job; he'd resigned from the naval career he loved and gone into the law.

Joe's thoughts about Preston and whether to help him were superimposed, like two blurred slides, with his Navy personnel experience. *Is this guy worth it? These rich guys have no yardstick, no base line. They don't know what the hell they can or can't do. The banks are probably in this, too. He wouldn't know the truth if it bit him in the ass. He brought all this upon himself. He's fallen off the mountain trail again. No way is this guy drawing me down into it again. I can't believe he would try to act like we have a relationship after all these years, and try to use that to get me to help him. It's all about the deal to him. I don't know if he knows what a real relationship is. He's not concerned about integrity or credibility, just money, and he's blown that. But he does love his wife.*

As Joe tried to sleep the argument continued, but his mind kept going back to the fact that Preston could lose his wife.

CHAPTER 11

Preston and Casey woke to the smell of meat cooking on the fire. In the brightness of the morning sun they each looked five years older. The pond was covered with a flock of mallards that had landed during the night, save the one Buck apparently had sampled, from the look of a nearby pile of feathers.

"Good morning," Joe said. "Would you like some meat? Coffee?"

Preston and Casey moved stiffly to the fire and picked up strips of venison with small sticks, as they had watched Joe do the night before. The meat, slightly burning Preston's mouth as he ate, tasted surprisingly good. They used left-over cups Sarah had thrown in the bag and drank the coffee.

"Preston, tell me a little bit more about yourself," Joe said.

"Well, I live in Manhattan – we do, my wife Marcia and I. We don't have kids. Marcia would like them, but I've been so busy with work, I didn't think it would be fair to start a family yet. To tell you the truth, Joe, I built quite a business. Wilson Holdings owns ten major automobile dealerships, all with upscale points. By that I mean franchises..."

"I know what points are, Preston," Joe interrupted. "Go on."

"Well, my stores are all over the country, and, if it weren't for some major problems at our store in San Francisco, we were doing pretty well, wouldn't you say, Casey?"

"Actually, no," Casey replied.

"Pretty well," Preston went on, ignoring Casey's remark, "except that we developed serious cash-flow problems. While we had considerable equity in our real estate, particularly in Manhattan, Atlanta, and

Houston, we had to mortgage that equity to help us with cash flow…"

Joe interrupted again. "Actually, Preston, I asked you to tell me about you, not your business. I'm interested to know more about you. For example, you indicated last night somewhere along the line that if I didn't help you, you would lose everything. Tell me, what is it that you feel you would lose? What is losing everything to you?"

"Everything I own, Joe. We'll lose it all. I'm on personal guarantees for all the flooring lines and the capital loans. My wife Marcia is on the guarantees as well. So we'll lose all our holdings, not only business, but personal as well. Our Trump Tower condo. Our plane. Our home in West Palm. And, of course, all the assets of the businesses and their income stream."

"If you lost all of that, Preston, what would you personally miss the most?" Joe asked.

Preston thought for a minute and then replied, "It sounds silly, Joe, but to tell you the truth, what I would really miss is my office in the General Motors Building. I like walking into the building in the morning, greeting the attendants, and taking the elevator up to the forty-fourth floor. I love my office. You should see the view. It's like looking down over canyons of beautiful buildings. When I'm up there, I feel like I'm on top of the world. Like I've really achieved something, like I'm a player."

"Anything else you would really miss?"

At this point, Preston's eyes filled with tears. He turned his face away from Joe and didn't speak for a moment.

"No, except… Marcia. I'll lose her, too."

"I suppose the full enjoyment of that view, however beautiful, is diminished by the dark clouds in your mind because of all the problems you're having," Joe said.

"That is so true. You have no idea." Preston felt strange opening up to this man in a way he had never experienced before, afraid and awkward, all unaccustomed feelings. There was nothing more he could say.

Joe broke the silence. "Preston, I've decided I will help you… on three conditions. Do you want me to go on?"

"Oh, God, yes."

"Okay. Let me put this in language you can understand. Here's the deal. I'll help you, providing you make a commitment to do three things, and these conditions are each non-negotiable.

"One: You tell me everything I want to know. You show me everything I want to see. And you do everything I tell you to do the way I tell you to do it.

"Two: You tell me only the absolute truth. You lie to me one time, and we are done. Instantly done. And I alone will judge whether you are lying to me.

"Three: If I ask you to do something for me, now, or in the future, no matter what it is, you will do it. No matter what. And this commitment is for life," Joe said as he crossed over in front of Casey and looked Preston straight in the eyes. "I want you to think very carefully. Are you willing and able to make a firm, irrevocable commitment to me on each of these three conditions? If you can, tell me now. If not, forget it."

Joe's words hung in the morning air. Preston sat still and stared back at Joe. Finally Preston said, "Joe, I want your help more than anything. I'm grateful to you for . . . "

"Cut it out, Preston," Joe interrupted. "Just answer the question."

Preston looked down for a moment, and then up at the sky. Finally he turned to Joe and said, "I can do the first two, no problem. But the third, hell, I don't even know what it will be. How can I agree to that?"

"Maybe you can't," said Joe, moving away from Preston.

Preston looked at Casey, and receiving no response, wondered whether Casey didn't know what to say or couldn't speak.

"Sometimes in life you have to have enough faith to make an irrevocable commitment," Joe said. "Some can, some can't. This is not one of your contracts with the bank. And it's not one of your lawyer retainer agreements either. Why am I responsible to help you? You never answered my question as to why I should. All of your responses are about the trouble you are in, about what you need. What about mutuality?"

Preston started to speak, and Joe held up his hand. "Not yet, I'm not finished," Joe said. "This, my friend, is about personal integrity. This goes directly to you. To who and what you are. Can you accept that? I'm done now. Just give me your answer, and it better be the truth." Joe sat down on a log near the fire.

Preston could feel the cool sweat running down his back. He noticed Buck staring as hard at him as Joe. He tried to weigh the pros and cons, to reason it out, but he was unable to focus. All he could think about was his fear of going down, and all that would mean. How could he commit now to do what Joe would ask in the future – not knowing what it would be?

Maybe you can't, Joe had said. If he couldn't, no deal. What did Joe mean about having enough faith to make an irrevocable commitment? Faith in what?

Then Preston realized he had no choice, that he had to make the commitment or else Joe would not help him. As to what Joe might ask of him in the future, if he did, Preston would cross that bridge when he came to it. Yet, there was something about Joe that made Preston afraid. This was not a man to renege on. Maybe he shouldn't agree. Preston paced back and forth in front of the fire.

Joe stood up and simply looked at Preston as if to say, "Well?" Preston took a big breath and then let it out. He had made a decision. "Yes, I am willing to make those commitments, all three, right now."

The three men stood, faced each other, and Joe and Preston shook hands.

Casey shook Joe's hand as well. Then he turned to Preston and hugged him for the first time.

"Let's go down the mountain," Joe said.

CHAPTER 12

Dinner at the Blooming Grove Lodge tasted pretty good to Joe.

"I hope you don't mind that I brought those fellas up," Larry said. "Didn't want them botherin' you, but that Preston fella seemed to know you and acted like it was pretty important."

"No problem, Larry. It was good of you. I had to come down sometime. Can't stay up there forever, much as I'd like to. Buck and I will stay here tonight if that's okay with you. I'll check my cabins in the morning, and then we'll head on back to Braydon."

"Of course. We always love to have you. That's a long drive to South Carolina, ain't it?"

"It's about twenty hours. I'm not going to push it. I'll take a couple of days; give Buck a chance to stretch now and then."

It was time to see what the rest of the world felt like again. On the trip down, Buck took in the sights and smells from Joe's open truck windows and hopped back and forth through the double back windows to the open truck bed. Joe avoided Route 81 and I-95 wherever he could, preferring instead to stay away from the big trucks and get as close to the ocean as possible. He smoked cigars, listened to music, and reflected.

Joe thought about the mountains, the time he had spent there. How they had changed with the increased activity in the park, all of the hikers, bikers, canoeists, and climbers. Realizing the mountains belonged to everyone, he was pleased and surprised that there had been so much growth. While there were trails, lean-tos and other indications of the park becoming a playground, there were still thousands of acres of real wilderness remaining. In fact, in certain areas where there had been blow-downs, trails were blocked and even became thicker. Because of the thickness, the game was still hard to find. The deer and other animals were full and large. There were actually more beaver than he had remembered, which meant more beaver dams, more back-up of wetlands, all with more benefit to the wild domain. The birds were plentiful and the beauty was still there. So was the quiet.

He thought about Preston and Casey. He figured if Casey made the same trip again, he'd probably have a heart attack. He liked Casey, but wondered what part his willingness to follow had led Preston into this mess. For a CFO, he surely missed a lot. On the other hand, he had a basic candor Joe liked.

Joe saw Preston as more complicated. He wondered whether Preston would have the character and the courage when it was needed. And could he be honest with himself and with his wife? Was he really afraid to lose her, or was he afraid of how it would look if he did? Would he honor his commitment to Joe?

Joe thought about how well one gets to know a man, what he's really made of, what he's really like, how he handles pressure and the fear of death, secretly chasing an enemy sub, so close a sailor could hit it, or hovering over a Soviet cable, tapping it and trying not to be caught. The guys Joe served with on those subs were the best. They were a family. His family.

He was sorry that his thoughts led him down a trail that led to family. He could feel the pain as he relived for the hundredth time the coroner's insistence that Ashley be subjected to an autopsy.

"It's always required in a violent death," the coroner had said. Joe knew too well the cause of death. What he did not expect to learn was that they were finally on their way to building their own family. There had been two deaths that night.

He forced himself to move away from these thoughts and concentrate on the project he had promised Preston he would undertake. As Joe drove his truck over the beltway around Washington he cracked the window, lit a cigar, and called his secretary.

"Joe, it's so good to hear your voice. I've missed you. We all have. How are you? Are you okay? Where are you?"

"That's a lot of questions, Alice," Joe laughed. "I've missed you, too. Not as much as Buck did though. I'm fine ... well, as fine as I can be. Buck was great company, as usual, and you know I love it up there."

"What made you leave?"

"That's a good question, Alice. You're good. I really appreciate you. I decided you needed work. You know, the kind you really love, sorting through boxes and boxes of documents."

"Oh, no, you're not telling me we're going to do another turn-around plan? I thought you were done with those. That will mean Braydon's economy is due for an uptick. The copy people. Trimax Office Supply. The coffee. More cigars. This is good. How many document clerks do you want me to line up?" Alice was obviously excited.

"It will be good to see you. Actually, I would like a couple of people to assist with the documents. The rest you and I can handle. Please keep it quiet that I'm coming back."

"Nice try, Joe. That won't work. As soon as you come rumbling into town in your truck with Buck, it will be all over. Get over it; you're going to have to say hello to a few people. I'll do what I can. When will I see you?"

"I don't want to spend too much time at the house. How 'bout in the morning, and we'll get started. In the meantime, call a man named Casey Fitzgerald who works as a CFO for a high-flying executive in New York City. He works for Wilson Holdings in the General Motors Building in Manhattan."

"And tell Mr. Fitzgerald what?" Alice asked.

"Tell him I'm back and ready to go. That I want to talk with him at eleven in the morning and to let his people know that they will be responding to his requests for a lot of detailed information and, in certain cases, phone calls from us."

"Aye aye, boss. This is great. Can't wait. See you in the morning."

Joe drove until late that night, stopping only for gas, a messy cheeseburger combo, and to let Buck stretch his legs. As he entered North Carolina, he decided to spend the rest of the night in a motel just off Route 17. He figured he would go directly to his office in the morning, thereby putting off the return to the house a little while longer.

CHAPTER 13

In the morning, Joe found his office and Alice exactly as he had left them. It was good to see Alice, her shoes off, feet propped against her desk, reading from her steno pad as they drank coffee and munched fresh Krispy Kreme donuts.

"As good as the mountains were, Joe, I'll bet they didn't have fresh donuts up there," she said as the phone lighted up.

Joe nodded, then picked up the phone. "Hi, Casey. Joe Hart. How are you doing?"

"Hanging in there. I'm glad to hear from you."

"I'm faxing you a list of what I need from you. I wanted to give you a heads up. The list is long and detailed. The package breaks down into two pieces. The first piece is comprised of authorizations and consents. The authorizations allow me to represent Preston. I have included Wilson Holdings since Preston apparently owns 100 percent of Wilson's shares, and therefore, there is no conflict of interest between the corporate entity and Preston. I did not include representation of Marcia but, as a personal guarantor, she certainly has a lot at stake. I will leave it to her to determine whether she would like independent legal representation, but I will not be representing her.

"In connection with the authorization from Preston and Wilson Holdings, I am representing him and the company only with respect to a strategic turnaround settlement plan. It's a limited engagement, Casey. In and out. Either it will work or it won't. If it won't, you won't be any worse off. If the bank agrees to undertake my plan, it will be up to you and your lawyers to follow through, do the transactional work. I'm not doing any litigation and my representation does not include any matters relating to criminal conduct or exposure. My authorizations will contain those disclaimers.

"Next, there are the consents, which permit me to obtain the information I need from the manufacturers, the banks, and anyone else who has information. Are you with me, Casey?"

"Yes, sir," Casey said.

"In addition to the consents, I would like you and Preston to write to Wilson Holdings' primary counsel..."

"Whitcock, Stevenson, Brookfield, Berry and Brown," Casey interrupted. "Andrew Brookfield is our main attorney there."

"I assume from what you and Preston told me in the mountains that Whitcock Stevenson has engaged in a thorough analysis of Wilson's financial condition."

"That's correct. They recommended Chapter 11 for Wilson Holdings and Chapter 7 for Preston and his wife."

"Did they cause an operational study of Wilson's dealerships to be undertaken? Did they do valuations of the dealerships and appraisals of the underlying real estate?"

"Andrew didn't mention anything about operational studies. I know there are appraisals of the real estate. I don't know about valuations of the dealerships."

"Well, in any event, I would like a letter from you to Whitcock Stevenson, attention Mr. Brookfield, explaining to the firm that I am representing Wilson Holdings, all of its subsidiaries, and Preston in connection with a strategic turnaround plan, and that I would like full copies of all their work product relating to their review and assessment leading to their recommendations, together with a copy of all of those recommendations."

"Understood," Casey said. "I will call Tom immediately and see that he has the letter. I'll request the info ASAP."

"Thanks, Casey. Make it clear to Mr. Brookfield that we are dealing with an urgent situation here, and that I would like all of the material FedExed to me within one week."

"He'll complain like hell, but I'll see to it," Casey said. "We paid those guys a fortune. It's time they did something to help us besides advise us to go screw ourselves."

"I'll call Mr. Brookfield as well, but I want him to have the letter before I talk with him. Now let's go back to the criminal lawyers. I imagine they'll advise Preston not to provide any more information than is absolutely necessary to the banks and/or the manufacturers. They will exercise legitimate concern about self-incrimination. Again, the stakes are high, because bank fraud – which they will explain – is a serious matter that, if proven, can have mandatory prison sentences of over twenty years. Upon learning that Preston intends to sign my authorizations and consents – which he should tell them and show them – they will no doubt raise hell and write disclaimer letters of their own, showing why this places Preston at risk, which it will. Life is full of choices.

"On the real estate side, form of ownership, copies of the deeds, current appraisals, mortgages, amortization schedules, maps and surveys, liens, encroachments, aerial photos, leases, and the financials. Then organize all of this in a package. Are you getting this, Casey?"

"I understand," Casey said. "It's a lot of detail. I'm not sure how much you really want given how much time there is and how long it will take to get it together."

"That's why I'm calling you as well as writing," Joe said. "Basically, I want everything. I realize this presents an immense burden, but that can't matter. It's the only way I can do what I need to do. When I say everything, I mean just that. You'll see the list, but consider the list an outline. I want you to fill it all in, resolving any doubt as to whether to provide it in favor of yes. Simply, it's full and complete disclosure."

"I get it," Casey said. "I just don't know if I can do it. I mean, I can do it, what I have or what's in my control. I'm worried about the records and materials in the other stores. The external items, the appraisals and the materials from people outside the companies. I don't know how fast I can get them to act."

"Casey, I don't care what it takes. Just do it."

"Okay... Jesus," Casey muttered. "I get the picture. On the personal side – current detailed financial statements for Preston and Marcia..."

"Yes," Joe replied, "for all lenders for the last five years. On the businesses, P&L statements, balance sheets, audits, operating statements, tax returns, and all other financials."

"Got it."

"When you provide the operating statements for the dealerships, be sure to give me a copy of each statement you provided to the manufacturer."

"You also want the operating statement we sent to the bank?" Casey asked.

"Casey, by now you must know I don't want to screw around. If you've got a problem with operating statements, you make it real clear and easy for me. You send me the statements the way you sent them to the manufacturer, the way you sent them to the bank, and the way you provide them for yourself. If those three are different, then give me each operating statement side by side, showing the differences. The same level of detail for the floor-plan-checks, the titles, the Manufacturers' Statement of Origin for each store. I want to know everything."

"When do you want all this?"

"I would like it all in my office, in uniform white labeled boxes, bound and clearly identified, within one week, no matter what it takes. In the meantime, FedEx a list of all the creditors – names, addresses, and amounts owed. Separate the lenders and make a specific list of all the litigation. I am also faxing you a letter for Preston to type on his stationery to each of the banks and all of the plaintiffs in pending litigation, explaining that he and the companies have retained me as workout counsel and that I will be in touch with each of them within two weeks."

Neither Casey nor Joe said anything further for a while. Joe could sense Casey's sweat over the phone.

"Okay, Joe. That's a lot. But I get it. I'll do everything I can. Thank you for helping us."

"You're welcome," Joe said. "Casey, have Preston call me himself. I don't want any wiggling on this, and I want to hear from him that he understands everything I'm doing and that he is fully on board."

"He'll call you, Joe. He'll call you right away."

CHAPTER 14

Preston fumbled for his cell phone. "Casey, what's up?"

"Joe called to tell me what he wants and when he wants it. Really simple. He wants everything in nice, neat boxes, labeled, in his office in one week," Casey said. "Five years of income tax returns, personal and business, operating statements, P&Ls, balance sheets, audits, all the real estate materials, financials.... He's faxed me a detailed list."

"Okay, so give it to him," Preston said.

"Easy for you to say," Casey mumbled. "But Hart wants documents from you – instruments for you to sign, consents, authorizations, letters to banks. And I'm going to need things from you also."

"What do you mean? I understand Joe needs consents, authorizations. All lawyers do. What are you going to need from me?"

"First of all, Joe spent a lot of time explaining. Forget what all the lawyers do. These are different. I'm sending them over now. You need to read these, Preston. They are very specific. He's only representing you and the companies..."

"What else is there?" Preston interrupted.

"Well, there's your wife. Joe talked about Marcia being represented by her own lawyer."

"He said that? He's saying Marcia has to get her own lawyer?" Preston was angry now.

"He's not telling you or her she has to get her own lawyer. He's saying he's not representing her, and it's up to her. He said he'd leave that to you and Marcia, but he did make it clear that he thinks you should consult a criminal lawyer."

"Why? Does he think we're in trouble on the criminal side? What did he say?"

"Preston, listen to me a minute," Casey said in as calm a voice as he could manage. "What Hart is saying is that the criminal thing is out there, that it's an exposure, and I think the reason he wants you to go to a criminal lawyer is so you will be fully advised. He's covering his ass, and he's being very straightforward about it. You can't blame him for that."

"I don't blame him. Get to the point."

"Well, the point I inferred is that he's going to tell the bank everything. And he says your criminal lawyers are not going to be very happy about that. In fact, he thinks they're going to tell you not to do that, or else you'll be incriminating yourself and the companies. So when they tell you all of that in writing, Joe wants you to sign off with him that they've told you all of that and that you still want Joe to go ahead, knowing that he's going to throw a grenade in there."

"Good Lord."

"You want to hear the part about what I want now?"

"Now you're beginning to sound like Joe," Preston said.

"I can't help it. I like the guy. You know right where you stand with him. He doesn't pull any punches. You gotta love it."

"Okay, we'll give Joe as much as we can. We'll do our best. Now, what do you want, Casey?"

"That won't work this time, Preston," Casey said, ignoring Preston's question. "We're in real trouble, and you know it. You either want to go along with Hart or you don't. This is one guy you can't screw around with. It's not a do-our-best situation. He wants it all, and he wants it now, and he won't do it any other way. I'm not going to be in the middle on this one. Either you're there or you're not."

"Jesus, Casey, where the hell did all this intensity come from? You've never been disloyal to me, and I've been damn good to you. You're making me nervous."

"Join the club," Casey said. "You asked me what I want. I want this mess to go away, now, and I want you to cooperate with Hart and keep your promise. You heard what your Harvard lawyer told you. Criminal fraud. Civil fraud. Bankruptcy. While I don't get to see her much, working my ass off for you, I happen to have a wife. And three kids. You've treated me pretty well – I can drive any car I want, and I make a couple hundred thousand a year. But none of that will do me much good if you're bankrupt or we're in prison. You can joke about it, but I like Hart. He's not like any of our other lawyers. It's scary doing it his way, but it's scary anyway. Like he says, life's full of choices. I've made mine. I'm with him. Are you? It's that simple."

"I'll get back to you, Casey." Preston hung up.

Five minutes later, Preston called Casey back, "I'm with him, too. I'm on my way over. Give him everything. I'll sign all the authorizations and consents, and I'll call Joe and tell him the same thing."

"Good. Glad to hear it," Casey said, relief evident in his voice. "We've got a lot of work to do. I forgot to tell you Joe wants you to call so he hears from you that you're 'fully on board,' as he put it. See you soon."

CHAPTER 15

Harry

Harry Klaskowski fidgeted in his overstuffed, blue leather chair, picked up his Perazzi MX-3 single-barrel shotgun, placed a Remington Premier Handicap Nitro 27 trap load in the barrel and pressed the muzzle tightly under the lower part of his chin. He placed his hand on the trigger, sweat pouring down his face.

At least this way it will be over. Mom doesn't care, and Dad will be a hell of a lot happier. No matter what I do for them, no matter what I do for anyone, it's never enough. They'll be better off, they'll all be better off, and so will I. But a note, I should leave a note.

Harry carefully lowered the gun and, leaning it against the chair, reached for the pad on the end table. He tried to write, but his hands were shaking too wildly. *I'm even screwing this up,* he thought. *The hell with a note. I'll call Joe and tell him what I'm doing. I owe it to him to tell him. Joe understands me. At least he never tried to change me. I think he actually likes me. One thing I do know, he's the only one who ever gave a damn.*

Harry picked up the phone on the end table and punched the speed dial number for Joe.

Harry was a large man, about six-and-a-half feet tall, who could really shoot. He'd first met Joe years ago at a skeet-and-trap shooting contest at the Wayne County Hunting and Fishing Club just outside of Marion, a small town in upstate New York. Harry liked Joe immediately. No pretenses. Before long, they were deer hunting in the Adirondacks and shooting geese in the southern tier of New York. Harry liked kidding around with Joe. He knew Joe got a kick out of his jokes and his big, booming laugh.

What really drew Harry to Joe was his confidence that Joe respected and accepted him for what he was. Harry thought he had come a long way since his childhood days in the Fishtown section of Philadelphia, or later when his family moved to Dunkirk, New York, on the shore of Lake Erie where he learned to fish and boat, and the mountains of northern Pennsylvania where he learned to hunt. He remembered how popular he'd been, a better than average student, three-letter man in high school. How after graduating, he'd enlisted in the Army and learned photography while stationed in Germany. In his spare time he'd studied music. He taught himself how to play the piano and accordion. Lord knows how many song-loving towns-folk bought him beers when he traveled by motorcycle on his days off.

Harry's thoughts drifted to his time after the service, his marriage to the lovely Polish girl he'd met at a cousin's wedding, how he returned to Dunkirk and became a professional photographer and music teacher. With growing businesses, hunting and fishing, and nightly live-concerts at Chautauqua, life could not have been better. Harry's heart pounded and head ached as he reflected on how it all went off track when his too-attractive wife forgot the part about being true. How long had it been since she left? He'd lost count of the years.

It seemed to take forever for Joe to answer the phone. Harry was slowly putting the phone back in its cradle when he heard Joe say hello.

"Joe, it's Harry." Harry paused, took a deep breath, then continued. "I've really made the effort, man, but there's no way . . . no way."

"What do you mean?"

After a moment of silence, Harry replied, "What I'm saying is I don't know if it's really worth living anymore."

"Woah. Hold on a minute. Let me get this straight. You're feeling as though there just isn't any point? Is that it?"

"No question, I'm telling you, no way. It doesn't make any difference, nothing does. I'm pulling the plug. Done. Leaving."

"Have you talked to Dr. Goldstein – I think that's his name?"

"Forget about Goldstein, man. That guy, apart from writing a few prescriptions so I can spend more money, isn't really interested in me. Just wanted to call you and say goodbye. You're the only one who ever cared."

"Where are you?" Joe asked.

"I'm at my apartment."

"How are you going to do it?"

"With a shotgun."

"Which one?"

"What the hell difference does it make which one?"

"I'm not sure," Joe said. "I was just wondering what specifically you intend to use, and whether you had thought that through? I remember your shotguns. You've got some beauties. You can really use them. I mean you can really run the targets at the trap shoots. Remember when you beat the hell out of me in Marion and again at the Northeast Grande in Syracuse? Harry, do you remember that?"

"Of course, I remember. I remember all the stuff we've done."

Silence.

"Are you there, Joe?"

"Yes, I am, Harry."

"What else do you want to know?"

"Well, now that you ask, do you have a will? What will your family's reaction be? How're they going to feel about not having you around? What're you going to do about your golden lab?"

"To tell you the truth, Joe, he means more to me than any of my family, what's left of them." Harry wiped tears from his face.

"I still have the picture you took of that dog," Joe said. "What a splendid picture. You can really shoot with a camera, too, Harry. And I'm not the only one who likes your pictures."

More silence.

Then Harry heard Joe ask, "Where are you right now? What are you wearing?"

"What are you, a goddamn reporter?" Harry said in a low voice.

"I just want to know."

"Well, if you must know, I'm in the family room, in my chair, and in my goddamn underpants."

"The blue leather chair?"

"Yeah, the one you love."

A long period followed, and neither of the men spoke.

Finally, Harry asked Joe, "What're you going to do today?"

"I'd like to be fishing," Joe answered. "I am going to fish soon though. Why don't you come down, fly into Charleston, and we'll see if you can still catch a fish."

Silence again, but this time a little shorter.

"That would be nice, actually, Joe. I don't know. I've got a lot to think about. Besides, I have a dog to look after, you know. You oughta understand that, Joe. By the way, how the hell is Buck?"

"Buck's great. Buck and I returned not long ago from a trip to the Adirondacks. You wouldn't believe how those mountains have regrown – even since you and I were there. The deer are huge. So are the black bears. More beaver. More birds. It was great up there. You would have loved it."

"Yeah, you're right about that. I bet you could've stayed there forever. Why'd you come down?" Harry asked.

Joe paused before speaking. "For a lot of reasons. I thought about staying up there, but a guy, actually two guys, found out where I was and came up and asked me to help them out of a bad business situation. I said I would, and so I'm down here in Braydon. I agree, you do have a lot to think about, Harry. How's your mother? Have you had a chance to tell your uncle about your trap shooting award? Have you spoken with the guys at the hunting club? They really need to hear from you, don't they?"

"Mom's fine. I do need to call her though, now that you mention it," Harry admitted. "I should call Uncle Ted, too. He does get excited when I call."

"Remember the time you and I were caught in that water spout on Lake Erie?"

"Hell, yeah," Harry said with a fuller voice. "I thought we would never get in."

"But we did, didn't we? We did get in."

Harry lowered his head, and in a soft voice, said, "Yeah, come to think of it, we did."

Another long silence.

"Joe, I'm telling you, I'm telling you, it doesn't work, it never will. I'm pulling the trigger. I'm going to blow my brains out."

"Harry, take it easy. Settle down. I'm staying on the phone however long it takes us to agree on a plan."

"Forget it. It's hopeless. What the hell kind a plan could work?"

"I'm talking about a plan for right now, Harry – this morning. I'm talking about a plan for a next step now," Joe said. "You're desperate now, and you can't think for yourself. You trust me, don't you?"

"Yes."

"Okay. Here's what I want you to do. Here's the plan. You put the shotgun down, now. You unload it. Do that right now. Harry? Do you hear me? . . . Have you done it?"

Harry pressed the tang on the shotgun, opened the breech, and removed the shell from the chamber. "Yes, dammit. I've done it."

"Do you have the shell in your hand?"

"Yeah."

"Put the shotgun in your gun cabinet now. Lock the cabinet. Tell me when you've done that and you've locked the cabinet."

"It's in there, and the cabinet's locked," Harry said.

. "Now, call Dr. Goldstein. Tell him you need to see him, right now. Call me immediately after you've called Dr. Goldstein. Will you promise you will do that, Harry? Right now?"

"Yeah," Harry replied.

"I'm counting on that, Harry. I'm going to wait by this phone for your call. I'm going to hang up now. I expect to hear from you in a matter of minutes, okay?"

Silence for a moment. "Okay," Harry replied and hung up.

Harry punched Dr. Goldstein's number, and after a brief discussion with his secretary, heard Dr. Goldstein come on the line. Harry told him that he needed help now, and reminded the doctor that he had instructed Harry to call him if he was in real trouble and that he could come over. The doctor told him he would see him right away. The next call was back to Joe.

"I did it," Harry said.

"You did what?" Joe replied.

"I called Dr. Goldstein, like you said. I'm going over there now. He's going to meet me at his office."

"Great, Harry. Promise you'll call me from Goldstein's office when you get there. Will you promise me that?"

"Yeah."

"I'm going to wait here by the phone until I get your call, Harry."

"I figured that," Harry said. "I'll call you from his office."

Twenty-five minutes later, Harry, ignoring the "No Cell Phone" sign, called Joe. "I'm here, Joe. I'm at Dr. Goldstein's office. He's going to see me now."

"What's his office look like, Harry?" Joe asked.

"Cut it out. I'm really here. Do you want to speak with the doctor?"

"No, Harry, I trust you. Good luck. Give me a call when things settle down."

"You got it, man."

Harry had called him before, been down, but never like this time. This was really a close call. Joe was exhausted, and the day had hardly begun. He wanted to be out on his boat, to be far away from any thoughts about guns or death. He figured the sooner he solved Preston's problems, the sooner he could do what he wanted to do, be where he wanted to be. He took a long, hot shower, dressed and took Buck for a walk. Then, after talking with Alice and reviewing the Wilson file, Joe decided it was time to call Preston's New York City lawyer.

"Mr. Brookfield, my name is Joe Hart, and I'm calling on behalf of Preston Wilson and his companies."

"Yes, Mr. Hart, I have a letter from both Mr. Wilson and Mr. Fitzgerald requesting a good deal of information from our firm. I have been expecting your call."

"Thank you, Mr. Brookfield."

"Call me Andrew, please."

"Fine, sir. I just have a few questions. First, did your firm undertake any operational studies of any of the dealerships?"

"No. We were not requested to do that."

"Andrew, let me ask you this: Did anyone from your firm speak with any of the manufacturers of the automobiles sold at any of the dealerships?"

"No. We were not requested to do that, either."

"Were there any valuations done of any of the dealerships?" Joe asked.

"The only dealership that had a valuation done to my knowledge was Manhattan Mercedes. It was ordered by the general manager of that store, as I understand it, in connection with a capital loan that the Greater Bank of Manhattan requested. I have not read the valuation, but I did see it in the list of materials being sent to you. Other than that, I am not aware of any valuations. That is not to say that there are not other valuations."

"How about appraisals on the underlying real estate?" Joe asked.

"There are a number of appraisals, but I'm not sure how current they are. Again, we did not request them to be done, but they were requested by banks, insurance companies, and title companies. I've seen to it that all the appraisals we have are included."

"Very well. Thank you for getting all this information to me in such short order."

"I'm happy to comply with the directions of our client, Mr. Hart. Fortunately, our firm has the required support personnel and assistants to gather all of this material and see to it that it is delivered to you within the required time frame. It is also fortunate that our retainer agreement with Wilson Holdings covers all of our costs and disbursements in addition to our time, which you can imagine is of considerable value."

What a pompous ass, Joe thought. *How much money have you already taken from Preston and his companies so that you could tell him he was going down and there was nothing you could do to stop it?*

"Thank you, Andrew. Is there anything else you feel I should know?"

"I can't think of anything else to tell you, Mr. Hart, but there is one thing you could tell me."

"Yes, sir, what is that?" Joe inquired.

"Why in the world are you going through all of this hopeless exercise? I doubt if Preston Wilson can get his hands on much more money. That is one of the reasons why, as you can imagine – lawyer to lawyer – our firm is looking forward to discontinuing our professional relationship with Mr. Wilson and his companies. You have to know when to get off the train, is what I always say." Mr. Brookfield gave a high-pitched laugh. "You and I both know that Wilson Holdings and Mr. Wilson are finished. They owe the bank millions, and there's no defense to that. The banks have been patient. We've held them off as long as we could. Preston will be fortunate if he doesn't go to jail. He should have known better, and so should his CFO, Mr. Fitzgerald. I don't understand why you're jumping in at a time like this, but it's fine with me. I wish you the best of luck."

Joe figured Andrew Brookfield had forgotten the question he started with, and, in any event, did not deserve an answer.

"Thanks for wishing me good luck," Joe said. "And thank you again for all of the information."

"You're welcome, Mr. Hart."

CHAPTER 16

The information Joe received from his inquiries filled four rooms in his suite of offices. With the help of Alice and a couple of interns from the university's business school, he sorted through all the documents and stacked them in piles throughout the office.

Joe placed a call to Alex Herman, an icon in the automotive business who had been a general manager, as well as Chief Financial Officer and Chief Operating Officer, for several mega-dealerships. Alex was an anomaly in that he not only had well-honed business skills and an astute perception of the business, but he also had one foot in the old school of dealers and the other in the new school. He grasped the value of the computerization, software, and service components of the dealerships, each operating as independent profit centers. He also knew that aside from modern advertising, finance, and buying, the business was still a people business.

"How the hell are you?" Joe asked when he heard Alex's voice on the phone.

"Great, Joe, you old son of a bitch. How the hell are you? Any fishing lately?"

"Not really. I'm tied up at the moment trying to help a client out of an automotive mess. To tell you the truth, Alex, it feels good . . . I needed to get immersed in this kind of thing."

"Yes, I'm sorry about Ashley," Alex said in a low voice. "How can I help?"

"If you've got time, what I would like you to do is visit six stores. As usual, they're spread around the country. Alice will fax you the list and all the details. They're owned by Wilson Holdings, Inc., a holding company owned by a gentleman in New York City named Preston Wilson. I have all the authorizations and consents, which include anyone acting for me, so in this one you won't have to be involved with anybody else."

"Understood. I'm working for you and reporting to you. I like it that way."

"What I'd like you to do is visit each store, look it over, get a feel for the site, the real estate, the way the sales and service departments are run, how the General Manager and Sales Manager are doing, your impression of the financial people, and how it all feels. Five out of six of these stores are in financial trouble. What I would like you to focus on is the operations aspect, just like you did for me in Syracuse and that store in New Jersey. That's what I'm looking for.

"Also, check with GMAC, Ford Credit, Subaru Acceptance, or whoever else is still providing floor plans these days, off the record, to see if they would be interested in picking up Subaru and BMW in the Houston store, and also check with Ford to see if they'll buy back the Ford Franchise. I would appreciate your doing the same thing discreetly with the new banks or lenders who are filling the gap on floor plans to see if they would pick up Honda, Porsche, Audi and Bentley flooring at the San Francisco Autoplaza. Bank North America is carrying Autoplaza's floor plan now."

"I take it these stores are upside down with Bank North America."

"Yeah, they are, but that's what makes these plans interesting. In any event, please get me your report ASAP. Sorry to do this to you, but I need the information and your read on it is important. Especially your thoughts on what can be done to make operations better."

"You got it, Joe. I'm outta here. I'll talk with you. I still want to know when we're going fishing."

"Right after this workout is done, we're fishing," Joe vowed.

"That's a promise I'll hold you to. I'll talk to you soon. So long."

With that call completed, and Joe having talked personally to each of the manufacturers' representatives, it was now time to reach out to the banks themselves. He wanted to start with Bank North America, the largest creditor. He obtained the name of the president, and, after explaining himself several times to various people, finally reached him on the telephone.

"Good morning, sir. I'm Joe Hart, and I'm calling on behalf of Preston Wilson and Wilson Holdings. I appreciate your taking my call."

"Well, I finally get to talk to the man who's causing such a ruckus around here," Tom Gallagher said in a good-natured voice. "You certainly are persistent; I'll say that for you. What can I do for you?"

"Well, first, sir, I appreciate the responsiveness of your bank in supplying all the information we have requested. I also appreciate your taking the time to talk with me personally. Wilson Holdings is in serious financial trouble. It owes substantial sums to your bank and other banks as well. Your bank should be paid in full. I have written a comprehensive turnaround plan for your review. What I would like to do, with your permission, is have a meeting with you personally to discuss the plan and how we can work together to make this happen."

"I like the part about Bank North America being paid back," Mr. Gallagher said. "How do you see this unfolding, Mr. Hart?"

"Permission to speak frankly and off the record, Mr. Gallagher?"

"Yes, and you may call me Tom. Go ahead."

"Well, sir, as I stated, Wilson Holdings is in serious financial condition. What I have tried to do in my plan is make a complicated matter as simple as possible. The reason for the plan in the first place is so that you and Bank North America will have in one place the information you will need to help you make the required decisions. The plan is a review and assessment of the current situation, how deep the hole is, what caused the difficulties, what we see as the immediate problem, what we need to fix it, and a detailed outline of execution steps to resolve the situation."

"Is that all?"

"That's enough, sir," Joe replied in a respectful tone. "You asked how I see this unfolding. Based on my experience, we will have a meeting around a long table in a large conference room. The bank will have several representatives present. Your people will remind us that we asked for this meeting and instruct us to go ahead and say what we

have to say. You will already have been advised by your counsel of the
gravity of the situation, and to say very little, leaving the matters in
their hands. When they speak, they will sternly advise us that we are
in default, that litigation is imminent, and that what assets remain are
being dissipated as we speak and, therefore, there can be no forbearance; that the only thing that can help the bank is if we are aware of
any additional collateral that can be pledged to the bank immediately."

"Well, that sounds about right," Tom said. "What do you have
for us, Mr. Hart?"

"I have a plan that can work if we can keep the lawyers in check
and focus on a business solution. I am a lawyer, but my entire
approach to this case is on a practical business basis. I'm asking
for an off-the-record, 'for settlement purposes,' honest discussion
about how we can construct this matter in such a way that Wilson
Holdings and Preston Wilson do not have to seek bankruptcy protection, your bank does not have to spend hundreds of thousands of
dollars on legal fees, and you can get your money back. I understand
that you require the input from your counsel, and that you have a
responsibility not only to your bank, but also to the regulators. I
suggest that we eat the elephant a bite at a time. I would like to have
the first meeting in whatever way you choose to do it, but sooner
rather than later, I would like to sit down with you without the loan
officers who are trying to defend their files and conduct and without the lawyers who would love to see this matter litigated. By then
you will have read my plan and you – and your people to whom you
assign these volumes – will see from the extensive exhibits that we
have provided you with a true detailed picture of what we owe, what
we have, and what we can do to clean up this mess."

"Well, Joe, this has been a very interesting conversation," Tom said.
"Frankly, I like the sound of it, although I'm sure my lawyers will not."
He paused a beat. "Let's have the meeting. I look forward to meeting
you. I'll get my people together. How does next Monday morning at
ten in our big conference room with the long table sound to you?"

"Thank you, Tom. We'll be there."

CHAPTER 17

Tommy

Joe woke to his phone ringing.

"Joe, it's Tommy."

Joe had met Tommy Greco in Vegas after he'd finished speaking at a J. D. Power Mega Dealers' Roundtable meeting and decided to relax at Caesar's Palace. Tommy had just come from a heavyweight-title boxing match and was shooting craps next to Joe. The short, stocky man was loud and funny, charming Joe and the entire table. They played together for six hours, Tommy signing as many markers. Tommy then talked Joe into going downtown to a favorite bar. The subject eventually turned to Tommy's being into Caesar's for over $350,000, and Joe learned that Tommy had a problem not only with the dice but with the ponies, too. Joe was tempted to say goodbye to Tommy and his gambling problems, but he told Tommy he was curious how he'd gotten into gambling in the first place.

"It's the way it was," Tommy said as he described his growing up in Niagara Falls, "on our side."

Joe lit a Graycliff Expresso cigar and listened, fascinated not only by the story but by the way his new friend talked. Far from his image of Niagara Falls, he learned about a small, heavily Italian community where early life for Tommy meant baseball, wrestling, church school, trying to avoid an abusive and alcoholic father, and a mother who, to make ends meet, "turned occasional tricks for the tourists that wanted more than the Falls." Tommy told Joe how the weights in Niagara High's gym became his friends, providing protection against being short and the fists of his father. "Besides, the girls love the muscles." When he dropped out of high school, he got a job working at a neighborhood bar.

Tommy told Joe, "The guys at *The Corner,* that was the name, Sammy the owner, they was my family. That's where my real education began. Everyone bet the games. There was rules, you know? You had to pay the guys or there were real problems. Just the way it was. Still is."

Tommy said he felt close to his older brother, until he became a priest. When Joe asked why that made a difference, Tommy dropped his head, explaining that his brother had "gotten too chummy with the altar boys," which Tommy couldn't "accommodate." Tommy told Joe he was All State in wrestling, how that helped him get the girls, too, why he hated Catholic school, and how, in addition to the tables, he loved betting on the ponies and basketball.

As Joe and Tommy talked into the night, Joe thought about how similar in some ways his and Tommy's early lives were, and what a difference education can make. His thoughts, as always, eventually turned to Uncle Howard and Aunt Lettie and how simple life had been with them, how lucky he was. Tommy was strong, rough but real, and he made Joe laugh. Joe knew he would stay in touch.

"Hi, Tommy. It's one in the morning."

"What are you doin' up at one in the morning?" Tommy asked.

"I can think of two reasons, Tommy. One, you called me and woke me up. And two, I have not been sleeping much anyway lately. What's on your mind?"

"I have a serious problem, which is sort of a dilemma, and I've been thinking about it hard, and I figured out there's a way out, but I need you to do something for me."

"Does this problem involve money?" Joe asked.

"It involves money, but not like what you're thinking. This ain't a gambling thing, and it ain't like I owe somebody, but it's complicated, and I need you to talk to a certain man and explain to him how a certain set of situations happened to happen," Tommy explained.

"Why does this have to be handled right now, Tommy? How about in the morning?"

"I'm trying to do what you and I talked about, Joe. You know, develop relationships with meaning and better myself. I got it figured out how I can become Frankie's go-through guy and if I become that, it will be like a job. And because Frankie's so classy, it would be like a profession. And then I could lay off the gambling."

"Who's Frankie?" Joe asked.

"You don't want to know. Period," Tommy said. "I'm getting you up now because it'll take you time to get here."

"Here?"

"I'm in Vegas, and I got this situation, which I'll explain to you in personable fashion, but I need you to get on a plane as early as you can in the morning so that you get here in the morning so that I will have time to talk to you before you do what I need you to do, which will only take you ten minutes. Time is of the importance."

"Tommy, I'm working on a case right now, and I've just scheduled a meeting for Monday morning that I must attend. If I can get a flight out in the morning, no matter what's going on with you, do you understand and accept that I will be leaving the next day to come back here so that I can be ready for my meeting?"

"You got it, Joe. Call me and tell me what flight you're coming in on and I'll be at the airport to meet you. Thanks, Joe. It means a lot."

Joe called the airlines and was able to get a 7:30 a.m. flight out of Charlotte to Las Vegas, although he had to buy a first-class ticket. He quickly packed, and dropped Buck off at Alice's house with a brief explanation that Tommy Greco had a "time is of the essence" problem that involved God knows what and that he needed to go to Vegas but would be back in plenty of time for Monday morning's meeting at Bank North America.

Joe enjoyed the flight; it gave him time to think through his presentation to the bank. Five-and-a-half hours later, Joe saw Tommy as soon as he left the security area.

Tommy stood as tall as a five-foot-four mesomorph with no neck could, and with a big grin grabbed Joe, pushed him back and pulled him forward and hugged him. Joe knew all of this was coming and went through the ritual. It was really good to see Tommy.

"Everything time-wise looks real good, Joe. Frankie will still be at the blackjack tables this morning if we hurry, and I got a driver who understands. He'll get us there. Oh, Frankie's playing at Caesar's," Tommy said, as they rushed to the tram and then through the halls of the airport, downstairs and to the black limo and waiting driver. When they climbed in, Tommy immediately poured himself a Johnny Walker black label on the rocks, and offered another for Joe.

"Okay, Tommy. Let's have it."

"Here's what went down. I'm in town for the Gibraldi-Houser fight. I check in at the Grand, leave my bag in the room, and then go down and put my wallet and everything but a few hundred in a safe-deposit box. I wander over to the Palace – Caesar's – to shoot some craps. I win a little and go to the cage to cash in. I see this guy who I recognize as Frankie Vittarone from Chicago. He walks up to the counter, carrying seven or eight racks of black and gray chips – up to his chin – with another guy, Jimmy, also carrying a stack of racks. There are four guys behind them. Frankie's wearing a gray silk suit with a gray silk tie on a gray silk shirt."

At this point, Tommy leaned over, grabbed the bottle of Scotch, and refilled his glass. Joe waved his hand.

"In his pocket, he's got a gray silk handkerchief. I mean, this guy's got the look, you know. He just stands there next to me, waiting for the woman behind the counter to take the racks. I hold onto my ten chips and say nothing. He looks at me and says, 'How ya doin'?' I tell him, 'Fine, thank you.' He says, 'What's your name?' I tell him, 'Tommy Greco, thank you.' He says, 'That's a funny name, Tommy Greco Thank You.' I tell him, 'Yeah, it is, thank you.'

"I cash in my chips, and Frankie and Jimmy hand in their racks of chips. The woman behind the counter asks them if they would prefer checks or cash. They say cash. She excuses herself for a minute, goes into the cage, and then comes back with another woman, each carrying stacks of neatly wrapped hundred-dollar bills. She turns to Frankie and asks him if he would like the cash now. He says yes, 'cause it's going in the safe-deposit boxes behind her. She counts out the stacks – which are five-thousand dollars each – until Frankie agrees that's the amount of his chips. The stacks are piled high on the counter, and there are now five or six security guys behind Frankie, Jimmy and me. She counts out the stacks for Jimmy as well and he nods.

"Then the woman sets down a large safe-deposit box in front of Frankie, and the other woman sets down the same size box in front of Jimmy, who's down at the other end. These are big boxes. Frankie opens his box right next to me and it's practically filled with stacks of c-notes, the hundred-dollar bills on their edge to make more room. He stuffs in as many stacks of the fresh money as the box will hold. He's actually forcing down the top. He's still probably got twenty to thirty grand left. He yells over to Jimmy – people all around – 'Hey Jimmy! You got room for more?' Jimmy shouts back, 'Yeah.' Frankie starts throwing the packages one by one over the heads of the security guards to Jimmy, who catches them and jams them in his box. I mean, here's these guys all dressed up watching the c-notes go over their head. You had to be there to see that," Tommy said through a fit of infectious laughter.

"So I'm watching all of this, and Frankie knows I'm watching, so Frankie and Jimmy decide they're going to eat. They ask me to join them. He's tellin', not askin'. I nod.

"I go back up to the Grand, spend an hour or so by the pool, back to my room for a shower and pick up my good luck brown leather sport jacket and go back down to shoot some more. Three markers later and being hungry, I go over to Caesar's and check in with the guy in front at the restaurant on the first floor. He tells me Mr. V is expecting me and points to the open restaurant across the hall. I go over there and see a section set up for Chinese food, only it's all blocked off with guards on each end. One long table, filled with a bunch of Asians and some heavy guys, some good-looking women, and one empty seat. There's Frankie at the end. He shouts, 'Hey, Thank You, over here. We're expecting you.'

"I take the seat. Everyone introduces themselves – first name only – the rest is small talk. Frankie shouts down from the end of the table, 'This is Tommy.' He tosses me a room key, tells me – and everyone else at the table – that's the key to my room in his suite, I'm to get whatever I want, and he tells me 'Just sign Frankie V to everything.' Everybody nods. I nod. Then the dinner's over. I tell Frankie, 'Thank you.' Frankie, Jimmy, and his group go over to the blackjack tables. Guards section the whole area off. They start playing heavy. I go back to the Grand.

"The next morning, I'm up early and I'm thinking I don't want to offend Frankie by not staying in his suite. So I check out of the Grand and go over to Caesar's and let myself in the bedroom on my side of the suite. Frankie is just getting up, and he's got some female company. I stay on my side and then a rap on the door, and it's Frankie, telling me it's time for steak and eggs. The three of us have breakfast, I say nothin'. Frankie leaves the waiter a $500 tip, in five black-and-purple chips, tosses two $500 gray chips to his girlfriend, suggesting she go shopping while he, his friend, Jimmy, and I go upstairs and take in some steam.

"We're upstairs at the health club, and, when we get to the counter, Frankie introduces me to his huge friend, Jimmy. Then Frankie takes out a safe-deposit box, and as he and Jimmy put all their personals into it – cash, rings, watches, keys, and a couple of crosses with diamonds in them – he looks over at me and says, 'One box is enough for all of us, right?' I'm not sure, but he looked at me, you know, when he said it, so I go along and put my diamond ring, my safe-deposit box key, and $500, which is all I have, in the box. Frankie takes the key to the box.

"Frankie goes first on the table for a massage. Jimmy and I are taking steam. First Jimmy clues me in that Frankie had heard some things about me and thought I might have potentiality. That's why he had receptivity about me. Then, Jimmy explains that Frankie's wife is coming in that night, that he gets the girlfriend. I nod but say nothin'. Then he takes a massage, and Frankie walks me out on the terrace in the sun looking down over the strip. He looks me in the eye and tells me how happy he is that I'm with him and wants to make sure I'm comfortable. I tell him I'm comfortable, thank you. He tells me he's up $850 K and that his group from the Pacific Rim is doing well. He tells me it really means a lot to him that he's got me to talk to, to spend quality time like this with. I tell him thank you. Then it's my time to get a massage.

"I come off the table, and everybody's gone. I get dressed, and it dawns on me, I would like to have a key to the health club safe-deposit box. I ask the guy working there if he knows where Mr. V went. He says, 'No, but he did leave this key for you.' I go to the box behind the counter at the health club, and there's my ring, $500, and the safe-deposit box key. I'm feeling better."

At this point, the limo had arrived at Caesar's. Tommy told the driver to wait and kept talking.

"I go to the Grand, to the safe-deposit box section, to get my wallet and more money, and close my box. I give them my key. I wait. They come back. 'Wrong key.' I tell them there must be a mistake. They ask for identification. I don't have any – it's in my box. I ask them to open the box. They ask for my room key. I tell them I don't have it, I've checked out. They tell me, 'Sorry, no way to get into the box without identification and without a key.' I'm fucked.

"I figured I would hang with Frankie, get to know him, let him see what I got, and become his go-through man. Now, he's got a key in his pocket, and it ain't going to open his box, and he's going to figure that out as soon as he goes to the box this morning, and then he's going to think of me and then . . . I'm seriously over-exposed. Or that's already happened and he thinks I'm running, and his guys are looking for me right now. Either way, this is not a good situation, Joe. And you can see that I wasn't screwing around when I said time is of the importance." Tommy took another drink.

"Not that it matters, Tommy, but it's 'time is of the essence.' In any event, what do you want me to do?"

"All you have to do," Tommy said, leaning over and looking Joe straight in the eyes, the veins bulging on the sides of his temples, "is go in there with me, we walk up to the blackjack tables, I whisper to the guard who stops me that you have to talk to Frankie. You're standing right next to me. Frankie's going to look at me, you know what I mean – really look at me. Then he's going to really look at you.

Then, I hope he will motion you in. You go in, go up to him, and tell him that I've got his key and he's got my key, that they got mixed up in the box. And then swap keys. That's it," Tommy said, clapping his hands and then holding them both up in front of his face. "That's it, Joe." He clapped his hands again.

"And have you given any thought as to why Frankie V. is interested in talking with me in the first place, or why he should accept what I'm telling him about the mix-up of the keys rather than you telling him? It seems to me this would be a good opportunity for you to earn his trust."

"Joe, this is one of those times in life when you got one shot, that you're either believed or not. You got what I don't – believability stamped on your forehead. I need you to talk to him. Swap the keys. We're done." Another clap of hands.

Joe could see there was no convincing Tommy to step up to this plate. Knowing he should have his head examined, he simply told Tommy, "Okay, stay with me." And with that, they both climbed out of the limo.

It was not hard to find Frankie in Caesar's. Three blackjack tables stood in a semicircle, with two pit bosses behind each table and five armed guards at the front of each, forming a tight ring, keeping the crowds away.

Joe walked straight up to the table at which Tommy had identified Frankie as the player on the end, standing, not sitting. He motioned to the pit boss behind that table that he would like to talk with Frankie. The security guards watched Joe and Tommy stand there, but nothing was said. The man behind the table adjusted his French cuffs and his tie, straightened his black suit jacket, and walked slowly over to Frankie and waited. After what seemed like a long time but was actually only a minute or two, the action on that hand was completed and Frankie looked up and nodded.

The man approached Frankie and whispered in his ear. Frankie looked over at Tommy, and at Joe. Then everything stopped. The next hand was not dealt. The other men at the table were watching Frankie for a signal as to what he wanted to do. Frankie pulled up the stool behind him and sat down. He put his arms up on the table, folded his hands, and looked down at the table. After three long minutes, he looked up again and motioned to the man at his side to come closer. He whispered in his ear.

The man approached Joe and Tommy and said, "Mr. V would like to talk to you gentlemen." Joe said, "Yes, sir," and started to walk towards Frankie. Realizing that Tommy had not moved, he stepped back, grabbed Tommy by the arm, and brought him along.

"What can I do for you gentlemen?" Frankie said, looking Joe over from head to foot.

"My name is Joe Hart," Joe said. "I've known Tommy Greco for a number of years. I live in South Carolina. He called me there last night at one in the morning and asked me to fly to Las Vegas to meet with you this morning to explain to you that you inadvertently picked up his safe-deposit box key from the health club you guys went to, leaving your key with him. He discovered that last night when he went over to the Grand to get his wallet out of his box. But because he had the wrong key and no ID, he could not get into his box. He needs his key, which you have. And he would like to give you your key."

At this point, Frankie had nodded yes over ten times. Frankie reached in his pocket and pulled out a safe-deposit box key. "You're tellin' me this key is Tommy Greco with a funny name's key?"

"Yes, sir, exactly," Joe replied.

"And Tommy Greco with a funny name's got my key?"

"Yes, sir."

Frankie stared at Tommy and Tommy stared back. Three blackjack tables watched all of this, and no one said a word. All action remained at a standstill.

"Tommy, how did you like the massage?" Frankie asked.

"It was okay, Mr. V, you know, it was okay. Thank you."

"There he goes," Frankie said. "Tommy Greco Thank You. I like you, Tommy. I like having you around. I think your pal Joe was a good guy to get up in the middle of the night and fly all the way out here to tell me about the keys. I like that. It shows a lot of respect. I like the way he calls me sir, too. It's good. So let's see the key, Tommy."

At that point, Tommy handed the key over to Frankie and Frankie gave his key to Joe. Frankie then told his group at the tables that he thought it was time for a break, and they all agreed. The group broke up and Frankie picked up the few chips left in front of him on the table.

"I'm gonna cash these in. You guys feel like walking with me over to the cashier?"

"Yes, sir," Joe said, and Tommy nodded again. They all walked over to the cashier and stood in line. Frankie soon exchanged his chips for cash. Then he put down the safe-deposit box key that Tommy had just given him and asked for his box, signing his name on the card. A moment later, the large box was placed in front of him. The lid on the box popped open and it was crammed full of hundred-dollar stacks. Frankie smiled.

"As I said, I like you boys. Tommy, you and I got to spend some more time together. Mr. Hart, sorry you had to come out all this way. Nice meeting you."

"Thank you," Tommy said. He reached out to shake Frankie's hand, but he had already turned and left. Joe and Tommy walked through the casino at Caesar's to the forum, where they went to Prada for some lunch.

"Joe, you're a stand-up guy. Thanks for coming. I knew it would go just this way. Done." Tommy clapped his hands and raised them again.

"You're welcome, Tommy, although I think you could have done it all yourself. However, you might want to think about a different career than being Frankie's go-through guy. This is a good time to let this one go and move on."

"Yeah, well, I have to do something other than just try to make money gambling. I wasn't aspirating to a made guy or nothing. I was just thinking of developing a relationship kind of thing where I would be like, you know, a private contractor. I don't mean a private contractor like that, but just in providing a go-through service, like in communications. Something like a communication facilitation kind of guy. I think I got some talents in that area. What do you think, Joe?"

"You've definitely got talent, Tommy. The challenge is how to channel it in a way that will work, and keep you out of trouble. I think we need to work on that a little bit."

"Sort of my continuing developmental program, right, Joe?"

"Yeah, Tommy. Something like that. Anyway, the pasta's great here, and it was really good to see you."

"Hey Joe, what do you say we shoot some craps, have some fun?" Tommy said. "You need some fun. We'll go to Angie's for some beers; maybe you'll do the Karaoke thing again. I love that shit." One night together, after Joe had had too many, he decided to try singing, and it had cracked up Tommy and the whole bar.

"Thanks, Tommy, but I've got to check on a friend of mine out here, and then I've got to get home. Time is of the essence."

"I understand," Tommy said. "There's nobody like you, Joe. So long." Tommy gave Joe the push-away-pull-forward hug, and said goodbye.

CHAPTER 18

Preston's secretary told him she had Marcia on the line.

"Hi, honey. I just got off the phone with Joe Hart, the attorney..."

"I know who he is. Let's have it."

Preston could hear the ice in her voice. "He's gathering material in preparation for meeting with the bank, getting his arms around it."

"Preston, dear, may I ask you a question?" Marcia's tone dripped with sarcasm.

"Of course."

"Why are you dealing with me about this over the phone? Is this one of your control moves? And why the hell do you have your secretary get me on the line? I'm your wife for Christ's sake. If you want to discuss this, and you damn well better, I suggest you get in your cherished Bentley and drive your butt over here now, and have the ... let's say courage ... to have this conversation in person."

"Settle down, honey. I know you're upset."

Silence.

"I'll come over."

"Do that," Marcia replied, and hung up.

Preston hailed a cab, arriving at the Tower a half-an-hour later. Marcia was waiting in the straight chair by the fireplace. He wondered why she always picked that chair when he was in trouble. He poured himself a Red Label on the rocks and sat down.

"Well?" Marcia said, watching him.

"Joe is preparing to talk to the bank. He needs all kinds of documents from us. Casey has the lists. He's getting it together. He's the guy to handle this . . . but it is our undertaking . . . "

"Get to the damn point. Are we in trouble? If we are, how much?"

Preston explained the stores' financial problems, including the
SOT, and that "a lot of money" was involved. When Marcia asked
what a SOT was, he explained that SOT is an acronym for Sold
Out of Trust – the condition a dealership is in when it has received
money from a bank to finance a car, called a floor plan, and has
sold the car to a customer, received the money, but not paid the
bank back for the amount loaned on that car.

Marcia rolled her eyes. "Leaving aside all of that mumbo jumbo,
which incidentally sounds dishonest to me, it wasn't two weeks
ago you told me 'not to worry, everything would be fine.' Now the
roof's caving in. Did all this just happen or did you suddenly get
religion and decide to tell the truth?"

Preston sank in his chair, looking at her.

Marcia pursed her lips. "Well dear, maybe I can make this go a
tad faster. What did Joe tell you he needs from me?"

Relieved at the question, Preston handed her a letter. "He wants
you to sign this."

"I need my own attorney," she said, reading the letter carefully.

"You don't actually need one," Preston replied. "Just a lawyer
covering his ass, making sure you are advised, as they put it."

"Very interesting," she said, more to herself than Preston. She
went to the kitchen and poured a cup of coffee, and returned to the
chair. "Is this the whole of it? Or is this one of those times when I
have to pull it out of you, piece by tiny piece?"

"There's another letter we need signed by you," he said, handing over another paper. "This one is from another lawyer. Joe is
thorough. He wants to cover all the bases." Marcia was already
halfway through the letter.

"This is from a criminal lawyer," she said, tears beginning to
form in her eyes. She held the letter up to the lamp and started
to read from it. *"Your signature below will memorialize your full
understanding of the multiple risks involved, and your voluntary
assumption of the risks, including exposure to criminal bank fraud,*

misrepresentation, deceit, and misappropriation of funds..." She put the letter down, and looked at Preston. "Have you read this?"

"Of course," Preston replied, trying to sound calm.

"You're trying to protect your little bottom, aren't you? You handle all this, get me to sign the damn personal guarantees, and now you want me to sign off on bank fraud. You're out of your mind, you selfish bastard. You think I'm pretty stupid, and you're a shining genius. Maybe we can get a cell together. What do you think? How the hell could you put me in this position?"

"Calm down, Marcia. You are not going to jail. I'm the one at risk, not you. I'll deal with it and it won't come down on you. Believe me, I'm the one affected."

"That's the problem. I don't believe you. What little faith and trust I had is long gone. Bang Bang like the song says." She cupped her face in her hands and cried softly. When Preston started to speak, Marcia held her hands up, palms out.

The only sound was the grandfather clock ticking in the vestibule.

Marcia rose, Preston springing up and standing before her.

"You know, Preston," she finally said, "I used to think you were tall."

More silence.

"I'll sign the damn letters," she said finally. "The covenants, the assumptions and all of that. I will consult a lawyer, one of my own choosing. And you will hear from my lawyer, and perhaps he will have some papers for you to sign."

Preston started to put his arms around her.

"Forget it," she said, pushing him away. "As you like to say, this conversation is over."

CHAPTER 19

Missy

After checking several casinos, Joe found Missy working as a cocktail waitress at the Frontier.

"Joe, what are you doing here?" Missy exclaimed as she balanced her tray of drinks on her side and hugged him. "How are you? When did you get here?"

"I just got in this morning. I had to come out to talk with a friend. Is there a place we can sit and talk for a little while?"

"Absolutely. I'm off in half an hour anyway. Let me tell my shift boss that I'm leaving now. She won't mind. It'll just take a sec."

Joe nodded, and Missy disappeared through a door that Joe had not noticed. A few minutes later she reappeared, having changed into black slacks and a simple white blouse.

Born Melissa Andrea Scarlatti at the Lyons Hospital in upstate New York, Missy had grown up to be a striking woman. Her dream was to escape the small town of Lyons and be a dancer in Las Vegas. She became a showgirl in Vegas, her dream later wiped out by marriage to a man who held himself out as an agent and promised her the moon. What he delivered was a lot of punches.

"Let's go to the coffee shop – it's fairly quiet now, and we can sit in a corner booth and talk," Missy said.

"Fine, lead the way."

Shortly, they were seated in the far corner, which, as Missy had indicated, was nearly vacant. She ordered a grilled cheese sandwich; Joe asked for apple pie and ice cream.

"Joe, it's so great to see you."

"You, too, Missy. Frankly, I'm glad you changed outfits. The

111

other one was a little too provocative for an old guy."

"You don't like my big boobs?" Missy asked, laughing.

"They're just fine. Actually, they're very fine," Joe said, trying not to look at them. "Let's hear how you're doing. That's what I really want to know."

The last time they'd talked was at the green-and-white cabins. Missy had gone through some pretty tough times with her husband. She'd told Joe she wanted to get as far away from him as she could, and Alice got a request for information from an attorney out here in connection with a protective order. Joe had no idea what happened after that.

"Why did you come back? What's going on? Is everything all right?"

"I'm trying to work my way back. I hate being a cocktail waitress. All the smart-ass remarks from drunks and gamblers. The assignments to distract this gambler or that one, feed 'em the booze. The whole thing. But I need the money and the tips can be good. I've got a friend who's working on getting me back on stage now that my face – now that I look better."

"You look wonderful," Joe said, meaning it.

"I took your advice and got the protective order. Sam was pissed, but so far he's left me alone. If I do go back on the stage, depending on what role I get, he'll probably start bothering me again. It's kind of ironic, you know what I mean? If I'm not doing well, he leaves me alone. As soon as I get back on stage and have a good dancing part, he can't stand it, and that's when he comes around. I thought the divorce would stop all that, but it didn't make any difference. So I'm damned if I do, and damned if I don't. But I just want to try to get back where I was. I felt great then, you know? Like I was alive and doing something."

So you put yourself right back in harm's way, right where this asshole is? "I guess I can understand that, but I worry about you out here. Do you have any real friends here, Missy? Somebody who can keep an eye out for you?"

"I've got some girlfriends and the church, but to tell you the truth I try to stay away from the guys, and by the time I'm off, I'm too tired anyway."

"There's a guy out here named Tommy Greco. He's quite a character, but it might be fun for you to meet him some time. He's from upstate New York, too. If you do meet him, get to know him, don't sell him short."

"What's he do?" Missy asked.

"Gambles." They both burst out laughing. "Okay. I wanted to check in. Is there anything I can do for you before I leave?"

"Joe, I know this is a touchy subject, and I don't mean to pry, but... I heard about what happened with your wife, and it made me sick."

"Thanks. By the way," Joe said, needing to change the subject, "Buck and I went back to the Adirondacks and hung out for a while. It was really great up there. So quiet. So gorgeous. Buck loved it, and so did I."

"I remember. It was when I was hiding. Different world up there."

"I probably would have stayed up there forever, but believe it or not, a guy with a business problem and his accountant came up into the mountains and found me and convinced me to come down and help them. So I did."

"Yeah, so what else is new? You had to come down sometime, Joe," Missy said, reaching over and holding his hand.

Joe took her hand away and patted it a couple of times. "Yeah, I had to come down sometime."

Missy looked directly into Joe's eyes for too long a time and said, "I'm not stupid, and you've been the best friend I've ever had. I want to help. No strings. Let's you and me go to my place. I want to be with you. Really be with you. You'll feel better. It'll do you good."

Joe motioned to the waitress and pointed to his coffee cup. "Missy, thank you. Please understand how much I appreciate the offer. I can't go with you. Clearly, part of me would like to. You're a beautiful woman, inside and out. But Ashley was... and for me, still is... my wife, and always will be. It's just the way it is. I hope you'll understand."

"I understand," Missy said, with tears in her eyes. "I knew that would be the answer. Besides, it's too early."

"It's not a matter of too early," Joe replied. "This is one mountain I don't ever want to come down from."

Neither spoke for a few moments. Then Missy looked at Joe, and breaking the silence, asked, "Why me?"

"Why me, what?"

"I mean, why have you taken such an interest in me? I know you're a good guy and that you believe in helping people, not just your clients but others, too. I know you and Ashley supported the Domestic Violence Shelter. I remember all my conversations with you back then. You helped me a lot. Don't get me wrong, Joe. I love you for it. The part that blows me away is that you've stayed in touch so long to make sure I'm all right and see what you can do to help. I just wonder why does a man like you look after a woman like me. I know why you're not doing it, and that makes me . . . want to know all the more why you do. And the others, too. Why, Joe? How do we get to be the lucky ones?"

There it is. "Why do you get so overinvolved with your men, Commander? Where's the detachment?" Damn it, I thought I'd left this bull behind when I left the Navy. Why can't it be as simple as lending a hand? But it never is. "Those are good questions. I'm not sure I have good answers. My wife asked me the same thing one time. Aside from my clients, there are a few people I have reached out to. Probably should have been more. Why them? Something struck a chord." *I probably need a shrink for the right answer. Look at Tommy. I don't know what's worse: an abusive alcoholic father and an unloving prostitute for a mother, or no mother and father at all. . . .* "When I look at you, Missy, and all that you've had to go through, I see who you are and what you can be. We can each use a few friends along the way. Besides, it makes me feel good."

Missy looked as if she were holding back tears as she sipped from her water glass. "God bless you, Joe. You're a great friend. They broke the mold when they made you."

Something in that moment made Joe reach way back in his memory, something about *"They broke the mold when they made you."* He vaguely remembered his mother saying something like that, but he had trouble remembering her. He wondered whether his mother was as gentle and kind as Missy, and if she had lived, what she would have been like?

"I don't know about that, Missy, but thanks. I'm glad to hear you're doing okay. I'm meeting with a bank Monday morning, so I've got to catch the red-eye back and have a day to get ready. You know where to reach me, if you need anything. Alice and Buck send their regards." Joe stood up to leave.

"Good to see you. I'll be in touch. Thanks, Joe."

CHAPTER 20

Preston knew the climate would be frosty for a while, but he was confident that he could bring Marcia around. *She'll be all right after she realizes I'm in the hot seat, not her. She didn't take any money, she didn't run the stores, she needs time, that's all.* Returning to the office restless and preoccupied, before he knew it he'd begun to walk uptown. Over one hour later, he found himself at 1040 Fifth Avenue, riding the elevator up to the twelfth floor. He knocked, and, using his key, met June Wilson in the vestibule.

"Hi, Mother," he said, putting his arm on her shoulder, and a kiss on her cheek. "You look marvelous, as always."

"Thank you, dear. It's so good to see you. Come in, sit down. You look like you just ran a mile." She was already heading for the bar. "Let me get you something to drink. Scotch?"

"Water would be fine. Thanks."

"How in the world are you, Preston?"

"Fine, Mother. I left the office, decided to walk, and here I am."

"I'm clearly the beneficiary! Are you still building empires, the conquistador?"

"Is that how you think of me?"

"Well, you've done well, have you not? Stores everywhere, real estate. How's the car business these days?"

"Cyclical," he replied. "Mother, let's not talk about me. How are you getting along? Are you ... happy?"

"That's an interesting question. Something must be on your mind. Oh well, let me answer you first. I'm as good as can be expected for a divorcee in her sixties. Better actually. I've got a great circle of friends and we look after each other. I practically live at the spa, except for shopping. Doctor Hutchinson is trying to get me to gain weight, a problem the girls tell me they wish they had." She got up and walked over to Preston, putting her hand on his shoulder. They were quiet for a while.

"I should make this walk more often."

"I agree."

"Wilson's built stores throughout the country. We own substantial real estate. But the car business is fickle. Same with real estate." Preston said.

"I'm told this co-op has gone straight up. I couldn't believe one similar to mine sold for 5.6 million."

"This is a *Candela* building, Mother; the real estate market in other parts of the country is not the same as the city. What do you say I take you to dinner?"

"That would be lovely, my dear. I just happen to be available tonight. Where shall we go? Will Marcia meet us?"

"Marcia is... tied up tonight. Just the two of us. You pick the place."

"Let me freshen up, and we'll be on our way."

They walked arm-in-arm to Bravos, a neighborhood favorite, where they sat in a quiet booth enjoying Chardonnay and seafood. During coffee, Preston leaned forward. "There's something I want to ask you, Mother – about Father."

"What about your father?" she asked, appearing to examine her cup.

"This is unpleasant, but I really would like to know. What was the main reason you insisted that he leave?"

June paused as if she were pondering the question. Finally, "I couldn't trust him."

"Was that because he failed at business, or the women, or what?"

"That was because your father was dishonest with me, with you, and with himself. The women were a part of it, although not as big a part as you might think. It was his lying about everything. The truth is he didn't want to spend time with me. And, there was far too much tension where you were concerned. Nothing to do with you, my dear. I hated that he didn't spend time with you, talk with you, do the things fathers do with their sons. Worse, I hated that he didn't want to, but pretended that he did. And the money. He always needed money and would work me to get it. I finally had my fill of the whole mess."

"I'm sorry."

"No need for that, my dear. I know how lonely you were as a child. I blame myself for that. You hated being forced to go to those private schools. I thought your father would visit you, do more, support you in sports. Instead he ignored you, and then compelled you to go on those wilderness trips. I never understood what all of that was about. Lord knows what demons drove him."

"What kinds of demons? Drinking? Drugs?"

His mother's eyes began to tear. "That's all I want to say. I've tried all these years not to speak disparagingly about your father to anyone, especially you. I'm sure I've let you down."

"You haven't let me down. Never have. I don't know what's caused me to go into this. Too much on my mind these days, I guess. Dad, business, Marcia. That's what you get when you build an empire."

"What about Marcia? Is she pregnant? Is that what this is all about?"

"No, Mother. I know how anxious you are, but Marcia is not pregnant. Ready to go? Let's get out of here, and follow your doctor's orders."

CHAPTER 21

Johnny

Alice finished binding the last of the twenty-four books that she and the interns had compiled. Each book was neatly labeled on the front center denoting the dealership, a description of the text, and the type of material in the exhibits. It was now 7:30 p.m. and Alice realized she was hungry. She figured Buck, who had been keeping her company all day, was hungry as well.

"How would you like to go to the Home Dairy for dinner, Buck? You can see your buddy Johnny, and I'm sure he'll have some roast beef scraps for you."

Buck sat up, ears erect, and, looking at her with his deep black eyes, cocked his head to the right.

"I thought so," Alice said. "Give me a minute to check the office and lock up, and then we'll go."

At the car, she opened the rear door of her Taurus long enough for Buck to hop in and they headed down to Braydon's Home Dairy on South Main Street. Stanley Niemeyer, a 275-pound baker, had successfully run this homespun, one-floor, cafeteria-style restaurant and bakery for thirty-four years. Alice enjoyed the country food and, because Stanley was a client of Joe's who loved dogs, and Buck in particular. Joe often stopped in for a meal in the kitchen, followed by a sample of Stanley's latest bakery creation. Stanley said he knew dogs weren't allowed in the restaurant, but he figured that didn't apply to Buck.

Joe had met Johnny through Buck, who'd developed a leftover-steak relationship with the Home Dairy's Chief dishwasher. Mildly

121

challenged, short and stocky, around thirty years old, Johnny had thin, gray hair, which he brushed across his balding head. He'd given Joe a lengthy dissertation on exactly how the food trays were placed on the cut-through windowsill by the customers at the end of their meals, how to bring the trays through the window, how to remove the dirty plates and guide the garbage down a stainless steel chute and into the disposal, using the spray device on the coiled hang-down washer.

Stanley, trying to shield Joe, had told Johnny to stay away. Joe countermanded the order, motioning for Stanley to settle down. He invited Johnny to join them at the small wooden table at the front of the twenty-foot-long baking table that separated the room from the ovens.

Joe liked Johnny and did not feel Stanley's sense of embarrassment around him. Besides, through Ashley's work, Joe knew about the community home for the mentally challenged where Johnny lived. Without the program, the state, struggling to find funds to care for these folks in homes, was increasingly leaving them on the streets to make their own way.

Joe told Ashley about Johnny, knowing that would not be the end of it.

On this evening, as Alice entered the Home Dairy, she could see that most of the dinner crowd had eaten and already left. As she came through the front door, she slowly passed by the five-foot enclosure in which, on four glass shelves, the cakes, pies, cookies, and other specialties were displayed. She could not resist at least a look, perusing peach cobbler, sweet potato pie, ambrosia, German chocolate cake, black velvet cake, and her favorite, key lime pie. She motioned to Buck, who proceeded down a hallway to the corner at the end of the dining area, sat down, and waited.

Alice loved the mixture of smells and held that experience responsible for her filling her tray with far more food than she needed. She paid Ida, the pretty, middle-aged woman who usually attended the cash register and always wore a clean, neatly pressed uniform with an elaborate colored handkerchief rising from the right front pocket, and a warm smile to match. There she found Buck, patiently waiting in the corner.

When she finished, Alice gathered her plates and utensils, placed them on the tray and carried it past Buck to an opening in the wall. Buck's tail was wagging as Johnny came to the window.

"Buck, how you doing?" Johnny asked. "Hello, Miss Alice, how you doing, too?"

"I'm just fine, Johnny, thank you."

"Johnny got special for Buck. Okay? Okay, Johnny give Buck steak? Buck likes steak. He can smell it. Okay?"

"Yes, Johnny, that would be nice. Thank you."

"Can Buck come back to kitchen? Mr. Stanley says okay. Joe told him it's okay. Johnny feed Buck. Leave Buck with Johnny. Okay? That good?"

"That's fine, Johnny, but just for a little while," Alice said, walking through the swinging door with Buck into the kitchen. Johnny had already found a nice piece of steak and a big bone, and had placed it on the floor, together with a stainless steel bowl of fresh water. Buck immediately began devouring the food.

"Johnny, I'll leave Buck with you, but just for an hour or so. I have to go down to Robins' Drugstore," Alice said.

"Late now," Johnny said. "Front door lock soon. Come in back door. Okay? Use back door, okay?"

"I will, Johnny. I'll come in the back." Alice waved goodbye and said to Buck, "Take care of Johnny."

Stanley had left a half-hour earlier, having closed up the front and turned the lights out. As he'd left through the back door, Stanley had instructed Johnny, when finished with the dishes, to sweep the kitchen again and make sure everything was clean before he left. Johnny continued with the dishes, all the time talking to Buck, who had gulped his dinner, drained the water bowl twice, and was now sitting at Johnny's feet. Then Johnny took the large floor broom and began to sweep one side of the room to the other.

Apart from his whistling, the kitchen was quiet.

Johnny heard the back door open and called out, "Hi, Miss Alice, Johnny in here, Johnny sweeping."

A large man, his head covered by a navy blue knit cap pulled down over his huge ears, and wearing dirty dungarees and an old camouflage jacket over an olive green T-shirt, quietly stepped into the kitchen. Buck seemed to hear the man before Johnny did and sat quietly, watching him as he moved past the large baking ovens and around the long baking table.

The man came up behind Johnny, who was whistling away and pushing the broom in the opposite direction. The man quickly threw his large right arm around Johnny's neck, pulling him back and up off his feet. Buck growled and Johnny struggled to get free, pushing the man back and turning around to face him.

"Kitchen closed," Johnny shouted at the man. "Go away! You not allowed in the kitchen. Johnny's kitchen. Leave Johnny's kitchen!"

"I'll be glad to leave your kitchen, Johnny boy," the man said in a menacing tone. "But first, why don't you show me where the safe is?"

"It's safe," Johnny said. "It's okay. It's okay. Just leave."

"Don't be a smartass," the man said, still holding Johnny's right arm. "I asked you nicely, Johnny. Where's the safe? I don't plan on asking you again." He dragged Johnny along the table to the area where Stanley had a small desk and a computer. "It's gotta be here, Johnny boy. Just show me where it is," he said, applying more pressure to Johnny's arm.

"Johnny don't know where anything of Mr. Stan's is. Johnny don't touch Mr. Stan's things. Johnny want big man now to leave. Hurting Johnny's arm. Not nice to do. Big man stop. You leave now."

"Okay, Johnny boy, you don't wanna do this the easy way, we can do it the hard way." At that point, they were under the lamp hanging down from the ceiling just over Stanley's desk. The man pulled out what looked like a military knife with a camouflage handle and a large blade, which curved up slightly at the end. He spun Johnny around and held him with his large left arm around Johnny's neck, his right arm and hand holding the knife high and to the right. He then started to bring his right hand down with the knife pointed at Johnny's chest.

"It would have been better for you to just cooperate with me, Johnny boy," the man said as he brought the knife closer to Johnny's throat.

It looked as though the huge man never heard Buck leap onto the baking table, run down it, and jump in the air as his mouth closed around the man's right arm, just below his wrist, crushing it. The big man screamed as the knife dropped to the floor. He released his hold on Johnny and fell forward with Buck on his back.

Johnny, scared to death and speechless, ran while the man scrambled to his feet, his right arm drooping at his side, and lunged forward toward Buck. Buck sat motionless, ears fully erect, staring at the man as he came closer. Buck gave out one loud bark, a sound that Johnny had never heard before. The man stopped for a moment. Buck lunged at his chest and pushed him back against the wall. Buck was standing full on his hind legs with his front legs and paws pressed against the man's chest and his mouth less than an inch from the man's throat. When Buck made a low, growling sound through his teeth, the big man froze.

Just then, Alice walked through the back door and called for Johnny.

"Johnny in here, Miss Alice. It's okay. Big man bad. Buck don't like big man. Buck mad now. Buck talking to man now. Man not saying anything. It's okay."

Alice could not understand, but knew something was wrong. She proceeded farther into the kitchen and then saw Buck with the large man against the wall. She was going to tell Buck to stop until she saw the blood on the floor and the knife.

"Come over here, Johnny. Come outside," she called. Johnny ran over to Alice and out the door. Alice called 911 on her cell phone. "We need help. Now. A man has broken into Stanley's Home Dairy. Through the back. He attacked Johnny. Oh, I'm Alice, with attorney Joe Hart. The man's still here. Come now."

Within four minutes, two policemen arrived. Alice told them to be careful and not to hurt Buck in any way, that he was Joe Hart's dog and that he knew what he was doing. The two officers entered the back door with guns drawn. Buck was still holding the man against the wall. At that point, Alice said, "Buck, here." Buck dropped down, walked to Alice's side, and sat quietly while Alice hugged him.

The police quickly took charge. Alice told Johnny to come with her and Buck, that she would drive him home. "Buck didn't like bad man," Johnny said. "Johnny Okay."

"Yes, you're fine, Johnny. You're right, Buck didn't like that man. I don't like him either. It's time for you to go home now, Johnny, and get some sleep." Alice's heart was still pounding but she tried to sound calm, at least until she dropped him off at the home.

Alice looked at Buck sitting quietly in the back seat. "Well, Buck, it looks like you did what I asked you to do. You took care of Johnny." Buck leaned over the front seat and rested his head softly on Alice's right shoulder as she headed home.

When Joe returned home from Vegas and drove over to Alice's house to pick up Buck, they met him at the front door.

"Hi, Alice. How are you doing? Hi, Buck, how you doing, fellow?"

"Everything's fine. All the books are bound and ready to go. Alex Herman's report is on your desk, and I brought a copy home in case you wanted to read it tonight." She reached onto the table in the foyer by the front door.

"Thanks, Alice. And thanks for taking care of Buck."

"You're welcome. I saved a copy of the paper for you." She handed him that as well. "Buck's quite a hero. He made the front page. He protected your friend Johnny at the Home Dairy and kept Stanley from being robbed as well. I actually saw it. It was scary, Joe. Buck is such a sweetheart, and he's so quiet. You forget how tough or strong he can be. I'm glad he's on our side, although I don't think the robber is. Anyway, you can read all about it in your spare time."

"Way to go, Buck!" Joe shouted, patting Buck on the head. "You're a hero. Next the police will want you on the force." Buck just quietly looked up at Joe, his tail wagging.

"How did things go in Vegas?"

"Fine," Joe replied. "Tommy is over his crisis and I was able to check in with Missy as well. All good," Joe said as he waved goodbye, heading to his car with Buck at his side.

That night, Joe studied Alex Herman's report, read about Buck, and went to bed early. Before falling asleep, he thought about Preston, Casey, and the meeting in the morning in Charlotte. He had arranged to see them for breakfast at a coffee shop near the Olympic Tower, where the meeting was to take place on the thirty-ninth floor in Bank North America's conference room. He knew the importance of the pre-conference discussion with Preston and Casey. He also understood they did not.

CHAPTER 22

The three men sat at a table in the corner of the coffee shop. Joe listened to Preston's questions as he finished his eggs, country ham, grits and coffee. Preston, apparently too nervous to eat, was only drinking coffee, while Casey worked his way through a stack of blueberry pancakes with fried eggs and syrup.

"I've told you what to expect," Joe said. "This is not going to be a pleasant meeting. I'm sure you'll find the small army the bank will amass to be intimidating, or at least overbearing and annoying. But remember, they do have a dog in this fight."

"What's that mean?" Casey asked, still chewing.

"I mean they have a vested interest in getting their money back, and they have a right to be very upset with you both. They didn't have to agree to meet with us in the first place. I'm glad they did, and I view this as a major opportunity."

"This is not my first meeting with a bank that is owed money," Preston said. "They're going to kill us in there. We don't have any defense. Let's just get it over with."

"Don't forget the ground rules," Joe said. "We're going to do this my way. You've already determined you have nothing to lose. You won't get in trouble for what you don't say. Therefore, I'd like each of you to say nothing. Other than 'Good morning' and that I'm handling this matter for you, zero. Also, there may come a time when I would like us to leave this meeting. If that should occur, I will get up to leave, and I would like both of you to immediately follow me. Avoid any body language or facial expressions during this meeting. If questions are put to you, refer them to me. If I do want you to answer,

I'll let you know, but I doubt that I will. There's not much you can tell these folks factually that isn't already before them in the books. Hard as it is, just sit there passively and quietly."

"I understand," Preston said, finishing his second cup of coffee and clanking the cup on the counter. "I haven't forgotten the ground rules. I'm with you, Joe."

"Me, too," Casey said, ordering a jelly donut for dessert.

"Okay, let's go," Joe said, once they finished eating. "I would appreciate it if you guys would help me with the carts to bring the books up to the meeting. My truck's around the corner."

They arrived at 9:40 a.m. and were the first in the conference room. It was just as Joe had imagined: thick, rich, tan wall-to-wall carpet and a thirty-foot-long mahogany table with eighteen black leather chairs. At each end was a matching mahogany credenza with a selection of coffee, tea, orange juice and soft drinks, a silver tray full of cookies, and other pastries.

A doorway opened at each end of the conference room, and the wall across from the entryway was glass, floor to ceiling. It was a clear, blue-skied, sunny morning, and the view of Charlotte from the thirty-ninth floor was imposing. The remaining walls were covered in light brown wallpaper, one with a large whiteboard and a tray of markers.

Joe placed his cart full of books and a yellow plastic box in the corner of the room. Preston and Casey followed suit. Then Joe picked a chair at the window side of the table in the middle and motioned for Preston and Casey to sit at his right.

At precisely ten o'clock, Tom Gallagher entered the room, followed by what seemed like an endless line of men and women.

"Good morning, gentlemen. I'm glad you could come," Mr. Gallagher said, with a broad smile, walking around the table and extending his hand.

Joe stood, followed by Preston and Casey. "Joe Hart, Tom. It's good to meet you in person. Thank you for setting this meeting up. This is Preston Wilson on my right, and Casey Fitzgerald, Wilson's CFO, next to him."

The men shook hands. Mr. Gallagher then moved to Joe's left and stood behind the chair at the end of the table. He introduced each of the bank's representatives and attorneys as they took seats at the table.

"There may be others joining us, but we will have to do with what we have now," Mr. Gallagher began. "I would appreciate it if each of you folks would pass your cards to these gentlemen so that they can keep y'all straight. Lord knows it's hard enough for me sometimes."

Each of the twelve reached in their pockets, wallets, or handbags and produced three business cards and pushed them across the table. Casey, apparently struggling to locate his business cards, could only come up with three. Neither Preston nor Joe offered any cards.

Joe, after carefully reading each card, placed it across from the person connected to the card, consulting the notes he had taken during their introductions. He took his time. Everyone sat quietly as he looked the group over, observing their clothes and body language, and studying their faces. Each was dressed in a professional manner, the men wearing conservative suits and ties, the women in suits as well. On his side of the table, Casey and Preston wore similar suits and ties. Joe simply wore gray slacks, a blue blazer, and an open white button-down shirt. A small Navy bar was placed in the right lapel of his sport jacket.

Joe rose, briskly moved to the corner to retrieve eight of the bound books, and placed them on the table. He then returned, selected six more, and placed them neatly in a row. Again he went back for the remaining five books, aware of the fifteen people watching and waiting.

He returned to his seat, folded his hands, positioned them on the table, and looked up at the group.

Floyd Ritter, BNA's general counsel, glanced at Gallagher, who nodded in return. Ritter leaned forward. "Well, Mr. Hart, you've got us all here. It's your show."

Despite Gallagher's in-house counsel taking the lead, Joe turned to Tom Gallagher. "Thank you for the opportunity on behalf of Wilson Holdings and Preston to go over our strategic turnaround plan, copies of which you have been provided."

Joe noticed that the only copies the bank representatives had brought with them were in front of Ritter, Bower, the corporate counsel, and Barenzo, the CFO.

"I trust that you have had an opportunity to review our plan. You will note that following the text of the plan itself there are numerous exhibits..."

Gallagher interrupted. "You certainly have put a lot of time and effort into providing us with a plan, Joe. I don't recall seeing a plan like this and with this much detail. Have you, Floyd?"

"Yes, we've seen a lot of plans. No matter how big and elaborate the plans are, they still have to represent the facts, and the facts here are uncontroverted that Wilson Holdings and Mr. Wilson owe us and a lot of other folks a lot of money. I want to hear what Mr. Wilson has to say about that." Ritter looked directly at Preston.

"There are a lot of ways we can conduct this meeting," Joe said in a low, even tone. "You came to this table voluntarily. So did we. This meeting is an opportunity for us to work together to reach a solution to problems that we, and I know you, take seriously. First, I..."

"I've got a question for you, Mr. Hart," Ritter interjected, cutting Joe off. "Why does the front of your book here state your plan is confidential and off the record?"

Joe focused on Ritter. "My understanding in setting this meeting up with Mr. Gallagher is that we could, for settlement purposes, have an honest discussion of how we can work this matter out in a way that helps the bank and Wilson Holdings and Preston as well..."

Ritter interrupted, "But why off the record?"

"I trust Mr. Gallagher, and I'm sure he has told you of our understanding. The writing is simply a safety net in the unfortunate event of any unexpected amnesia."

Bower's face broke into a broad grin. Ritter's did not. "There are obviously some serious issues in this matter that we want to be able to speak frankly about today. To begin with, Wilson Holdings indeed does owe Bank North America a considerable amount of money..."

Ritter, sharply cutting Joe off, asked, "Just how much money do you admit that you owe us, Mr. Hart? How much in total?"

"Hold it," Joe said directly to Ritter and putting his hand up. "I don't owe your bank any money, Mr. Ritter. Nor do I owe you the effort, study, and energy I have put into solving the bank's problem for you. I have been interrupted four times this morning, three by you, Mr. Ritter. As I said earlier, we can conduct this meeting in a lot of ways. One is for us each to actively listen to one another, without interruption. I'm good for those four interruptions, but any more and I decide to leave this meeting." Joe surveyed everyone across the table. No one said a word.

"Good, then I'll continue. The amounts of debt are detailed in the plan. For Charlottetown Motors, the cap loan is five million, but is not yet due by its terms, and the interest is current. However, we believe the SOT to be in excess of eight million dollars…"

"Eight million dollars," Mr. Olsen, the COO exclaimed, cutting Joe off. "That's outrageous! That's criminal! You've got to be kidding!"

Joe slowly stood, moved around the table, and briskly strode out the door without saying a word. Preston and Casey followed. Before they got to the elevator, Bower came running down the hall.

"Joe! Wait up," he said, sounding out of breath. "Olsen didn't mean to interrupt you. He wants to apologize. This SOT issue hit a nerve. He's feeling on the spot. I ask you, please, come back in. There won't be any further interruptions."

Joe turned, nodded to Bower, and at that moment his cell phone vibrated, displaying a call from Harry. Joe sat down on a window ledge in the hall and stared at the phone. He decided he would have to return the call, nodded again to Bower, then to Preston and Casey, and walked slowly back to the room. He took his seat and motioned for Preston and Casey to take theirs.

"Sold out of trust deserves attention," Joe said. "It is, however, only one piece of the puzzle. In my review and assessment of Wilson Holdings' overall situation, my first task was to undertake a critical analysis of Wilson's present condition. This involved four questions: One, why and how did Wilson Holdings get into financial trouble? Two, what is required to fix the difficulties? Three, how long will it take? And four, is it worth the time, money and effort?"

He glanced around the conference room. Good. He had everyone's attention. He continued. "The short answer to how Wilson Holdings got into this mess is that Mr. Wilson is a very effective and successful automobile dealer. His first store, Manhattan Mercedes, did well. So well, in fact, that he expanded to California, acquiring a dealership there and expanding it into San Francisco Autoplaza. The expansions continued to Georgia, Texas, Illinois, and here in North Carolina. The stores became bigger and bigger. When one store got in trouble financially, Wilson Holdings helped it out with money from another store. This was a classic case of robbing Peter to pay Paul. Beyond that, each store has its own story, each of which has been explained in detail in the history portion of the plan. Then came the market crash, unemployment, uncertainty and the bank contraction. You know all about it.

"In determining what is required to fix the difficulties, I first centered on how deep the hole is, individually by store and altogether. I started with all the work that Wilson's prior law firm did when they reviewed this problem and ultimately recommended bankruptcy protection. Then I reviewed the current financials, including information that I obtained from your bank.

"Operationally, I brought in a gentleman named Alex Herman. Those of you who have heard of Mr. Herman know that he is highly regarded in the automotive world, not only with the manufacturers and dealers, but he also has a deep reach into the auto financial end. His comprehensive operational analysis is included in the exhibits. He finds that the management in most of these stores was incompetent, allowing operating capital to grossly exceed the revenues generated by the various dealerships, but he believes that each of these stores has the capacity and potential to be profitable. I have a ways to go, but let me stop for a moment to see if you have any questions."

"I have a question," said Steven Cutter, the litigation counsel for White & Polk. "Let's go back to the SOT. How can Wilson Holdings be expected to pay our bank back, let alone recover and turn around if, by court order, the stores are restrained, if not shut down, with the proceeds going to the bank and your clients perhaps going to jail?"

"I agree with you," Joe replied. "It certainly is not in the interest of Mr. Wilson or his company or the bank for that to happen. Let's put the SOT elephant on the table. As you are aware, Mr. Cutter, the SOT condition is simply a case of the dealership taking in money from the sale and not, for whatever reason, paying it back to the bank in as timely a fashion as required. In a sense, the same thing is done with a float. Just as with a float, the policies in practice at the bank and the dealership need to be examined. How long, as a matter of practice, did the bank give the dealership before it had to cover its checks? One day? Two? Seven?"

Joe knew that the SOT issue was both alarming and confusing, even to bank officers. Part of the reason the bank had difficulty monitoring the floor plans was that they didn't fully understand the automobile business. Joe saw the bank's pattern of acquiescence and lack of due diligence as tantamount to implied consent.

"Mr. Hart, Elaine Trevor here. Please call me Elaine. Are you suggesting that this bank is responsible for your client's stealing our money by not paying the bank back in accord with our floor plan agreement?"

"I am here trying to facilitate a workout, Elaine; I don't have my lawyer hat on – and hope not to put it on. Neither am I a judge or a jury. What I am looking at is, what did Wilson Holdings intend? And what did the bank know and to what extent did it acquiesce in or consent to the SOT situation? Part of my job, as I see it, is to get your bank as much solid information as I can about this entire situation, including the SOT and its amounts.

"There was no intent to steal any money from the bank; no money went into Preston's pocket or any other person's at Wilson Holdings. Instead, the money was used to finance the other stores and certain real estate acquisitions." There was, Joe stressed, no criminal intent. "What they are guilty of, however, is a lack of supervision of their financial and operations people, combined with some major errors in judgment."

Silence reigned as everyone in the room absorbed what Joe had just said and the candor with which he had said it.

"Let's take a break for coffee," Tom said, and with that, Casey moved directly to the tray with all the cookies.

During the break, Joe made a point of going around the room, shaking hands, saying a few words to Tom and each of the other twelve representatives. Twenty minutes later, everyone resumed their places at the table.

Steven Cutter, the litigation attorney, opened the discussion. "Leaving aside your, 'consensual SOT theory,' I am still troubled by the existence of enormous debt and no demonstrated program for its repayment. Your client is clearly in default and has no defense on the notes. You know that. Trust me, we will successfully move for judgment this week in each of the jurisdictions on all of the notes that are due. In addition, within days we will have Temporary Restraining Orders against each dealership in which we have an interest. Inasmuch as the stores have all cross-collateralized each other, we will have no problem receiving all of the corporate assets."

At this point, Casey leaned over and whispered into Joe's ear, "Except East Bay." Joe patted him on the arm and nodded his understanding, but held his finger to his lips.

"Because of the personal guarantees by Mr. and Mrs. Wilson, we also are entitled to proceed directly against them for judgment on all of this debt. Beyond that, your construction of the SOT will not stand up. We could turn the facts over to the attorney general's office in each of the applicable states and see if they view the SOT as warranting a criminal indictment, including for bank fraud, which I believe carries a mandatory sentence of at least twenty years. I don't mean to give you a haircut, Mr. Hart, but I am wondering, what is your response to that?"

Joe rose and walked to his left, where he had placed the yellow plastic box. He brought it over and set it on the table. Joe opened the box and took out a handful of keys. "This box contains the keys to all of the stores in which Bank North America has a security interest and liens. Life is full of choices. Wilson Holdings has admitted that it owes you money. The plan before you is directed to getting you paid back. Both Wilson Holdings and Preston Wilson would like to help do that. You may not want their help. You may want to run all of these dealerships yourself. You may want to manage the real estate and determine what to do with the leases, and in the case where real estate is owned, what to do with the property. You've already had a lot to say about what was done with the property owned by Wilson Holdings in Manhattan, as I'm sure your New York representative has told or will tell you." He nodded to Sally McCormick. "I'll make it easy for you. If you don't want our help, you take the keys to these stores and you run the business."

The room was silent for nearly a minute. Finally, Bobby Bower spoke. "I, for one, don't want to be involved with running these stores. We're not car guys. Of course, I don't make these decisions. But I'm interested in whether I heard you right. What were you saying about our having something to do with the real estate in Manhattan? What is that about?"

"I can answer that, Bobby," Sally McCormick jumped in. "The Manhattan store is located at 9th Avenue and 57th Street. The store is approximately ten thousand square feet in a sixteen-thousand-square-foot, two-story building. Wilson Holdings leases the property from General Contractors and Holdings, a New York City developer. Wilson, in turn, sub-leases six-thousand square feet to our bank, which has a corner retail office. I believe that is what Mr. Hart is referring to, right, Joe?"

"That's the tip of that iceberg," Joe replied. "I readily concede that there is no problem with the bank's prosecution of its rights to collect the money it has loaned. There are issues, however, with the bank's defense."

"Defense of what?" Floyd Ritter asked, his voice rising in anger. "What does this bank have to defend?"

"Again, Mr. Ritter, I'm not here with my lawyer hat on. But since you asked, the defense I was speaking of would be the defense to counterclaims based on lender liability principles, should this matter go into litigation, which I have made clear that I hope it does not."

"And what issues of lender liability do you, Mr. Hart, in all serious-ness, contend could possibly apply to the actions of this bank that would provide a defense to the debt you have admitted on behalf of your client?" Steven Cutter appeared patronizing, sarcastic.

Joe held his eyes for a long moment and then quietly said, "The first is a conflict issue dealing with the structure of the capital loans and mortgage financing by BNA on the Charlottetown Motors property. From a lender liability point of view, I will refer to that as the 'equity kicker problem.' The second is a control issue. The nature of the involvement of the bank in Wilson's business affairs. I can discuss these things with you as the bank's counsel separately, if you like, rather than get into technicalities here," Joe replied, nodding to each lawyer in turn, and finally at Tom Gallagher.

"No, you go right ahead, Mr. Hart," Cutter said. "As long as you are making this up out of whole cloth, I am sure we would be interested in what facts you have to support these ridiculous claims."

"Okay, if that's what you want," Joe said. "Wilson Holdings had a lease on the property where Charlottetown operates. The owner offered Wilson a chance to buy it. Wilson informed BNA of what it saw as an opportunity to kill three birds with one stone. By owning the property, Charlottetown Motors would be free to expand and renovate the existing store. Doing that would satisfy pressure the store was getting from Porsche and Audi to upgrade the facility – which would in turn allow the store to get more allocation of product – which it needed to be competitive and profitable. In addition to those two features, Wilson felt the property could be bought at a reasonable price and, given its location, would only increase in value."

Joe went on to explain that the loan Wilson obtained from BNA to buy the property included profit participation by the bank, a 10 percent equity kicker, but BNA had encouraged Wilson to proceed with the loan and mortgage, despite his reservations. Wilson's commitment to Porsche and Audi to expand, together with pressure from BNA, forced him to accept the loan, which, Joe explained to an increasingly gloomy room, might well be characterized by the IRS or by a court as an equity investment rather than a loan. BNA, moreover, had increasingly involved itself in the day-to-day running of the store.

Joe looked over at Tom Gallagher and quietly said, "I wanted to discuss this with you, Tom, privately.

"So what you really have here, Mr. Cutter," he went on, "is sufficient participation by the bank in Wilson's business, including decision-making, policy, sharing of profits and equity, to be a partnership or joint venture, regardless of an attempt by the bank to make the stripes on the zebra go away. If a court finds that this is a partnership or joint venture, there are a whole host of adverse legal and tax consequences, concerning which I will leave to your legal team to advise. The bank has a conflict of interest. Actually, Mr. Cutter, as a partner with Wilson, you may want to come over to this side of the table and help us figure a way out of this mess."

"Folks," Tom Gallagher said, standing up to his full six-foot-four height, "I believe that we all could use some lunch about now. I'd like everybody back here in this room at one o'clock sharp." He then walked over to Joe and moved into the corner. "Joe, let's you and I have that private talk upstairs. The chairman of the board is going to join us in the boardroom. Okay?"

"Absolutely," Joe replied. On his way out of the room, Joe stopped for a moment and addressed Steven Cutter. "Thanks anyway," he said, "but I have a barber in Braydon named Sammy. He takes care of giving me my haircuts."

CHAPTER 23

Tom led Joe up the back stairs to the next floor and into the spacious corner office of the bank's Chairman of the Board. "Terrence J. Perkins," he said, introducing a fiftyish-looking clean-cut man of medium build with blond hair, dressed in a tan suit nearly identical to his own.

Perkins stepped forward and shook Joe's hand, looking as if he were studying his face. "I've heard a lot about you, Mr. Hart. Tom here likes you and tells me you can be trusted. I'm happy to meet you. I'm sorry it's under these circumstances."

"I'm happy to meet you as well. I don't know if Tom still likes me after this morning."

"How could I not still like you, Joe?" Tom laughed, putting his big hand on Joe's right shoulder. "You've told us you owe us eight million in one store alone, not to mention all the other money, and then you told us we've screwed things up, and finally, that we're partners. Who wouldn't like a guy like that?"

"Let's go have some lunch," Perkins said as he led the way to a small room with four tables, white linen table cloths, and expensive silver. Alone in the dining room, they sat at a small table while the waiters brought iced tea.

"I understand you're from Braydon."

"Yes, sir," Joe said.

"I'd prefer you call me Terry," Perkins said. "I'm younger than Tom here, better looking and a helluva better fisherman. I'm from Wilmington, North Carolina, Joe. Grew up there."

A waiter presented sheets of paper and pencils for the selection of lunch. The men quickly filled out the sheets and handed them back, each ordering salads with grilled chicken.

"Wilmington is a wonderful city," Joe said, remembering his trips with Ashley during the Azalea Festivals. "I've been there a number of times. George Bisby, an attorney friend of mine from Wilmington, took me to the Cape Fear Men's Club for lunch, which I loved. I played golf a couple of times at the Cape Fear Country Club, too."

"I know George. Good man. He's a big boater, keeps his boat on the waterway next to Dockside."

"I've been there, as well. Right across from Wally's."

"Pusser's now," Terry said. "You fish?"

"You bet. It's what I wish I was doing today."

Terry smiled.

The waiter brought the salads, and the men ate quietly. When they finished, Tom began, "Joe, I appreciate the fact that you told us about the SOT. We knew there was a SOT, but we didn't know how bad it was. Wilson's people didn't tell us, and neither did their fancy firm in New York City, I might add. I also appreciate all the work you've put into your plan – you've made our work a hell of a lot easier, and you've given us a lot of information we didn't have and would normally have to fight to get. I know you're getting pissed at Cutter, although you're not showing it."

"No, Tom. This is serious. I'm not upset with Cutter. He's a litigation lawyer, and he needs to demonstrate to you how clever and smart he is so that you'll feel better about making this into a federal case and paying his firm a few hundred thousand dollars or more."

Tom and Terry looked up at each other. "What do you think of Floyd Ritter?" Tom asked.

"I think he's sitting in a tough seat," Joe answered. "He's one of your vice-presidents and also your general counsel. As much as he'd like to treat this as a simple foreclosure on a few loans, he knows that it's a lot more complicated than that. He's doing what lawyers do. It's not always easy."

"What do you think of Bobby Bower?"

"Are you going through the whole list?" Joe asked with a smile.

"We'll never make your one o'clock deadline. Actually, I like Bobby, even though he's a lawyer." Tom and Terry burst out laughing at that one.

"We've checked into your background a little bit, Joe," Terry said. "You don't get to be a commander of a Navy sub without being able to read men and lead them, too. Also, Floyd has checked you out with the bar and the judges, and they all hold you in the highest regard."

"Thank you," Joe replied, looking at his watch. "Tom, it's five to one if you really want to make it back to the conference room in time."

"Let 'em wait," Terry interjected. "Okay, Tom?"

Tom nodded, and Terry continued. "What Tom really wants to ask you is what you think of Mr. Wilson and his sidekick, Mr. Fitzgerald. We know they're your clients."

"I'm glad you asked," Joe said. "It's an important question – in fact, central to the tough decision you have to make in this case. What's the story with these guys? Are they good guys or bad guys? Are they crooks, as your lawyer has suggested? Can you trust a dealer who's eight million out of trust? What should you do with them?"

"You got that right," Tom said. "Those folks aren't from around here, and we don't know them. Our loan officers know the general managers of the stores and their bookkeepers and so forth. And some of our other people have met Wilson and Fitzgerald at the bank and at closings. But neither Tom nor I know either one of them."

"Well, speaking frankly – and now you know, Tom, why all of these discussions have to be off the record – I'll tell you my view of these men, for what it's worth. I'll start with Casey. I think he's an honest guy. He's worked for years for Wilson. He's steady, good with numbers, and a good transactional accountant. But he's always looking in the rearview mirror. He has a problem seeing the big picture. He's not strategic. He's too reactive and accepting. He didn't or couldn't get underneath exactly what was going on with these dealerships, didn't ask the hard questions. Also, Preston had him spread way too thin. With six stores spread all over the country, Casey was way over his head. He didn't manage the oversight of these stores the way he should have. He should have had systems in place that would have raised red flags. He also should have had a couple of comptrollers working for him that were smarter than he is.

"As to Preston, he's a charismatic visionary. He's smart and he's got a lot more depth than is immediately evident. He's not transparent. It takes awhile to peel the onion. He wants to be recognized as a major player, a highly successful businessman. His initial success added fuel – in the form of an outsized ego – to his already huge ambition. Preston got in trouble because he tried to get there too fast. He has a focus problem. He really didn't know how bad his businesses were doing overall. He was too busy planning the next acquisition and playing big shot."

Joe stopped talking and took a long drink of water. He looked first at Terry and then Tom. "Preston probably would have gotten away with it but for the economic meltdown and all of the turmoil that has followed. Perhaps that is behind us now, or, if not, will be soon. I'm sure you guys have had a lot to think about as well – and you can't sit on money forever.

"But back to Preston, he's acted in a dishonest way, not by stealing, but by breaching the trust of others. I'm not talking about the SOT, because I think, to the extent that he had any knowledge of that, he figured the bank knew about it and it was just part of his loan structure. And to a certain extent that is the case, although any SOT is wrong. Mistakes were made – and not only by Wilson." Joe paused a beat to let that sink in.

"I think this whole mess has scared Preston to death, and he's learned a lot. He has to start telling his wife the truth, and more importantly, he has to start telling himself the truth. Preston's biggest fear is being a financial failure. I'm certain of that. That's why he's a good bet for you. Why not ride the horse? Let him work his way out of this mess and carry you out as well. You wouldn't be able to hire a better man to run this company from this point forward if you can shift paradigms and forget what's happened in the past. But that's hard to do. I believe that Preston is now committed to lead his company out of the hole and back to success. Going forward, I believe he'll keep his word."

"I tell you what," Terry said. "You just said a mouthful. Very interesting."

"Where do you see this going from here?" Tom asked.

"That depends a lot on you. As I said when we first talked on the phone, I need you to keep your lawyers in check. You saw this morning how they wanted to draw me into all the legal side of things. If you make this into a big legal case, you will be fulfilling your lawyers' every wish. Except for Bobby, who strikes me as a sensible business-man who really wants to find a way to work this out, just as I believe you do. Get the lawyers off my back, and let's not concentrate on litigation. You both know no matter how the case comes out, only the lawyers will win in litigation. Also, I would really rather leave the loan officers out of these discussions so that we can concentrate on how to solve the problem. These loan officers and anybody who works with them are part of the problem itself. They helped create it."

At this point, Joe could see the strain on Tom's face as Terry picked up his linen napkin and refolded it. Joe continued, "I haven't disclosed today all of the specific information I have about all the screw-ups by various people in your bank who handled the loans and the businesses. It isn't just Charlottetown. There was a big problem in Manhattan as well, but I didn't want to embarrass Sally.

"Rather than the drum beating, which is wasting our time and will only result in litigation and/or bankruptcy, both of which will not have a happy ending for the bank, what we need to concentrate on is how to turn Wilson around and get the money to pay you back. Besides, the government will appreciate your using some bailout money to help a worthy dealer out and get people back to work."

Tom and Terry looked at each other, as Terry refolded the napkin again.

"Joe, thanks for having lunch with us," Terry said. "Where do you keep your boat?"

"At Charleston City Marina," Joe replied. "Her name is *Mountain Stream* and she's in slip D-7."

"How the hell did you come up with that name?" Tom asked.

"Well, I love the mountains, I love the mountain streams, I love boating, and I like to take my boat to the Gulf Stream fishing, so *Mountain Stream*."

"Sounds right to me," Terry said. "In fact, it all sounds right to me. Tommy?"

"I got it," Tom said. "Joe, I'll ask Floyd, Steve, and Elaine to sit out this afternoon's part of the meeting, and I'll have Mike, Frank, Dorothy, and Sally meet upstairs and be on call if you need them. I'm going to leave Bobby in, as well as Lou, our CFO, and Jim Olsen, our COO. They're a nervous wreck about all of this, but they're good with the numbers, and they're going to need to understand and sign off on whatever we're going to do. The same thing's true of Barry and Debra, our commercial VPs. They're good people, sensible and bright. Why don't you go down and talk with your people, and I'll go down and thank everybody on our side for their efforts and explain that I think it would be better if we made the group a little smaller at this point. Do you need me to stay in, Joe?"

"Absolutely," Joe replied. "I wouldn't mind if Terry came in as well."

"Tom will tell me what's going on," Terry said. "I've got to sell all of this to the Board once you get it worked out, if you do. I'd better stay out of the meeting at this stage."

"I understand," Joe said. "But I would like to be able to give you a call if I need to and talk to you directly. Do either you or Tom have any problem with that?"

"No, we don't," they both answered.

"And you come to Wilmington and we'll see how good of a golfer you really are," Terry added.

"I only impersonate a golfer," Joe said with a smile. "I'd rather we go fishing."

"I'll tell you what. That's going to happen."

"Good. Thanks for lunch. Let's go to work."

CHAPTER 24

Joe found Preston slumped in a chair in the corner of a small conference room, with his hands on his knees. Casey, two chairs down, was reading the sports section of *The Charlotte Observer*.

"This is a disaster," Preston said, rising. "I knew this would be bad, but I didn't know they'd blow us out of the water. They're going to shut us down, and that one guy, Cutter, that son of a bitch wants to see us both in jail. He's not going to let up. It's pretty clear to me that Cutter and Ritter are really tight, and those two lawyers are obviously running the show." Preston paced in circles. "The president is going to do whatever his lawyers tell him to do. That's obvious. He hasn't said a word."

With tears in his eyes, Preston collapsed in his seat. "I'm fucked," he said. "So are you, Casey."

"I'm not fucked," Casey said. "I'm actually feeling relieved. We're finally dealing with all this, not in the state of . . . suspension we've been in. Something's going to happen. I will say that I'm disappointed in the food." Then Casey looked up at Preston and with an exaggerated scowl, said, "They brought us some tiny sandwiches and tea. Can you believe it? A big bank like this, and we get tiny sandwiches and drink tea from tiny cups."

"What the hell is the matter with you, Casey? We're going down the chute, and all you can think about is food."

"Preston, save the lectures and settle the hell down. I'm not as dumb as you think. I talk about food as a distraction. Well, I do like it. But it's like sports. You're the only guy I know I can't talk sports with. I know you're feeling cornered. So like I've done for too many

147

years, I make myself the goat to try to make it easier for you. You know what? I'm not doing that anymore. Screw the food. At least talking about it. By the way, you won't want to hear this but, I think you're only listening to their side of the table. I'm listening to Joe on our side. Like he said, they need time to absorb all this. Hell, we do, too. You're just freaking out because you're scared. I'm scared, too, but I'm glad we've got Joe sitting here with us doing the talking and the thinking. Like I said to you on the phone, you either want to go along with Hart or you don't."

Preston looked like he'd been kicked in the stomach but didn't say a word. After a while, Joe asked, "How about those Red Sox, Preston?" At that point, all three burst out laughing.

Finally, Casey turned to Joe. "I really appreciate what you are doing. So does Preston, believe me; he's just scared and hasn't gotten around to telling you yet. We're both with you 100 percent. Whatever way it comes out."

"Thanks, Casey. Actually, it's going reasonably well at this stage. If anything, we're ahead of the game. But it's not over until it's over. It's a process, as I explained earlier. We have to take it a step at a time. But we've taken a few steps. This afternoon's meeting is going to be with a much smaller group. The lawyers, except for Mr. Bower, the bank's corporate counsel, are going to take a rest, as are the loan officers. They'll be on standby. This afternoon I expect we'll concentrate on next steps and execution issues. In other words, how can we structure the workout to get the bank repaid without foreclosures and litigation?"

Preston sauntered over, wrapped his arms around Joe, and hugged him. He still had tears in his eyes. "I'm a horse's ass, Joe. And I do appreciate what you're doing. And I do have confidence in you. It's me I don't have confidence in, but I'm working on it. Casey's right. I am scared . . . really scared . . . but I'm ready to keep going."

"Preston," Joe said in a soft, even voice, "this is a turnaround and a workout. That's what we're doing here. You'll have plenty of time for soul-searching with time left over to beat yourself up. None of that is what we need now. Once we get this ship off the rocks and heading back into deep water, we have to execute on the workout plan. You're going to be central to that. You think this is all about money. It's not. As much as the money's important, the bank needs to determine whether they can believe *you*, whether it should bank on *you*. In the past, you've given them every reason not to trust you. I need you to demonstrate to these guys that you are aware of what has gone wrong and have the capacity *and* the desire *and* the will to turn it around and make it right.

"The president of the bank and the chairman asked me privately what I thought of you. I told the bank that I believe you are committed to leading this company out of this mess and back to success, and that I believe you will keep your word. You may be having a bunch of self-doubts right now, but I believe you can do this. I need *you* to believe it now."

Joe could see a subtle change in Preston's eyes. He knew he had hit his target. "Don't let 'em see you sweat. They, too, have a lot to think about. Don't underestimate Tom. He's a switched-on guy, and I think he wants to help us. At least, help us help him and the bank. And that's always a good sign. Let's go back in and keep working."

The three men walked back to the conference room and to their seats. This time only five sat across the table.

"Tom will be here in a minute," Bobby Bower said. "In the meantime, Lou Barenzo, our CFO, has some things he wants to check with Casey on a couple of the stores. Do you mind if Lou talks with Casey directly?"

"Not at all, Bobby. Come on over, Lou."

With that, Lou picked up his full briefcase and the bound book for Charlottetown. He sat to the right of Casey, placing his books on the conference table, and his briefcase on the floor to his right. Casey swiveled his chair around. "What do you have?"

In a soft voice, Lou said, "Looking at Charlottetown, I've got a list of the last floor plan check. Mr. Hart's correct, we should have checked these a lot sooner and a lot closer. Can you help me with the SOT, particularly the cars we don't have, starting with the transits?"

"Sure, that actually is in the exhibits," Casey said, reaching over the table to the light blue books in front of Joe. While Casey and Lou reviewed the exhibits and talked quietly, Preston was again looking out the window, and Joe excused himself to make a call to Alex Herman. Joe had arranged with Alex to fly to Charlotte the night before and hang out at the Sheraton next to the airport until he needed him.

"Hi, Alex. Joe. What are you doing?"

"Just sitting out on the balcony, smoking a cigarette, and watching the planes take off and land, Joe. It's real challenging. Thanks a lot for flying my ass to Charlotte."

"You're welcome," Joe said. "Are you dressed?"

"That's none of your business, Hart," Alex quipped.

"I'd like to have you join us this afternoon. We're meeting on the thirty-ninth floor of the Olympic Towers downtown. I'm sure the people at the front desk can tell you the fastest way to get here, and they may be able to arrange a car for you, or you can take a cab. The bank has a copy of your report. I just want them to see what you look like in person and to listen to your silky bullshit."

"That'll be a relief for them if they've been listening to you all morning," Alex said. "I suppose you want to time my arrival?"

"Actually, I do," Joe said, waving at Tom, who had just walked by and into the conference room. In a softer voice he said, "It's two-fifteen now. Can you walk in at, say, four?"

"You got it," Alex said. "And I'll even get dressed."

Joe went back into the conference room to his seat and addressed Tom. The air was lighter with the lawyers out of the room.

Tom leaned forward, as if he were taking in everybody in the room. He raised his right arm and then brought it slowly down, the fingers on his large right hand spread open and perpendicular to the table. "You all have got a big job to do and a small amount of time to do it in. Sometimes you've got to decide whether to fish or cut bait. This is one of those times. I'm asking you to work together to get this done. I know it's a little complicated. Let's put our heads together and see what we can do. Joe?"

"Thank you, Tom. Putting aside litigation, bankruptcy, and all that, we need to focus on just what Tom said, how to make this work. To give us the time and room to do that, we need to immediately have an agreement to withhold any legal action by all parties. The point is, from a legal point of view, everything stands still so we can concentrate on the workout."

Wilson would provide a legal paper acknowledging the debt, a Confession of Judgment, which they could hold in escrow. He went on to explain additional ways in which the bank could feel confident.

"I've made arrangements with major accounting firms in each city where Wilson's stores are to come in and do a full-scale audit. I'm not talking about a compilation or a review, but an actual audit. They're expensive, but it will provide an independent, certified statement of exactly what the story is financially in each store. That will be the starting point. Assuming the bank allows the flooring to continue, the proceeds from the sales will be independently logged and reported on a daily basis with a weekly trust reconciliation. That information will not only go to Wilson, but also directly to the bank. Any time even one vehicle is out of trust, the bank will have the option to consider it a trigger event, cancel the line, and take whatever other action it deems appropriate.

"The stores obviously need money to operate. They each have to be adequately capitalized. As part of the forbearance agreement, Wilson will agree that no monies except for ordinary business expenses will be taken out of the revenues, including no loans to officers and no salaries to Preston."

James Olsen and Barry Hazelton were each taking notes on yellow pads as fast as they could write.

"I recommend that the eight million SOT amount on Charlottetown's flooring line be transferred to a capital note to BNA. A recent appraisal of the real estate shows that it's now worth fifteen million, more than enough to cover BNA's capital loan." Joe knew the bank feared the current real estate market collapse and would be skeptical of appraisals, believing they would be self-serving. "BNA has a first mortgage on the property for 3.8 million, and a second mortgage for five million to secure the cap loan."

Joe went on to outline his plan for each of the dealerships. He could see from their expressions and body language that the bank's finance guys were paying attention to the details and the lawyers could care less. He watched Lou rise from his chair and raise his hand.

"I know how you feel about being interrupted, Joe, but I want to ask you a few questions at this point, because, as I see it, we're going ass over teacup further into the hole. I understand we want to try to work this out, but the bank's risk is getting greater, not less. This just doesn't compute."

"I think it does, Lou. But you have to see all the pieces." Joe approached the whiteboard, selected a black marker, and drew squares denoting each of the six dealerships. "In order to make this work, we have to sell certain assets. We want to make those assets as strong as we can before we sell, and we want to sell the assets that are strong enough to be sold quickly." He pointed to the board. "Houston is warming up, real estate wise, right now, and this property is in a prime location for automobile dealerships. The value is in one of the exhibits, which Casey can find for you. Those franchises, together with the hard assets and blue sky are worth fifteen million, even without the added 6.4 million equity in the sale of the real property.

"We follow the same strategy for Charlottetown. The only other store with SOT is San Francisco, and it's only $646,000. BNA should renew the cap loan for at least another eighteen months. With proper management, San Francisco can be profitable, pay off the SOT, and make the cap loan secure. The franchises are strong."

"Can we take a break, Tom?" Debra Seabrell asked.

"Good idea," Tom said, and they all got up and moved to the credenza where, in addition to coffee, tea, and soft drinks, fresh fruit and cookies had been brought in.

Lou and Paul huddled with Barry and Debra in one end of the conference room, apparently deep in discussion as they sipped coffee and nibbled cookies. At the other end, Bobby was talking to Joe with Tom.

"I know this is all in the plan in one place or another, Joe," Bobby said, "but these folks are having a lot of trouble with all the 'what ifs.' You know, what if the Texas store does not sell or brings much less than its valuation? What if the real estate doesn't sell? What about the commission on the real estate? What about the commission on the sale of the store, for that matter? All of that eats away from the bottom line."

"Good points," Tom said. "What about that, Joe? What I'm worried about, even if all of that can be worked out, is how are we – I should say I – going to be able to sell the idea to our Board that this bank should lend millions more to Wilson, when the idea was to get us paid back?"

"Well, Tom, sometimes you've got to prime the well. The pluses will take care of the 'what ifs.' If we have to, we can sell Atlanta Motors. While the valuation on that store is good, I hate to sell more stores than necessary because when this mess is all cleaned up and turned around, I'd like to have BNA continue to make money. Manhattan Mercedes is a strong store, too. A lot can be done with it, including with the real estate. In fact, Tom, I'd like to have you call Sally back."

Their conversation was interrupted when Barry came over to them, munching on a large Krispy Kreme donut. "Mr. Hart, with all due respect, you've done all the talking and we haven't heard a word from Mr. Wilson. Honestly, I don't see how BNA can lend more money – in fact, a lot more money – which is what you're asking us to do. How do we know that Mr. Wilson isn't just going to take that money and run? And what if the property doesn't sell? Or the stores don't sell? He could end up in bankruptcy anyway. Hell, the other creditors could force Wilson into bankruptcy if we didn't. It only takes three, doesn't it, Bobby?"

"Yes, three creditors could force an involuntary petition of bankruptcy."

"And Joe, how can the bank have confidence that these stores are going to suddenly turn around and become profitable, and that's how we'll get paid back? What if they don't?"

"All good questions," Joe said. "It's frustrating as hell, isn't it?"

"It sure is," Barry replied. "It's a huge problem."

"Well, let's sit down and keep working at solving it," Joe said. "It can be done. And it beats the hell out of the alternatives." He looked at his watch and smiled, noticing that it was almost four o'clock. They all took their seats around the table just as they heard a knock.

"This is Alex Herman," Joe said to everyone. "With your permission, Tom, I invited him to join us."

"Glad to meet you, Mr. Herman," Tom said, standing up and shaking his hand. "Happy to have you join us. Sit anywhere you like." Alex went around the room, then took a seat at the end of the table facing Tom.

"You have Mr. Herman's report," Joe said. "I've known Alex and worked with him on automobile turnarounds for several years. I met him when we both were asked to speak at a JD Power Super Round Table for mega-dealers in Atlanta. He's been in the business for a lot of years, and in addition to knowing what he's doing, he can be trusted."

"Thank you, Joe."

"Alex, I have represented to these folks that while you've found substantial problems with these dealerships, you believe they have the potential to be successful. Successful enough, in fact, to generate sufficient net profit to pay the bank back."

"First, let me say that I am pleased to meet you, Mr. Wilson," he said, looking directly at Preston. "You have done a commendable job in building these six stores. I am particularly impressed with the way you've managed the mixes of the product, as well as your relationships with the manufacturers. In my experience, it's very unusual to see stores in the bad financial shape that these stores are in and still have the loyalty and support of the manufacturers. Each of these could have stopped sending product any time they wanted to. To a manufacturer, however, each has allowed the pipeline to stay open, knowing that if they shut it off, the dealerships would die. They know their cars have been sold. And they obviously want to keep the franchises open. That means they still have confidence in you, Mr. Wilson, which, under the circumstances, says a lot.

"I visited each of the sites. Every one is in a good location. The dynamics are good, the streets are good, and each of the stores is positioned perfectly in between other dealerships who are selling good product, but not necessarily in competition. For example, East Bay, which is doing great, by the way, and very profitable, is selling Porsche and Audi in between a smaller Mitsubishi store and a small Volvo store. The sports car traffic is generated, but the surrounding stores are no real competition. All six of the stores are well-situated.

"From an operational point of view, Manhattan Mercedes, Atlanta Motors and East Bay are all doing pretty well. They've got good programs and the GMs and sales managers there are pretty good. Their service departments are strong, and so are their warranty departments. Each department is an independent profit center, as it should be.

"Houston, San Francisco and Charlottetown suck from an operational point of view." The room erupted in laughter, everyone appreciating Alex's candor. "I would fire the general managers, as well as the entire bookkeeping department in Charlottetown and San Francisco. I can go into the details with you later, if you want. These stores are potential gold mines, but they've been dragged down by incompetent management and lack of controls. It's not the sales department that's the problem. It's the lack of management, financially and otherwise. Bad people obscure the solidity. What these three stores need is fresh, strong talent in virtually all the management and financial positions.

"There are a lot of other ways that the control of operations can be exercised. First of all, with due respect to Mr. Fitzgerald, the CEO needs to be visiting these stores constantly to know what is really going on. A conference TV could be set up to permit the head office to be talking to these dealerships weekly, if not daily. I'd like to see a lot more open communication with the bank on a constant basis. The dealership and the bank need to work together to constantly understand what is going on. If you answer the questions on the daily snapshot form honestly, there's no room to wiggle and everybody gets a clear picture.

"I know this has been brief, and to some extent, oversimplified, but, as Joe said, you have my report. The point I would make is the basic ingredients – location and franchises of value, and the support of the manufacturers – are in place. They can clearly be turned around with good management and proper controls, because they have the capacity to be profitable, highly profitable."

"Thank you, Alex," Joe said. He could tell, looking around the room, that the bankers were impressed. The real question in Joe's mind was whether Alex had been persuasive. Joe knew that to convince a man against his will leaves an unconvinced man still, and he was well aware of the negative mindset many of these bankers would have a hard time overcoming. On the other hand, he felt that Bobby, at least, got Alex's point that the dealerships had the capacity to ultimately be profitable.

"We've covered a lot of ground today," Joe said. "I appreciate your patience."

Then he turned to his right and looked at Preston. "Preston, the one man these folks have not heard from is you. As I said to you after lunch, this company truly needs your leadership, your will, and your commitment to make this work. Talk to these people."

Preston did not know where to start. He froze, saying nothing, his head spinning. The room was silent. Finally, Preston pulled himself up and looked at everyone at the table. Then he stared out the windows, and back at the group.

"I love looking out the windows from up here," Preston began. "It's such a great view, looking down over everything. I have a stunning view from my office in New York, too. I love it. What I realize now is that I needed to be looking out from the ground floor, not the top floor. I needed to be going into my stores more and looking at everything. I needed to understand what was really going on and what I could do to help. I didn't do that. Instead, I just looked down, thinking the view was clear.

"I've been doing a lot of thinking since my high-priced lawyers in New York so eloquently informed me that my company was in terrible financial shape and that there was nothing they nor I could do about it except go bankrupt. I don't want to go bankrupt. I've made a lot of mistakes. I owe you folks and others a truckload of money. If I can correct those mistakes, if I can pay you back the money I owe you, if I can make my business successful again, then they will only be mistakes. Mistakes that have been corrected. If I can correct these mistakes, I will not have failed. I don't want to fail. Please give me a chance to correct these mistakes. You won't be sorry you did."

The room was silent. "This has been quite a day," Tom Gallagher said, breaking the silence. "I suggest we all go home and think about this. Bobby, I would appreciate your convening a meeting tomorrow afternoon with Lou, Paul, Barry, Debra, Floyd, and myself. Oh, and ask Sally to join us."

Pointing at the whiteboard and holding up one of the books of the plan, Tom said, looking at Lou, "I ask that you and Paul take all the information and work on that tonight and tomorrow morning." He then looked at Joe. "If any of my folks need to call you, Alex, or Casey in the morning for clarification on any of these points, may they do so?"

"Absolutely," Joe replied. "We're all spending the night at the Sheraton. We can come back here in the morning, if you like."

Joe, Preston, Casey, and Alex gathered the books and moved them to Conference Room C, stacking them at one end. Joe asked Casey to take the yellow box, to return the keys to the dealerships. After they rode the elevators down to the outside of the building. Casey said, "I'm starved. How about a big steak at Morton's?"

They smiled and headed for Morton's on foot.

CHAPTER 25

By the end of dinner, the crowd at Morton's had thinned out and the room had become quieter. Preston and Casey were having after-dinner drinks and engaged in a serious discussion of their business. Joe was pleased to hear them talking about that rather than rehashing the day.

With Preston and Casey totally engrossed, Joe was working on Alex. "You did a good job today."

Alex raised his glass of Merlot and nodded.

"You know what Wilson needs," Joe said.

"Here it comes," Alex replied. "I like Atomic Motors. They've been good to me. It's been a good run. And I've accomplished a lot there."

"It's your call," Joe said. "I haven't even mentioned this to Preston or Casey. It's just that in the event that you may feel that you have largely finished your work at Atomic, you may want to consider a new challenge. Wilson needs an overall operations manager with experience, understanding and horsepower. You know that."

"You asked me to analyze the stores from an operational point of view. I did that. I'm sure you got your time at bat today, and your plan, as usual, was dynamite, but we don't know what the bank is going to do, do we? There may not be any business to be operations manager of."

"Between us, I believe the bank is going to think hard about all the information they've been asked to digest. Wilson has some problems, but so do they. They've got a lot of explaining to do with their regulators. They need help, too. They don't want to lend more money, but their other choices are not viable. Bankruptcy would be a mess. Lawyers would have a field day. Foreclosure only leaves the bank with more problems, and in the end, the bank won't get what it wants and needs most – to be repaid. Our plan is their best hope for that."

"I agree with all that, Joe, and these are good guys, although a little screwed up. But what has it got to do with me?"

"Alex, you've been a hell of a field major for a lot of years. Have you ever thought of being a colonel? Or even a general? This is an opportunity – assuming Preston agrees, which he will – for you to be group vice president in charge of all operations. If you listen to your own report, you believe these dealerships have the capacity to be highly profitable. Isn't it time for you to be providing hands-on leadership, with a piece of the holding company in the bargain?"

"How big a piece?" Alex asked, pouring himself some more wine.

"Fifteen percent?" Joe replied. "No buy-in."

"Hmm, that's interesting," Alex said. "But again, we don't know that the bank will allow these businesses to continue."

"The bank is going to meet all day tomorrow and thrash this around internally and with their lawyers. We know what the lawyers are going to argue, but I believe, while the bank will scale down the loans I've asked for, they will, in the end, buy the program if they know there will be a major management change. They need to know that there will be experience at the wheel, somebody who will communicate with them, work with them. That's you."

"Well, now that you've got my future planned, how much will I be paid?"

"Ask Alex Herman," Joe replied. "He makes those kinds of management decisions. He knows what's best for the company, and he understands bonus structures. Alex, have a chat with Preston; I want to talk with Casey for a minute."

Alex got up, moved around the large round table, and went over to Casey. "I don't mean to interrupt you guys, but the Captain would like to have a few words with you, Casey. Can we switch seats?"

"Sure." Casey sat down with Joe, carrying a large plate of German chocolate cake with ice cream on the side.

"Hi, Joe," Casey said. "You did a masterful job today. Unbelievable. I learned a lot, too."

"Thanks. It's a process, and we're moving along. I need to talk with you about part of that process."

"Go ahead."

"Casey, assuming that the bank lets the business run, what do you think is the most important thing needed to make it work?"

"More dinners like this," Casey said, as he attacked his dessert.

"Right. We can talk about this in the morning."

"Let's get it over with tonight. You want me fired, right, Joe? I'll do whatever you ask."

"No, I don't want you fired. I just want you to answer my question. What do these stores need most right now under these circumstances?"

"To begin with, we obviously need sufficient capital. In terms of management, each store needs a strong general manager – a hands-on type the bank will respect. And each department needs to be an independent profit center. Overall we need better controls. All of which I should have addressed."

"If the bank gives you the chance, do you feel you're in a position to provide that now?" Joe asked.

"Probably not, although honestly, I do think I have a lot to add. Also, I never heard Preston talk like he did today in my whole life."

"What do you think is in the best interest of the company?"

"I think we need a guy like Alex to take charge and run the place. That's what I think."

"How would you feel about working with him? Retaining your position as CFO and having Alex be a VP/COO in charge of overall operations."

"I'd love it, Joe. I'd love it. We could really get things organized and, as Preston said, we could learn from our mistakes. Preston's been talking to me all night about that. I'm telling you, he's really into it. The real question is, will we get the chance?"

"One more thing, Casey," Joe said. "I think it's time you had a piece of this company. You've worked long and hard and you've been totally loyal to Preston and the business. How would you feel about 15 percent, no buy-in?"

Casey looked up at Joe, dead serious for a change. "It would really mean a lot to me. It would mean a lot to be able to say that I'm an owner. It would also mean a lot to my wife. I guess it would be an answer to a prayer if all this could work out. I hope we're not dreaming."

The waiter brought the check, which Preston picked up. Joe stood, raised his wine glass, and said, "Gentlemen, we've had a good dinner and a good night. Let's go back to the Sheraton and get some sleep. We've still got work to do tomorrow."

"Aye, aye, Cap," Alex said, as they clinked their glasses.

On the way to the parking lot, Preston made a point of walking with Joe. "I hope I didn't mess things up in there this afternoon," he muttered.

"Quite the contrary," Joe replied. "You spoke from your heart. Nothing like the truth. As my Aunt Lettie used to say, it will set you free. I'm proud of you, Preston."

"You don't know how much that means to me, and how grateful I am to you. I don't know how this is going to come out, but I'll never forget all you've done for me."

"Thanks. I don't know how it will come out, either, but I believe the bank is going to struggle with loaning more money and letting the businesses go forward – compounding their risk – unless it has an anchor of stability in terms of management."

"A guy like Alex, for example?"

"Exactly. And when you talk to him, which I hope you will do tonight, I suggest you ask him what role he would like to play. You'd be damn lucky to get him, and it would be a big risk for him. I'd let him set his own salary, make him VP, general manager of operations, and COO, and give him 15 percent equity in Wilson Holdings with the other 15 percent going to Casey."

"Fifteen percent to Alex and 15 to Casey? That's 30 percent! I've never given any ownership up."

"Look at the donut, not the hole. Seventy percent of something is a lot better than 100 percent of nothing. Anything over 66⅔ percent gives you two-thirds majority and all kinds of corporate control. On the other hand, Casey and Alex will work their hearts out and feel that they're really a part – as owners – of turning this company around and growing it. It will be the best investment you've ever made. Besides, not having a guy like Alex running these companies is going to be a deal-breaker with the bank."

"You're right, you're absolutely right. I'll talk with Casey and then with Alex first thing in the morning."

"Good," Joe said. "But do it the other way around. Let Alex know how much you want him and how much you need him and that he will have a direct line to you, as will Casey. Casey will understand that. You're lucky to have such a loyal friend."

CHAPTER 26

While Preston, Alex, Casey, and Joe were having breakfast at the Sheraton coffee shop, Lou Barenzo, the bank's CFO, was already meeting in his office with Paul Olsen. Lou, focused on the numbers, Paul, on operations, were locked in argument.

"We've got a meeting this afternoon, and you and I have got to be together before we go in there."

"You don't get it, Lou. The reason you have the SOT is because of operational issues. If the bank lets these dealerships go forward without turning the faucet off now, we'll have more SOT because there's no controls in place. If we put our own people in place in the stores, then we'll know precisely what we've got."

"Hart wants us to transfer the SOT in Charlottetown to the capital loan and then increase it by five hundred thousand, secured by consolidated first and second mortgages. If you believe the MAI appraised value, we've got a ratio of 90 percent on the mortgages. Are you willing to loan the money and accept that risk?"

Paul looked at his notes. "I understood Hart to say that Houston is sitting on a lease with an option to purchase at a fixed price that can be sold for more. So the sandwich is 6.4 million in gross proceeds, just from the equity in the real estate." Paul walked to the board and spelled out what the store could be sold for, the payoff of the cap loan, and ultimately how the bank is paid back. After several hours, they managed to find common ground, agreeing that the bank would be in an improved position.

"Don't forget," Lou said, "If Houston's sold, it sure as hell doesn't need four hundred thousand dollars working capital. We should have that money applied toward our debt. And we're entitled to 10 percent of the equity of that store when it's sold." So much for common ground.

"I want to forget that, Lou," Paul said. "I'm going to clearly recommend this afternoon that BNA waive any interest it has in the equity kickers. I don't know who drafted those documents, but it's a hornets' nest. This is a good opportunity to get out of it clean."

"We don't have to give up the four hundred thousand!"

"The store needs working capital until it's sold. Let's leave fifty thousand in for working capital and take 350 thousand and apply it to debt."

And so it went for the rest of the morning.

The afternoon meeting was convened by Bobby Bower at two-fifteen in the large conference room. The first item Bobby brought up concerned Manhattan Mercedes. "I'd like some straight answers on what really happened with the sub-lease, Sally."

Sally explained the pressure she was under from the real estate department to make Wilson extend the sub-lease, and that, while it made her uncomfortable, she got Wilson to go along.

"Well, there's nothing wrong with that!" Floyd Ritter said.

"There's a lot wrong with that," Tom jumped in, his face red. "But it happened. Let's hope we don't have to defend ourselves over that someday. Let's turn to Hart's plan. Lou, where are you and Paul?"

"We're essentially in agreement. We can't approve the plan in its present form. We don't agree with the proposed numbers. We feel it would be an error in judgment to allow these businesses to continue with incompetent management, confirmed by Wilson's own expert, Alex Herman," Barenzo said, turning to Paul.

"If we did do the plan," Paul interjected, "and Wilson sold Houston, I for one do not think we should take 10 percent of either the real estate or the store."

"That's totally naïve," Floyd Ritter said, having had a part in drawing up those documents. "In any event, I think it can be fairly said at this point," he said, standing up, "that the bank does not have an affirmative vote from either of you gentlemen, you cannot buy into this plan. Tom, I move we reject the plan, and give White & Polk the green light to proceed with foreclosure and TROs immediately."

"Sit down, Floyd," Tom said. "I appreciate your input, as always. Let's go a little slower. What do you think, Bobby?"

"I'd like to ask Lou and Paul a couple of questions. It seems to me that your objection is to the incompetent management going forward and that you don't trust these folks. Correct?" Lou and Paul both nodded. Bobby continued, "Let's suppose, for argument's sake, that there was a strong management in place, and that the management could be trusted. Would you then accept Hart's plan to get us paid back? I don't want to be in real estate or the car business."

After two more hours of debate, Tom returned to his office, had a long talk with Terry Perkins, and placed a call to Joe.

"How you doing, Joe?"

"I'm fine, Tom. How is Wilson doing?"

"Joe, here's where we are. We like your program and appreciate all the work you have put into it. We can't approve your program, however, loaning more money with the knowledge that Wilson lacks competent management that can be trusted to run the businesses going forward. We believe to do so would be irresponsible. That's our biggest problem. You know I wanted this to work, and so does Paul, but it is not within our control to get over this hurdle. I'm sorry."

"I understand," Joe said. "You're a good man, Tom. Let me ask you this. What kind of management would make the difference to you?"

"Well, as one of the guys said today, and don't quote me on this, your own expert was pretty clear in demonstrating how incompetent the people in Wilson's stores are. In fact, he even said he would fire a couple of the GMs. Wilson needs a man like that. Somebody Preston Wilson can trust and we can, too. Wilson needs a real powerhouse right now, with the experience and the ability to make all the things happen that are called for in your plan. Hell, you know it, Joe. It all comes down to execution."

"I agree," Joe said. "Suppose we could find a man like Alex, with all his horsepower and experience. Does the bank really want to throw away this opportunity to get back on track and avoid all the expense and pitfalls of going forward through the minefield if Wilson had a man like Alex to get the job done?"

"No, we don't," Tom replied. "If you could produce a man like Alex immediately, I can bring the others around and we'll go forward with the deal. There would be a few changes in the numbers, and your operating capital amounts would not be as high, but essentially, your plan would work. Where are you going with this, Joe?"

"It's not where I'm going, Tom. It's where Wilson and the bank are going. And it's a good place. Preston has already cut a deal with Alex Herman, who's willing to leave Atomic Motors and join Wilson as vice-president, general manager of operations and COO, reporting directly to Preston. He's also going to have 15 percent of Wilson's stock, and Casey will have 15 percent as well. Preston is totally committed to turning this business around. He meant every word of what he said to you yesterday. Admittedly, there's a lot of work to be done, issues to be resolved. But you now have before you not only a plan, which you like and believe can work, but also the strong management to make it work, and the ability to trust that management."

"Damn, don't you just keep stirring the pot. I'll give you a call in the morning."

"Thanks, Tom. Call me in Braydon, please; my work here is finished, and I'm going home."

"Come in," Preston said to Joe as he opened his door. "Sorry," he added. "I was on my computer catching up on my e-mail. How are things going? Have you heard anything?"

"I spoke with Tom," Joe replied. "Have you spoken to Alex?"

"I talked with him in the car last night on the way back here. He spoke with me at breakfast and again about an hour ago. He's with us, Joe, if we have a chance." Preston smiled broadly. "I've spoken with Casey as well. He was delighted. I never realized how much ownership meant to him all these years. He's still worried, though."

"Good," Joe said. "I am very glad to hear that about Alex, especially since I've already told Tom. I'm happy about Casey, too. He's a good guy."

"He sure is," Preston replied. "I think I've taken him for granted. Another one of my mistakes. What do you think will happen with the bank?"

"It's in their hands now," Joe said. "We've done what we can do. Tom will let me know. I'm done, Preston, and it's time to go home. I've already checked out. I'll try to catch Alex and Casey. If not, tell them I said goodbye and that I'll be in touch. By the way, how are things going with Marcia?"

"Not well. Not well at all. Remember when you asked me to sign all those authorizations and consents?"

"Of course."

"Well, I showed her your letter. We had a big fight. She was shocked. She had no idea we were in such bad shape. She got scared, especially when I told her the part about getting her own lawyer if she wanted to. She took that the wrong way. I showed her the criminal lawyer's letter and she went over the top. I told her we were going to Charlotte to talk to the bank, and that there was a chance that things could work out. She asked me why she should believe anything I said. I pray that she doesn't leave me. I guess that's my other big workout."

"Good luck with that," Joe said. "I assume you're going home now."

"Yup. Thanks again for everything, Joe," Preston said, opening his arms to give him a big hug. "Send me your bill."

"You're welcome. I'll talk with you later."

After dropping Casey off at his apartment in Murray Hill, the taxi driver delivered Preston to his Trump Towers condo. Preston waved absently at the doorman and hurried to the elevator. Eager to see Marcia, he was sure she would want to know what was going on. He wished he had shared more with her about his situation, but he'd soon take care of that.

He was happy to be home, back to his familiar surroundings. He put his bag down in the foyer and went into the den looking for Marcia, surprised that she was not at the door. He had called from LaGuardia and left word on her voicemail, telling her that he'd landed. In the past, he would have just come home. Not finding Marcia immediately, he roamed around the eighteen-room apartment, calling for her. Silence.

Finally, he went into the kitchen and checked the refrigerator to see if she had left him a note on the little magnetic pad she kept there. The pad was wiped clean, devoid of even the customary shopping list. He walked into the den, picked up the remote and turned on his 72-inch flat screen plasma TV, settling into his Italian leather easy chair with his feet on the ottoman. He surfed a while, but nothing held his interest while he waited for Marcia to return.

She's probably yakking with one of the neighbors, he thought. *Or picking some things up at the 93rd Street Deli.* He decided to take a shower, freshen up, and change into comfortable clothes. When he finished, and Marcia still had not returned, he grabbed his bag, threw it into the closet, and slammed the door.

Preston wandered around the apartment and, as he went by the front hallway again, he saw a small white envelope sitting on the antique credenza under the mirror next to the empty basket where Marcia usually put the mail. He picked it up, noticing that it was Marcia's personal stationery and that the envelope bore his name. He opened the envelope and took out and read the one page it contained.

Preston, I hope you had a good trip, and I hope it was successful. I have given a lot of thought to you, to me, and to us. It should be no surprise to you that I have been unhappy for some time. I've tried very hard to be the wife you have wanted me to be. In the process, I have lost something, and I fear what I have

lost is me. I need time to think about all of
this. I'm going to visit my mother, and I may
spend some time with Ann, my roommate
from Smith (you know, the one you never
liked). I also want to talk with my lawyer
some more. There is plenty of food in the
refrigerator, all the things you like. I'm not
taking my cell phone. Please don't call me.

Marcia

CHAPTER 27

Corey

Joe walked into his office feeling refreshed and chipper, having slept the whole night, for a change. As usual, Alice was there earlier than she needed to be.

"Hi, Alice. How are you doing? Thanks for looking after Buck at the house."

"I'm doing well," Alice said. "It's never a problem looking after my hero. He's such a sweetheart. How did things go?"

"As I expected. It's up to them now. I like Tom Gallagher, the bank's president. I enjoyed meeting Terry Perkins, the chairman. He's from Wilmington. Good guy."

"So you like Tom and Terry. A little male bonding? That means they aren't full of themselves and love to either hunt or fish."

"You're right. It was fishing, and a little golf. But you're wrong about the male bonding. Why do women always bring that up? This was business, remember, Alice?"

"Yeah, all business. When are you going to Wilmington to play golf?"

"I'm not, but I might go there to fish."

"I knew it. How did Preston and Casey do? And how did the bank like your plan?"

"Preston did fine. Casey ate well. The bank liked the plan, to the extent that they read it. Some of them are probably still reading it. Their lawyers didn't like it, I'm sure. I brought Alex in. He did a good job."

"I bet you got 'em," Alice said.

"We'll see. In any event, I'm done with this deal. Our work is finished."

173

"Good. Then we can bill these guys, right? You didn't get any retainer, and we do have a lot of time and expense in this."

"You can prepare a bill. What I'd like you to do is to prepare a detailed bill showing what you did and all of your time. I'd like you to bill your time at $100 an hour. Also, you should have a bill from Alex, but he's got added time and expense from coming to Charlotte. Also include the time for the summer interns, and all the out-of-pocket expenses. Then send a bill to Wilson Holdings, attention Casey Fitzgerald."

"Got it. But you haven't billed my time before, let alone at $100 an hour. And I didn't hear you say anything about your time."

"In this case I don't want to bill for my time. It was time for me to come back to Braydon, and this case got me to do it. I almost enjoyed it. I want your time billed, and I want the money from your time to go directly to you, with no argument from you."

"You can't do that, Joe."

"I just did. Stop arguing, Alice; I don't want to have to fire you for insubordination. You've always worked hard; you've always given me your best. And apart from your over-inquisitive personality, I find you to be a fantastic secretary, office manager, and everything else around here, not to mention a shrink to my clients. I just want you to know how much I appreciate you, and that I'm grateful for all you've done for me, and for hanging around all the time I was up in the mountains."

"Thank you," Alice said. "That's very thoughtful and much appreciated. Oh, by the way, your friend Mr. Corrigan stopped by while you were gone. He's such a dignified old man. He said something about teak in your boat. I tried to take a good message, but he just laughed and kidded around with me and I never did understand what he wanted."

"I'll go see him," Joe said, with a big grin on his face.

Joe couldn't help but smile every time he thought about Corey Corrigan. His full name was Cornelius C. Corrigan, but everybody called him Corey. Corey had been seventy-two years old when Joe met him five years before. Six-feet-tall, white curly hair shining against his black skin, and thin as a rail. Ashley and Joe had wanted to have the den in their home on South Live Oak Parkway remodeled, with three walls of bookshelves and the fourth set up for the elaborate sound system Joe envisioned. But Joe sought a finish carpenter, one who really understood and appreciated wood. He'd heard about Corrigan Yachts, a boat building company along the waterway north of Charleston, so he and Buck went there one day to look it over. That's when he met Corey, the son of the late Cornelius Calvin Corrigan, Sr., who had inherited the small yachting company from his father.

Joe was immediately aware of the man's quiet confidence and humor. And Alice was right, he had a true sense of dignity. Corey's dark brown eyes actually sparkled, not only when he talked, but all the time. He had a kind way about him, a gentleness, not only in the way he moved, but in the way he spoke. He was the kind of man you would pick, if you could, to be your grandfather.

Corey had turned the large shed where the boats had been handmade one at a time into a woodworking shop. Joe loved the shed – the look of it, the smell, the raw wood stacked on the right side floor to ceiling, all the clamps, miters, chisels, and other tools neatly hung on the wall over a woodworking bench with vices at each end, and the saws in the middle of the shed, with large exhaust tubes hooked up to take away the sawdust.

Corey gave Joe the grand tour of an adjoining building where more wood was stored to age, having had its bark cut or stripped, and another where a small tractor, a forklift, and other heavy machinery were stored. Corey showed Joe the block and tackles and the power chain lifts, allowing heavy objects being worked on – and formerly the yachts – to be lifted while stanchions or other metal and wood braces could support them.

Corey took Joe into the old house where he lived alone, explaining that his wife had died and his daughter would come by from time to time and straighten the place up. The house was a two-story wood frame with a large, hand-laid, fieldstone fireplace on the south end of the living room. On the mantle hung an old picture of a striking black man with hair standing straight up. Corey pointed to the picture and proudly said, "That there is Frederick Douglass, born in a slave cabin in 1818. He became a very famous man."

The front had a walk-around porch directly facing the waterway, with a long, sloping front lawn, filled with old oak and maple trees. At the end of the lawn there was a small wooden dock with a twelve-foot john boat and an old outboard motor tied up.

After the tour, Corey invited Joe to sit out on the front porch in one of the two rocking chairs to smoke what he called a "ceegar" and gaze at the water. Joe accepted the invitation with delight. He and Corey, with Buck at their side, settled on the porch, Corey talking about everything and nothing at the same time, with it all coming back to boats. It dawned on Joe that Corey had never asked him what he wanted. Joe loved the man.

Joe finally told Corey about how he and Ashley wanted to refinish their den. He explained that he wanted the right kind of wood, with the right look and the right grain and that he wanted the bookshelves to be built in without any holes and fasteners to hold the shelves. Corey, rocking gently, with Buck's head on his knee, had said, "You don't want them removable shelves, you want what they call today 'built-in' shelves, and you want them all fitted, not just glued or nailed. And you want 'em curved in the right places. And then you want the kind of wood that just gets better with time, you know, looks real good years later with all that light coming in the window. I would use bird's eye maple."

Joe hired Corey that day, no contract, no plans, no discussion of money, and asked him to come to the house, look it over, and just do it the way he thought he should. When Corey showed up several months later, he spent the whole time drinking iced tea, talking with Ashley in the backyard, except for one quick look in the den. Ashley, too, fell in love with the old gentleman. Half-a-year later, Corey did the work. Joe still admired the bookshelves, the cabinet holding the television, and the bird's eye maple with its tiny knots, growing lovelier every day. When it was finished, Corey had simply asked Joe whether he liked it. When Joe said that he loved it, Corey said okay and told him the price. It was far less than Joe was prepared to pay, but he felt if he argued with Corey to take more, it might offend the man. He gave him the money in cash.

Since then, Corey had, in his own time, refinished the inside of Joe's forty-three-foot Riviera Sportfish boat in cherry wood. Joe was delighted with that and next wanted Corey to finish the cockpit with an overlay teak floor and fit teak on the step to the salon and the two side steps. Corey hadn't gotten to that. Joe was glad to hear that Corey had stopped by, and was eager to see him.

He left the office and picked up Buck at his house. Buck leaped in the back of Joe's truck, but Joe asked him to hop up in the cab. Buck bounded through the sliding windows and sat erect in the front seat with his head out the window as they headed for Corey's house.

When they arrived, they heard Corey in the woodshed working on the lathe, turning what looked like wood into a furniture leg. Buck jumped up with his front two legs on the bench and licked Corey's face, his tail wagging back and forth rapidly.

"How you fellas doing?" Corey asked with a smile. "Come on, Buck, let's go to the house. I got some fish I want you to sample." With that, Buck jumped down and headed for the house. Corey strolled to the refrigerator and got out some fresh perch that he had fried. They ambled out on the porch, and Corey set the fish gently down on the front step, together with a bowl of water. While Buck ate it all in what seemed like one gulp and loudly lapped up the water, Joe and Corey took their seats in the rocking chairs.

"I hear you came out to see me," Joe said.

"Nope," Corey said. "Just working out here, young fella."

"Well, you stopped by to see Alice, didn't you?" Joe said. "I thought maybe you wanted to tell me that you were ready to finish the teak in the cockpit of *Mountain Stream*."

"What's *Mountain Stream*?" Corey said.

"It's the name of my boat, remember?"

"I know you got a boat, young fella. Boats are good. Especially the wooden ones. They don't make 'em in wood anymore. What kind of boat have you got?"

"It's a Sportfish. A 43, made in Australia by a company named Riviera. They don't make the 43 anymore, but it was one of the best boats they ever made. It's five years old now, but I can't see buying a new one. Mine runs perfect, and I love the woodwork you did in the salon when we changed the windows and fit in the TV. What a fine job you did with that wood, with the fit and finish."

Corey looked puzzled. "I did that job? What kind of wood did we use?"

"Cherry. Exquisite cherry, which you had right here in your wood-shed. I wanted to use teak, but you talked me into cherry, and I'm glad you did. But you and I talked about putting teak in the cockpit, you know, the floor and the stair to the salon and the steps on port and starboard."

"We can do that," Corey said. "I'll have to take a look at your boat, figure it all out. We can do it. How about some iced tea?"

"Sure, Corey. I'd love some."

Corey simply sat there, until Joe heard a knock at the back door, and a middle-aged, heavyset woman with brown hair and a kind face walked in through the house and out to the porch.

"Hello, Dad." She ambled over to give Corey a kiss on the fore-head. "My name is Barbara Johnson," she introduced herself. "I'm Corey's daughter. I just came over to check on him and make sure he didn't leave a pot on the stove with the gas going and burn the house down," she said, resting her hand gently on Corey's shoulder. She had Corey's dark brown eyes, without the twinkle.

"Nice to meet you, Ms. Johnson. My name is Joe Hart," he said, getting up to shake her hand. "Corey has done some woodwork for us, my wife and me, in the past. I think the world of your father."

"Everybody does," she said. "Please call me Barbara. If y'all will excuse me, I'm going upstairs to do some cleaning, especially in Dad's bathroom and bedroom, and then the kitchen. Can I get you anything to drink, Mr. Hart?"

"Joe, please. Some iced tea would be great. Thank you."

In a short time, Barbara returned with two iced teas, handing one to Joe and the other to Corey. Then she went upstairs.

"Your daughter seems like a very nice lady, Corey."

"She fusses over me. She wants me to be neater. She picked out these pants I'm wearing. Thought my dungarees weren't right anymore. And she makes sure I wear a belt, which I need to do to keep 'em up. She cooks a lot for me, too. Very nice girl, Barbara. Always has been. Married to an engineer. I can't think of his name right now. Nice fella. No kids yet."

"Corey, I have to get back. If you feel like it, give me a call and let me know whether you want to put the teak in my cockpit. Okay?"

"I don't use the phone much," Corey said. "But I'll come and find you one day. Where do you live?"

"We live in Braydon, on South Live Oak Parkway. You refinished the den in our home. Did an excellent job, with bird's eye maple, remember?"

"Bird's eye maple is good wood. It ages good, too."

"It's nice to see you again, Corey. I'll come out and visit you again soon."

"You do that, young fella. And bring your dog. I would like that. We can sit out on the porch and talk. And you're the fella that likes going in my shop and seeing all the wood, right?"

"Yes, sir, Corey. I'm that fella. Joe Hart. I love going to your shop, and I love talking to you about your wood. You're a real woodworker, Corey. It's a lost art. I'll come see you soon." With that, Joe shook Corey's hand and headed through the house, Buck at his side.

When Joe got to his truck, Buck hopped in the back. Joe sat there, thinking of the man Corey once was, the man he was now, and it saddened him, like losing a friend.

Joe started the engine and was about to leave when he saw Barbara running up. "Is everything all right?" he asked.

Barbara had walked around to the driver's side and was looking at Joe through the open window. "Everything's fine, but I wanted to talk with you privately about Dad. I try to keep my eye on him, and I do his bookkeeping, what's left of it, and his checks, look after the house, and make sure he's got plenty of food. I remember your name from the files, and I know that Dad did some work for you and Mrs. Hart a few years back. He also did some work for you on your boat."

"Yes, ma'am. Corey did a masterful job refinishing the salon in my boat. You should see the fit and finish of the cherry he put in that boat."

"I know. He does good work, just like my grandfather did. I guess it's in the genes. He's starting to slip, Joe. I just wanted to mention that to you. I overheard you say you wanted him to do some more work on your boat. I don't know if that's going to happen, and I didn't want you to be thinking it would and then not have it happen. He's forgetting a lot, and he's only seventy-seven. You may not see it when you talk to him, and he looks great, but, ... " Barbara started to cry. "His doctor says he's got Alzheimer's. It breaks my heart."

"I understand," Joe said. "I could tell, talking with Corey on the porch. But he still needs friends, Barbara. He still needs people to talk to. And he still needs to work with wood as long as he can."

"I know, I know. He's a proud man. And with good reason." Barbara wiped her eyes. "I apologize for carrying on like this. Thanks for coming out here. I hope you'll come again. You're right, Dad loves talking to you. He's talked to me about you before. Says you're one of the few young fellas who understands wood and boats, and people, too. And he likes your dog," she added, reaching in the back and petting Buck.

"I'll be out again, that's for sure," Joe said. "I don't mean to pry, Barbara, or to be intrusive, but I'd like to ask you, does Corey have other family who can help you take care of him? You're doing a wonderful job, but it's a big job, isn't it? I know it takes a lot out of you to look after your dad. Is there anybody who can give you a break now and then, help a little with it all, particularly as the situation gets worse, if it does? I hope it doesn't, but chances are it will."

"It's really just me. My husband's an engineer with GE and he travels a lot and is too busy to look after Dad. I'm his only daughter. But I understand what you're saying. Thank you. I know the time will come when we'll have to put Dad in a place that can help him better, but, to tell you the truth, he's getting along all right now living here. He would hate it, leaving here. He's lived here all his life."

"Keep up the good work. I'll be back." Then he drove off, wondering what he could do to help his old friend. He waved at Barbara, who stood alone watching him drive away.

CHAPTER 28

Joe woke up to a gorgeous day. Early as it was, the sun was already shining, and the sky was blue, without a single cloud.

"Come on, Buck," Joe said. "This is not a work day. This is a fishing day!" Buck, sensing Joe's mood, reacted with excitement, running around Joe in circles, inviting him to play. Joe got down on the floor to wrestle with Buck and then found the dog's favorite large rubber bone, tossing it to his exuberant buddy over and over.

Joe loaded some bait in the back of his truck, along with a bag of clothing, lunch, and dog food and drove to Charleston City Marina. As he walked up D dock, he was glad to see a stream of water coming through the hull from the water-cooled pump, telling him that his air-conditioning system was functioning. He climbed into the cockpit, Buck jumping in behind him.

Joe climbed up to the bridge, cleared and placed the aft lines, hopped back in the cockpit, nudged his boat forward slightly, hopped back down and cleared and placed the bow lines on the pilings. He then climbed back up to the bridge and called Alice on his cell phone, told her he was going fishing offshore and would be back before five. Joe had previously always left word with Ashley when he was going offshore; now he did the same with Alice. Old habits die hard, and Joe believed in a float plan.

He moved his boat slowly out of the slip, down the rows of other boats, around the seawall, and out of the marina, waving at other fishing boats heading out to sea. He went under the bridge and passed the Coast Guard vessels on his left, following the markers out of Charleston's expansive harbor as he had done many times before.

He listened to the purr of his quiet electronic diesel engines, enjoying how clean and smooth they were with exhaust expelled underwater.

Eventually Joe turned a few degrees to port, leaving Fort Sumter on his right, and headed out the long inlet. He set his plotter for a point to the east twenty-six miles offshore – where the depth would be over 280 feet at the beginning of a ledge on the western side of the Gulf Stream. The waves were not even seven feet, and the southeast wind was gentle and refreshing. He switched on his stereo, turning the volume way up, slipped in a Johnny Cash CD, and listened to "Ring of Fire" blare through the marine speakers on the bridge. He shouted, "Hi, I'm Johnny Cash!" as loudly as he could, exhilarated at being at sea again, away from bankers, lawyers and problems.

He thought of his friend Harry Klaskowski, and how, in addition to hunting, he enjoyed fishing and being on the water. He thought about calling him, but he just wasn't up to hearing Harry's depressed voice that morning. Then his thoughts turned to Ashley; he tried to push them back and out of his mind, telling himself, *this is too pleasant out here to think about that. It's time to fish.*

Out of sight of land, Joe knew from his plotter that he was getting close to the waypoint. As he slowed his vessel down, he saw three dolphins playfully following him on his port side. He hoped they liked Johnny Cash as much as he did. He brought the vessel to a stop, and set the plotter to the sea buoy at the channel entrance to Charleston Harbor. He activated the autopilot so that his boat would move slowly along his homeward course as he fished.

He climbed down into the cockpit and readied two fishing poles with Penn reels, placed bait on each, and let the lines slowly out. When they were where he wanted them, he set the reels and placed the rods in the holders on port and starboard. Then he sat in one of his two chairs in the cockpit, petting Buck and watching the lines. After half an hour, he noticed action on one of his lines, jumped up and grabbed the rod to starboard and hooked what he hoped was a king mackerel. As he reeled it in, he was not disappointed. Minutes later, he saw action on the port side, again grabbing the rod and reeled it in, this time catching an even bigger king mackerel. He shouted for joy as he put his second catch in the fish box.

He went in the cockpit and got a bottle of water for Buck and a can of Miller Lite for himself. He fed Buck the water from the bottle, took a sip of his beer, and, noticing that the Johnny Cash CD was starting all over again, he climbed onto the bridge, reached up to the CD player, and took out the disc.

As he reached down to the drawer to take out another disc, he saw a flash before his eyes, his vision going black, then white. Something was wrong. He felt a slight flutter over his right eye that seemed to disappear into his head. He'd never experienced such a feeling, rarely even getting a headache. His head started to throb and he became dizzy and disoriented. He reached for his VHF radio, but his head felt as if somebody were hitting it with a hammer. His vision blurred and he thought he was seeing either double or triple as he stood in front of the seat on the bridge, trying to see the gauges and controls. He fell forward, his right hand hitting the twin disc gear lever, throwing both engines into forward gear at full throttle. He had fallen into a big black hole. Then there was nothing.

Until the horrible sound of his bow crashing against metal. It was a sound he would never forget and one that he had, for a lifetime of boating, sought successfully to avoid. His vessel had hit red sea buoy #1 dead center, then rolled hard along her port side. Joe felt something licking his face hard as he woke up, and the first thing he saw was Buck. He sat up, petted Buck's head, and looked around, trying to get his bearings. He realized that he had been lying on his back in the cockpit at the foot of the ladder. Then it came to him that his boat was still under way at about five knots and seemed to be holding to the sea buoy. Joe managed to crawl up the ladder and look at the plotter, his head clearing a bit. He recognized exactly where his boat was, having freed itself from the sea buoy only a thousand yards or so from the perilous seawalls on his starboard and port, marking the channel to the inlet. By now there were other boats in the area. He hit the standby button on the autopilot, instantly regaining the ability to manually steer the boat. He pulled back on the electronic controls and steered through the inlet.

Whether out of habit or skill, he brought the boat around the seawall and back into his slip, stern first, and shut the engines down. He fixed the bow lines on the posts to his bow cleats, and slowly pulled himself along the side of his boat and up on the dock, retrieved his stern lines, and climbed back in the cockpit to secure those lines on the cleats.

Then he collapsed in the fighting chair, Buck still licking him, and tried to figure out what in the world had just happened. There was no trace of anything wrong. Then he remembered the sea buoy and the awful sound of the crash.

He clambered out of the cockpit to the dock and, calling Buck to follow him, examined the port side of his boat and could see damage to the fiberglass hull and the bow rail, which was completely bent backwards. There was a large scrape on the port side of the bow, and the anchor under the bow pulpit was bent, but Joe saw no structural damage.

Joe knew that his vessel could be repaired. What he did not know was whether or not he could say the same for himself. He would see Dr. Worthington in the morning.

CHAPTER 29

Joe awoke at six in the morning, as he did each morning, without an alarm clock. Even as a boy, he'd never needed to be awakened. To his surprise, he felt fine. No headache, no trace of what had happened the day before. Not even tired. It didn't make sense. He took Buck out for a run, had breakfast and then, thinking about yesterday, called Dr. Worthington's office. He told the receptionist that he would like to see the doctor as soon as he could, that it was important. She asked him to wait a moment, and Bob Worthington got on the line.

"Hi, Joe. Good to hear your voice. What's going on?"

"I'm not sure, Bob. I went fishing yesterday and something happened to me while I was out there. I apologize for imposing, but I would feel a lot better if I could see you and tell you about it."

Bob must have heard the tone of Joe's voice. "Come right over."

"Thanks. I'll be there shortly."

Joe played catch with Buck, kissed him, told him to stay, and drove to Dr. Worthington's office at the University Medical Center. While he had seen the man for routine annual exams, he really thought of him more as Ashley's doctor, and a family friend. Bob and his family belonged to the same church, and before Ashley's death they would see them there and occasionally socially, too. Bob and Joe had gone fishing together a couple of times.

The receptionist smiled and said she would tell Dr. Worthington that he was there. He could see she already had his chart in hand.

He was led into a small examining room where he was shortly joined by a nurse with a big smile.

"The doctor will be here in a minute, Mr. Hart. I'm just going to check you in – all routine," she said in a pleasant and reassuring manner. She had him stand on the scale and noted his 160-pound weight in the chart. She took his temperature and measured his blood pressure, each reading normal. Then she smiled again and said the doctor would see him in just a moment. For some reason Joe felt like climbing up on the exam table and taking a nap. He felt strange, but he was not sure why. Instead he sat on the small straight chair and waited nervously for what seemed like a long time.

Dr. Worthington was a clear-eyed, slim man in his mid-fifties, sandy brown hair, a few inches taller than average, with a pleasant warm face. He shook Joe's hand, and with his other hand grasped his arm.

"How are you Joe? It's been a while, hasn't it?" He looked at the chart. "About a year. You still look in great shape. Tell me, how are you feeling? What happened?"

"Thanks for seeing me, Bob. I don't know what happened. That's what worries me. Always been in good health, work out regularly, plenty of exercise. Buck sees to that."

"How is Buck?"

"Fine. Just fine. Not sure what I'd do without him."

"Can you describe what specifically is causing your concern?"

"Yeah, sorry, Bob, little off today. It was yesterday, out fishing, just me and Buck. About ten miles off shore, nice day, set my boat on slow return course, my rods up to fish for kings. Caught a couple, good weather, everything good, music going, great to get away, back on the water... Bob, I actually felt happy for a change. Went up to the bridge for something... I don't know, to change a CD, then I remember feeling funny... strange... then I lost it."

"Is that all you remember?" Bob asked in a gentle tone.

Joe looked around the small examining room, thinking how surgically cold it was. He noted the crisp, white paper covering the examining table next to the chair he was sitting in. He probably could not have taken a nap on that table anyway. Then he noticed the expression on Bob's face and that he had been asked a question.

Question... what was the question? Oh, anything else? Is that all I remember? Think! He looked up over the examining table and saw a large, round light. *Yeah, the light.* "Sorry, Bob, my mind was drifting a little. I do remember something else. There was a flash of light – blinding, bright light – but it only lasted a second, and then black. I must have blacked out."

"You're holding your right eye right now, Joe. Did something happen to your eye?"

"Oh... I'm not sure. My eye hurt, my head, yeah that's affirmative, head hurt a lot, like a hammer pounding it."

"What about your vision at that point Joe? Could you see?"

"My vision was fine. Maybe a little blurry. I'm not sure. I felt a little dizzy at that point... I think I remember falling, but that's it. I lost it, blacked out."

"Did you call for help? How did you get home?"

"No, no call for help. It happened too fast. No time."

"What do you remember next, after blacking out?"

"The next thing I remember was a crash. Then Buck licking my face, licking hard and fast. And he was pulling on my shirt. That's what I remember next."

"Where were you then?"

"I was in the cockpit, next to the stairs to the bridge, lying down. I got up. I told Buck to stop licking me. He did, and then I asked him if he was okay. I looked him over. He seemed good. I got him some water. I drank some, too."

"What happened next?" Bob asked, continuing to take notes as he spoke.

"Well, I went up to the bridge. We were at the sea buoy to the inlet. Can you believe that? My autopilot was set, for home I mean. I was hung up on the sea buoy for a minute, freed her, and brought her back. I saw damage to the vessel, so I must have hit the buoy. That's it, Bob. That's what I remember."

"Wow. You had quite a day. This was yesterday at about what time, when you had these feelings, when you blacked out?"

"Not sure of the time. It was about three when I got to the slip. I looked the boat over, got Buck more water. We drove home. I fed Buck. I wasn't hungry. We walked, he did his thing, we played quietly in the den, I fell asleep on the couch. I slept all night. That was unusual. I got up this morning, felt fine, like it never happened, just a bad dream."

"But it did happen," Bob said. "I'm sure of that. How do you feel now, Joe?"

"How do you know it happened, Bob? That I'm not losing my mind?"

"There's nothing wrong with your mind, Joe. There is a large ecchymosis developing on your upper forehead and over your right eye." Bob pressed that area gently. "Does that hurt?"

"A little."

Bob asked Joe to remove his clothes and put on one of those tie-from-the-back, loose gowns Joe hated, and then left the room. A few moments later Bob returned and asked Joe to first sit on the examining table and then lie down while Bob checked him over, head to foot, palpated his ankles, moved his arms and legs, and examined eyes and ears. Before Joe climbed off the table, while his legs hung over the side, Bob tapped the bottoms of his feet with a small stainless steel mallet with a rubber wedge on the end.

"Let's go over your chart and history, Joe. But before we do, I have not seen you since Ashley's funeral. Obviously, that was an ordeal, to say the least. How have you been feeling since then and up until yesterday?"

"Physically?" Joe asked. "Fine."

"How about other than physically, Joe? Obviously, you've had a pretty bad time of it. Major adjustment. We haven't seen you in church since Ashley's funeral. What have you been doing with yourself? How have you been getting along?" Bob asked gently.

Joe looked directly at Bob and smiled his appreciation. "You're right. It has not been the best of times. But I'm getting along fine. Or at least I was, until yesterday. I took some time from my practice and went up to the mountains in the area where I grew up. That was good. Then I became involved in a case for a client, which I just finished. But getting along fine, looking forward to spending time on my boat, fishing, maybe a little diving. Or at least I was."

"Well, let's see if we can figure this out and get you back to your boat. Any signs of eye problems, severe headaches, that type of thing, before yesterday?"

"No. None."

"We need to run some blood work, urine analysis, routine work-ups. Joe, I want to refer you to radiology for an MRI, and perhaps a brain scan, and also to the neurology department for a work-up. Something is going on, but I don't know what it is. We need to get to the bottom of it."

"What do you think it was? What do you think happened to me yesterday?"

"I don't know. I'm an internist, Joe. It could be nothing. Maybe a tiny mini-stroke. Or trauma from your fall. It could be a lot of things. You look and sound good to me, generally speaking. We need to see the results of the blood work, the chemistry, see how all of that is functioning. We need some more tests. We need to look at your cardiovascular system, neurological system, rule out some things, make a comprehensive diagnosis." And then, looking at Joe's file, Bob said, "By the way Joe, we show Ashley . . . who would you like us to list in case we need to get in touch with a family member?"

Joe thought about that. *A family member?* He thought some more. "Other than Buck? Put Red Barnes down. Red was my exec. We served together on a submarine during my Navy days. I'll give you – him – medical authorization to talk to one another, handle consents for me if I am unable, that sort of thing. Will that work?"

"That's fine. I'll make some calls and we'll get you admitted for tests this afternoon."

"Let me make some calls first. I want to talk with Red, and then to my secretary, make some arrangements. All of this stays strictly with us, right, Bob?"

"And all your doctors and medical support people, but that would take an authorization, which means you and Mr. Barnes in accord with your instructions," Bob said.

"Exactly. Thank you for working me in, for everything. I'll call you this afternoon."

"Please do. I don't want to worry you, but I do want to get to the bottom of this as soon as possible."

CHAPTER 30

Joe picked up the phone on the first ring. "Hi, Cap," Red said. "You must be pushing the java, picking up the phone so fast. How the hell are you?"

"Hi, Red. Thanks for getting back to me so soon. How're you doing?"

"You want me to give you the details of how lousy my golf game is and how bored I am at work? Come on, what's up?"

"I'm not exactly sure. I went fishing yesterday, and while I was out there, impressing Buck with my ability to catch king mackerel in rapid time, I blacked out. Because I'm a genius, I was able to bring my vessel back to port without knowing it. I guess I woke up when my bow hit the sea buoy at the end of the Charleston inlet. I brought her back to the slip from there."

"I hope you were at least drinking Guinness or Bass Ale," Red said, "instead of Coors Light. I don't get the part about how you brought her in. Tell me about that."

"The best that I can reconstruct it, smart ass, was that I had set my autopilot for a reverse path home with my waypoint at the buoy and had the engines forward at full slow. Then I passed out and somehow managed to fall on the gear, pressing the electronic fuel and transmission controls full ahead. The autopilot took my vessel to the buoy, and the impact woke me up."

"Buck with you?"

"Yeah."

"He probably drove. Is he okay?"

"He's fine. Would you like to hear about me, shit head?"

"Not unless you're dying to tell me. If you're going to tell me you're injured and can't walk or whatever, then I have to drive down to that small-ass southern town of yours, stay over in your house, which hasn't been cleaned since you know when, and then I'll have to stock the refrigerator with some good beer and listen to all your stories again. Who would want to do that?"

"I don't know," Joe said. "Some asshole who is bored with his job and plays a lousy game of golf. Somebody like that."

"When are you gonna tell me what you really want me to do, Joe? The reason you called?"

"Okay, I've been to the doctor here in Braydon. He's an internist, a good guy. I told him about the blackout, seeing a flash of light, then black, hammering headache, being out for what I figure was probably an hour, at least. He says it could be anything, something, or nothing. He wants me to be admitted to the medical center down here this afternoon for a series of tests. Not just blood and urine analysis, but MRI, possibly CAT scan of my brain, full neurological and cardiology workups.

"That all sounds fairly heavy to me. I think he's worried, but he doesn't want me to be worried. He asked me for a family member for consents and to follow my progress, that sort of thing. I gave him your name and contact details. I told him you were my exec on the *Trader* – I just said we served together on a submarine during my Navy days – and that you, but only you, should receive any information you want. Is that okay?"

"Quit busting my balls. The consent part's fine, and I get the fact that this is on a need-to-know basis, and that unless I hear to the contrary from you, I will be the only one who needs to know. Understood. But I don't like hearing about the symptoms. Also, if I may speak frankly, I don't think you should screw around with the medical center down there."

"What's your recommendation?"

"Skipper, I think you should get your ass up to Bethesda Naval Hospital. You're a former commander, you may recall, and you can go in there in a heartbeat. They'll handle it all, and they've got great medical teams, as you know from the work they did with some of our guys. You're not going to like these tests, and you're going to be impatient as hell waiting for the results. And then you're going to want straight answers, whatever it is. With due respect to your family doctor, Joe, I'd feel a lot better, and so will you, if you go up there now and get squared away. I'll meet you there."

"Thanks Red, good advice. I'll do it. See you there."

Joe hung up and called Alice. "Hi, Alice. How're you doing?"

"Good, Joe. How's the fishing going? Are you ever coming back to work?"

"Caught a couple of nice kings and some big bill fish, Alice. Weather was great, and it felt really good to get out there."

"Joe, you got a call from Mr. Gallagher at the bank." She gave him Tom's numbers.

"How did he sound?"

"Like he was anxious to talk to you, just as we all are," Alice said with a laugh. "I told him you were out of the office and that I would get the message to you. I didn't tell him you smelled like fish."

"Alice, I need to impose upon you again," Joe said.

"It's never an imposition. You know that. What can I do?"

"I would appreciate your looking after Buck for a few days, starting this afternoon. I've got to go to Bethesda, Maryland, for some routine medical tests. Apparently the Navy thinks I'm getting old and needs to look me over. When they see what great shape I'm in, I'm sure they'll be sorry they wasted their time. But, orders are orders. Would you please check around, call the airlines and get me on the earliest flight you can – Dulles, Reagan, as close as you can get me to Bethesda – and arrange for a rental car I can drive from there."

"I understand; you mean this afternoon?" Alice asked.

"Yes, I have to go as soon as possible, so figure it all out and let me know where I'm leaving from and when."

"Are you going to call Mr. Gallagher, or how would you like that handled?"

"I'll try to reach him now," Joe said, "and I'll keep in touch with you by phone. And Alice, thank you for all that you do for me. I don't know how I would get along without you."

"Thanks, Joe. I'll take care of everything here," Alice said and hung up.

"How y'all doin', Joe?" Tom asked. "Good to hear from you."

"Doing fine, Tom. How are you and Terry?"

"Terry's his old, miserable self. Still trying to get me on the golf course with him so he can teach me another lesson.

"Joe, I got an answer for you. We're going to do it. We've made a few changes in the plan, nothing serious, just cutting back a little on the amount we loan. But we're going to enter into a forbearance agreement now and essentially follow your plan. I'm assuming your boy, Alex, is still in the picture and will be available and active, just as we discussed."

"Alex is in, Casey is rejuvenated, and Preston is focused and committed."

"Good. Then we need to get together and approve all the paperwork and get it done."

"You don't need me for the paperwork, Tom, as long as you keep your lawyers honest and don't let them screw up our deal. Have your lawyers do the paperwork, and Alex and Casey can be immediately available to get you what you need. The rest is transactional and will take some time. Alex can hire local lawyers where required to do that part of the paperwork for Wilson. Preston will sign what he needs to sign. I think the bank made a good decision, Tom, and I don't think Preston and the others will let you down."

"I hope not, too. I'd feel a lot better if you'd stay involved in all of this. I really enjoyed working with you. We could use someone like you at our bank, you know. Teach us how to do this better."

"Thanks, Tom, but I figure you and Terry can do the work and are doing the teaching very well. As I told you in Charlotte, my job is over. Besides, I've got some serious fishing to do. I'll call Preston, Casey, and Alex and tell them of your decision and ask them to be in touch with the bank immediately. Who would you like to be the point man for them?"

"Have them call Bobby. He'll take it from there. I wish I were going fishing with you, Joe. Have a good trip, and thanks again for all your help."

"Thank you, Tom, and Terry and the bank. Now we've created the opportunity, let's hope the bank and Wilson work together and take advantage of it. By the way, I enjoyed getting to know you and working with you, too. So long, Tom."

"So long, Joe."

Joe next looked up Preston's cell phone number and punched the call.

"Hey, Joe," Preston said, unmistakable eagerness in his voice. "Any news?"

"Yes, that's why I called. I've heard from the bank. They're going to do the deal. A few changes in the amounts being loaned, but essentially, they're following our plan right down the line."

Silence on Preston's end. Joe waited. Finally, Preston spoke in a barely audible voice. "That's really good, Joe. Really good. Unbelievable. You did it. You actually did it. Once again, you saved my ass. My life. What do we do now?"

"Gallagher asked that you contact Robert Bower. He's going to act as the lead man."

"I'll call Casey and Alex immediately," Preston said. "Also, I don't know if this is the time to discuss this, but I got a legal bill from your office, and it can't be right. It's way too low and there was no charge for any of your time. I assume you'll send Wilson another one with all your time on it."

"Negative. I'm not billing you for my time, Preston, because Wilson needs all the money it can get its hands on right now. It is important, however, that the bill we did send you gets paid immediately, because my secretary worked long and hard on this matter, as did the interns. There are out-of-pocket disbursements to be covered, and I want to make sure that Alex gets paid right away."

"Thanks. I'll see to it that the bill is paid today. When will I see you again?"

"We'll get together, Preston. I'm going to take some time off, spend time on my boat, and catch up with friends. I'll be in touch with Alice, but I expect it will be difficult to reach me for a while. How are things going on your other workout?"

"Marcia is visiting her mother at the moment. Then she's going to visit her college roommate. I've got a lot of work to do on that score, Joe, but I'm taking a chapter out of your book, you know, thinking of a plan and taking it step by step."

"I hope it works out, Preston. Good luck."

"Thanks, Joe. Have a great time on your trip. You certainly deserve a vacation. And Joe, once again, thank you for all you've done for me and especially thank you for believing in me. That means more to me than you can ever know."

Joe's next call was to Worthington.

"Hi, Joe. When are you coming in?"

"Bob, I'm not coming in. I've reviewed my health insurance program and talked with Red Barnes. Red's pretty good at sorting this kind of thing out, and he recommended that in view of my status as a former commander in the Navy, I should go to Bethesda for the workups and have their team of medical experts make the diagnosis. Red tells me this will end up being cost-effective for me, as well. I trust Red implicitly, and I'd ask that you cooperate with him fully. I realize this may be overkill, and that whatever is going on with me may be nothing at all and not serious, but by training and inclination, I am taking it seriously. I hope you'll understand and accept my decision."

For a moment, Bob was silent. And then, he said, "Of course I do. I hadn't thought of Bethesda, but, given your naval background, it probably makes sense for you to go there. While I believe our university medical center is quite capable, there's no question that the Bethesda Medical Center enjoys an excellent reputation. I'll cooperate with them fully, of course, and provide them with all the records I have here."

"I appreciate that," Joe said. "And I will ask those folks to be in touch with you and keep you advised. I know that you care about what's happening to me, and I am grateful for that. Thank you for all of your help. I'm leaving for Maryland now. I'll be in touch."

"You're welcome. My prayers will be with you."

Joe packed his bag and dropped Buck off with Alice, who never ceased to amaze him. Not being able to make any satisfactory commercial arrangements within the time frame Joe had asked, Alice arranged for a small private plane to fly him from Charleston Airport directly to a private airfield in Bethesda.

CHAPTER 31

Joe had dozed off and was gently awakened by a physician's assistant in a green gown who advised him that a doctor would be in shortly. Upon the doctor's arrival, Joe was surprised that he was such a young man, probably in his early-thirties, obviously fit, and with military bearing. Dr. Burns, addressing him as "Commander," explained that he was going to ask a few questions and examine him. The doctor had a thick chart with Joe's name and identification number on it.

"The last thing you remember was a bright light and then blackness?"

"Correct."

"And just prior to that, your head felt like it was being hammered, you had a severe headache?"

"Yes, sir."

"And do you have a headache now?"

"No, sir. But I'm a bit tired."

"I can understand that, Commander. Anyone would be tired, going through all the procedures we have here. Sorry about that. How did you feel in the days prior to the event? Have you been having any headaches, any trouble with vision, any change in strength on one side of the body as compared with the other?"

That last one surprised Joe. "No."

"Numbness, pain, heaviness or clumsiness in an arm or leg? Any trouble with handwriting?" Actually, Joe was doing less and less handwriting these days, anyway, preferring to dictate to Alice.

"No, sir. I really have not, other than waking up once in a while with a minor headache, which goes away after my shower or if I take an aspirin. Those other symptoms you asked about have not been a problem."

"How much alcohol have you been drinking lately?"

Joe looked at the doctor for a moment and replied, "Not much, really. In fact, I can't remember the last time I had a drink. Maybe two weeks ago."

Looking at the file, the doctor asked, "And you don't smoke cigarettes, never have, but do occasionally smoke a cigar?"

"Correct, no cigarettes, a cigar once in a while when called for, and I don't inhale."

"When you wake up, do you ever find that you have bitten your tongue?"

He answered no, thinking, *There are a few times when I wish I had bitten my tongue.*

Then the doctor asked Joe whether he had ever had a seizure. Joe wanted to know precisely what he meant. "Well, have you ever blacked out before? Have you ever lost consciousness before?"

"No, sir." Joe told him he was not aware of any seizure history but that his parents both died when he was ten years old, and he really didn't know. The questions went on. Irregular heartbeats or murmurs? Unusual back pain? Incidents of constipation?

"Let's take a look at your eyes, Commander." Then he asked Joe to stand and face the wall. As Joe did, it occurred to him that there was nothing on the walls in the examining room. As he thought about that, the doctor asked Joe to close his eyes, open them, and take two steps backward and then forward, before he had him lie on the table while he used the handle end of his steel and rubber tomahawk to stroke the sole of each of Joe's feet upward from his bare heel. As Dr. Burns did so, beginning with the right foot, Joe, with his head propped up on the pillow, observed his great toe pointing upward.

"Is there any room in this examination for questions, or should I just keep quiet?" Joe asked.

"You may ask anything you like, sir. I'm just not sure how much we will be able to tell you until we have the entire picture. There are a lot of pieces to the puzzle. At the moment, I'm assessing whether there are any electrical problems. I'm focusing on the passing out. Passing out can be the result of some potentially serious conditions, although not necessarily. I am a little concerned about your waking up with headaches, and I am finding, on the physical side, a little weakness in your right hand."

"Where did you pick up weakness in my right hand?"

"From your handshake, for starters, and watching you climb up on the table. I want to see the results of your MRI and CAT scan. That'll tell us a lot more."

"Do you have an idea of what you may be looking for?" Joe asked.

"There are a fair number of possibilities. Some unusual infections can do this, or it could be a blood vessel abnormality, such as an aneurysm, or even a growth or tumor."

Joe hated all this testing. He missed Buck. And he missed Alice. He was eager to see Red. Most of all, he missed Ashley. She would be at his side, quietly reading, waiting, smiling at him. She would know just what to say, what not to say, and when. Joe felt more loneliness than he had at any time since Ashley's death. He wondered if something were to happen to him, what would become of Alice, although he had already provided her with life insurance and a well-funded retirement. Who would keep her from being bored, keep her keen mind and wit engaged? Who would make her feel needed? And who would take care of Johnny, Missy, Tommy, Harry, and Corey, that group of his friends whom Ashley had – hopefully in jest – referred to as his 'collectibles?'

Joe's thoughts were interrupted when another doctor came into the room. This one was in his mid-forties, stern, on the tall side, with short, black hair.

"I'm Dr. Gordon," he said. "Chief of neurology, and I've been looking over your file to see if I could lend a hand. It's nice to meet you, Commander." He shook Joe's hand. "I've read your file, not just medical, but some of your service file as well, trying to get a full picture of your background. You had an impressive career, Commander. Very interesting, especially the part that was declassified for me to take a look at your history. I won't discuss it further, except to say you'd be my first choice to get the job done and keep it secret in the bargain."

"Thank you, sir. What, if anything, can you tell me so far?"

"The purpose for all this testing is to assist in reaching a differential diagnosis. Your loss of consciousness is known as syncope. Syncope can have many diverse possible causes, both innocent as well as serious. Generally, the vast majority of causes will involve conditions of either the brain or nervous system, cardiovascular conditions, and metabolic conditions. While there are some other very unusual conditions, 98 percent of people presenting with syncope will have a cause that falls into one of these three categories.

"I want to have a chat with Dr. Burns here to get his input. Subject to that, I have preliminarily ruled out cardiovascular and metabolic causes. That leaves the brain and nervous system. You did not indicate any symptoms relating to your spinal cord. No back pain, no urinary retention, and no new onset of constipation. Your Babinski reflex was positive. You may have noticed your right toe pointing up instead of down. For these reasons, and some weakness on your right side and right hand, we are interested in the MRI and CAT scan results. We should have them in the morning. In the meantime, I'm sure you'll be glad to get back to a more comfortable room, have a good meal, and get some sleep. I'm sorry we had to put you through so much in such a short period of time. Tomorrow morning, after breakfast, I'd like to meet you in my office at 1100 and we'll go over the results of all of the tests and hopefully be able to tell you, with reasonable medical certainty, a definitive diagnosis."

"Thank you, doctor," Joe said, "and thank you, Dr. Burns."

Shortly thereafter, a male nurse brought in a wheelchair and transported Joe to a private room. He climbed in bed, with the nurse standing by. Another came in and asked him what he would like to eat and drink, and he asked for a large cheeseburger with onions and a Coke. She smiled and said, "I'll come as close to that as we can."

Just before he fell asleep, he noticed a man with short red hair over in the corner, reading a boating magazine. "How the hell did you get in here, Red? How did you find me?"

"I used to work in intelligence, Skipper. Back when you had a memory, you would have known that. Go to sleep."

CHAPTER 32

Joe was wheeled into Dr. Gordon's office at 10:55 a.m. It was a large, rectangular, dimly lit room with rosewood paneled walls and no windows. Instead, the wall on the right was lined with diplomas, and the upper half of the wall on the left was illuminated with a soft white light. Dr. Gordon sat behind a large metal desk covered with files, Dr. Burns was in one of two armchairs in front of the desk. He motioned Joe to the other. Dr. Gordon leaned forward on his desk. "How are you feeling today, Commander?" he asked. "Is everybody treating you all right around here?"

"Just fine, sir," Joe replied.

"Yesterday I spoke with you about the MRI. As you know, the MRI consists of scans, or images, of your brain. Essentially, the MRI is a way of making a picture of the brain using magnetic energy rather than X-rays. In your case, the scans are quite impressive. Let me show you some films." Dr. Gordon said, getting up and moving from behind his desk to a table on his right. "Most of the pictures that we'll look at today are cross sections through the head, done serially so that they're stacked on top of each other."

Dr. Gordon pointed to the portions of the MRI study that pictured Joe's nose and ears. As he moved his finger across the brain images, he pointed out a mass higher up in the front of the brain that involved areas known as the frontal lobes and the corpus callosum, or the part of the brain that connects the two sides.

The mass had a different appearance from the other part of the brain, the brain tissue that surrounded it looked swollen. It also extended into the area on the left side known as the basal ganglia.

Dr. Gordon then put up another sheet of pictures. "Commander, these pictures show where contrast dye had been given to you. As you can see, the mass is even more obvious here."

Joe experienced a cool, drawn-down feeling in the back of his neck. His stomach was queasy, his shoulders ached, and his heart was pounding. He felt hot and cold at the same time. He also sensed he was weak, but he was standing in a firm manner and he heard himself ask, "What does this all mean for me, doctor? I understand I have a mass. What I would like to know is, can it be treated? How do we get rid of it? And will I be okay?" What Joe didn't hear was the intense edge to his voice.

Dr. Gordon put his hand on Joe's shoulder and suggested that Joe sit down in front of his desk. He poured a glass of water from a silver water pitcher. Now Joe caught himself observing the water pitcher with too much attention, yet he could not help himself. He did manage not to start a conversation about it. Instead, he realized how good the cool water tasted. Then he found himself dwelling on how important cold water is, and wondering why he did not drink more of it. His mind wanted to follow that course, but, recognizing its absurdity, he decided the only thing he could do was listen to Dr. Gordon some more. He was not sure, however, he wanted to hear anything else Dr. Gordon had to say unless he was going to be told this was not a serious problem and could be taken care of.

At this point, Dr. Burns moved his chair to more directly face Joe. "Do you remember when I asked you to turn away from me yesterday during my physical examination?" he asked. "What I noticed then was that your right arm drifted downward slightly from the original position. When I asked you to stand at the side of the exam table and close your eyes, you seemed a little wobbly.

"We don't have all of the answers today, but we have enough to make us feel, based upon the information we have reviewed, that you have a tumor of the brain that's called a glioblastoma multiforme. It's still possible that something else is producing the findings, such as an infection, but we don't think so."

Dr. Gordon interjected, "We're going to get you started on

Dilantin, to decrease the possibility of a seizure from the irritation of the brain. I'm also going to prescribe a second medicine called Decadron, to reduce the swelling of the brain."

"Is this tumor malignant?" Joe heard himself ask. He felt as if he were outside the room, looking in at a conversation that he was having. "Do you mind, Doctor, if we bring in Commander Barnes? He was my exec officer on the *Trader* years ago, as you may have read when you reviewed my file. He's here in the hospital; I saw him last night. I'd like him to hear this."

"He's not only in the hospital, he's right outside the door, practically asking for a court martial trying to get in here. Please ask Mr. Barnes to come in, Dr. Burns." Sure enough, Red was standing on the other side. Joe looked over at Red, who simply smiled back and didn't say a word.

"Commander Hart tells us that you served with him as his exec on the *Trader* several years ago," Dr. Gordon said.

"I can't discuss that, sir, but I do know the man," Red said with a smile.

"I'm sure you do. You both have very impressive records. Let me get to the point. Commander Hart has a brain tumor, which caused him to sustain syncope, which is a loss of consciousness. The tumor is called a glioblastoma multiforme. Commander Hart, may I call you Joe?"

"Yes, sir, please do. And call this guy on my right Red, if you would, so he doesn't get a swelled head."

"Joe, you asked whether or not the tumor was malignant. We'll need to schedule a CT guided stereotactic biopsy. The neurosurgeon will take a small piece of the tissue in the area of the mass through a twist drill hole in the skull. Although there is risk of causing harm to the brain any time surgery is performed, Dr. Raymond, our chief of neurosurgery, sees the risk as minimal, and the benefit is that we'll know the diagnosis. I'm sure you'll want to ask him questions. Ask him whatever you like. And, Joe, as you well know, you're not married to the opinions of Dr. Raymond, or mine either for that matter. We've been in touch with Dr. Worthington. There's always room for second or third opinions."

There was silence in the room. No one said a word for quite some time. Dr. Gordon poured another glass of water for Joe, and one for each of the others in the room without asking if they wanted any. They all drank. Joe and Red looked at one another for a long time, neither speaking words, each speaking volumes.

Joe broke the silence. "I would like the biopsy as soon as possible. I would also like to talk to you, Dr. Gordon, alone."

"Of course. We can talk tomorrow at 0900."

"With your permission, doctor, I would like to talk with you alone in fifteen minutes, and I would like to be alone from now until then."

"Fifteen minutes it is," Dr. Gordon said. "And you can stay right in this office." With that, he walked out of the room, followed by Dr. Burns. Red waited a moment, looked at Joe, and told him he would be outside the room. With that, he got up and left as well.

Joe rose and poured himself another glass of water, rushed into the bathroom adjoining Dr. Gordon's office, relieved himself, and stood in front of the mirror, splashing cold water on his face and fighting the urge to throw up. He didn't want to leave the bathroom, so he sat down on the toilet, arms resting on his legs, holding his head. His mind was spinning, but he was also organizing, thinking, gaining control. After fifteen minutes, he washed his face again and dried it, came out, and sat back in the chair. Moments later, Dr. Gordon came back into his office, locked the office door, and sat at his desk. He looked at Joe.

"How much do you know about glioblastoma, Dr. Gordon?"

"More than I would like to, in some ways," Dr. Gordon gently replied. "In addition to neurology, I have been trained in oncology, and while rare, we have seen more of these tumors over the years than we would like."

"I realize that you don't have the results of the biopsy, but it seems to me that you have reached a diagnosis, tentative at least, of this glioblastoma. What I want to know is, is this tumor malignant?"

"Glioblastoma, if that is what you have, is a malignant tumor of the brain tissue that is a kind of cancer. It can be treated with radiation therapy, which, in some instances, depending on the size and location of the tumor, can induce a phase of remission. The tumor, however, often recurs in a short period of time. It can also be treated with chemotherapy, but unfortunately, this treatment prolongs life only fifteen extra days in a typical case. Surgery is an option in certain cases but is not a cure for these tumors and, because of the location of your tumor, is not viable. There are several other kinds of experimental treatments that have shown some promise. However, it is a very serious tumor problem, and if we are correct, cannot be cured."

Silence again. Dr. Gordon seemed to wait for the question both he and Joe knew was coming. Finally, Joe asked it.

"Assuming the biopsy is positive, that I have this type of tumor, how much time do I have left?"

Dr. Gordon remained silent for a while and then, walking around his desk and sitting next to Joe, he said, "The average time from diagnosis until death in a patient with a biopsy-proven glioblastoma is a little more than one year, although the time for any given patient can vary significantly from that figure all the way from less than six months to more than two years. I told Dr. Raymond that I had reviewed your record, met you, and told him that you are going to want the facts, all the facts. I asked him specifically, given the location and appearance of your tumor and the brain swelling, what did he truly believe you had left in useful time. Dr. Raymond told me, and I am sure he will tell you, that given your age, good health generally, and the size and location of the tumor, it is likely that you will live approximately six months, assuming the biopsy confirms our impression. Even with radiation and experimental therapies, he could not be optimistic because the tumor involves both sides of the brain, the corpus callosum, and even the basal ganglia on the left.

"Naturally, we will go ahead with further consultation with other neuro-oncologists in our department to be sure we have not overlooked any possibility of new treatment options that might have the potential to prolong your life. And we are only doctors, Joe. We don't make decisions as to when people die. I may be wrong. You may have much longer, and we'll keep working on it."

More silence.

"Let me ask you three questions, Dr. Gordon: again, assuming the biopsy is positive, the tumor malignant, and that I have approximately six months to live, what will my life be like during these six months? Will I know when the time has come? And how will I know it?"

"It is hard to say with certainty how you will do from this point forward. Given your history of good health and being in good shape, it is not unlikely that you will proceed relatively normally during this period. You may experience headaches, perhaps some constipation, and it is not unlikely that you would have a decrease in your motor response efficiency. Medication will mitigate the likelihood of seizure and abate the swelling in your brain. It's entirely possible that for several months you will feel physically normal, or close to it. Of course, the stress is incalculable. If anyone, however, has a history of handling high stress in an exemplary manner, from what I have read, it is you.

"As to your last two questions, will you know and how will you know it, those are very interesting questions. At the very end, you will clearly know it because you will have an episode something like the one you had on your boat, but one from which you will not wake up. As far as how you will know it, I can tell you that I have observed in some of my patients over the years with this particular disease that towards the end – a day or two – and it's hard to be specific, they smell a very pungent odor, one they clearly recognize, like burning leaves, oil-based paint, ether, but in fact, there is no precipitating agent for the smell."

"You mean I smell the odor, but it's not there?"

"Exactly," Dr. Gordon said. "That could happen."

Joe rose and shook Dr. Gordon's hand. "Thank you, Doctor. I want to share something with you in confidence."

Dr. Gordon nodded, and Joe continued.

"You know, there were times when we were at sea and down for considerable periods. A submarine is smaller than you think, and the quarters are close. Sometimes the work we did got a little hairy.

One of my favorite times would be when the job was completed, our orders successfully carried out, and we would be in a position to surface. Once in a while, under those circumstances, we would surface in time to see a clear, calm ocean with the warm afternoon sun shining on the bridge. I would happen to have a cigar to light up just at those moments. Nothing like a good cigar at a time like that."

"Did you bring any cigars with you to the hospital?" Dr. Gordon asked.

"As a matter of fact, I did," Joe replied.

"You know, Commander, sometimes I feel a little closed-in in this office. There's a little balcony that can be accessed by the first door on the left of the entrance to this office. When the weather's decent, sometimes I sit out there, get some fresh air. I believe that door is unlocked."

Joe shook Dr. Gordon's hand again and walked to the door. When he opened it, he ran into Red.

"Red, we need to go AWOL for an hour. We're going to have a cigar."

CHAPTER 33

After breakfast, Dr. Raymond came in. About Joe's age, a few inches taller, with a shaved head, the doctor had small bright blue eyes and a cool demeanor. He introduced himself and explained that as a neurosurgeon, he was part of the team evaluating and treating Joe. Mechanically, as if checking off his to-do list, he recited that he had reviewed all of the test results and had conferred with Dr. Burns, Dr. Gordon, and the neuro-oncologist and radiation oncologist assigned to the case. He told Joe that the biopsy had been scheduled for that morning, and explained the procedure, including, in great detail, all the risks. He asked Joe whether he had any questions about the biopsy procedure or otherwise. Joe recognized Raymond's professional skill as a surgeon but, trying to hide his immediate dislike for the man, said, "No, sir. You have my informed consent. I'm ready to proceed."

"Excellent," Dr. Raymond replied and left the room.

Shortly, two nurses came in to prepare Joe for the biopsy. He was sedated and taken by a gurney to the surgical wing where he was further prepped, and the procedure performed.

When he was returned to his room and recovered, he noticed Red sitting in the chair. Red gave him a wave and asked him how he was feeling. Joe told him he felt fine, a little dry, and took a sip of water from the tray in front of him.

Later that day, Dr. Gordon and Dr. Raymond paid Joe a visit. Dr. Gordon took the lead as they walked in, but Joe beat him to the punch.

"Malignant, correct?"

"Correct," Dr. Gordon replied. Dr. Raymond stood stoically without saying anything.

   Silence for a long moment.

"Well," Dr. Raymond said, "if you don't have any questions, I have to get back to my wing."

"No questions, Dr. Raymond," Joe said, before the surgeon turned and left.

"I'm sorry, Joe," Dr. Gordon said. "Can I get you anything?"

"Is that door still unlocked?"

"No, but it will be in a minute," Dr. Gordon replied with a smile. "By the way, I made sure there were two chairs and a table out there this time, and an ashtray as well."

"Thanks, Dr. Gordon."

"You're welcome, Joe," Dr. Gordon said. "And it's Henry. In fact, please call me Hank. You'll be free to leave here soon. Let me know if there's anything you need. And I'm available to talk any time you want."

"Thanks, Hank," Joe said. "You deliver a strong pill, but you do it in a nice way." With that, Dr. Gordon shook Joe's hand, then Red's, and left the room.

Red came over and sat on the edge of Joe's bed, carrying a red canvas bag, looking like he was going to the beach.

"What's in the bag, Red?"

"Six bottles of cold Sam Adams just in case I have to go sit with you on that balcony and smoke another one of those lousy Graycliffs."

"Let's do it now," Joe said.

"You might be rushing it a bit," Red replied.

"I intend to, Red. My timetable's a little shorter these days. By the way, any chance you could free yourself up for a boat trip in the immediate future?"

"That would be really difficult," Red said. "I'd have to make arrangements, get everything lined up, talk with some people, prepare. I don't think I could go before tomorrow morning. Come on,

I'll wheel you to the balcony."

"Sounds good," Joe said, reaching for two cigars, a cutter, and his favorite lighter.

CHAPTER 34

Joe called Alice and told her he was ready to head home. "Of course I will bring Buck to meet you," Alice reassured him. "How did all of your tests go?"

"They're pretty thorough at Bethesda. They looked me over head to toe. But I'm still here. I had no idea how big Bethesda Naval Hospital is. Huge. Anyway, Alice, I'm ready to go fishing, but I need you to make some calls for me."

"Go."

"Please call Taylor Grant at Grant Marine in Charleston. Tell him you're calling for me and that I need some work done on my boat as soon as possible. Ask him to pick it up at my slip. Tell him the keys are where I usually hide them. The boat needs to be hauled and a fair amount of fiberglass work done. His glass guys will see the damage. Ask him to repair the glass, the bow rail on the port, and the anchor mount on the bow. While that's being repaired, tell him I'd like to have his electronics people install a new ITT night vision system with a screen on the bridge and on top of the bridge, an HDTV satellite antenna for the TV system. Oh, and on the bridge, have him replace the two seats behind the wheel with two new Stidd admiral-style seats, electric, white." Joe waited a minute to give Alice time to catch up.

"I would also like cameras placed in each room in the boat, the cockpit, and the engine room, all showing on the screen on the bridge. He'll know what I mean. Also, have him install three titanium underwater lights in the hull under the swim platform, and underwater cameras. Give him my American Express credit card number, the one I use for my boat, and tell him I'd appreciate his getting it all done one week from today, that I'm planning to go down the coast and over to the Bahamas. Oh, and ask him to be sure to have the bottom pressure washed when he hauls the boat. Did I go too fast?"

"You haven't gotten ahead of me yet," Alice replied.

"You're right about that," Joe said with a laugh.

"That's a lot of material," Alice said. "It's probably going to cost a bundle."

"Probably will. What the hell, we only live once. Also, Alice, would you please figure out a way to provision my boat for Red and me with as much food, water, plates, utensils, sheets, pillowcases, all that ... as much as you can put on the boat? Call Red; he can tell you exactly what kind of beer he'd like. There's a large cooler in the cockpit. There are people at the marina that can help you do that. Just ask the dock master. I don't want you carrying any of this, but I would appreciate your arranging it."

"I'll do it," Alice said. "I assume you're going to handle the fishing gear, or whatever you call it. Are you taking Buck?"

"Absolutely. That reminds me, please arrange with Buck's vet for a certificate from him showing that Buck has had all his shots and is in good health. The certificate needs to be dated the day I leave so it will be current when I take Buck into the Bahamas. I don't want to have Buck get caught up in any quarantines."

"I get it," Alice said. "I'll make sure that there's plenty of dog food, and plenty of his chewies, too. I'll talk with the vets, and I'll check with Bahamian immigration people through the internet to see the fastest and most efficient way of clearing Buck."

"Thanks, Alice. Let me know the flight arrangements. I'll see you and Buck soon."

CHAPTER 35

"**W**here we headed, Skipper?" Red asked, stowing his gear in the starboard cabin.

"I thought we would head down the coast to St. Augustine, spend the night there. The next day, we should be able to make it to West Palm, and we can spend the night at Sailfish Marina. Then we'll head out to the Bahamas, Nassau first. How's that sound?"

"Sounds like a good plan to me," Red said, looking in the cooler. "Ready when you are. I can't believe you got bottled Bass Ale!"

"Thank Alice."

Joe fired up the engines and they headed out the harbor on their way south. The seas were two to three feet with a northeasterly wind. Skies clear. As they were pushed along by the following sea, Red and Joe relaxed on the bridge, enjoying the day and each other's company. There was little need for words between these two old friends.

They arrived at the St. Augustine Inlet in early afternoon and proceeded to Camachee Cove Yacht Harbor, where they enjoyed a good steak dinner, a few after-dinner drinks in the cockpit, and spent the night. Buck devoured the bones.

They awoke to a clear sky with the same soft, northeasterly wind at their back, heading out the inlet and south along the coast. They arrived at Lake Worth Inlet about an hour before sunset, idled into Sailfish Marina, and savored dinner. Joe loved that time of day, and relished the moments at sea and in port, as, apparently, did Red and Buck.

The next morning, they set out for Nassau. Again, the weather was perfect, the seas only a light chop. The wind had shifted, coming from the southwest, and on the way over, Buck looked excited as a large school of dolphins evidently decided to keep company with the *Mountain Stream* on the port side. Red and Joe took turns at the helm, and at one point Joe took a nap in one of the comfortable teak chairs in the cockpit with the warm afternoon sun on his face. They arrived in Nassau Harbor shortly before six, put in at Hurricane Hole, and cleared customs and immigration with Buck, thanks to Alice. That night after dinner, with Buck guarding the boat, Joe and Red sampled the action at the crap tables at Atlantis Casino on Paradise Island. Cigars and Sambuca had become the after-dinner nightly ritual in the cockpit.

"I'm really getting to like these damn cigars," Red said. "What kind are they? There are no labels."

"Well, it's a long story. The short version is these cigars are made with Cuban tobacco that actually came to the United States between 1956 and 1958 and therefore was pre-embargo. I call 'em 'pre-revs.' Eventually they got the tobacco certified, worked out a deal with customs, had the cigars made in Ecuador and brought back in. But customs put a quota on the amount of tobacco they could bring back in so enjoy these while you can. I don't think there will be any more like these, and time is running out."

"Is there a metaphor in this story, Joe?"

"Yes, unfortunately, there is, Red. When I was alone with Dr. Gordon, I pressed him on how long I've got. The bottom line was about six months. Let's enjoy these while we can." If he was shaken by the news, Red didn't show it.

"You got it, Skipper."

The next morning, they left Nassau harbor and turned east, heading for Eleuthera. It was a head sea with five to seven footers, so the going was slow. After four hours, they arrived at the entrance to the Lower Bogue, which was southwest of Harbour Island, and which gave protection from the wind and waves. At that point, Joe called a man named Woody, a local icon who arranged to meet Joe's boat at a waypoint not far ahead and guide the boat through the shallow waters of the Bogue. Joe put *Mountain Stream's* controls in neutral as Woody swung his little outboard motorboat around the stern and pulled up to Joe's swim platform, tossing Red his bow line. Then he climbed in Joe's boat, his arms full of packages. Neither Joe nor Red needed any guidance through the Bogue, but Joe liked Woody and the way he talked, and he loved all the fresh stone crabs he brought with him.

They gabbed as they proceeded along the shallow waters at barely two knots, and then they broke out into the ocean side briefly, around the bluff, and into the sound. They arrived at Valentine's Resort and Marina, where they paid Woody and prepared the stone crabs for a pre-dinner treat.

After they had gotten to know Harbour Island as well as they wanted to, which included a wildly charismatic singin' and stompin' Sunday service Joe dragged Red to, they left Eleuthera for Great Abaco Island. The weather was clear and the wind steady at about fifteen knots from the west as they made their way along the thirty-two-nautical mile crossing, past Hole in the Wall at the southern tip of the island, and up to Little Harbour. The sound was calm and flat as they cruised to Marsh Harbour, their destination.

Joe could have stayed at the Conch Inn Hotel and Marina, a five-star facility with lots of amenities and new floating docks. Instead, he chose the older Marsh Harbour Marina, preferring the down-home atmosphere and remembering the barbecues at the Jib Room. He also thought Buck would be a lot happier there.

That night, after another good dinner, sitting in the cockpit, Joe asked Red if he needed to get back.

"I'm okay, Joe," Red replied. "I'll stay here as long as you'd like me to."

"I appreciate that, Red, but I know you've got a life of your own and things to do. I can't tell you how much I've enjoyed these last few days with you. It's been wonderful. I know you're staying with me in part because you want to make sure I'm all right. I'm doing fine. I've got Buck here with me and I plan to stay put in Marsh Harbour for a while. My cell phone works here, it's comfortable, and there's an airport with commercial and private planes that go back and forth to West Palm Beach, Fort Lauderdale, and Miami every day. If I need something, I can get it here, and you'll only be a phone call away... and Red, there will come a time when I'll be calling you to come."

"Okay, Joe. Thanks for telling me that. I'll fly out in the morning."

"Good. I know you need to get back, and I think you should. I'm going to ask a guy to fly over here and spend a little time with me, so you don't have to worry about me being alone – although that's not a problem, either."

"Who are you going to have come over?" Red asked.

"Well, I want to call Harry, a buddy of mine I used to hunt and fish with. I want to see if he's able to come over because I don't think he's ever been in the Bahamas, and I know he'd love the bone fishing and fishing in the ocean. He's also a professional photographer, and I think he would appreciate all of this," Joe said, pointing to the entire area and the harbor.

"But before I call him, I need to call a... client of mine. I just finished a business deal for him and I want to sit in a relaxed atmosphere and have a chat. None of this, of course, has anything to do with my physical situation, which remains strictly between you and me."

"Aye aye, Skipper. How about some more Sambuca?"

As it turned out, Preston flew in on Continental, the same airline Red was taking out, and the two unknowingly passed each other in the airport. Preston hired a taxi and within a few minutes was at Marsh Harbour Marina, where Joe and Buck were waiting for him in the Jib Room. Preston remembered Buck from the mountains. He was still uneasy around the dog, but, realizing that he was going to be sharing space with him on a small boat, decided he had better make friends in a hurry. Buck was mildly receptive.

"He figures you're with me, you must be all right," Joe said, clearly picking up on Preston's sensitivity and Buck's attitude. "He'll put up with you."

Joe showed Preston to his starboard quarters and explained the systems in the boat. Preston was starved, so Joe grilled him some hamburgers on an electric grill set on the cooler in the cockpit. He made an extra three for Buck. Preston relaxed that afternoon, as they sat in the cockpit talking and took some walks. He thought the area was charming, the harbor and especially the beach across the road on the sound side. He told Joe how energized Casey was, and, in detail, what a great job Alex was doing.

"I had no idea what a huge difference a really good operations man makes. And you were so right about giving Casey and Alex a piece of the ownership. Casey's a different man. He's not just following anymore. He talks about the company in terms of 'our company' now. I've never seen him so with the program." And so it went, for hours, as Joe listened patiently, with an occasional nod, and when necessary, bolstered by another cigar.

Preston was relaxed and excited at the same time. There were some real changes in him since he last saw Joe in Charlotte. More confident, more positive. Definitely more comfortable with himself. Joe didn't ask about Marcia, apparently not wanting to spoil the good mood. Preston would have said something if there was good news to tell.

After dinner, when the stars and full moon lit up the sky, Joe fed Buck again, not that he needed it. He played with Buck awhile, and then took him for a little walk by himself. When he came back, Preston was sitting in the cockpit with his feet up on the little teak table in front of the chairs.

"Are you tired?" Joe asked.

"Not at all, Joe," Preston said. "This is wonderful here. The weather is perfect. What a night."

"You're not sleepy? You're sure you don't want to turn in?"

"I really don't, Joe, if you don't mind. I'm happy just sitting here. But if you're tired, please go ahead and go to bed."

"No," Joe said, sitting down in the chair next to Preston with Buck settling in at his side, close enough so that Joe could pet his head.

"Do you feel like talking? Or actually, listening to me talk?"

"Of course," Preston said. "I've been yakking all day. I'd love to listen to you. I should have asked you earlier how you were doing. One of the things I'm working on is trying not to be so full of myself. It's a struggle, particularly when I get excited."

Joe got a fresh cigar and slowly lit it. "This doesn't bother you, does it?"

"No, not at all. Actually it smells good."

"Preston, thank you for flying down here. Apart from thinking you would enjoy this, and I'm glad to see that you are, I have something else I want to talk to you about. I'm sure you remember our conversation in the mountains, when you asked me for help."

"I remember every bit of that, Joe. I've thought about it many times."

"Well, then, you will remember there were three conditions to which you agreed. You have already performed the first two. You've told me everything I've wanted to know, shown me everything I wanted to see, and you've done everything I wanted you to do the way I've asked you to do it. And I believe you have told me the truth. I now am asking you to do something for me, to fulfill commitment number three."

"Absolutely, Joe. Whatever you ask. What do you want me to do?"

"I would like you to look after . . . six . . . friends of mine."

"Sure, I'd be glad to, Joe. What do you want me to do for them?"

"I'd like you to get to know them, have them get to know you, earn their trust, and take care of them." Joe was silent for a moment, and then he looked into Preston's eyes. "For the rest of your life."

"I don't understand, Joe. Who are these people? Do they need jobs? How do you want me to help them? Do you want me to hire them?"

"These are . . . friends of mine . . . I like them." Joe said, thinking but not wanting to hear himself say, *I have become involved in their problems.* "I talk to them once in a while, see them now and then look after them in a way. They're a small group. My wife, Ashley, referred to them as my 'collectibles.' I don't know why she said that, but I want you to get to know them; use your judgment and your feelings to determine how you can best help them. Let me tell you a little bit about them, to give you a feel for them. Let me start with Johnny. Johnny is a mildly mentally challenged dishwasher who works at the Home Dairy in Braydon."

Preston burst out laughing. "You've got to be yanking my cord, Joe. Come on, what are you talking about?" Joe was not laughing with him; his face had a stern grey look. "You're not serious, are you?"

"I'm as serious as a..." *brain tumor...* "heart attack," Joe said. "Johnny's a good guy, hardworking, straightforward, and he loves Buck. He can probably teach you how to get along with Buck. He doesn't need much attention, in a fundamental way, because the state takes care of him in terms of room and board, and he has a good job at the Home Dairy. What he's in short supply of is friends. That's what he needs. Somebody to talk to him from time to time in a sincere manner. Somebody to listen to him, teach him."

Joe could see Preston tighten his lips in a thin line.

"Then there's Harry. Harry is a professional photographer, when he's able to work. He's also an expert marksman, an award-winning trap and skeet shooter. He also likes to fish, hunt, camp, anything in the outdoors. He's bipolar. So you have to get used to the mood swings. Sometimes they're pretty severe. When he's down, he's really down. He has a psychiatrist, and he has medication – which, when he takes it, seems to work pretty well for him. But he needs somebody to talk to and somebody to listen."

Joe wondered whether he was going too fast. While he understood Preston's conceptual difficulties and need to process, he found Preston's resistance annoying.

"There's Missy, a former dancer in Las Vegas who's now working as a waitress. She divorced a husband who was too quick with his hands and battered her around a lot. When she's not scared to death, she's a delightful lady.

"Then there's Tommy Greco. He's a little too fond of the crap tables, and he has a bit of a problem with gambling across the board. But he's fun, a good guy at heart, and would do anything for you.

"Another one is Corey, a wonderful older gentleman and a highly skilled finish carpenter. He learned woodworking from his father, who used to build yachts north of Charleston. He's a lovely man, but he has the beginnings of Alzheimer's. He has a daughter who looks after him, but she has a family to take care of as well, and it's quite a burden. He, like the rest, can really use a friend. And the last one is a person who..."

At this point, Preston jumped up from his chair, looked at Joe and said, "Wait a minute, Joe. You must be crazy. What are you doing?"

"This is not about what I'm doing, Preston. This is about what I'm asking you to do. Go find these people. Alice has their addresses and phone numbers and I will ask her to give them to you. Find them, earn their trust, and help them. That's what I ask."

Neither spoke for a long time.

Preston paced around the cockpit, and sat down again. He stared at Joe, looked down at the floor of the cockpit, gazed up at the stars, back at Joe, and down again. Finally, he turned to Joe and said, "I don't mean any offense, Joe, and I'm well aware of how much you have done for me. I'll never be able to repay you. But what are you doing with these people? If I heard you right, you're talking about a retard, a Vegas showgirl, a manic-depressive photographer, some Italian gambler, and an old man with Alzheimer's. And you're telling me these are your friends, and you want me to help them? Forever?"

Joe shifted quickly in his chair, spoke in a different voice. Buck's ears shot up as he recognized Joe's tone. "Let's get a few things straight. I don't believe Johnny is a retard, Preston, although he is, fortunately or unfortunately, depending upon your point of view, classified as *mildly retarded*. In fact, I don't look at any of these people the way you've described them. But you know, Preston, it really doesn't matter. It doesn't matter how I view them. What matters is how you view them. I'm not asking you to sponsor them in your country club or even take them to your charitable balls. I'm asking you to go to them, earn their trust, and take care of them. Forever."

The conversation stopped for a few beats, with only the whine of a distant outboard motor being heard.

"Joe, I want to be honest with you. I don't think I can do that."

"Preston, I want to be honest with you. You don't have a choice."

Joe got up, patted Preston lightly on the shoulder and went to bed. Buck got up and followed.

Preston sat in the cockpit, staring at the stars as if they could give him some answers.

I can't believe Joe has gotten himself involved with these people, these 'collectibles,' whatever the hell that means. Why? Why would he do it? Why would a man like Joe, a guy with a career like his, assume responsibility for them?

And now, he asks me to do it. And just when my business looks like it's going to go and things are looking up. Even if I could offer money to these people or to Joe for these people. I know what Joe's going to say. "This is not about money." And then he'd remind me that none of this is negotiable anyway. I gave him my word that I would do whatever he asked. I can still hear him up in those damn mountains, "Are you willing and able to make a firm, irrevocable commitment to me on each of these three conditions? . . . Maybe you can't. Sometimes in life you have to have enough faith to make an irrevocable commitment. Some can, some can't . . . This . . . is about personal integrity . . . goes directly to you. To who and what you are." I'm screwed.

I've got to do something. Joe's over the top . . . but there's something about him . . . what will he do if I don't come through? I hate it, but I've got to do it. Joe's right. I don't have a choice. The question is . . . what is it I actually have to do? I'm going to bed.

CHAPTER 36

J oe woke at six, saw Preston was still asleep, and took Buck for a long walk to one of his favorite beaches. Eventually, Preston, looking as if he were still half asleep, wandered down the dock and joined them at the Jib Room.

"Morning," Preston said, as he poured himself some coffee and waited for the young owner's helper to come back in from the kitchen.

"Good morning. Sleep okay?"

"Fairly well," Preston replied. "I tossed and turned a bit. A lot to think about. I'm embarrassed about last night, Joe. I sincerely don't get what you're doing with these people or why you're doing it."

"I believe that," Joe said.

"In any event, the bottom line is, on this one, it's mine to do or die, not to question why."

"I believe that, too."

"So, I'm in, Joe. Where and when do you want me to start?"

"As I said last night, Alice can give you the contact details. She has their full names and addresses, telephone numbers, all their contact information. The one I'm most concerned about at the moment is Missy. I saw her not too long ago in Vegas. She's the one I would look up first, because she's under a lot of stress, which she gets directly from her former husband. While you're out in Vegas, you'll probably be able to connect with Tommy Greco, too. I'd start there. As far as when, I'd like you to start right away."

"Okay," Preston said. "Let me ask you this. What are you going to do?"

"Well, I'm going to give Harry a call today, see if he might want to take a vacation and fly down here for a few days and relax. Depending on where he is with himself, he can be a hell of a lot of fun. Once you've connected with these people, it can sort of take its course. I have faith in you, Preston. I believe once you get going with them, you'll know what to do."

Joe paused, noticing Preston drop his head, and then went on. "I'm at the point in my life where I'm into the moment, sort of taking it a day at a time. You know, I've spent a lifetime trying to..." Joe could still see his Uncle Howard's face that evening on the mountain, his words burning into Joe's head... *Do what the other fella can't. Be what the other fella ain't. And then help the other fella*... "do what I could to accomplish some things and help some people along the way. There comes a time when a man just has to go fishing or play golf or climb a mountain or whatever. I've done my mountain climbing, and now I just want to fish."

"Sounds good to me. I'll give Continental a call and see if I can get a flight out today. If not, tomorrow."

Joe knew the moment Harry answered that he was up. "How you doing?"

"Great, Joe. Good to hear from you. Where are you?"

"That's why I'm calling you. I'm in the Bahamas on my boat. The weather's good, and I was wondering whether you might be interested in flying down and joining me. There's an airport right in Marsh Harbour, and several flights directly from West Palm and Fort Lauderdale. What do you think?"

"Wow! I hadn't thought about that. I've got some time. Actually, the timing's great. I finished two weddings last week, and I don't have anything scheduled right now. I'd have to check out..."

"Don't worry about the cost of the airlines," Joe said. "I've got tons of frequent flyer miles that I'll never use up. I'll arrange the tickets from here and have them electronically transferred to you there."

"Man, that's great, Joe. Just let me know when."

"Today's Saturday. I'm thinking Monday. The flight gets in at

10:35 am. Get your gear together, and I'll meet you at the airport. Don't forget to bring your scuba gear."

"Great, Joe. Great! I'll see you then. And thanks for the tickets. I can't wait! See you soon."

"See you soon." Joe and Buck went back to the boat and, in an hour, were joined by Preston.

"I've made some calls to my secretary and checked in with Casey. Still no word from Marcia. She's been gone awhile. Anyway, I've made arrangements to fly out today, Joe, four-thirty this afternoon. I called Alice and got Missy's address and phone number. She works at the Frontier."

"I know."

"Are you going to talk with these people ahead of time, or am I going to just call them cold turkey and introduce myself?"

"I'll try to call them and tell them that you're somebody I'd like them to meet and vice versa."

"That's all you're going to say?"

"That's enough," Joe replied. "Get to know them."

"I know, get to know them, have them get to know me, earn their trust, and take care of them."

"Good, Preston. You're doing good."

CHAPTER 37

When Harry arrived Monday morning, Joe was at the airport to greet him. He could see Harry squeeze his oversized frame through the doorway and down the steps. What was left of his thin, blond hair was combed across his large head, trying to hide the baldness. His face, rounded by too many years of eating too many Snickers bars, had closed around his bright blue eyes, seeming to reduce them in size. He wore his khaki trousers high around his waist with a large belt, an attempt to contain his huge belly.

After Harry had cleared customs and come through the door, Joe was amazed by the size and volume of his luggage. In addition to the gigantic backpack he wore and the bag in his left hand, he was rolling an outsized bag with his right hand, and a porter was following behind with a huge cardboard box.

"Joe, great to see you!" Harry exclaimed, setting his bags down and throwing his big arms out. At that moment, as many times in the past, Harry reminded Joe of the beefy, uninhibited men he knew as a boy in the Adirondacks, full of energy, wearing a smile, always looking ready to pick up a chainsaw and take down a gargantuan tree.

"Harry, good to see you again," Joe said, shaking his hand. "You sure you brought enough gear?" he asked, laughing. "Where's your lab?"

"I left Scooter with a friend at home. I didn't want to put him through the hassle of flying, cooped up in a cage with the luggage."

"How's he doing?"

"Great, Joe. Really great."

"So what's in the box?" Joe asked.

"Surprise for you," Harry said as they made their way to the taxi and, with the help of the driver, loaded all of his luggage.

They had barely left the airport when Harry reached in his backpack and pulled out a Cannon XL Rebel digital camera, quickly attached a 300-mm lens, and began shooting. "Great spot, here. Look at those buildings. Look at the color of that water."

When they arrived at the Marsh Harbour Marina parking area, Buck was waiting in the cockpit, tail wagging.

Joe and Harry grabbed some lunch in the Jib Room – Greek salads with fresh fish on top – and caught up. Harry did most of the talking, and Joe was delighted to see him so upbeat, particularly remembering their last conversation. After eating, they sat watching the boats come and go in the harbor. Then Harry looked up at Joe with a peculiar expression that Joe couldn't read and asked, "How far are we from the ocean?"

"Not far, really. We can go out this harbor, up the sound past Treasure Cay, then a straight shot. We can probably be out there in less than an hour. You want to go fishing this afternoon?"

"Really just like to ride out there this afternoon, if you think it would be fairly calm."

"We can do that. I think today will be surprisingly flat."

Looking at the camera around Harry's neck, Joe asked, "You want to take some shots? You want to go now?"

"Yeah, I'd like to do some shooting. Let's go."

Buck, hearing the word "go," was already up, tail wagging.

Joe headed out the harbor, up the sound, past the rocks at Whale Cut, and into the ocean. He was right, it was flat, the sun high and strong, bouncing off the water. The engines purred along at cruise, and before Joe knew it, they had gone five miles. He brought the boat down, put the engines in neutral, and climbed down in the cockpit to see whether Harry was getting the shots he wanted. He couldn't believe what he saw.

"What are you doing, Harry? What is this?" Joe asked, looking at Harry assembling some kind of metal frame in the middle of the cockpit.

"This is just somethin' I thought you might like to have," Harry said with a big smile. "It's what was in the box. Have you figured out what it is?"

"Not yet. What the hell is it?"

"Well, see if this helps," Harry said as he placed the top piece on the contraption, bolted it down, and attached a heavy, coiled spring.

"Sorry," Joe said, "no clue."

"Okay, see if this helps," Harry said, reaching in his bag and pulling out a round clay pigeon. He told Joe and Buck to get back a little, as he set the pigeon in the handle at the end of the swinging arm on the frame and pulled it back against the frame. Then he pulled a small lever on the left, the arm swung out swiftly, and the clay pigeon was hurled out of the cockpit and into the air.

"Whoa!" Joe exclaimed.

"That's trap," Harry said with excitement in his voice. "Now, all you've got to do is hit it."

"Great. With what?"

"With this," Harry said, opening the door to the salon and bringing out a single-barrel shotgun, unlike any Joe had ever seen.

"How the hell did you get that past customs?"

"It didn't seem to be a problem," Harry said. "I had it checked on the plane, noted as a shotgun, with the shells in a separate shotgun box, all properly declared. I showed all that to the customs guys, signed the forms, no big deal. They said if I had any handguns, they would confiscate those, but I told them I just had the shotgun. Are you gonna talk all day, or try to hit a pigeon?"

"So this is the shooting you had in mind? Yeah, I'm ready. Give me a second and let's put Buck inside, though, to protect his ears." Joe opened the salon door, hopped up to the bridge, killed the motors, and climbed down the ladder.

"I brought along a pair of noise shields, too," Harry said, handing the headset to Joe. "You stand to my right and I'll load her up." Harry brought over an open box of clay pigeons neatly stacked between dividers, took a pigeon from the top, and placed it in the device. Harry handed Joe his shotgun. "When you're ready, say 'pull.'"

Joe admired the shotgun. "Tell me about this gun. I'm used to a Remington 1100, and I've seen several other shotguns over the years, but none like this."

"It's a Perazzi MX-3. As you can see, it's single-barrel. It's got a great feel, a great weight, and the sights are unbelievable. We're using standard trap load. Put one shell in at a time."

Joe held the gun up, sighted it, brought it back down, and then did it again. It felt amazing in his arm. He put a shell in the chamber, locked it back down, and sighted it one more time. "Pull!"

Harry pulled the lever, the pigeon went flying, Joe fired, and the pigeon exploded. Before long, Harry and Joe were haggling over the size of the bet, Joe wanting it as high as he could make it, sure that Harry would win. Joe hit the majority of his, missing when Harry sat on the side of the boat, rocking it. "You're throwing the game!" Joe complained with a smile. Joe couldn't count the pigeons he and Harry shot that afternoon, taking turns working the trap-shoot device. They shot until the entire bag of pigeons was finally emptied. Joe could not remember having so much fun in a long time. Harry did do some shooting with his camera, too, including candid shots of Joe.

Sitting comfortably in the new Stidd seats, they laughed and joked all the way back to Marsh Harbour. Joe was always amazed at what an interesting guy Harry was, all the things he had done, which he was glad to hear about again – the trap and skeet shooting contests; his photography underwater on scuba; his cabinetmaking and wood-working; the instruments he played; his hiking; camping; fishing for trout in the mountain streams and making his own flies; his cooking and baking – on and on. The list seemed endless.

"You know, Harry, there's something to be said for diversity of interests."

"What do you mean?"

"I was just thinking how fortunate you are to have such a wide variety of interests, so many different things that you know how to do. A lot of people are good at one thing or another, but that's all. Or at least that's all they're interested in. Sometime I'd like to have you meet a guy I recently did some work for. His name is Preston. He owns automobile dealerships and is all tied up in his business. I've mentioned you to him." Harry nodded.

When Joe pulled into his slip, Harry was busy taking shots with his camera. It had been a long day and a good day.

CHAPTER 38

Although Preston would have preferred to stay at the Bellagio or one of the other newer, upscale casinos, he figured it would be better to stay at the Frontier, easier for Missy. When he checked in, Nevada being three hours behind New York, his room was not yet ready. He tried Missy's cell phone, but getting no answer, he roamed around the casino and wandered into the coffee shop. He checked back with the reception desk; his room still was not ready, but the young man behind the counter told Preston he had a message and handed him an envelope. His expression soured as he was reminded of the last envelope he had opened. This was a brief note from Missy explaining that she was working the morning shift in the casino and would be off at twelve-thirty, suggesting they meet in the coffee shop at one. Preston checked his watch and, noting that it was 12:45 p.m., set out for the coffee shop, wondering how he would recognize her.

Preston left his name with the hostess, explaining that a Miss Scarlatti would be joining him, and sat down in a corner booth with red and white leather upholstery. Preston was lost in thought. The business, Marcia, everything that had happened to him in the last few months swirled in his head, and now he was embarking on this strange inherited project. His thoughts were interrupted by one of the most attractive women he had ever seen, standing in front of his table with her hand out.

"Hi, I'm Missy."

Preston started to stand up and come out of the booth, but Missy waved him to sit down.

"You're fine," she said, joining him at the table. "Nice to meet you, Mr. Wilson. How was your flight?"

"Easy. It was comfortable up front; I read a little and slept most of the way."

"Never flown first class," Missy said with a smile. "Must be nice. Anyway, glad you made it safe and sound. Where are you staying?"

"Right here, the Frontier, waiting for my room to be ready."

"Yeah, it takes awhile, particularly when the busloads come in. Probably it'll be ready around three-thirty or four. My shift started early and I'm starved. Do you mind if we order?"

"Not at all. I'll call a waitress over."

"You don't need to. She'll be here in a minute. She knows what I want anyway. Everything's pretty good here." Missy looked Preston over. "So tell me," she said, "how long do you plan to be here?"

"I'm not sure, Miss Scarlatti."

"Missy. And I plan to call you Preston, unless you've got a better idea."

"No, Preston is good." The waitress strolled over, and they ordered, Missy nodding when the waitress asked whether she wanted her usual.

"So what brings you here? All I know is that you know Joe. How do you know him?"

"I first met Joe, actually, when I was a kid – fifteen. My father dragged me up to the Adirondack Mountains for some father-son bonding. I hated it. Joe was helping his uncle, who was a guide for my dad and me. I thought he was a weird guy, Joe's uncle, but I knew a lot less than I thought I did then.

"Joe actually saved my life. I lost my footing and fell down into a deep crevice in the mountains. Somehow, the old man lowered Joe by a rope down to where I was, Joe got a rope around me, and I was hauled out of there. Pretty scary, although I acted like it was nothing. I didn't see Joe for another thirty years, but I tracked him down a few months ago. Ironically, he was up in the same mountains. I had gotten myself into a pretty bad business mess – I own some car dealerships around the country and some real estate, and I owed the banks and others a lot of money – and I'd heard that Joe was a lawyer specializing in getting business people out of messes like that."

"So you're a car guy?"

"Well, yes, I'm in the automotive business."

"You don't look like a car guy."

"No? How's that?"

"I see a lot of guys out here. Vegas gets a lot of dealer conventions, NADA, I think they call it, and a lot of other meetings involving automobile dealers. You don't have the car-guy look, that's all."

"What's the car-guy look?"

"Oh, a touch harder, gold necklace, bracelet, rings, no tie, shirt open, unbuttoned at the top. You're not even wearing a Rolex."

"I know what you mean. To tell you the truth, I don't think of myself as a car guy, either. I'm not on the sales side. I own the companies. I'd like to think I'm on the business executive side, as CEO and chairman of my companies."

"I see," Missy said. "Anyway, back to Joe. He does get a lot of people out of messes. Doesn't have to be business. He's that kind of guy. So he agreed to help you?"

"Yes, and he did. It was unbelievable. He wrote a plan and presented it to the main bank I was in trouble with. It was a very comprehensive plan. Frankly, I didn't think we had a chance. I thought I was done. But somehow, Joe convinced the bank to give me another shot. Unreal. I still can't get over it."

"That's Joe."

"How did you meet him?"

"Actually I met Joe's wife Ashley first. She was running a domestic shelter."

"A domestic shelter?"

"Yeah, a place where spouses who have been knocked around, battered, can go for help. What a fine woman. I couldn't believe she was spending her time doing that. Anyway, I got help.

"It's complicated. I wanted to get as far away as possible, where nobody would find me. Went to New York, upstate, a rural area. I was hurting for money, stayed in a small motel, cabin really. It turned out Joe owned the cabins. He was up there looking things over. That's when I first met him. He's been looking after me ever since. Anyway, I'm happy to meet any friend of Joe's. I'm just wondering what all of this has to do with me, though."

"This is a little weird, I know," Preston said. "All I can tell you is that Joe really wanted me to meet you and get to know you. He obviously thinks a lot of you. Joe knows I'm married, so it's nothing like that. I know it sounds funny, but he just wants me to get to know you."

"That's not so funny, Preston, not so hard to understand. I like the fact that Joe wants people to get to know me. Makes me feel good, important. Tell me about your wife. What's her name? What's she like?"

"Her name is Marcia. She's about your height. She's very pretty. And she's smart." *A lot smarter than I've given her credit for.* "We live in Manhattan. She used to teach psychology at Columbia. Now, she's helping schools set up gifted-children programs. She's got a lot of friends. People love her."

"How about you, Preston? Do you love her?"

"Of course."

"Any kids?"

"No, not yet."

They were quiet for a while as they ate their lunch. Preston worried that this was not going as well as it should.

Missy excused herself for a moment, telling Preston with a warm smile that she had to powder her nose. But before returning to the table, she reached in her handbag and took out her cell phone. She punched Joe's number.

"Hello?"

"Hi, Joe, it's Missy."

"Hi, are you okay? Is anything wrong?"

"I'm fine. How are you? Where are you?"

"I'm down in the Bahamas fishing. Had a great day. Actually, I was shooting trap on the back of my boat out in the ocean with a friend."

"How do you shoot trap from a boat?"

"You don't, usually. My friend Harry is pretty clever, and he rigged up a device to do it."

"I have to go, Joe, but I wanted to ask you: there's a guy here named Preston Wilson. He called me and said he was coming out, wanted to meet me, and said he knows you. He said you encouraged him to meet me. I'm having lunch with him right now. I just ducked out to go to the ladies' room. Is this guy for real?"

"I'm glad he's out there, Missy. I did suggest that he meet you and get to know you. He's not a bad guy. Born with a silver spoon in his mouth, trying to work his way out of a few problems."

"Sounds like he's got a silver corncob up his ass."

"That, too," Joe said, laughing. "But, Missy, he could use your help right now. Don't be too tough on him; it's hard being rich. Get to know him and see if there's any way you could be of help, would you?"

"Jesus, Joe. That's the first time you've ever asked me to do anything. Of course I'll help any way I can. I'm glad I caught you. Keep having fun down there and catch some fish."

"Thanks. Great to talk to you. I may be *incommunicado* for a while – the reception can be bad down here. I hope things continue to go well for you. You're quite a lady."

"Thanks," Missy said, her eyes moist. "Talk to you later." She returned to Preston just as he was hanging up his own cell phone.

"So what do you and Marcia do together?" Missy asked.

Silence for a moment. "Well, to be honest, Missy, I've been tied up with my stores, my business, flying around the country, and I haven't done a lot with Marcia lately. I come home from a trip, I'm tired. We talk a little, have a drink, that sort of thing. Once in a while we go to the opera and the ballet. Marcia likes that. And to dinners with her friends, business associates. She works out at the club. She stays in good shape."

"What's really going on, Preston? Are you having problems with Marcia? Talk to me."

"No, well, why do you say that?"

"I don't know. Just listening to you, sounds to me like there's more to the story, that's all. It's not a problem. You don't need to tell me anything. I've got enough problems of my own to deal with. So what are you going to do here while you're in Vegas? Gamble? See a show? Hook up with a woman? What?"

"Let's start over," Preston said, realizing he was getting in trouble. "I came here to get to know you. I haven't started out very well. I should have asked you a lot more about yourself. I would like to know more about you, if you're willing to talk to me about you. And let me be more forthright about Marcia. I'm too used to giving evasive answers, and I don't want to do that now. I apologize. The truth is, my wife left me a couple of weeks ago. She wrote me a note telling me that she was going to see her mother and then her college room-mate. Lord knows why she needs to see her."

"You mean the roommate?"

"Yes."

"You don't like her, I gather."

"Not really."

"Do you like her mother?"

"Not really, either."

"Marcia got a boyfriend?"

"No, or at least I don't think so. I never heard anything about that. God, I hope not."

"Have you tried to reach her?"

"No, she told me in the note that she wasn't taking her cell phone and not to call her."

"She took her cell phone with her, Preston. She's probably wonder-ing why you haven't tried to call her. She must want time to think. She must have been under a lot of pressure. Have you ever done anything to hurt her?"

"You mean physically? God, no. Why would you ask that?"

"Just asking. She must have left you for some reason. Why do you think she left?"

"You're right about her being under pressure. I had her sign a lot of personal guarantees in connection with my corporate debt. Then, when it looked like things were going to blow up, that the banks would foreclose, including on the personal guarantees, I had to get her signature on some consents and that brought the whole matter out about the risk to her in signing the guarantees. There was even discussion from our criminal lawyers about going to jail because we hadn't paid the bank back when we should've. She wasn't really at risk in terms of jail, but she was pretty upset. Mainly, she was upset because I hadn't told her about the deterioration of my business. She said she thought we were in this together."

"She sounds like she loves you. She just hates that you used her for the guarantees and weren't honest with her. Mostly, it sounds like she hates that you didn't tell her about what was going on."

"That's pretty much what she said when we last talked, or I should say, argued. Then I got a note, which I'm still not sure I understand."

"Tell me about the note," Missy said, pouring herself another cup of coffee. "This is getting interesting."

"I was on my way down to Charlotte for a big conference with the bank there, which Joe had arranged. She told me she hoped I had a good trip and that the meeting would be successful. She knew I was a nervous wreck about it, not that I said that. She said she'd been thinking a lot about us, and she's tried hard to be the wife I wanted her to be. That bothered me. I'm not sure I understood it. And then she talked about losing something, and that she thought what she had lost was her. I read the note over and over, and I still don't understand that."

"What's so hard to understand about that, Preston? Jesus. You're working all the time. You told me that. You're running around the country, being a big shot CEO. You don't spend time with your wife. You have her sign a bunch of guarantees, putting her 'at risk,' as you put it, and then you don't level with her when things start going south. You don't include her, you don't talk to her, and yet you tell me you think she's smart. She's trying to figure out where she fits into all of this because the woman she was is apparently not the woman you expect her to be. She lost herself. I get that. Why don't you get it?"

"I never thought of it that way."

"I believe that," she said, thinking, *You belong to an exclusive club of men – the All About Me Club. No wonder you wouldn't think of it that way.* "You've got to lighten up a little. Try looking at things from other people's point of view. Try to put yourself in Marcia's shoes. It's pretty understandable that she'd be talking with her mom and a former roommate somewhere. If she hasn't got a boyfriend, it's only a matter of time, I can tell you that. If you want your wife back, you better figure out where she is, go to her, and let her know you love her before it's too late."

"I'm not sure where she is..."

"Get over yourself, Preston. People can find people everywhere. Trust me. You know where her mother lives, don't you? Start there. If you really need help, I've got a friend in the casino cage that can find anybody. Give her Marcia's birth date and a few other details, and she'll tell you where she is."

"This is amazing, Missy. Thank you. You've given me a lot to think about, and I will. I'll try to reach her. Believe me."

Preston took a deep breath. "You must be tired, having worked since early this morning."

"I am. And my feet ache. It's funny, my feet didn't bother me when I was dancing up there on the stage. But walking around the casino floor, bringing drinks to God knows who, and having them stare at my boobs – that makes me tired."

"I can understand that," Preston said. "Tell me about your dancing. You look like a dancer. I can sure see you up on a stage. What happened?"

"My ex-husband happened," Missy said, looking around a bit nervously. "In fact, I've been sitting too long with you right now. He's always watching me."

"What has he done?" Preston asked.

"It's a long story. Let's just say he can't stand to have me dance, he can't stand to have other men look at me – because he loves me so much – so he demonstrates his love in a lot of ways that get pretty ugly."

"Does he hit you?"

"He has, many times, including in the arms and face, almost to the point where he made sure that I would not be able to get on the stage. That's why I had to get away, why I went to New York."

"He assaulted you. There have to be laws against that."

"Yeah, there are plenty of laws. And they're not worth a damn. I've got a protective order against him right now. It's illegal for him to bother me in any way, even talk to me or be around me. If he decides to, that court order won't be worth the paper it's written on. That's just the way it is. And if I leave Vegas, I leave the very thing I want to do most. It's a Catch-22. In any event, I've talked to you longer than I should have here. If you're around tomorrow, I get off work about the same time, and if you feel like it, we can have lunch. But we should get together in another restaurant, someplace quieter and off the strip. There's a nice place between the strip and downtown called Charley's."

"I would really like that." Preston gave his cell phone number, told her his room number, and told her he would find Charley's and meet her there at 1:30 p.m., if that worked for her.

Preston sat there for another hour, thinking about the amazing conversation he just had. *I came here worried about what I'm doing here talking to her, and she spends all the time enlightening me. Incredible.*

CHAPTER 39

Preston, checking at the front desk, was pleased to find that his room was finally ready. After he shaved and showered, all the time thinking about his conversation with Missy, he threw himself into the large chair by the desk, put his feet up, and gazed out the window at the strip. Then he remembered he had told Tommy Greco he would call when he got in. He dialed the number Alice had given him.

"Greco," Tommy said.

"Hello, Mr. Greco. My name is Preston Wilson. We spoke briefly on the phone and arranged to meet out here. I told you I'd call when I got in."

"Yeah, I remember. What's it you want?"

Silence for a moment. *I can't see telling this guy I'm here to get to know him and earn his trust. Now what?* "Is it possible, Mr. Greco, that we could meet someplace, have a cup of coffee?"

"You hittin' on me? I'm not that kind of guy, you know what I mean? You still haven't told me what you want. My time's valuable, Mr. Preston."

"Well . . . I'm at the Frontier."

"Good for you," Tommy said.

"Where are you, Mr. Greco?"

"I'm in an important business meeting at the moment with some significant business associates. We're discussing some opportune situationals in which we believe a healthy economic environment could happen."

"How long do you think you'll be? Would you be able to meet for dinner?"

"Now you've asked me two questions. I can meet for dinner, you doing the lifting."

"Doing the lifting?"

"Yeah, you know, picking up the tab."

"I can do that."

"Next, as to how long I'm going to be, that depends on the progression of our discussions here. One of my associates is a dickhead, and that makes our progression a lot slower."

Preston could hear a commotion over the phone. "Sorry," Tommy said, "my last pronouncement created the unintended effect of a commotional, which then I, in turn, had to resolve."

Preston could not believe he was having this conversation. He wanted to quit, but knew he had to keep going. "Where would you like to have dinner, Mr. Greco?"

"How's Barrymore's Steakhouse, end of the strip?"

"Good. Does six o'clock work for you?"

"No, it don't."

"When would you like to have dinner?"

"I have to go over to Caesar's, check some action, see a few people. How's eight?"

"Eight it is," Preston said, glad the negotiation was over. "I'll see you at Barrymore's Steakhouse at eight."

Tommy hung up. Preston did, too, staring at his phone, before he called Barrymore's and made a reservation for two. After a nap, he showered again and dressed for dinner, deciding that tonight's meeting did not require a tie and that his blue blazer and an open blue Oxford shirt would be enough.

Barrymore's consisted of three large rooms with a fourth private room in the back. The décor was heavy English, a lot of wood, gas lights behind stained glass, white tablecloths, heavy china. As the maître d' took Preston to his table in the second large room to the left, he told Preston over his shoulder, "I think it was a wise decision for you to go to your table now if you are expecting Mr. Greco. He customarily arrives a little late."

He was right. Preston sat in the restaurant for forty minutes, munching on bread. When Tommy finally arrived, he appeared to do it in a burst, coming out of nowhere, walking in and sitting down all in one motion. Wearing black slacks, a black belt with a silver buckle, and a black shirt, open at the top, he seemed to have no chin. And no apology for being late.

"So you're Wilson."

Preston stood up and extended his arm. "I am. Please call me Preston, Mr. Greco. It's good to meet you." Tommy shook his hand with an iron grip.

"Pleased to meet you, too," Tommy said. At that point, a tall, thin waiter who looked like he had been on Social Security for a while came to take their drink orders.

"Would you like some wine?" Preston asked.

"I'll just have a beer," Tommy said. "You go ahead."

Preston ordered a bottle of Merlot. Tommy seemed to change his mind and ordered Chianti. "So, Preston, what's the deal? What's going on? I don't have a problem with you buying me dinner, but tell me, what's going on?"

"We have a mutual friend, it seems. Joe Hart. He's the one who suggested that I meet with you."

"You know Joe?"

"Yes," Preston replied, his legs bobbing.

"How do you know Joe?"

"I first met him years ago when I was a kid up in the Adirondack Mountains. More recently, actually a month ago or so, I asked Joe to do some work for my company, Wilson Holdings."

"What kind of work?"

"My company owns several large automobile dealerships around the country. A few of the dealerships had developed some financial difficulties with the banks providing them floor plan financing and loans..."

Their conversation was interrupted by the waiter, who had brought their drinks and now wanted to take their order: two eighteen-ounce New York strip sirloins, Preston's well done, Tommy's rare.

"And so your guys went SOT," Tommy asked, "and put you in jeopardation?"

"Actually, that's just what happened," Preston said after waiting a beat and suppressing a laugh. "I was in serious financial trouble, a lot of zeroes behind the numbers. I asked Joe to help me out of it, although I had real doubts that anything could be done. Joe figured out a way to turn it all around. He met with the lead bank. It was amazing. I still can't believe it."

"Yeah. Joe could do that. So Joe asked you to look me up?" Tommy tore into his steak with a large, black-handled steak knife. Holding the knife up in his beefy right hand, he looked at Preston and said, "I love these fuckin' things."

"Yes. He asked me to find you and get to know you."

"Why? If Joe needed me for something, he'd just call me."

"No, it's not Joe needing you for anything. It's that Joe thought I should meet you. That I should get to know you, and vice versa, as he put it. May I call you Tom?" Preston asked.

"No. Tommy. So you flew all the way out here because Joe thought it would be good if you met me?"

"That's right," Preston replied. "And so you could get to know me, too."

"You sure you're leveling with me?" Tommy said. "You're not looking for money, some financing to help with them car dealerships? I know people with money, you know. I can be a facilitational guy."

"Actually, my meeting you has nothing to do with money. Thanks to Joe, the banks are restructuring our debt and providing the flooring plans we need. Our workout is on track, actually better than I expected. What are you doing here, Tommy? Can you tell me a little bit about you?"

"I'm a businessman here in Vegas. I..."

Tommy's answer was interrupted by Preston's cell phone. Preston looked at it and was about to shut it off when he noticed that it was Missy's number.

"Tommy, I've got to take this," he said. Tommy nodded, picked up his steak knife, lavished a huge piece of butter on the last piece of bread in the basket, shoved the bread and butter in his mouth, and ordered more.

"What? Missy. Are you all right? What?" Preston could hardly hear her soft voice, which sounded as if she were crying. He heard enough to know she was in trouble. "Where are you? Where is that?" Preston said, asking Tommy if he had a pen. Tommy nodded and reached in the side pocket of his trousers. Preston grabbed it and wrote on a napkin. "I'll be there shortly," he said and hung up.

"Who's Missy?"

"She's another friend of Joe's that I met just this afternoon. She sounds like she's in trouble."

"We're out of here," Tommy said, getting up from the table and motioning to the waiter for a check. The waiter rushed it over, handing the bill to Tommy. Tommy glanced at it and handed it to Preston.

"Here, pay it in cash and let's go," Tommy said.

Preston, glancing at the check, left a $100 bill on the table. Tommy reached in his pocket and matched Preston's bill. Then they left.

Outside the restaurant, Preston started to look for a taxi, but Tommy told him to get in the black limousine, which Preston hadn't noticed.

"Is this yours?" Preston asked as they got in.

"It's a convenience that is appropriated to me on certain occasions," Tommy said. "Give me the napkin."

Tommy gave the driver the address and told him to step on it. The limousine took off, and within fifteen minutes they found themselves in a quiet neighborhood of inexpensive townhouses close together, all looking alike. Preston knocked on the hollow sounding door. Missy opened it slightly, and then, seeing Preston, took off the chain and motioned him in. Tommy followed.

"This is Tommy Greco, Missy. Tommy, Missy Scarlatti. Tommy is a friend of Joe's, as well. He and I were having dinner when you called. I hope you don't mind my being here with him, but the way you sounded, I really thought I should come right over."

"Tommy Greco!" Missy said, as she motioned for the two men to sit on the couch in her small living room. She was wearing sunglasses and her hands were shaking as she lowered herself into the chair next to the couch. "Joe mentioned your name to me, said I ought to meet you some time. It's good to meet you, Tommy. I didn't mean to interrupt your dinner." She lowered her voice. "I just wanted to call and cancel tomorrow's lunch. I'm not going in to work in the morning."

"What happened? Are you all right?"

"I'm all right," Missy said, rising to get a drink of water. "Can I get you guys anything?"

"No, nothing," Tommy said. "Preston here just bought me a big dinner. I can't believe you and I live in the same town and both know Joe and don't know each other. What a coincidental. Anyway, any friend of Joe's is a friend of mine, and I'm pleased to meet you."

"Missy. Please call me Missy. I agree with you; us living here, both knowing Joe. We should know each other. Preston, too. I spent some time getting to know him this afternoon. I enjoyed the talk, but I apparently spent a little too much time."

"Did he see us talking?"

"Who?" Tommy asked.

"My ex," Missy said.

"Okay, I get it," Tommy said. "Take the shades off."

Missy shook her head no. "There's nothing we can do. If I call the police and tell them that he's violated the protective order, they can arrest him. Then he'll get out, then he'll find me again. Then . . . it'll be worse."

"There's got to be something that can be done, Missy. Obviously, you've got a lawyer. Can you call your lawyer and see what he recommends?"

"It's a she," Missy said. "And I know what she recommends. She wants me to leave town, go hide, just like I did the last time this happened. I went all the way to New York and hid in a motel up in the mountains, a place that Joe owns. He looked after me all that time. I could have stayed there, but I wanted to come back. I dreamed about being a showgirl out here, a dancer, and for a while, and with a lot of hard work, I made my dream come true. Like I told you this afternoon, Preston, if I leave here, I'll never get back in the show. If I don't..."

"I think we should call the police," Preston said.

"I don't," Tommy said. "Missy, what's your ex-husband's name?"

"Sam O'Brien," Missy said in a whisper.

"This prick's Irish?" Tommy asked. "And you're using your maiden name?"

"Yes to both," Missy said. "I'm from Lyons, New York, originally."

"I know Lyons," Tommy said. "Small little town between Buffalo and Syracuse, right? I knew some vending machine guys up there. Also, a great area for... well, a lot of book comes from up there. Good to know you, Scarlatti." Tommy smiled. "So where's Sammy the Prick work?"

"He used to work as a stagehand for the show at the Aladdin. Now he works for some company that does stage management for different shows on the strip. I haven't talked with him in a long time, tried not to, and I don't really know where he's working now."

"What's he look like?" Tommy said. "Got a picture of him?"

"I burned the pictures," Missy said, looking down as if she were trying not to cry. "But he has to have an ID picture on file somewhere."

"What's his birth date?" Preston asked, wishing he were more involved in the conversation and feeling useless.

"December 4, 1974."

Tommy took a small piece of white paper from his shirt pocket and jotted down the date.

"Do you mind taking them glasses off, Missy, so we can see what it looks like and whether we can get you something to make it easier?"

"Yes, I do, Tommy, but thanks. I know the drill. All too well. I've got a compress, I've got medicine, I'll take care of it. Thanks."

"Okay," Tommy said. "We'll leave you alone. You get some rest." Tommy wrote a number on a card and gave it to her. "Stay in tonight and tomorrow. Keep the door locked. He shows up tonight, and you have any more trouble, you call me at this number. It was good to meet you."

"Again, thank you. I can't believe you're helping me like this, Tommy," Missy said.

"No problem," Tommy said. "I'm from Niagara Falls, our side. I know what it's like to have people after you, mistreating you ... in a lot of ways. My father knocked me around a lot, and my brother ... well, he became an abuser in a different way. I also know what it feels like to try to make a life for yourself; try to improve ... like reach another level ... and then things keep holding you back. I'm a little rough, Missy, in my presentation. I'm working on it. I think you're a first class lady. To be honest with you, I hope we can see more of each other, and I mean that in a respectful way. Like I said, you've got my number."

"You know where to reach me as well," Preston interjected and handed her his card. "I would appreciate it if you could call me tomorrow on my cell and tell me how you're doing."

With that, Preston and Tommy stood and headed to the door. Missy touched Preston's arm lightly. "Thank you for coming over, Preston. You, too, Tommy. You guys didn't have to do that." Her eyes sharply focused on each of them.

Preston and Tommy left the apartment and walked to the waiting limo. Tommy asked Preston where he wanted to go.

"Frontier," Preston answered. Tommy leaned forward to the driver.

"I really feel awful about Missy," Preston said. "Her ex-husband is insanely jealous and can't stand to see her talk with another man, or even be looked at or admired on the stage. She told me about it this afternoon. He's been haunting her for a long time. Apparently, the law is of no help in a situation like this. I wish I wasn't the one she had been seen talking to. What a mess."

"It ain't about you. It wouldn't have mattered whether she was seen with you or some other guy. This guy's a prick. He needs an educational. Don't worry about Missy. She ain't gonna be bothered anymore by this guy."

Preston didn't know what to say to that, so they rode along in silence for a while. At the Frontier, Tommy turned to him and asked, "You shoot, Preston?"

Again, Preston didn't know what to say.

"Hey, I'm talking to you," Tommy said, whacking Preston in the arm. "You play craps?"

"No, I don't know how to play craps. Anyway, I don't gamble."

"You shittin' me? You a car guy, you gamble. How about cigars? You smoke cigars?"

"No, but I like the smell of them."

Tommy told the driver to hand him the box of cigars in the front seat. He grabbed a handful. Then he told the driver to wait. He turned to Preston and showed him the cigars.

"If you like the smell of cigars, trust me, you're gonna love the smell of these babies, and the taste. And it's time you learned to shoot craps. We'll start here at the Frontier, but we'll probably end up at Caesar's. You go in and get comfortable, whatever. I've got a few phone calls I've gotta make. I'll meet you at the crap tables in a half an hour."

CHAPTER 40

Preston reached for his watch. He looked at it and then looked again. It was noon. He couldn't remember what time he'd finally gotten back to his room, but he knew it was early in the morning. He had met Tommy at the tables at the Frontier, where Tommy took him to a crap table not in use and explained the game. He told Preston where and how to bet and which numbers on the table to stay away from. He advised him to bet "right way" with three chips on the pass line, and then to keep it simple, depending on the number, back them up with three chips more for a 4 or 10, four chips for a 5 or 9, and three chips for a 6 or 8. He showed him how to bet all the numbers and how to take odds on them. Preston was ready, surprising Tommy with how fast he was picking it up. Tommy took him down to the end of a table with a $25 minimum, and they began to play. Preston was leery at first, but it didn't take long, when the shooter made his point, for Preston to like the payoff on the odds and the amount he won. Besides, he loved Tommy's lingo and style at the tables, and got a kick out of the other players, too.

For several hours, Preston forgot about automobile dealerships, Missy, or any other problem. He wished Marcia could see him now, shooting craps and smoking cigars with Tommy Greco. He wondered what she would think. They kept at it way into the night, leaving the Frontier for the Mirage, and then ending up at Caesar's. Preston vaguely remembered Tommy's limo dropping him at the Frontier. He did remember, at the end of the evening, Tommy telling him that, for a shithead, he was an okay guy.

Preston's message light was not on, and his cell phone showed no messages. He shaved and showered, wondering about Missy. Why didn't she call? He made a reservation for a San Francisco flight, called Alex, checked out, and called Tommy to thank him, and let him know where he could be reached. Tommy asked if Missy had called.

At the airport, before Preston boarded, he tried Missy, relieved when she answered.

"How are you doing? I was worried when you didn't call this morning."

"I'm a lot better today. Thanks. Took some Tylenol PM, slept late, then got something to eat. I'm doing a lot better, I really am. And it's been quiet here. No problems last night and none today. Like I told Tommy when he called, I'll take it a day at a time, but I am going back to work."

Preston said he'd be in touch, and made sure she had all of his numbers. "By the way, I want to thank you for the conversation you had with me yesterday afternoon. I'm sorry that talking to me got you into all of this. I got a lot out of our conversation, particularly the conversation about Marcia. You helped me, Missy. Thank you."

"I didn't do anything, really. And don't worry about my talking to you. Wouldn't have mattered whether it was you or some other guy."

"That's what Tommy said. My plane's being called; I'll talk to you later."

"Talk to you, Preston. Have a good flight. I hope you find her."

It was a short flight to San Francisco and Alex was waiting out front in a new Cadillac Escalade.

"How you doing?" Alex said, shaking his hand as Preston climbed in the front seat. "Good to see you."

"You, too."

"Where you been?" Alex asked as he drove them to the dealership.

"I was coming straight out, but I stopped in Vegas on the way."

"No kidding? I didn't know you were a Vegas guy."

"I didn't either," Preston said. "I've been to Vegas a few times for conventions, and put a couple of quarters in a slot machine every now and then, seen some shows. But this trip was different; I really enjoyed it. Got a lot out of it."

"That mean you won, got lucky, or both?"

"I won a little money, but the good part was seeing some friends. Tell me about the dealership. How are we doing? Give me the details."

They talked business the rest of the day. Alex took him on a tour, introducing him to each employee, pointing with obvious pride to all the improvements these people had made. Although he had been there before on several occasions, it was as if Preston were seeing his own dealership for the first time. He could feel the respect that the managers, salesmen, and other employees had for Alex, and he admired Alex's easy but in-control manner. When he got to the financial department, he was surprised to see Casey, working alongside the bookkeeper and controller.

"Casey! I didn't know you were coming out here."

"I didn't either, but Fred, our bookkeeper, had some questions and I thought it would be better to talk about it personally, and handle it hands-on. Fred's been doing a good job."

Preston reviewed financial reports with Casey and Alex, then the three of them met in a private office to go over the current status with the bank. Preston was impressed and delighted with the progress, and with how satisfied the bank seemed to be, under the circumstances.

Within half an hour, the conference room was packed, with the door open and other employees standing outside the room. Preston realized this was the first time he had met any of them.

"Thank you," he said, addressing the group, "for being here." Everyone laughed. "Seriously, I really do want to thank each and every one of you for the job you are doing. It's no secret that this dealership, and some other dealerships of Wilson Holdings, ran into financial difficulties. I take responsibility for that. I realize today that I am meeting most of you for the first time. That should not have been the case, and I take responsibility for that, too.

"This afternoon, I took a detailed look around this store. Thanks to the leadership of Alex, Casey, and each of you, I can see tremendous change. For one thing, I don't ever remember seeing the service area floor so clean." Everyone laughed again. "No, I'm serious. I never have. That says a lot. And in a way, it's emblematic of what's going on in this store and all of our stores from this point forward. With your help, we're going to be squeaky clean in every department, financially and otherwise; in all of our dealings with the bank, with our customers, and with each other. I promise you that. And I thank you for staying with me and for giving me 100 percent. I'm proud of you and I hope that down the road, you will feel proud of me, too. Thank you."

Preston sat down, but everyone else stood and filled the room with applause. He looked around at Alex and at Casey; they all grinned.

After dinner Preston made a series of phone calls, at last locating Marcia.

"I'm so glad I found you and that you took my call. I have so much to tell you. I won't take your time tonight, except to say that our business situation – yours and mine – is in better shape now in many ways than we've ever been. Our meeting in Charlotte went exceptionally well – thanks to Joe Hart – far better than I expected. I'm not going to jail. Neither are you. No one is. The banks are working with us, Marcia, and we're going to pay them back, without any exposure on your part."

"That's good news. Very good."

"I wanted to tell you that, but that's not why I called. I called to tell you that I've been a horse's ass where you're concerned for a long time. I want to apologize. You deserve far better from me. I really would appreciate it if you would give me the opportunity to talk to you. Please. It would mean a lot."

"I'm with my girlfriend now, as you somehow have figured out. When did you want to talk?"

"I'm flying back to New York from San Francisco in the morning,"

Preston said. "There really is nothing more important to me right now than to talk with you as soon as I can. You tell me where and when. I'll be there."

"Really?" Marcia said. "I just got here from Mother's house, and I would like to stay with Ann a few days."

"That's a good idea," Preston said.

"Really?" Marcia said again. "How about we talk at the condo in a few days, say next Friday. I have to pick up some things there anyway. How would that be?"

"That would be just fine. Great. Thank you. I'll be there, and I'll look forward to seeing you on Friday. I appreciate it, Marcia. And I love you. I really mean that."

"I'll see you Friday," Marcia said and hung up.

"Was that him?" Ann asked.

"I can't believe he found me. It's weird. I don't know if I'm happy or sad."

"Maybe both," Ann said. "I'm pissed that you have to go through this. Why can't he leave you alone?"

"I'd like to think it's because he loves me."

"He loves himself, Marcia. That's who he loves."

"Actually, it's the other way around. I wish he loved himself more."

"What are you going to do? Are you going back?"

"I need some clothes, and Pres wants to talk, so I agreed to meet him next Friday. I don't know, Ann. When I was little, my favorite doll broke. I took it to my dad, God love him, and he looked the doll over. He said, *'Well, honey, we can try to fix it, or we can get you a new one. If we fix it, it won't be perfect. If we get a new one, it won't be your favorite.'* That's the way I feel now. I love Preston, and there's a good man underneath all this. But I can't wait forever for him to come out. I'll lose myself in the process."

"Wow."

Marcia started to cry. "There's more. I'm pregnant."

"Oh My God! Is Preston..."

"Yes, of course he's the father."

"Jesus. Let's pig out on a huge pizza."

"And some Sam Adams! ... No, wait, hold the beer."

CHAPTER 41

Preston called the airlines to change his flight. Since Marcia wouldn't be in the city until Friday and he had almost a week, he'd go to Braydon, meet Johnny, and look up Mr. Corrigan. Joe had said he wanted him to connect. At least he'd get started with these people as soon as possible, and after meeting Missy and Tommy, he could see why.

On the plane, his mind was full. What a difference a few weeks could make. Autoplaza in control and doing well; Casey a different guy; Alex. Getting to know Missy, Tommy. And Marcia. And maybe even himself.

Driving into Braydon late that afternoon, Preston was surprised at what a delightful town it was, beginning with Braydon's welcome sign. Preston loved New York City, but he saw for the first time why somebody might like to live in a place like this. Downtown consisted mostly of two-story wooden buildings, many with balconies overlooking the street. Flowerpots accented the balconies and the windows and the quaint stores, each adorned with a colorful display. Plenty of places to park and no parking meters. And it was quiet – no honking horns, no sirens, just people and traffic moving calmly along the clean sidewalks and streets.

Preston first went to Joe's law office. He wanted to meet Alice in person, catch her before she left for the day. He was surprised to find that Joe's office was actually in an old, restored house. He met Alice and found her delightful and charming, the type of woman to whom one feels invited to tell everything. Preston was doing just that.

They talked about Braydon for a while, sitting on the front porch drinking iced tea. What a contrast from Whitcock Stevenson. If only Brookfield could see him now. Preston told Alice what a wonderful job Joe did in Charlotte, and how he somehow convinced the bank to go along with his plan. Alice listened and smiled. Preston told her about his visit with Missy and meeting Tommy Greco.

"Missy's quite a pretty young lady, isn't she?" Alice said.

"She certainly is. And smart, too. Insightful." Alice simply smiled and rocked in her chair.

"And tell me about Mr. Greco; he's quite a character. How did that go?"

"He tried to corrupt me with gambling and cigars."

Alice laughed. "Where are you off to now?"

"I passed the Home Dairy to see Johnny on my way into Braydon."

"Yes, on South Main Street."

"I need . . . want to meet him, Alice. Can you tell me a little bit about him? How did Joe become friends with Johnny?"

"I'll let Johnny speak for himself, but I will tell you that Joe's wife Ashley, bless her heart, did so much for us. Apart from her work with charities and cancer, the unemployed homeless were among her major concerns, which led her to look into the mental health departments of our state. She encouraged the development of an outreach program to put mildly mentally challenged patients who qualified to work in the community.

"What really upset her, and Joe, was that Johnny's mother and father had apparently dumped him in the state's mental hospital as an infant. There is no evidence that Johnny is actually retarded, but having grown up in a mental institution that's all he's ever known. Joe couldn't get over what happened to Johnny, and he's looked after him ever since."

Alice and Preston were silent for a while.

"Do you think he's there now, and that I could meet him?"

"Yes, but I suggest we call Mr. Niemeyer, the owner, first, explain the situation to him. Would you like me to do that?"

"I really would. Thanks."

"Hello, Stanley," he heard Alice say. "How are you all doing? I

swear, I can smell you baking up something delicious right now."
Laughter. "I'm calling you to ask if it's all right with you if a friend
of Joe's from out of town comes down there to see what really good
Southern food tastes like." More laughter. "And good baking, too.
Oh, and Stanley, while he's there, he wants to meet Johnny. You
know how Joe goes on and on about Johnny, how much he likes him.
This fella's heard so much about Johnny from Joe, he wants to meet
him himself. Would that be okay with you? Right. In the kitchen.
Okay, good to talk with you, Stanley. Bye now."

"Thanks, Alice," Preston said. "Would you like to join me for
dinner?"

"I thought you'd never ask, Mr. Wilson. And it's about that time.
Before we go, unless you've already made arrangements, we should
see about getting you a place to stay tonight."

Preston had completely forgotten about that. Alice made a call,
and suggested that Preston follow her to the Home Dairy, where
they could park out back.

As they walked in, the smell of the pastries filled Preston's nose.
He followed Alice, filled his tray, and enjoyed a sumptuous meal.
When Stanley Niemeyer came by their table to say hello, he wore a
full, white apron and a baker's cap at least a foot high. He left freshly
made raspberry tarts on their table.

Following dinner, they took their trays to the serving window,
where Preston saw Johnny at work.

"Hi, Johnny," Alice called through the window. "We're coming
into the kitchen. I've got someone who wants to meet you."

"Hi," Johnny repeated with a broad grin.

Alice led Preston through the swinging doors to the kitchen and
over to Johnny's workstation. Johnny was busy clearing the china and
silverware off the trays, pushing the uneaten food and napkins into
the garbage drop. He was covered with sweat, his white apron dark
and soiled in front. Johnny turned around and smiled.

"This is Preston Wilson," Alice said. "Mr. Wilson lives in New
York City, Johnny. He's a friend of Joe's. He came here to meet you.
Mr. Niemeyer said it's okay."

"Hi, I'm Johnny," he said, holding out his wet hand for Preston to shake.

Preston shook Johnny's hand with a trace of reluctance.

"I'll leave you two to get to know each other," Alice said. "Thank you for dinner, Preston, and for our delightful talk this afternoon. Call me if there's anything you need. I hope you enjoy your visit to Braydon. If you leave before I speak with you, you come back and see us soon." With that, she said goodbye and left through the back door.

Preston did not have a clue where to start with Johnny, who had simply gone back to work, clearing the trays and feeding the dishwasher. Preston had never seen a man working as a dishwasher in a commercial kitchen. After a while he sensed a certain rhythm in Johnny's actions.

"That's a pretty neat operation," he called to Johnny over the noise.

Johnny said nothing, kept working.

"It's good to meet you, Johnny. How's it going?" he said in a loud voice. Nothing.

Finally, Preston tapped Johnny on the shoulder. Johnny turned around quickly, the dish sprayer hanging down in his right hand. As Johnny turned, the hot spray hit Preston right in the face, and then proceeded down the entire front of his polo shirt and Italian leather belt and trousers. Within seconds, he was dripping wet.

"Uh oh. Man got wet. Johnny sorry. What man want?"

Preston just stood there, dripping. *At least the water's clean and hot,* he thought. "Call me Preston," he said.

"What's Preston?" Johnny asked.

"My name. My name's Preston, Johnny."

"Funny name. Funny name," Johnny said. "Pressdon?"

"Close enough." He paused. "I like that machine," Preston said, pointing first to the dishwasher and then the rest of the apparatus. "Show me how it works."

"Pressdon all wet. All wet. Johnny get towel." With that, Johnny went to a linen cupboard in a corner and brought Preston a large, white towel, a smaller one, and a white apron. Preston wiped his head and face with the hand towel and blotted his shirt and pants to soak up as much of the water as he could. He looked at the apron for a while and decided what the hell, he had gone this far. Johnny smiled.

"Johnny got helper," he said. "Johnny show Pressdon how."

Johnny showed him how to reach out and catch the trays, how to clear them, use the sprayer, and load the machine. Preston went through the whole process once, thanked Johnny, then moved away from the table and took his apron off.

"Don't feel bad, Pressdon. Get better. Need practice. Okay." Johnny finished off the last of the trays and then, with great care, washed all of the equipment down and dried it.

Preston stood by and watched, admiring Johnny's efficiency. Then Johnny took off his apron, soiled white T-shirt and his white pants, and stuffed them into a commercial washer. From a narrow locker he pulled out clean blue jeans and a shirt. After he dressed, he went up to a small mirror on the back wall, combed his thin hair, and turned to Preston.

"Johnny turn lights off. Johnny go home now. Pressdon leave now. Pressdon good start. Pressdon learn. Takes practice. No feel bad."

With that, Johnny turned all the lights off, took Preston by the arm, and led him out the back door, setting the locks on the door before he closed it.

"Where do you live, Johnny?" Preston asked. "I can give you a ride home."

"Johnny live at home. Johnny can walk."

"I'll be glad to drive you there," Preston said. "Can you show me where it is?"

"Johnny not supposed to get in car."

"It's okay, Johnny. I'm a friend of Joe's."

Johnny appeared to think about that. "Okay," he said and climbed in Preston's car. When they drove out of the parking lot and onto Main Street, Johnny pointed the way to his home, and in a few minutes, Preston pulled up to a large, beige-colored house with a wraparound porch.

"Johnny live here," Johnny said. "Johnny get out now."

Preston pulled over to the curb, shut the rental car off, and got out and walked around to the passenger side as Johnny got out.

"Thanks for showing me how to wash the dishes, Johnny. It was good to meet you."

"How's Buck?" Johnny asked.

"Buck's great," Preston said, happy to finally have a conversation with Johnny. "I saw him with Joe not long ago on Joe's boat in the Bahamas."

"No trouble for Johnny with Buck. Buck likes Johnny. Buck no like the bad man. Buck hurt bad man. Bad man not come back. Bad man afraid. Buck Joe's friend. Buck Johnny's friend. Pressdon practice. Pressdon be good dishwasher."

"Okay, Johnny. I'll come see you again." Preston shook his hand.

"Know what?" Johnny asked, taking Preston by surprise.

"What?"

"In movies when bad man get shot, not really dead."

Preston thought about that. "That's right, Johnny. But what about when the bad man gets stabbed?"

"Oh, then he's dead."

Preston burst out laughing. Johnny sat quietly.

"Why Pressdon laugh at Johnny?"

Still laughing, Preston told Johnny, "I'm not laughing at you. It's just what you said is funny."

Johnny stared at Preston. "Not nice to laugh at people. Johnny knows. Johnny not stupid. Pressdon got funny name. Johnny not laugh. Johnny not stupid, Pressdon, just 'retarded.'"

Silence. *He's right, he's not stupid. I wish I could say the same for me sometimes.*

"I'm sorry, Johnny. I really am. I don't think you're stupid, and I didn't mean for you to think I was laughing at you. I won't do it again."

Johnny stared at Preston for several moments, and then said, "It's okay. Don't feel bad. People make mistakes."

Preston wondered what on earth he could say. Finally: "Johnny, do you know how to play catch with a baseball?"

"Johnny good catcher. Good thrower, too."

"Could you and I do that some time?"

"Johnny good. Johnny and Pressdon do that some time."

"I'll be back to see you Johnny, that's a promise. Thanks for spending this time with me."

"Bye. Johnny go now," he said and walked up the steps, onto the porch, and into the home.

Preston drove to a nearby motel, where Alice had made arrangements for him to stay, and dialed her.

"How'd it go with Johnny?" Alice asked. "I'm sure he appreciated making a new friend."

"It went pretty well, Alice. But I think I'm the one who got more out of it. I hope I'm not calling you too late."

"No, not at all. Is there something you need?"

"Yes, well, I just wondered, do you happen to know where I might go to get information on educational opportunities for mentally challenged individuals like Johnny?"

Alice was quiet for a minute. "Actually I do. Joe has an entire Johnny file. Hang on a minute. Actually there are two cabinets relating to Johnny – several files of Ashley's and others Joe developed. Give me another couple of minutes."

In a couple of minutes she had it. "Here it is. There's one called *'Educational Opportunities for Those Left Behind.'* Joe got into this in a big way before Ashley died, but he hasn't touched the file since. I'm sure he won't mind your looking at it."

"Thanks a lot, Alice. By the way, do you have anything in there on Johnny's background?"

"I think so. Wait, I'll check."

After several minutes, Alice came back to the phone.

"Ashley did considerable research on Johnny's history. There are three of her folders on that."

"Great. Thanks, Alice. I'll pick them up in the morning on my way out, if that's okay?"

"Of course. See you then."

Chapter 42

Preston woke early, checked out, and drove to Joe's office where Alice had coffee and the files waiting.

Preston drove to Charleston, then north along the route Alice had given him to Corey's house. He made good time, arriving shortly after ten, rang the doorbell, and at last knocked on the door. No response. Checking the number of the house against his notes, he could see Corrigan Yachts' faded name painted against the old barn behind the house.

Preston hoped he had not come this far to miss Corey Corrigan. He decided to check the entrance facing the waterway, but again no one answered. He did notice a cigar in an ashtray, still lit, with smoke, on a porch table in front of two rocking chairs.

He noticed that a large sliding door to the barn was open. Preston strolled in. It was quiet, the smell of wood and sawdust permeating the air. Past an impressive selection of saws and power tools to an open door, the strong, cool breeze came through the building.

"It's nice in here, ain't it, young fella?" A man in blue denim overalls seemed to come out of nowhere. "What can I do for you, young man?"

"Hi, are you Mr. Corrigan?"

"One and the same," Corey replied. "People around here call me Corey. What's your name?"

"Preston. Preston Wilson," he said, shaking Corey's hand. "You have a nice place here. I knocked at your house looking for you, but no one answered, so I came out here to find you. I hope you don't mind."

"Why would I mind?" Corey said. "Always glad to see young people. You like wood?"

"I do," Preston replied, glad that Corey seemed so willing to take him in and show him around. "I like the smell of it in here."

"If you like the smell, that's a good first step," Corey said. "Come with me; I'll show you around."

Corey pointed out various pieces he had made and pointed out different features – the fit, the grain. He explained the equipment, the tools, the lifts. Preston liked Corey immediately; he found the man charming. And he was impressed with his work.

After the tour, Corey told Preston it was time for a cigar and suggested that they go to his porch and sit for a while. Corey shuffled to the rocking chair on the left and sat down, motioning for Preston to join him. Corey reached in the breast pocket of his crisscrossed coveralls and pulled out a cigar. He bit the end off and spat it out, felt in the right pocket of his coveralls, and pulled out a box of wooden matches. He lit the cigar and turned to Preston. "Barbara tells me I'm not supposed to have more than one of these a day," he said with a smile. "Want one?"

"Yes, actually, I do," Preston said. "Thank you."

Corey reached in the same breast pocket and pulled out another cigar and handed it to Preston, then gave him the box of wooden matches. Preston bit off the end the same way he'd watched Corey do, spit it out, and lit his cigar. Far from the quality of the cigars he had had in Vegas with Tommy, and it made him want to spit, but he kept the comparison to himself.

The two men sat on the porch, rocking and smoking as if they had known each other thirty years instead of thirty minutes. Corey never asked Preston why he was there or what he wanted; he simply accepted him. He did ask if Preston wanted some iced tea. Preston said yes, so Corey went into the house and returned with two glasses of iced tea stuffed with a bunch of green mint.

"That mint's what makes it good," Corey said, as they sipped their iced tea and smoked their cigars, watching boats go up and down the waterway.

"Are you doing a lot of woodwork these days?" Preston asked.

"You bet, young fella. I'm keepin' busy."

"Is Barbara your wife?"

"My wife's gone," Corey said. "Barbara's my daughter. Looks after me. She's a fine girl."

"Can you give me her address and phone number, Corey?"

"She's a fine girl. Whaddya do, young fella?"

"Call me Preston, please. I'm in the automobile business," Preston said. "And I own some real estate. I know Joe Hart, and he suggested that I get to know you."

"Joe Hart?"

"Yes, you know Joe Hart, I believe, Corey."

"We used to make big yachts, you know, right here – wooden yachts – real boats, not like today. My daddy taught me to make boats. He was good. Real good. His daddy taught him. You like boats?"

"I do, generally," Preston replied. "I don't know a lot about boats. I've been on some really big boats, cruise ships, that kind of thing, and not long ago, I was on Joe Hart's boat in the Bahamas."

"A wooden boat?"

"It's fiberglass, I believe," Preston said. "But I know it's got a lot of fine wood inside."

"Tell me about the wood inside, young fella. What kind of wood? Cherry? Teak? How is it fitted?"

"I think it was cherry, but I'm not sure. There were curves in it and different kinds of wood, or different colors, at least, all made together, very smooth, first class."

Corey just listened and smiled. "You feel it with your fingers?"

"No, I just looked at it."

"Should've felt it with your fingers. Remember that. Always feel it with your fingers. Can't just look good. Got to feel good. Remember that, young fella."

They watched more boats pass by and Corey commented on each one. "That's a cruising hull. That's a planing hull. That one's fiberglass. That one's wood. She ain't got enough power, she's too low."

"It sure is nice out here," Preston said.

"I like it here," Corey said. "Don't want to leave. It gets a little lonely sometimes. Barbara comes out when she can, but she's busy, and she's got a husband, too. He don't come around much, and when he does, he can't wait to leave. My friends are all gone. I've outlived them all. There is one young fella who comes around now and then. Sits right here where you're sitting, and smokes cigars, too. He always brings good ones for me to smoke. And he brings ice cream.

"He knows boats, too. Knows 'em real good. And he loves wood. He don't just like it. He loves it. I can tell, you see. He tells me I've done work for him. I really like that young fella. He'll be back."

Preston figured he was talking about Joe.

"I'm sure he will," Preston said.

Then silence for a while. "What do you do, young fella?"

"I'm in the automobile business."

"Do you like boats?"

"Yes, I like boats," Preston replied.

Silence.

"Say Corey, you ever think of selling this real estate? It's probably worth a lot."

Rising, and turning to face Preston, Corey's eyes became coal black as he stared at Preston for what seemed like an eternity.

"This land has been in my family for a long time, son. Longer than you been around. We're boat builders. You understand? Been good at it for years and years. *Skilled* at it. That's what made us free. My great-granddaddy worked with Frederick Douglass." Corey slowly sat down. "Would you like me to get you some more iced tea?"

"No, thank you, Corey. I'm sorry if I offended you." Preston paused, and slowly put his hand on the old man's knee. "I really am sorry."

Corey nodded. "That's all right, son. You didn't understand."

"No, I didn't. I'm going to leave you now. I've got to drive back to Charleston and then fly to New York City to meet my wife."

"What's your wife's name?" Corey asked.

"Marcia."

"I bet she's a nice lady, ain't she?"

"She really is."

"You love her?"

"Yes, I do."

"That's good," Corey said. "Real good. Would you like some more iced tea?"

"No, thanks," Preston said, getting up. "I enjoyed talking with you, and I'll come out and talk with you again sometime. What kind of ice cream do you like?"

"The same kind that young fella always brings me. I forget the name, but it's real good."

"Okay. I'll bring you some of that and a couple of cigars, too."

"That'll be awful nice," Corey said, walking with Preston to his car. "Maybe I'll have a little piece of wood made for you next time. Maybe one of those fancy canes, or a nice little wooden box. You like boxes?"

"Sure I do. Thanks; you take care," Preston said, getting into his car, waving goodbye, and making a note to see if Alice had Barbara's address and phone number.

Preston drove back to Charlotte and boarded a plane to LaGuardia, glad to be heading home. He could now understand why Joe was so fond of Corey and why he would be saddened that the old man's mind is slipping away. He wondered how long Corey could continue to live there alone and what would happen to his home, his wood-working art, when he was gone.

Preston felt a real sense of accomplishment since he had left Joe in the islands. He'd covered a lot of ground, and he would be home in plenty of time to get the apartment ready for Marcia on Friday.

While Preston was surprisingly impressed with Charleston and Braydon, New York City's landscape felt good. With the help of the doorman, Preston brought the files into his condo, where he spent the next three days reading them and thinking about Johnny... and Marcia.

He was also surprised by his own interest in Johnny's files. He'd spent hours reading Automotive News and other trade magazines and articles, and endless time studying real estate, but he could care less about fiction or other writing not relevant to his business. After meeting Johnny, and now reading all of his background, he had to admit it was not only of interest but compelling.

Preston thought Marcia would enjoy reading these files. He'd regarded her as an intellectual but considered her input to be of no practical use. Yet here he was trying to understand all of this, figure out how to help Johnny. He knew that Marcia would be able to make sense out of what he was looking at and not be intimidated or overwhelmed. She would sort it out, organize it, and love doing it. He knew nothing about mental illness, and had, until now, avoided any involvement with other people's problems. He found this type of information confusing, and disturbing.

In reading Ashley's comments regarding Johnny, he could see how upset she was with the failure of people to recognize his needs and give him the right kind of help. She was incensed that Johnny's parents had dumped him in an institution for mentally challenged patients in a small village in upstate New York, and she hated the fact that the institution was for the mentally defective. She questioned whether Johnny was actually mentally retarded and could only imagine how horrible it must have been for him to only know the institutional environment as a child.

It was unclear whether Johnny's IQ had been established and, if so, at what age, but in any event his IQ scores would have been affected by many factors including how thorough the testing was. One of Johnny's early reports showed an IQ of 80 to 85 and he was termed mentally retarded. Then mildly retarded. Johnny was transferred to another state institution in the mountains in the western part of North Carolina bordering on Tennessee, and the next reports from the later institution reflected a cognitive and intellectual impairment; in other words, borderline intellectual functioning. Like the state school in New York, the North Carolina institution also suffered a lack of funds and paid limited attention to the developmental or educational side.

A memo from Joe indicated that if Johnny was not considered mentally retarded, he would not be eligible to receive the education and help that he needed. At the same time, there was a big push to refer to patients like Johnny as mentally challenged, as a more politically correct term. Labels such as these, according to Joe's view, were commonly used as a means to avoid the expenditure of time, energy and dollars to give a patient like Johnny the kind of special education he needed. It was clear from their files that Joe and Ashley were disturbed by the way Johnny had been treated, and were focused on what educational opportunities could be realized now.

Preston could see that Joe was exploring programs including tutoring, but his efforts appeared to have ended when Ashley died.

Preston wished Marcia was there to help him. He admired her ability to make sense out of research and connect raw data to practical results. He thought of other areas in which Marcia had helped him and others throughout the years. He had either taken that for granted or been too self-centered to notice it.

He realized that he had never told her that.

CHAPTER 43

Marcia walked in to the penthouse she and Preston had shared for years and picked up the envelope he'd left for her in the foyer alongside a vase of red and yellow roses. Unaware that Preston had arrived earlier, she put her suitcase down, took her jacket off, and read the note.

> Dear Marcia,
>   Welcome home! I wanted you to see these flowers first and to tell you that I have missed you terribly. I fixed ~~lunch~~ dinner for you in case you're hungry. I can't wait to see you.
>   Love, Preston

Her first impulse was to rip the note up and throw it in the basket. Instead she turned it over, left it on the table, and glanced toward the expansive living area.

"Preston?"

The sound of her voice apparently gave Preston hope.

He crossed the foyer and tried to pull her into his arms. She gave him a slight hug, and at the same time gently pushed him back.

"Flowers and this note?" She said, "Straight out of the soaps. Did you really cook dinner?"

"Well, I did cook lunch, but my timing was off. I got here a few hours ago, so I ordered dinner and had it delivered. Are you hungry?"

"Actually, I'm starved."

"Then let's go," Preston said, pulling her toward the table by the window. "Sit. You sit, I'll serve."

"Come on Preston, cut it out," she replied.

Preston was worried that she was not buying any of this, but he did see her take in the candles flickering on the table. When he came out wearing an apron, his hands loaded with dishes, Marcia burst out laughing. He served her a salad while she poured herself some water. Then he offered her Peking duck, garlic chicken, rice, pepper steak. He even set out the wooden chopsticks Marcia had bought him years ago, which he had never used.

"I should leave you more often," Marcia said with a smile.

"I hope you never leave again. So much has happened to me in the last couple of months – to us. I want to tell you all about it. But first, tell me how you're doing. How are you feeling?"

"Hmm... that's different. I'm okay, Preston. It was good to see Mother, for a while. And it was good to see Ann. She's great."

"What's she doing now?"

"Well, she's an editor for a newsletter. She's meeting a lot of interesting people, and she tells me she feels good about using her skill sets to the fullest."

"That's good," Preston said.

"It's been a long time. I never felt I could take the time to go see her."

"I probably contributed to that feeling," he said. "Stupid of me." Preston thought about his conversation with Johnny.

Marcia put down her water glass, disbelief registering in her eyes. "What in the world has happened to you? Is it real, or is this just to put you in my good graces again?"

"Long story. I hope you'll hear me out."

"Okay," Marcia said, sitting back in her chair. "Go ahead. I promise I won't interrupt, or at least I'll try not to."

Preston began with the search for Joe Hart to save his business. Joe, a lawyer who specializes in turnarounds, was not available. In fact, no one knew where he was because his wife had been killed in a drive-by shooting.

"How awful!" Marcia exclaimed.

Preston told her how Joe had withdrawn to the mountains. He explained how he'd actually met Joe when he was fifteen, how his father had dragged him into the mountains for forced vacations, and the story about his falling in the crevice and how Joe got him out.

"You never told me any of this."

"I know. It was all wrapped up with my father, what he was and what he wasn't. I never realized how much that and his breakup with mother affected me. Didn't want to talk about it. Guess I was scared I'd end up the same way."

Preston went on to tell Marcia how he'd found Joe up in the Adirondacks, how they camped there, the fire, the wilderness. He eventually explained the three conditions Joe required to help him and his unequivocal acceptance.

"You agreed to do whatever he asked, not knowing what it would be?" Marcia asked incredulously.

"I did. I was afraid of failing and," he said, reaching across the table and taking his wife's hand in his, "I was afraid of losing you. Joe said things to me up in the mountains I will never forget. He told me that sometimes in life you have to have enough faith to make an irrevocable commitment, and how some people can and some can't. How it's about personal integrity, who and what you are. No one ever spoke to me like that, and I'll tell you, Marcia, it went into my head and heart like a laser beam."

Preston then described the detailed turnaround plan Joe drew up, the meeting in Charlotte where he and Casey were not allowed to say a word, not even gesture.

"You kept quiet the entire meeting?"

"You had to be there. The bank's lawyers were attacking us like crazy, and it sounded like we had no defense. For the first time in my life, I was not in control, and I knew it. Also, you had to see Joe, the way he responded to the attacks, the way he reasoned with the bank, brought out errors on their part, the whole thing.

"But Marcia, he really had faith in me." He swallowed around a lump forming in his throat. Other than Marcia, no one had ever shown that faith in him. "He gave the bank his word that I would keep mine."

He described the moment when Joe had asked him to speak to the bank, how he had no idea what he would say, what he should say. How he went to the window and looked down, and it came to him. He described as best he could what he told the bank.

"I don't remember what I said exactly, but I know it was the absolute truth. I told how I felt, how I had screwed up and knew it, and that I knew what I needed to do to fix it. I came right out and told them that I was afraid to fail, and that I was not going to, that they could count on it. I remember how clear it seemed to me at that point."

After they finished dinner, they carried the dishes to the kitchen, and, for the first time in their married life, washed the dishes together, Preston talking the whole time. They made coffee, strolled to the living room, sat on the floor before the low table in front of the sofa. He told her about Joe directing him to give 15 percent of Wilson Holdings to Casey, and another 15 percent to Alex.

Marcia's eyes grew wide.

"You gave 30 percent of your company away?"

"I did. Seventy percent of something is better than 100 percent of nothing," he echoed Joe. He explained what the new success meant to Marcia and to him, his eyes tearing up as he spoke.

He told Marcia about the phone call from Joe asking him to fly to Marsh Harbour, that Joe wanted to talk to him. How he flew there, spent time with Joe on his boat. He told Marcia in detail about their conversation that night.

After several hours of discussion, Preston realized he'd talked too long. "Are you tired? You just got home. Do you want to rest?"

"Not on your life. Keep talking. Forgive me, but you've never been this open . . . this vulnerable."

Encouraged by Marcia's enthusiasm, Preston went on, explaining how horrified he was at the thought of taking responsibility for Joe's 'collectibles.' He thought Joe was crazy to ask him to look after these people who had become so important in his life. It still puzzled him somewhat.

Preston stood up and wandered around the room, fired by the enthusiasm he already had for his new friends. He told Marcia about Missy, about Johnny, Tommy and Corey. He told her how worried he was about what he would say to her, to Marcia, what they would have to talk about. He had been such an ass where Marcia was concerned.

He described going to dinner with Tommy, what a character he was, how he got a phone call from Missy, how her ex-husband had beaten her up because of seeing her talking with Preston. How Tommy went to Missy's apartment to make sure she was okay, and how Tommy told him that night she wouldn't have to worry anymore. How he was glad to hear that, but also afraid that he could somehow be drawn into whatever would happen. He talked about shooting craps, the cigars.

"You shot craps in Vegas," she said, "and smoked cigars? Are you sure you're my husband?"

Preston gave her a kiss on the cheek and went on. Told her about his trip to San Francisco. What he was feeling when he called her from there, how glad he was to hear her voice. His trip to Braydon, how stupid he was to have thought of Braydon as some hick town. He described its beauty: the trees, the streets, the architecture, the flowers, and most of all, the people. He recounted his time with Alice, going to the Home Dairy and meeting Johnny, getting soaked. At that point, Marcia was laughing hysterically.

"I would have given anything to see you soaking wet, in an apron, washing dishes with Johnny!" she exclaimed. "Absolutely anything!"

Preston sobered and added, "There's more I want to ... need to tell you about Johnny. Marcia, you'll understand what I want to talk to you about better than I do. I'd like to ask you to help me on this ... and a lot of other things."

Preston could see from Marcia's expression that she was trying to process all of this. He had to get it out, and he was thankful for her willingness to listen. Reaching over and gripping her right arm, he smiled warmly at Marcia.

He then detailed his trip to Corrigan Yachts, his time with Corey. He described what a neat man he was.

"I still have two of Joe's collectible's to meet – a bi-polar guy named Harry, and one other. I need to talk to Joe about those two, but he's in the Bahamas and can't be reached by phone right now."

Several cups of coffee later and way into the night, Preston reached the end of the story. Marcia simply sat and stared at him.

"What?" Preston asked.

"Well... wow... what a story. It's been a long day. I'm tired. Let's go to bed...."

"Really?" Hope and a surge of male hormones sent a rush of blood to Preston's head.

"Really, as to the sleep part. We need to go slow here, Preston. But it has been a good night." Marcia said, taking his hand and leading him to the bedroom.

Preston woke smelling coffee, feeling great. Until he saw Marcia, already up and dressed, packing. "What are you doing?"

"I told you I needed some things here, Pres. I'm going back to Mother's."

"But what about last night? You aren't staying? Marcia, please. I need you."

"Last night was wonderful," Marcia said, clicking her suitcase shut. "And I do love you. You slept like a baby. I woke up around four, with a lot on my mind. It takes time to build trust, Preston. Even more to rebuild it. There's a lot of scar tissue to deal with."

She bit her lip and turned away. "To be honest, I'm not sure I want to come back. I need time. Time to think about what I want, for a change. What I need."

Chapter 44

After more than a week with Joe in the Abacos, Harry had taken more than four-thousand shots. When he downloaded the pictures onto Joe's computer, Joe was fascinated by the range and diversity of the images. He found out how two people could look at the same thing and see it differently.

They ate fish they had either caught or speared on one of their dives, and lobster they caught at night. They hung out at the beach, at the local bars. And they talked. Instead of Harry winding down with all of this activity, he seemed to be energized, his energy endless. Each day he wanted to see more, do more, and talk more. Finally, late one afternoon, sitting on the cockpit, Joe decided they needed to get serious.

"Harry, you and I have had a great time down here."

"We sure have, Joe. I've loved it, man. And we're just starting. I want to explore the other islands. We could go to Eleuthera. I've never been there, but I hear it's great. We could go farther down, too. We could go to Puerto Rico..."

"Hold it, Harry," Joe said. "The water's a lot different between the Bahamas and Puerto Rico. That's a rough stretch. And what about your job? I've loved having you down here, but it's been almost two weeks. How much time away can you really afford?"

"Oh, that's not a problem, Joe. I could take a month. I could take two months. This is great."

"Have you got the resources to take two months without earning money?"

"Oh, yeah, that's no problem. I can make it when I get back."

"Well, that's good. So I take it that you haven't needed to see your doctor lately, you've been on an even keel, health-wise?"

"I've been feeling great ever since you called, and I'm loving being down here."

"I don't want to prick any bubbles, Harry, but how were you feeling a few days before I called?"

Silence for a moment.

Harry clasped his hands between his knees and looked up, his expression somber. "Not good, Joe. I was having a series of problems then. You know, my weight, no energy. I wanted to stay in bed most of the time. I couldn't work. I lost my steady job shooting weddings and a few of my freelancers."

"Were you seeing your doctor?"

"I went to him; he changed my medication. That helped a lot. What with being bipolar and all, the medication has to be exactly right, or it really screws me up. And sometimes my doctors just don't get it right. That's why I have these problems. But I don't have any problems now."

"Do you have your medication with you?" Joe asked.

"I did, but I ran out the third day. Don't worry. I don't need it now. In fact, it only causes me more problems."

Joe paused, searching for the words to impress on Harry the seriousness of his situation. "Harry, I'm not a doctor, and I'm not in any position to give you advice. I love having you here keeping me company and doing all the things we're doing together. It's been fun, more than you know. But I would feel better if you went back, checked in with your doctor, and had your prescriptions refilled while you're still feeling good. I'm being selfish here, Harry. I may not be in a position... with the bad telephone reception down here... to take another phone call like the one we had one time."

Neither said anything for a long time.

Finally, Harry responded. "I'm sorry about that, Joe. Sometimes, like then, I wonder why it's worth going on. I was going to end it that time, but after talking with you, I decided it would be better to keep going. You know what I mean?"

"Actually, I do," Joe said quietly, looking down.

"I think you're right, Joe," Harry said, getting up from the chair, grabbing the hose, and refilling Buck's water bowl. "I've been putting it off, but I do need to go back. I hate the medicine, but my doctor tells me I've got to take it, or else. Besides, I miss Scooter. It's just that it's been great down here, hanging out and not having to worry about any of that. Do the planes come in here every day?"

"You could catch one at 11:15 a.m. You've got a round-trip ticket with an open return, and I can call this afternoon, if you want."

"I guess that's the thing to do," Harry said. "It's funny, every time I'm down, I'm trying to get up. Every time I'm up, my doctor tells me I'm a little too happy. Either way, I'm screwed."

Joe clapped his friend on the back, wondering how many more times he would have a chance to fish with his friend Harry. "We're all screwed in one way or another, Harry. Let's just remember the good times and try to have more of them."

Harry and Joe sat in the cockpit with a couple of after-dinner drinks that night and then got a good sleep. After breakfast, then after they ran out of clay pigeons, Harry and Joe rode together in the taxi, had coffee, and said their goodbyes. "Thanks for everything."

"Thank you, Harry. Your pictures are great, and your company is even better. I've had a good time with you. I appreciate you. I want you to know that."

Harry gave Joe a big bear hug, waved goodbye, and waddled through security on to his gate.

Joe took the same taxi back to the boat, reflecting upon how much fun it had been with Harry. Uncomplicated. Easy. But he was tired, weary. He had done a lot physically in the last couple of weeks, and Harry's pursuit of happiness had been increasingly intense. He decided to do nothing the rest of the day.

When he returned to the boat, he sat quietly with Buck, reading, grilling a hamburger. He fell asleep in his chair in the cockpit. He awoke an hour later, drank a bottle of cold water, and decided he should refresh his will. His current one left everything to Ashley.

He went into the salon, sat at the table, and hooked up his computer.

He had drawn up many wills in his career and was trustee and/or executor in many estates. He pulled up a form will, and started filling in the blanks.

He skipped over the funeral instructions. Ashley had always wanted Joe, when the time came, to have a full Naval funeral and graveside service, and she insisted that he buy two plots in the Braydon cemetery so that she could join him. They had picked out the plots together in a serene section, near a large live oak tree and with water in sight. What Joe never anticipated was that he would be joining Ashley, instead of the other way around. He would have preferred no service, to simply be cremated and have his ashes spread at sea. But he knew how much the full service and burial would have meant to Ashley, and he had made his commitment. He had to talk with Red about the necessary red tape.

He made Alice his executrix. He also made a specific bequest to her in the amount of $100,000, with an expression of his deep gratitude and appreciation of her service, loyalty and support over all the years. He left her his house and furnishings, and to her and Johnny, he left Buck. He made a specific bequest to Red in the amount of $100,000, with his boat, truck, fishing gear, his Navy ring, and all of his jewelry. The rest of his estate he divided in half, one part a gift in Ashley's name to the top five charities that she worked so hard for, the other half to the Bethesda Naval Hospital and the American Cancer Society, earmarked for medical research, prevention, and treatment of brain tumors.

He read the will over and printed it out, placed it in a file, returned to the cockpit, and took another nap.

CHAPTER 45

arcia's two weeks with her mother were intense but, on
balance, helpful. So were her telephone conversations with
Ann. But most of all, it was her replaying over and over in her
mind her recent time with Preston that made her decision. She
still loved him, perhaps now more than ever, and she knew he
needed her. She also knew he was really trying, really reaching out
to her. She had to give him and herself another chance. Besides, it
wasn't just the two of them anymore. She must go back. Marcia
headed for New York.

Having Marcia home again gave Preston more energy and spirit
than he had felt in the last ten years. A few days after her return,
Preston had his lawyers transfer 50 percent of his shares in Wilson
Holdings to her. He was determined that she really be part of his
business, not simply share the risk. As the days went by, he invited
Marcia to join him in trips to his dealerships, and was delighted that
she accepted and seemed to enjoy coming along. More and more he
realized how smart and effective Marcia was, how much she understood of the strategic side of business. And everyone liked her.

It was not all business. Preston flew to Vegas with Marcia and introduced her to Tommy and Missy. At one dinner, Marcia discovered
that Preston had been instrumental in talking with a talent agent,
arranging for Missy to have an audition as a dancer in a new show at
the MGM Grand. Marcia delighted in watching Tommy and Preston

smoke cigars and shoot craps together. After a couple of lunches with Tommy, she came to understand that he had a lot more depth and substance than she had originally thought. Preston appeared to enjoy the time he spent with Tommy, finding it relaxing, and to hear Tommy's practical take on ideas from people in Preston's organization.

Preston also made a few trips to Braydon, checked in with Alice and Johnny, and drove over to see Corey, taking him three different kinds of ice cream until he discovered the man's favorite, black raspberry. On his last trip, just as Preston was leaving, Corey had handed him something wrapped in brown paper, tied with soft, white string. When he got home, Preston unfolded the paper and found an elegant wooden box made of cherry with bird's eye maple inlay. When he opened the box, he found a scribbled note on a torn piece of brown paper. It simply said, *"Don't forget to feel the wood, young fella."* Preston kept the box on top of his dresser in his bedroom with his favorite watches and rings in it.

He made several attempts to reach Harry, but was never able to talk to him on the phone. Harry had apparently moved, and there was no answer on his cell phone. Alice said she would do what she could to try to track him and the sixth 'collectible' down. These were the only two of the group Joe had mentioned that Preston had not connected with yet, and he wanted to meet them as soon as he could.

When another three weeks passed and Preston had not been able to reach Harry, he decided to give Alice a call.

"Good to hear from you, Preston. I haven't called about Harry because I haven't been able to reach him, either. I had trouble reaching Joe, too. I learned later that he'd gotten together with some fishing buddies in Nassau and that they'd gone to Eleuthera, where there was no cell reception. Harry was with Joe for a couple of weeks, but then he came back. Joe hasn't heard from him either but wouldn't have been able to anyway."

"How's Joe doing, Alice? Catching a lot of fish?"

"He sounded pretty good. Definitely catching a lot of fish. Swimming with Buck. I think he's having a good time," Alice said. "He didn't say so, but I kind of got the feeling from the tone of his voice that he might be having enough fishing and is ready to come home."

"Maybe he misses work."

"Could be," Alice replied. "I know we miss him, that's for sure. I'm sure Harry will check in somewhere along the line. He goes like this for periods when Joe doesn't hear from him, and then, after a while, he gets in touch. I'll call you if I hear."

"Thanks, Alice. Good to talk with you. Say hello to Joe. And be sure to tell him Alex and Casey are doing an outstanding job. We're in touch with all our banks every day. Each of the stores is turning around. We're following Joe's plan, which is a masterpiece, and it's working. I still can't believe what a great job he did. Anyway, I don't want to burden him with business issues, but I would appreciate your letting him know we're doing well and that the banks are happy. And how much I appreciate what he did for us."

"I'll let him know," Alice said. "I'm sure he'll be glad to hear it."

Over the coming weeks, Marcia became increasingly interested in Preston's new friends, and particularly how much enjoyment he seemed to be getting out of talking and being with them. He told her how Johnny was abandoned as an infant by his parents, left to an institution, that he actually was not retarded, how Johnny might be able to receive special education, and about Preston's discussions with a speech therapist. He told her about a plan he had that would involve all of the group, something about a restaurant with entertainment where Missy could be involved in the show, Corey could make the bar, Tommy could be the bartender and head of security, and Johnny could be in charge of the dishwashing staff in the kitchen. Marcia thought it was a little crazy, particularly since Missy wanted to be a showgirl in Vegas, not some restaurant. She didn't want to throw a damper on his idea, but she let him know her thoughts. "Doesn't Missy want to stay in Vegas? I thought she had something going with an agent, a chance for her to get into a show."

"She does, and the agent's still working on that. But these shows don't last forever, and I'm trying to figure out some type of long-term solution or plan for all these people to use their individual skill sets, work together in some enterprise, and be able to have a revenue stream, a source of money that each of them can count on. And at the same time, have the enterprise build equity. Maybe it's not a restaurant, maybe it's something else. I just want to find a way that works for them going forward. Something that will give them security."

"You've got it all figured out," Marcia said, pleased to see Preston worried about other people instead of himself. At the same time, she worried about Preston's proclivity to control. "I understand what you want to do for Missy and the others. But what they want is important. Before you go too far with your planning, you might want to talk with them."

Preston's attitude toward her was entirely different and wonderful. Marcia was heartened by Preston's new-found sensitivity, not only to others but in the way he regarded her. More respect, more interest in what she had to say. Even noticing when she was feeling a bit queasy in the morning, and wondering why.

Preston studied Marcia's face as if reading her mind, and smiled. She smiled back, wondering whether she could trust her growing sense that she could be herself, that Preston would love the real her, and whether this was the time to tell him.

Preston asked Marcia to sit down, explaining he had something important to discuss.

He looked hesitant before the out-pouring of words: "Honey, I want to have ... to start a family. I know I've been selfish about ... a lot of things, but I really want ... a little Marcia. What do you think?"

Tears ran down Marcia's face. "Well, Preston, your timing's pretty good. If you want us to have a baby, I think that can be arranged. Sooner than you think."

Preston simply stared and then jumped up, her words fully sinking in.

"You mean..."

"Yes, my love, you're going to be a daddy."

Chapter 46

Joe was happy to bring the *Mountain Stream* back to Marsh Harbour after spending a few days in Nassau, then three more weeks fishing with his buddies. Before pulling into his slip, Joe stopped at the end of the dock to fuel his boat and chat with Ed, the dock master. After the crossing, Buck was eager to jump on the dock and spend time on land before he plunged in the harbor for a cool swim.

With the boat back in his slip, Joe gave Buck a fresh water bath and cleaned his ears, and gave his boat a thorough wash-down and cleaning. With the boat finally clean, Joe began to dry it with a shammy, starting at the bow. Buck sat in the shade of the cockpit and watched him work. It was hot, and Joe was working up quite a sweat, but the labor felt good and island music coming from the speakers on the bridge added a bounce to the shammy.

When he got to the cockpit, Joe dropped the shammy, smelling the strong and distinct odor of electrical wires burning. He figured he must have a fire in the engine room. He ordered Buck off the boat and shouted, "Fire!" to the dock master, worried about the fuel tanks at the end of the dock and wanting to give him time to react. Then he grabbed the large fire extinguisher in the salon, knowing that water would not help if the diesel fuel ignited.

He carefully opened the door to the engine room, staying to one side to avoid any flames bursting out. He hoped to get to the electrical wires before that happened. The dock master and two others came running to his boat as he opened the door. He yelled for them to stay back. The door opened, and he was relieved to see no flames. He rushed into the engine room with a flashlight in one hand, fire extinguisher in the other. He searched for the smoke and burning wires. He could not find either, but he knew they were there from the strong smell. He called for help, and the dock master hopped on the boat.

"I've got electrical wires burning somewhere in the engine room, Eddie," Joe said, "but I can't find them. Would you have a look?"

"I don't smell anything," the dock master said, climbing into the engine room. After about five minutes, he came out and joined Joe in the cockpit. He looked confused. "I don't smell anything, Joe, anywhere in the engine room or on your boat. Your batteries look good, all the connections look good, the wires look good. I think you're in good shape down there."

Joe jumped back in the engine room again, this time just with the light. He stayed in there ten minutes. Then he came back out. The dock master was still on his boat.

"You're right, Eddie," he said. "Sorry I yelled fire. I just wanted to be careful, because I was sure we had an electrical fire, and that's part of the drill."

"Well, I'm glad you don't," Eddie said. "I'm glad you're in good shape. No problem, Joe." He went back to the end of the dock, where he was working on another boat. The others had already left. Joe stood there alone with Buck. He ruffled the old boy's ears and stared off over the water.

"Well, Buck, my boat's in good shape. I'm not." He picked up his cell phone and punched Red's number.

"Hi, Joe. What's up?"

"Red, it's time. Come now," Joe said and hung up.

Joe packed a small bag with a few things, including his wallet, computer, the file that contained his will, his passport, and Buck's papers. He went through his boat and cleaned out the refrigerator and freezer, carefully stacking all the food, frozen lobsters, fish, and drinks in cardboard boxes. He carried the boxes off the boat and down the dock to the Jib Room and into the kitchen, where he found the owner, whom he always called Buddy.

"I'm going to be gone for a while," he said, "and I want you to have all of this. Go ahead and use it, eat it, or sell it to your guests."

"You sure you don't want some of this, Joe? These lobsters look great, and there's a ton of fish here. I'll be glad to keep this for you in our freezers."

"No, Buddy, I want you to have it. I want you to use it. I'm not sure when I'll be back. Please use it up. And I want to thank you for all the wonderful meals I've had here, the great service. We've had some outstanding times, and you've always made me, and Buck, too, feel at home."

"Hey Joe, you're part of the family. So is Buck. You know that. Stop acting like you're never going to see us again. We'll be waiting for you when you get back. We'll do it again."

"That sounds good," Joe said. "Nothing I'd like better than to do it again. I've got to shut the boat down now, and Buck and I have to get to the airport. I'll leave the key to my boat on the counter. Call us a taxi, would you?"

"You got it, Joe. Have a great trip."

At the airport, Joe checked with Continental and learned the next flight would not be in until 3:30 p.m. That meant he had more than four hours to wait. He sat down with Buck. He tried to keep calm, employing the same techniques that had served him well in his Navy days. The discipline was there, but this time seemed different.

As he sat there, he could not help but play his life out in his mind. He thought of his Uncle Howard, his Aunt Lettie, and the mountains. Playing baseball, his teachers, getting into Annapolis, his time there. Then his submarine duty and meeting Ashley that night in Charleston.

His thoughts were suddenly interrupted by a hand on his shoulder. "How you doin', Cap?"

"How did you get here, Red?" Joe said, standing up. "The plane's not due in for another three hours."

"You said now, Cap. I've got a private plane waiting, a Lear jet. Let's go."

Joe hugged Red, and Red introduced him to the captain.

"Right this way, sir. You don't have to go through the normal procedure or security. We're ready to take you and your dog right now. Our plane's right over there," he said, pointing and reaching for Joe's bag.

"Thank you, but I'd rather carry my bag." Within ten minutes, they were in the air, headed for Charleston.

"Thanks for coming, Red."

His friend simply nodded.

"I've drawn up a will, Red." Joe showed it to him. "I'd like to ask you and the captain to witness my signing it."

Red nodded and went up to the cabin, put on headphones, and told the captain what Joe wanted to do. The captain nodded. Red came back and told Joe to go ahead and sign the will. Joe did. Then Red signed over one of the witness lines, and took the will to the captain. The captain took off his headphones, turned to Joe, and asked him if it was his signature on the will. Joe said yes. The captain saluted and signed his name over the other witness line and handed the will back to Red.

"Would you keep this original, Red, and give it to Alice as soon as you can. She'll know what to do with it. And I need to talk with you about a few things."

Buck, who had been sitting in his seat looking out the window, turned and looked at Joe. His ears perked up and he slowly climbed down from the seat and edged over to Joe, sat down, and leaning against his legs, put his head on Joe's lap.

"I figured that, Cap. Are you up to it now?" Red asked, the pain showing in Joe's face.

"This is a good time," Joe said, petting Buck's head and then leaning down and kissing him. "And I'd feel better having the conversation while I know I can. First of all, thank you for being my friend. Thank you for all you've done. For always being there." Joe stopped talking for a while. Joe and Red heard only the muffled sound of the jet.

Then Joe continued. "I promised Ashley I would have a full Navy funeral and burial service. I never dreamed she would go before me. I don't really care about the ceremonial part, you know. But I told her I'd do that. I don't know if I can still do that now. Can you try to arrange it? If you can, for Ashley, I'd like our Navy guys to do what they do at my funeral. I'd also like them to do what they do at the gravesite. I don't want an open casket. But I would like a casket made of fine wood. Cherry, if possible. The one to talk to is Clayton Anderson at Anderson Mortuary in Braydon. He'll know how to handle everything at the funeral. Except that the formal Navy ceremonial component will be different. Just tell him that's the way I want it. Also, Red, if you can pull it off, I'd like Buck involved, somehow."

"You've got it."

"Oh, Red, there's one other thing. There are six people I have sort of looked after in some ways, tried to be a friend to, helped them do what they couldn't do. In one way or another, they needed a hand."

Joe fell silent again and stared out the window of the plane, seeing nothing. After a few minutes, he looked back at Red.

"Alice is the executrix of my will. She's done it many times before, and she'll know what to do. You should be in touch with her, because you're one of the beneficiaries. She'll handle that. She's going to look after Buck, too, and my house, so none of that's a problem. I'm leaving you my boat and my fishing gear, among other things, but don't feel you have to keep it if you don't want to use it. You can either use it or sell it and use the money, whatever works for you. The same with my truck. I guess that's it, Red. Do you have any questions?"

Red was silent for a while with that confident serenity that was their common legacy from their Navy days. Then he looked at Joe and said, "No, I don't. Everything understood. I'll get it done. Would you like something to eat?"

"There's food on this plane?"

"Yes, sir. Nothing but the finest," he said, handing Joe a large tray of gourmet sandwiches, cheese, fresh fruit, pickles, and potato chips. Then Red reached in a cooler and brought out a cold bottle of Sam Adams for Joe and a bottle of Bass Ale for himself.

Before long, they landed at the private airfield at Charleston, where a limo was standing by. They went directly to Joe's office, where Alice was waiting.

Joe entered with Red and Buck behind him. Alice appeared to be worried. "Joe, it's good to see you. Are you okay? All Red told me was that you had decided to come home, and he thought you might want to see me. Do you have some work you want me to do?"

"I do want to see you, Alice. Let's go in my office and have a talk."

Joe disclosed his situation, explained the will, and reviewed all of the arrangements. He told Alice how much he appreciated her always being there for him and his clients and his friends. When he informed her he was leaving her his home, and Buck, Alice could not hold back the tears. She reached for him, grabbing and squeezing his arm.

"Joe, there are not words ... or if there are, I don't know what to say. I admire you so. May I ask you a question?"

"Of course," he said.

"You are always so calm, even ... now. Have you ever been afraid of anything your entire life?"

"I'm not going to be able to give you a long answer – what that question deserves, Alice," Joe said, knowing that he was beginning to have a seizure, starting to see flashes of bright light. "Actually I'm a little scared right now. I've experienced fear in big ways and little ways all my life. When I've been able to beat it, in the end, I've felt exhilarated. But there was always fear, mainly of the uncertainty of life." As Joe talked, he felt weak and strange, like he was listening to himself from another place. He saw his Aunt Lettie, heard her voice, felt himself slipping, then saw Ashley. He kept going, but his voice was fading: "In terms of living the only thing I have feared is living life without meaning and love, and you made that fear go away. When you died, a part of me died, too."

Alice knew he wasn't talking to her anymore. "God bless you," she whispered, squeezing Joe's hand as if willing him not to go. But she let him gently push her back as he closed his eyes, and fell flat on the floor, fading away.

CHAPTER 47

Preston approached Anderson Mortuary, holding Marcia closely at his side. He'd been shocked when Alice had called to say that Joe was gone. He could neither believe it nor accept it. Joe was such a major, unselfish force. How could he be dead?

Two men in black suits at the front door bordered by a white column on each side greeted Preston and Marcia. Once inside, they were directed to a room on the right. Before entering, Marcia walked to the registry laid out on a small stand with a light, glanced over at Preston, and signed their names. The room was large and rectangular with pastel green walls, lighted by several tasteful lamps and further illuminated by six windows bordered by heavy dark green velvet trim. In the front was a pipe organ attended by an elderly woman with short gray hair, wearing a black robe.

The wall-to-wall carpeted room was divided by a five-foot-wide, thick runner, which formed an aisle between neatly ordered straight-backed armchairs. To the left at front was an ornate pulpit. In the center and two steps up was a platform. Even though Preston and Marcia arrived early, so many people were already seated that Preston worried whether they would find seats. As they walked in, he immediately surveyed the room but did not see a casket. He wondered why there were no ushers at that moment, but they were finally able to settle in near the back.

Joe's in-laws were seated in the front row on the left, joined by Alice, Red and Reverend Barrett. Trying not to look too obvious, Preston scanned the room. He recognized Casey and Alex, sitting together. He questioned why there was a block of empty seats in the right front. In a moment, a group of lawyers from the Braydon County Bar filed in and sat in that section. Preston thought he saw Corey with Barbara, but he was not sure. He couldn't see everyone, and he wasn't sure whether Missy and the others were there.

At last, the room was packed and quiet except for the soft but unfamiliar music coming from the organ. That, too, ended when an eight-man Navy color guard entered the room. Each member wore a crisp, white naval uniform with a black silk tie folded at chest level, a white belt fastened by a shiny brass buckle, and a white cap perched on his head. Two sailors carried flags – the U.S. flag, and the Navy flag – each held in front by a blue leather strap and a shiny brass holder. The flag bearers marched smartly down the aisle, with three other sailors on each side of a closed cherry casket covered by the American flag. Everyone in the room stood, eyes fixed on the color guard as they proceeded down the aisle, all in perfect step. The casket was followed by Buck. As the casket went by, several people softly cried. At the front of the room, the guardsmen carrying the flags did an about-face, with the bearer of the American flag standing on the right, that of the Navy flag on the left. The six sailors carrying the casket carefully placed it on the stand. They then joined the flag bearers, three on each side, where they remained at attention. Buck lay down directly in front of the casket, putting his head between his extended front paws.

Reverend David Barrett rose, turned, and faced the audience. He ran his hand over what hair was left on his head, looked out over the room through thick, black-rimmed glasses, smiled warmly and for a few moments said nothing. He then opened the memorial service with a prayer, followed by warm sentiments about Joe and Ashley.

"It was not long ago that we were gathered here in shock and grief for the passing of Ashley Hart," Reverend Barrett reminded everyone. He spoke of their obvious love and devotion, how caring and sensitive each was, not only to each other, but through their generosity of spirit and contributions to the community of friends and loved ones, all of whom they reached in one way or another. Preston was struck by how Reverend Barrett continuously referred to Joe and Ashley together, in essence combining them.

The Reverend finally finished and said, "And now, we will hear from a few close friends." Preston was jarred by the word "friends," immediately feeling annoyed at himself. *I should be up there speaking. But I don't think I can do it.*

Reverend Barrett called selected people, who came forward to the small lectern. It was as though they picked up Reverend Barrett's theme, or perhaps in their minds Joe and Ashley simply could not be separated. Preston was surprised that this was not the case when it was Ashley's father's turn. He spoke eloquently about Joe as a husband, son-in-law, friend and former Navy commander. One comment especially struck Preston: "Joe treated my daughter and the death of my daughter, not surprisingly, with honor and dignity. What made Joe unique was not only his sense of duty, but his humor and his humanity. Men like Joe are certainly not common."

Red spoke briefly, clearly upset. When he finished, he turned to Joe's casket, raised his right hand to his head and gave a slow, final salute.

As each person spoke, the common thread was how generous Ashley and Joe were, how they cared, and how they now finally could be resting together in peace. A few spoke of personal experiences they'd had with one or the other, and some tried lamely to interject humor. It seemed all bases were covered.

As each man and woman spoke, Preston felt another heavy weight on his chest. He was not certain exactly what he felt, but he knew the list included remorse, regret and guilt. Remorse for what he and so many others were losing. He was sure that many would not at first, or maybe ever, know the extent of their loss. But Preston knew that Marcia would not forget Joe, even though she had never met him. Hell, he'd saved their marriage and the man she loved.

Then there was regret. To begin with, the regret of having Joe gone. And for not getting to meet his last two collectibles before Joe died. To develop a relationship with each of them, help them. And for Joe to see, or at least know, that it was being done. At the same time, he was well aware that Joe had never once asked him how he was doing with his commitment, how he was getting along with the collectibles. He imposed zero accountability upon Preston and gave him 100 percent faith and trust that he would keep his word. Preston wondered if that was why Joe's Navy buddies held him in such high respect. He already knew the depth of feeling that Tommy Greco, Johnny, Missy, and Corey had for Joe, and their connection with him. And he knew he would find the same with the other two.

And guilt. Good old guilt. Something Preston had sidestepped for years but had fostered in others with a passion. Guilt was a tool in his toolbox, a capital M in his manipulation of others. Preston knew well the value of well-administered guilt, the assistance it had provided in shaping and molding conduct and enhancing his ability to control the behavior of others. He knew how it could help him get what he wanted and, to him, it had been natural to use it. After all, he had learned from two masters. He watched his mother and father use guilt in a million ways. He remembered well how his father controlled him in the same fashion, could hear his father's words, *"What do you mean, you are not going with me to the mountains, Preston? How can you not go? You know that I have set aside this week for you and me to be together. You know how much this costs me. You know that I had to twist your mother's arm to get her to go along with letting you go with me, knowing the dangers of being up there. Don't you want to be a man? Are you afraid of the bears? Are you afraid you won't be able to cut it?"*

Preston had quite naturally learned the art of administering guilt. Only he'd raised the bar, used it as an art form with his department heads and managers. When they didn't respond fast enough to his emails and text messages, he fired off rebukes, demanding to know why he was being ignored, intentionally forgetting that his messages were not even hours old. He knew his employees were afraid of being fired, and more importantly, he knew that they would feel guilty about letting him down, inasmuch as he continuously played on that theme. He'd extended the same treatment to his friends when they wouldn't visit him at his house, or play golf at the country club. "What do you mean you're not coming? Marcia and I were really hoping to see you. What do you mean we can't play a foursome this Friday? We were counting on that." But in the last year, the guilt tables had slowly turned. He increasingly felt the guilt himself, and he hated it. He hated it enough to try his best not to let others feel what he did. He understood that he was gaining, growing, that it was working.

Preston was suddenly jarred into the reality that the service was over, that the last of those chosen to speak had said their kind words, and Reverend Barrett was standing before the assembly again, about to close the ceremony. Preston looked up to the top of the room, staring at the ceiling, thinking about Joe.

He saved my life as a kid, he saved my life as a man, and he taught me how to live the life he saved. I promise, Joe, I will remember you for the rest of my life.

A large man in his late-forties wearing a white shirt, gray tie and black jacket with gray trousers high around his waist and carrying a large manila envelope and easel in his left hand stood up and walked down the aisle to the podium. Reverend Barrett was as surprised as everyone else. Preston wondered who he could be. The man approached the podium and set up the easel directly to his right, facing the crowd.

"My name is Harry Klaskowski," he said in a booming, clear voice. "I have known Joe for many years, and I have only two things I would like to say today. First, Joe and I had a lot of good times together. Second, he's the reason I'm alive." Harry then took a photograph out of the large envelope and placed it on the easel. There was a soft murmur and audible gasp in the room. The picture showed Joe on the bridge of his boat looking forward with a relaxed smile on his face and an expression of hope in his eyes. The sun was shining down on him. Harry said, "I thought you might like to see this picture." With that, he returned to his seat.

So that's Harry Klaskowski, Preston thought. *What a good guy. I'm going to enjoy getting to know him.*

Then Tommy Greco, sitting behind Preston in the back of the room, abruptly stood up.

Oh, God, here it comes, Preston thought. Tommy walked as only Tommy could, in a burst, straight to the end of the aisle, up the two steps to the podium, head bent slightly to the side like he was about to whack anybody who stepped in his way. He bent the mike over with his large, beefy right hand, and with his hand still covering the mike, looked up briefly and then down again.

"I want to say something here about Joe. Nothing is certain about nothing, if you know what I'm saying. And this problem with Joe going is no exception. Who would have thought it? What're the odds of a guy like this catching it like this and bam! It's over. I have to tell you, I was shocked when I got the call from Alice. And why him, for Christ's sakes? Of all the guys, he never did nothing to nobody, except try to help them out. That's all he ever done. His whole damn life, if you'll excuse my French." Then Tommy looked out over the people and jabbed his pudgy right index finger straight at them. "I'm here to tell you, Joe's going upstairs. If anybody's getting in, it's him, you get what I'm saying? I lay it nine to one, he gets in, and I'm not afraid to say it right now. I love you, Joe."

Preston felt the muscles in his throat tighten, and he tried to fight the tears. He was holding his own in the battle until he realized Tommy was not quite finished.

"And there's one more something I want to say. This is not pertaining to Joe directly, but in a way it is. I want to thank you, Joe, for Missy, a classy lady, and for Preston. He was a real case in the beginning, but I have to tell you, he's got a heart. And that's all I have to say." Then Tommy in one continuous series of movements climbed down the stairs, wiped his eyes, walked down the aisle and straight out the back of the room and outside.

Next Johnny stood. He was so short most people couldn't see him, but he pushed his way out from his seat on the left, and waddled down the aisle to the podium. He climbed up, but his head still was lower than the top of the podium, and there was no way he could reach the mike.

It was apparent that everyone but Johnny, Alice, and Preston felt awkward about the situation, and most verbally wondered who in the world this weird little man was.

None of this seemed to faze Johnny. After all, he had lived with it all his life. Besides, it was Joe who'd convinced him that it didn't matter what people thought about the way he looked, that what mattered was how he acted and how good he was. Joe had taught him to smile and laugh along with the people who laughed at him, to just keep doing his job, and it would work out, and it had. But Johnny apparently wasn't accustomed to speaking to a group of people. He was sweating profusely, the perspiration dripping through his new dress shirt, a shirt Preston had taken him to buy, and through his jacket, too. The room was silent. After a while, he spoke in a soft, low voice.

"My name is Johnny. I wash dishes. Do it good. Joe a friend of mine. Joe loves Johnny. Joe talks to Johnny – that's me – like there was nothing wrong with Johnny . . . with me. Joe has Buck," Johnny said, looking back and down at Buck, who, hearing his name, perked up his ears and looked at Johnny.

"Buck a friend of mine, too. Buck loves me. Johnny takes care of Buck. Buck takes care of Johnny, too. Bad man afraid of Buck. Buck don't like bad man. Johnny takes care of Buck, Joe. Don't worry, Joe. Johnny takes care of Pressdon, too. Pressdon not bad, Joe. Pressdon doing better now. Don't worry, Joe. Johnny be okay. Johnny, oh . . . Johnny, . . . I . . . going to *school*. Joe gone now. Not like movies. Joe not living anymore. Joe died. Bye, Joe. Johnny loves Joe." And with that, Johnny waddled back to his seat and sat down.

Reverend Barrett looked over the gathering, seeming to sense there were others who wanted, needed, to say their goodbyes to Joe.

A tall, slender woman in her late-twenties who had been seated in a middle row on the left side stood and crossed over to the aisle. She wore a black tailored suit with a white pearl pin. She looked as elegant as Preston had ever seen her. She took her place at the podium and adjusted the mike with poise.

"Good evening. My name is Melissa Scarlatti. First, I want to thank

Reverend Barrett and all those who spoke today for their kind words about Joe. I want to thank Mr. Klaskowski for his words and the wonderful picture he took. And I especially want to thank Tommy and Johnny for what they said and how well they said it. There are no words that can adequately express my feelings at this time. I have had a lot of difficulties in my life. I won't go into them now, as I don't believe this is the time or the place. But I will say that Joe Hart is the reason I'm here today. He took an interest in me, guided me, protected me, and taught me more about life than anyone else ever has. He cared about me. And he did that at a time when no one else did. That kept me going. I've seen a lot of guys, and I know something about how they act. I also know something about how they feel and what they really want. Joe was unusual. He was the real thing. He never took advantage and he always treated me with respect."

Missy stopped and glanced around the room at all the people watching and listening to her. In a barely audible voice, she went on. "Joe could have had any woman he wanted. He sure could have had me. There was a time after his wife died that I made sure of that. But not Joe. I loved him, and I think he knew that. He's the only man I know that not only knew that loving someone and being in love were not the same thing, but who also respected the difference.

"After his wife died, I was trying to encourage him to move on, you know? Go on with his life. I figured he was still young, and he needed a woman. But Joe loved his wife. That was it. He said something to me about that that I never forgot. I wrote it down." She reached into her purse and pulled out a piece of paper and unfolded it. "He said," as she read the paper, "'that's one mountain I don't want to come down from.' There will never be another like him. He was the most unselfish man I ever met. Also, Joe had a way of looking around the corner and into the future. He knew Tommy, God love him, would look out for me. And just like Tommy and Johnny said, I, too, want to thank you, Joe, for Preston. Tommy's right, he's got heart. I'll never forget you, Joe, as long as I live."

With that, Missy stepped down from the podium, walked down the aisle with her head high, and took her seat.

Way to go, Missy, Preston thought as he reached over and squeezed Marcia's hand.

Barbara Johnson, Corey's daughter, walked slowly up to the podium and introduced herself. She explained that Corey wanted Joe and the others to know that he was here, but unable to speak. She explained how much Joe had meant to her father, how he always treated her dad with respect. She added that Corey was quite fond of that other gentleman, Mr. Wilson, and that she appreciated his coming by, too. Then she sat down.

There seemed to Preston to be a special feeling pervading the room, a quiet and an energy at the same time. His gaze moved up from Reverend Barrett and over the organist to a large window in the right-front side of the room. The sun was setting, and it cast a strong beam of warm light through the window and on Joe's finely finished wooden casket. After a moment of silence, Reverend Barrett stood, looked out over the group, raised his arms, and gave the Benediction.

Immediately thereafter, the guardsmen holding the flags marched to the middle of the aisle, turned, lowered their flags, and strode to the back of the room. The three from each side walked in unison to the casket, carefully picked it up, turned it, and carried it slowly through the aisle and out of the funeral home to where the hearse was waiting. Buck walked behind the casket, never taking his eyes off it. After that, Red followed with Alice at his side. There was not a dry eye in the room.

As the Navy pallbearers and sailors marched by Preston, followed by Buck, Preston could feel his hot tears falling on his hands. Marcia took Preston's hands in hers. He looked at her through his tears and with an incredulous smile on his face, he said, "That son of a bitch. *I'm* the sixth Collectible!"

JAMES J. KAUFMAN

An attorney and former judge, James J. Kaufman has published several works of non-fiction. In *The Collectibles,* his debut novel, Kaufman draws heavily from his experiences in law, the world of business, and interaction with people from widely different backgrounds. The founder and CEO of The Kaufman Group, Ltd., he assists companies world-wide to meet challenges, restructure, and flourish. Kaufman lives with his wife, Patty, and his golden retriever Charley, in Wilmington, North Carolina. He is working on *The Collectibles* screenplay and a second novel. Visit the author at **jamesjkaufman.com**. For additional copies of this book or other information regarding *The Collectibles,* please email the publisher at **downstreampublishing@gmail.com** or write to Downstream Publishing at PO Box 869, Wrightsville Beach, NC 28480.

Author photograph: Patricia Roseman